BY HIS
OWN HAND

BOOKS BY NEAL GRIFFIN

Benefit of the Doubt
A Voice from the Field
By His Own Hand

BY HIS OWN HAND

NEAL GRIFFIN

A TOM DOHERTY ASSOCIATES BOOK
New York

BY HIS OWN HAND

Copyright © 2018 by Neal Griffin

A Forge Book
Published by Tom Doherty Associates
175 Fifth Avenue
New York, NY 10010

www.tor-forge.com

Forge® is a registered trademark of Macmillan Publishing Group, LLC.

The Library of Congress Cataloging-in-Publication Data is available upon request.

ISBN 978-0-7653-9558-0 (hardcover)
ISBN 978-0-7653-9559-7 (ebook)

Our books may be purchased in bulk for promotional, educational, or business use. Please contact your local bookseller or the Macmillan Corporate and Premium Sales Department at 1-800-221-7945, extension 5442, or by email at MacmillanSpecialMarkets@macmillan.com.

First Edition: April 2018

Printed in the United States of America

0 9 8 7 6 5 4 3 2 1

To the strong women I love, who continue to shape my life.

My wife, Olga Diaz
My mother, Grace Coggins Probasco
My sisters, Meme and Ellen
And my daughters: Shelby, Emma, and Julia

ACKNOWLEDGMENTS

I remain deeply indebted to a core group of supporters, friends, and colleagues at Team Forge, particularly Melissa, Kirsten, and Karen. And also, my agent and friend, Jill Marr, with the Sandra Dijkstra Literary Agency. Thanks to all of you for standing by me.

To my friends in law enforcement (you know who you are) who gave me access to their specialized areas of expertise. Thank you and I hope I represented you well.

When I was a young Marine back in the early 1980s I remember serving with a number of WM's, which is the acceptable acronym for women Marines. Two in particular still stand out in my mind. Their names were Michelle and Heather. By the time I met them, they were both in their early twenties and had already established themselves as non-commissioned officers. They were consummate professionals. They were hard charging dedicated Marines. They never asked for or expected preferential treatment because of their gender. They were both very good at their jobs.

The reason I remember Michelle and Heather so vividly is because of the abuse they endured in the workplace. Every day they came to work, Michelle and Heather had to overcome the disparaging comments, the sexist attitudes, and the gender bias that ran rampant in the armed services. And both of them did endure it and still got the job done. Not on occasion. Not once in a while. But *every day.*

As a police officer, I also served with many women: Kathy, Lynn, Holly, Molly, Diana, Julie, Bry, Linda, Shannon, Therese, Janice, and so many more. Women who work in a challenging profession, overwhelmingly dominated by men. It takes a special breed of individual to survive a decades-long law enforcement career. The women who do it are nothing short of extraordinary.

As the husband of an elected official who is the only woman on the council she serves, I see the duplicity and double standard that has been painstakingly designed to constrain the influence of women who enter politics at any and all levels of government. And yet my wife, and hundreds of women like her, still answer the call to fight the good fight and serve their communities and their country.

This book is about strong women in difficult circumstances. Women who don't give in. Working women who fight against sexism and bias by being better at what they do than the men around them. For that reason I'd like to acknowledge all of the women who I've had the honor to work with in my military and law enforcement careers.

Semper Fi. Stay Safe.

BY HIS OWN HAND

ONE

Detective Tia Suarez drove the plain-wrapped Crown Vic down the rutted fire lane until its high beams lit the yellow tape that blocked the narrow wooded road. The sight struck her as odd, if not damn near comical. Cops and routine: inseparable partners. Three o'clock in the morning, surrounded by miles of heavy forest in a remote corner of Waukesha County, Wisconsin, there probably wasn't much in the way of mopes and lookie-loos, but by God, the yellow tape had to go up.

Considering the nature of the call, Tia figured it best to leave room for other vehicles to come and go. She steered her newly assigned squad off to the side of the road, but the car fought back. The power steering had crapped out a month ago just as the odometer hit 150K, and the lumbering sedan was granted a long-overdue retirement out of the patrol pool. That's when some pencil-neck geek in the mayor's office got the big idea to strip off the red-and-blues, slap on a coat of battleship-gray paint, and call it a detective car. When Tia complained to the city mechanic, he shrugged and said, "Get in line." She maneuvered in behind the lone marked cruiser and killed the engine but the car refused to die, coughing and sputtering like a four-thousand-pound emphysema patient.

Twenty minutes removed from a warm bed, Tia sat balanced on the greater Milwaukee yellow pages, listless and still waking up. The phone book provided the support missing from the seat springs, long since worn out by a decade of weighted-down patrol cops who pushed the sled twenty-four hours a day, seven days a week. Such was life in the Newberg PD, where the most recent round of politically driven budget cuts hadn't been with pens and pencils, but hatchets and cleavers. A long sip of the hot coffee she'd brought from home provided an energetic lift, but she couldn't help but think a shot of Patron would sure as hell liven the drink up a bit.

"Thirty-seven days," she said out loud, glancing at herself in the rearview mirror. With a quick shake of her head, she pushed off against the near-constant temptation and turned to the task at hand. Time to get to work.

Tia gathered up her writing pad and pen, ignoring the department-issued computer tablet and body-cam recorder buried in the center console. Not for the first time, she wished the feds in Washington would fork over some grant money to replace her car, instead of handing out whiz-bang monitoring equipment that was just more Big Brother bullshit. She slammed the console shut and grabbed the five-cell flashlight from the charging dock between the seats, then tucked the twenty-inch metal tube under her armpit, preferring the substantial steel to the lighter and brighter Mini Mags most young cops carried nowadays.

A pen, a spiral notepad, and a five-cell. Old school or just stubborn? Hard to say. The way she saw it, technology in law enforcement had gone too far. There were time-tested methods of police work that couldn't be improved on by electronic gadgets or pre-populated drop-down forms. Methods that sure as hell included handwritten detective notes made at a crime scene. But Tia had to admit, even at the fairly young age of thirty-one, her way of doing police work was fast becoming eccentric.

Through the windshield she saw the beam of a flashlight bobbing in the darkness, twenty or so yards into the woods. Still balancing the hot coffee, Tia used her shoulder to push hard on the door, but the tilt of the road made for a tough angle. She got her boot into it, kicked the door all the way open, and pulled herself to her feet. Scalding liquid sloshed over her notepad, windbreaker, and jeans, just before the door swung back and knocked the cup out of her hand. The coffee pooled on the soiled remnant of floorboard carpet, the latest addition to the car's long list of deviant odors.

Tia looked down at her soiled jacket and blue jeans, mumbling obscenities that would have her well-meaning but pious Catholic mother lighting candles for a month. She tore off a chunk of soggy pages from her pad and dropped the wet, shriveled sheets onto the pool of coffee. Good as new, she thought, looking at the now fresh writing surface.

"Try doing that with an iPad," she said as she finally dragged herself out of the car.

A cool breeze whipped through the trees and blew across her face, signaling rain might be on the way. A chorus of a million or so cicadas and the steady snore of nearly as many northern leopard frogs filled the night air, accompanied by an obnoxious, all-too-familiar voice from somewhere up ahead.

"Ah, shit." Tia rolled her eyes.

Him.

Again her number ran through her head, but with noticeably less conviction.

Tia slammed the car door, along with the door in her mind that led to a dangerous way of thinking. If she got through the day, her number would be thirty-eight. All things considered, pretty impressive. No reason to think back further than that. Bygones. History.

Bury that shit. But now, she had to suck it up and spend a little one-on-one time with the most relentless prick on the Newberg Police Department. Times like these left her feeling that sober living was highly overrated.

Standing at the tape line, she whistled loudly and gave two quick bursts from her flashlight, but the deep voice droned on without pause. She whistled again and called out, "Yo, Jimmy."

The talking stopped.

She yelled out, "Am I okay to walk in from here?"

"Yeah," the voice came back. "You're good."

Tia ducked low to pass under the tape. As she stood up on the other side, a stunning white light swept across her eyes. Turning her head away, she raised an arm to block the beam.

"Damn, man. Watch it."

The beam dropped to the ground and Tia tried to blink away the thousand points of light, knowing she'd be seeing spots for the next hour. A young trainee she'd passed a few times in the hallway at the PD walked toward her. She squinted hard and jammed at her eyes with a thumb and forefinger, making no effort to disguise her irritation.

"You're that new hire?" His name came to her. "Puller, right?"

"Yes, ma'am. I'm Officer Puller. Sorry about that." He stood awkwardly in a uniform that even in the low light appeared a bit baggy, but pressed and new. He was rail thin—Tia put him at about a buck-fifty, including the stiff leather gun belt that cinched a waist so narrow there were no empty spaces between the items of issued gear. A light dusting of acne covered his pale, fuzzy cheeks and Tia figured he probably shaved every other week, whether he needed to or not. Perfect, she thought. We're recruiting from Newberg High School.

"Show some light discipline, all right? Guys can get pretty pissy when you sweep up like that. Point it at your feet. That'll give you all the light you need." Tia looked deeper into the woods. "You riding with Youngblood?"

"Yes, ma'am. Last phase of field training. One more week."

"Knock off the 'ma'am' shit."

"Uh, yes, ma'am," he said nervously. She really had him flustered. "I mean, right. Okay."

Vision clearing, Tia managed eye contact. Cowed like a puppy that had shit the carpet, the kid didn't show much in the way of command presence. More like a crisis of confidence. No surprise, considering who was training him. "Dispatch called me out. So where's this dead body at?"

Puller looked back over his shoulder and pointed with his flashlight, orienting the beam toward the ground. "Right over there, next to where Officer Youngblood is standing."

"Really? *Next* to where he's standing?" Tia didn't try to hide a growing sense of frustration. "So tell me, has he trained you in the concept of an inner perimeter?"

Puller stared back, slack-jawed, as if trying to answer a trick question. Tia pushed past, done with the clueless trainee. She walked up to Youngblood, who was talking on his cell phone. She hung back ten feet and he gave just the barest jut of his chin in acknowledgment. She put her left hand on her hip and her right on the back strap of her Glock 23. A bell rang in her head, signaling the beginning of round one.

Officer James "Jimmy" Youngblood had recently been named the department field training officer, after the previous FTO had left to join the force up in Green Bay, where cops were paid much better and the overtime policy was all-you-can-eat. Youngblood got the FTO job after being turned down a third time for a detective's shield. Most cops, Tia included, figured his appointment had been some kind of consolation prize.

"Gotta go, Stan. She's here. Wait for me at the station. I'll be there in twenty minutes." He paused, then laughed and said, "Yeah, no shit."

Youngblood looked Tia up and down in a way that signaled his last comment had something to do with her. She tried to let it go but her effort was halfhearted, and when he ended the phone conversation and turned to her, the challenge in her voice was obvious.

She stood with her hands on both hips. " 'No shit,' what?"

"Huh?" Youngblood tucked his cell phone into a cargo pocket of his trousers.

"You said 'no shit' just now. 'No shit,' what?"

"Just talking to Hansen." Youngblood gave a dismissive shrug and Tia picked up on his satisfaction at so effortlessly getting under her skin. He did his best to convey confused innocence. "We're blowing out of town tomorrow. Coupla days in Vegas."

Knowing she'd given his juvenile nonsense more acknowledgment than it deserved, Tia decided to push back from a different direction. Her gaze shifted to the dark outline on the ground, less than two feet from where Youngblood stood.

"What? We don't train inner perimeters anymore?" Tia looked to the ground and picked up on the trampled leaves and boot prints in the dirt. "In kind of close for a DB, aren't you?"

Youngblood launched a gob of tobacco spit over his shoulder. He shoved his hands under his external load-bearing vest, making his arms resemble chicken wings. Like most senior officers, Youngblood wore black, military-style gear instead of the traditional blue uniform required for trainees and probies. He turned back to Tia, dark flecks clinging to his thick mustache.

"Yeah, it's a dead-body call. But for a crime scene perimeter, you need a crime." His face displayed a well-practiced look of deadpan disinterest. "Last I checked, when it comes to suck-starting a shotgun, it's still a free country. Anyway, here's your stiff."

His flashlight clicked on and the intense beam lit a ten-foot circle on the ground. Tia studied the body, starting at an ordinary pair of high-top tennis shoes, traveling up past jeans and shirt to neck and throat. After that, there was a violent departure from the expected. A mass of red, chunky gel, the size and roundness of a small truck tire, replaced what had once been a human face. A shotgun alongside the body served as the scene's exclamation point.

Tia drew a breath through clenched teeth and turned away. *"Ah, Jesus."*

"Sorry, Suarez." Youngblood laughed. "Didn't figure on you being squeamish. You need a minute? A tissue, maybe?"

Tia ignored the apology, knowing the shock treatment had been intentional. She'd seen more than enough dead bodies, mostly during her three years in Afghanistan. But this one, fresh, violently violated, and obviously youthful, made a strong impression. Youngblood went right on yucking it up.

"I wish you could've seen your face just now. Fucking priceless." He feigned a high-pitched squeal, waving his hands in the air. *"Oh, Jesus. Oh, Jesus."*

She stared back, determined to match his disdain. "You done dicking around? Can we get on with it?"

"Take it easy, Suarez. Calling you was just routine." His voice carried the same attitude she'd seen since her first day in the department, almost eight years ago. The guy couldn't accept the idea of women cops. It didn't help that even though he had four years seniority on her, Tia had transferred to the Investigations Bureau while Youngblood still pushed a patrol sled. Most of the patrol dogs had convinced themselves that she only made detective because of her brown skin and female gender, but Tia knew better. The career kick-start for a double minority might play in the city, but in a small town like Newberg, it didn't count for shit.

"Your buddy Sawyer wants one of you to come out on all unattended deaths involving a weapon. I'd say this qualifies."

" 'One of you'?" Tia was determined to make him say it.

"Detectives." He sniffed, his voice resentful. "One of you detectives."

Tia let it fester. *That's right, dipshit.* Detective.

Looking him over, Tia was reminded how the upside-down life of graveyard patrol played hell on the body. The black watch cap pulled down to just above Youngblood's eyebrows couldn't hide his pasty complexion or the meaty sag of his jowls. The Glock forty-caliber was strapped low against his thigh, the tactical nylon belt mostly buried under the hang of his ample gut. Too many midnight drive-through burgers followed by beer and eggs for breakfast. Then a fitful two or three hours of daytime sleep before heading back to work loaded up on Red Bull. Yeah, Youngblood was looking rough. Ten more pounds, she thought, and he could carry an extra pair of handcuffs under one of his sagging man boobs, along with a backup thirty-eight in the crack of his fat ass.

She pulled out her pen and notepad, shook off her shock and sorrow, and saw the scene for what it was: the unexplained death of a human being, in need of investigation.

"Give me what you've got."

"Time of call was zero-two-eleven. We got to the scene at zero-two-thirty-eight. By then, the RP had split. We—"

"Whoa, whoa, whoa." Tia cut him off, looking at her watch. "Twenty-seven minutes? On a dead-body call? Damn, Jimmy, I got here faster than that and I was sound asleep. Where were you coming from?"

The trainee looked at his feet but Youngblood avoided the question, saying only, "Busy night."

"All right, but what do you mean the RP split?"

Youngblood spoke as if every question was a personal inconvenience. "I mean he split, Suarez. He's gone. Guy called Dispatch, ID'ed himself as Henry. We show up and there ain't no Henry. Just the stiff."

"No RP? On a DB?" Usually the reporting party on something as significant as a dead body would stick around. Losing the RP was a lousy way to start the investigation.

"Yeah. Well, whatever." Youngblood hunched his shoulders in a show of obvious disinterest and offered no further explanation.

"Dispatch got recall info, though, right? Captured the number?" she asked, prodding. "Have you reached out? Tried to get him to come back?"

"Ask Dispatch. All I know is we got a call about a body off county Highway Twelve, a mile north of the campground. Took us a good twenty minutes to find the guy. Hell, my trainee practically tripped over him."

"Wait a sec," Tia looked up, pen poised over paper. "You mean another twenty minutes, after the twenty-seven it took you to arrive on scene?"

"No." Now Youngblood was flustered. "I mean—yeah, so what? We had to search around. Jesus, Suarez, what's with the third degree?"

"Take it easy, Jimmy. I'm just trying to get the time line straight. So we can figure time of death, right?"

Youngblood scoffed, "Because it really matters what time this guy blew his face off?"

Tia ignored him and moved on. "So, this Henry guy. Have we tried calling him back or not?"

"Like I said," Youngblood enunciated each word, *"ask Dispatch."*

Tia looked him up and down. *This guy's our training officer?*

Granted, in a case like this, the first patrol officer's only job was to freeze the scene, then document and pass along all activity up until the arrival of detectives. But most cops actually took the initiative to start the preliminary investigation. Check out the crime scene. Locate possible witnesses.

Not Youngblood. The man dodged more work than any cop in the department.

Trapping the Maglite under her arm, Tia pulled out the pair of blue latex gloves she'd shoved into the pocket of her jeans before leaving her house. She slid on the first then snapped the second one on her wrist. Meeting Youngblood's gaze in the bouncing ambient light, she made no effort to hide her opinion of the man's ability. "The guy found a body, Jimmy. We probably ought to have a talk with him. But no worries. I'll handle it."

"Relax, Suarez." Youngblood did his best to downplay his own incompetence. "He'll turn up. Probably just got a little spooked. How many folks you know have the sac to hang out at two o'clock in the morning with a headless body? In the woods, no less. But it don't even matter. This shit ain't exactly complicated."

"Is that right, Jimmy? You got it figured?"

"Damn right. This here's the human chum of a fella who was by no means just toying with the idea." Looking at the body, Youngblood nudged it with his boot, like a boy might poke at a dead cat with a stick. "Whoever he was, he was *not* fucking around."

Tia's frustration boiled over. Taking a quick step forward, she reached out to shove at his 250-plus pounds, to no effect. "Knock it off, Jimmy. Holy shit, man. This is a *crime scene,* get it?"

He shook his head dismissively and pushed his hands deeper into his vest. "Whatever, Suarez. Like I said, I got travel plans. Just do your thing so we can get out of here. I gotta take a piss."

With that, he walked over to a nearby tree. His shoulders hunched up and she heard the sound of his zipper.

"Oh, hell no," she shouted. "Keep walking."

Youngblood muttered objections but moved further into the woods, until his dark silhouette dissolved into the night. She heard the strong stream hit leaves and dirt, coupled with the sounds of other bodily functions.

"Pig," she said out loud. She wasn't talking about his occupation.

The trainee took a step back, into the shadows, probably not certain how to deal with two cops who so clearly despised each other. Tia figured that was a good place for him.

"Get on your radio, Puller. Ask Dispatch to try the RP's number. Get them to come back out."

Puller began to fumble with his radio and Tia turned her attention back to the body. Irritating as Youngblood might be, his assumption was hard to argue with. First impression was that the death was a straight-up suicide. Still, the other officer's dismissive attitude aggravated the hell out of her. She closed her eyes for a moment to clear her thoughts; a roll of far-distant thunder helped quiet her mind. She took a deep breath and checked her watch. Be daybreak before too long.

"I'll be damned, can you believe it?" Tia looked down at the dead body and to the general area of where the eyes might have been. "I made it to thirty-*eight*."

TWO

The Wisconsin night sounds faded away, along with the irritating distraction of the two patrol officers. Tia began what was for her a crime scene ritual—a mental cleansing, of sorts, a concentration on known fact and nothing more. *All we have is a body. A dead one for sure, but that's it.* Anything beyond that was speculation. In her mind, she held the one key question. The question with a single truthful answer but a thousand imposters. Limitless masquerades. The one question she would hold herself to resolve.

What really happened here?

Tia clicked her flashlight on, instantly transforming dark, muted tones of black and gray into bright, Technicolor, 3-D images, still and silent as if frozen in time. In the center of the circle of light lay the body, supine on a bed of hard dirt, twigs, and dried leaves, mostly birch with a few maple mixed in. The legs were awkwardly crossed and pulled up close to the torso. The arms stretched out to the sides, dramatic and biblical. Along the right side of the body, in a position consistent with self-infliction, was what Tia immediately recognized as a Remington 870, single-barrel, pump-action shotgun.

The 870, long known as the field artillery of law enforcement, had been carried by generations of patrol cops, until finally replaced by the sexier and much sleeker M-class of military assault rifles. Tia still preferred the shotgun. In a close-up gunfight, the Remington was unmatched for reliability and deadly effectiveness. If you don't believe me, she thought, looking at the ground, get a load of this guy.

Before moving closer, she scanned the ground, studying every leaf and chunk of dirt. After a full two-minute, 360-degree examination of the immediate terrain surrounding the corpse, nothing of evidentiary value jumped out. Tia lowered herself to her knees. She knew the importance of avoiding unnecessary physical contact, but one issue needed to be cleared up, and under the circumstances there was only one way to do it. With a gloved hand, she grabbed the crotch and squeezed, confirming her first instinct. Male parts. That settled, she directed her light on the area that had been the head.

Strange, she thought. The first undisturbed flesh was near mid-throat. Not so much as a remnant of a chin or jaw. Not a hint of lips or teeth. Eyes, nose, mouth: all gone, replaced by an exploded mass of tissue and cartilage. Countless strands of red flesh, with the thickness of spiderwebs, stretched uniformly toward what had been the top of the head. That meant the wound had been inflicted not through the mouth, but from somewhere under the chin.

A deviation from the norm, but not unheard of. In shotgun suicides, most determined individuals went with an intraoral discharge. Or what Tia referred to as the "wrap your lips around it and let 'er rip" approach. Hollywood bullshit. Then again, Tia figured people were entitled to improvise on something like suicide. Show a little individualism.

She'd long since come to realize there are no hard-and-fast rules about gunshot suicide. Just general guidelines. In the end, getting the job done was all about good barrel placement, steady trigger pull, and a strong sense of personal commitment. Practice rounds were highly discouraged. If she were handing out letter grades, this fella had definitely earned an *A* for effort.

Adjusting her light, Tia ducked down for a sideways view. Both ears were still in one piece and attached, along with the back third of the skull, which was covered in thick, black hair that extended down past the collar. All consistent with a bottom-to-top trajectory. What was left of the head rested among a red-stained halo of leaves and dirt. She played the beam over the blood pattern. All seepage. No sign of high-velocity spray. He was either sitting or standing when the fatal injury occurred.

She sat back up and took a breath. So far, it all made good sense.

Next, the hands. Brown—not tan. Youthful. Could be Latino. Maybe Native American. Her attention was drawn to a tattoo on the web of the right hand, between the thumb and forefinger. At first, it looked like some sort of symbol formed with crisscrossing lines. She kept staring until it dawned on her: letters. *HTH*. Crude, uneven, in drab green ink. Self-made for sure. She bent down for a closer look, resisting the temptation to adjust the position of the hand to get a better angle. She guessed the faded ink was at least a year old. Tia pulled her cell phone from a pocket and took several pictures. She hoped there would be some ID on the body, but if not, the tattoo might be helpful in figuring out who he was.

A question occurred to her and she spoke, without looking up.

"How'd he get here?"

"Say what?" Youngblood, back from his nature hike, was leaning against a nearby tree, texting on his phone.

"Car. Bike. Anything in the area?"

Youngblood shrugged so Tia turned her attention to the trainee, who was still doing his best imitation of a tree stump.

"How about you, Puller—notice any sign of transportation?"

"No, ma'am." Tia sensed a reluctance to offer up anything that might contradict his FTO. "I mean—no."

"Any luck on getting hold of the RP?"

Puller spoke quickly, as if glad to finally be making a contribution. "Dispatch said it went to voicemail."

"Yeah?" Tia said. "Right to voicemail or after it rang a few times?"

"Uh, I didn't ask." Puller began to fumble for his radio.

"Forget it. I'll deal with it later." Tia couldn't let the teachable moment pass. "But always ask. It makes a difference."

Having the reporting party on scene would help but everything about the body said suicide. Screamed it, actually. She had half a mind to start digging through his pockets. With any luck she'd find a suicide note. Hell, maybe he was even one of those lost souls thoughtful enough to have included a list of next of kin. Phone numbers. Addresses. A litany of regrets and apologies. Or a "This is all your fault so deal with it" letter. Either way, a note would clear this shit up quick and she could be back in bed before daylight.

She carefully lifted the T-shirt with two gloved fingers, just enough to light up the smooth, hairless skin of the stomach. Damn near baby skin, she thought. Bit of a belly, but no more so than your average teenager. Kid was young. Maybe sixteen or seventeen, eighteen tops.

Youngblood shrugged himself off the tree and moved in. "I'm gonna go ahead and call the meat wagon. Get 'em headed this way. We got rain comin'."

Tia ignored him, slipping her latex-covered hand under the shirt to lay her palm against the skin. The body was cool to the touch. She gave a light pinch. Still soft and supple. She pulled the shirt a bit higher and again used her flashlight, this time to light up the back. A slight reddening of the skin showed early signs of settling blood in the area where the body rested against the ground. Nothing indicating postmortem movement. Definitely DRH: died right here.

Tia once again sat back on her heels for another mental assessment. No known method of arrival, but he could have walked in or parked somewhere out of view. No movement of the body, so no way it was a dump. Mechanism of injury and death was obvious. Weapon accounted for. Position of gun and body consistent with self-inflicted fatal wound. Yeah. Everything pointed to suicide. *But damn*. No rigor and just the early stages of lividity. The kid was fresh.

She went back to the wound area with her flashlight, leaning in for closer examination. Dark areas of chunky coagulation had begun to form, but she saw no insect activity. She looked to her watch.

"Tell me again. What was the time of call?"

Youngblood inhaled deep through his nose and blew it out, doing his best to sound annoyed. "Zero-two-eleven."

"Not even two hours ago," Tia said, under her breath and mostly to herself. "That's really cutting it close."

"Cutting what close?" Youngblood asked.

"I'm just saying, he wasn't dead long when the call came in."

"Yeah, whatever." Youngblood began to punch numbers on his phone. "Like I said, I'll call the wagon and get a waiver. My trainee's got a bunch of reports to write, plus this one. He needs to get at it."

"Not yet."

Youngblood stopped, looking up. "What?"

"Hold off on the transport." Tia smoothed out the dead boy's shirt and gave his chest a sympathetic, almost maternal pat. "I think I'll have an investigator from the ME's office come out and have a look."

The uniformed officer cocked his head. "An MEI? On a suicide? What the hell for? This time of night, it'll be an hour before they roll! out."

Still kneeling next to the body, Tia said, "He ain't gonna complain, Jimmy."

"Oh, for shit sake, Suarez." Youngblood held out his phone. Again, Tia heard his frustration at having to deal with any cop who didn't have a penis. "Just let me handle the notification. I'll tell it right and they'll waive off on the response."

In the never-ending effort to save another tax dollar, all county police departments had signed a memorandum of understanding with the county medical examiner. Police officers who attended a one-day training course on death investigations were allowed to determine manner of death in cases that were obviously natural causes, accident, or suicide. In Newberg, Chief Sawyer had added a stipulation requiring a detective make the call if the death involved a weapon. Tia knew the decision was hers.

"Yeah, I'm sure you could keep this pretty simple." Tia stood, being sure to step well away from the body before wiping off the leaves and dirt that clung to the knees of her jeans. "And I agree, it looks like a straight-up suicide. But protocol says if there are any significant extenuating circs, the ME's office will be notified prior to removal of the body and respond to the scene."

" 'Protocol'? 'Extenuating'—" Jimmy threw his hands in the air and practically shouted, "What are you talking about? There's a dead dude with no face lying by a shotgun in the middle of the damn woods. What the hell 'extenuates' that?"

The near-half-hour response time, lack of a reporting party, and no sign of transportation seemed to be the textbook definition of "extenuating circumstances," but Tia wasn't going to argue. A quick assessment by an investigator with the ME's office would confirm the finding of suicide and she knew that was the appropriate course of action. For Tia, this was just another example of having to deal with the alpha-male mentality of graveyard patrol officers. She answered calmly and even tried to smile.

"If you need to split, Jimmy, then go. I'll take care of the report."

"Can't do it. Need to check the death investigation box for his training book," Youngblood responded, hooking a thumb in the direction of his trainee. "Believe it or not, I'm supposed to cut this hot mess loose at the end of the week. We might not get another body before then."

Tia looked at the brand-new cop, who again obviously wanted to be anywhere other than at the center of a disagreement between a detective and his FTO.

"Leave'm with me," Tia said. "I could use a scribe. I'll drop him off at the PD when we clear." When Youngblood looked at her with distrust, she couldn't resist adding, "What? You think I'm going to infect him with lady-cop germs or something?"

"Exactly." Tucking his phone away, Youngblood let loose with another gob of chunky tobacco spit and went on with disdain, "Trainee Puller already comes across a little too sissified. I've spent the last two weeks trying to get him to put some damn bass in his voice."

Glancing at Puller, Tia saw the young cop's expression mixed anger with embarrassment. She regretted having walked him right into a fanging from his jerk-off FTO.

"Tell you what," she said. "I'll have him do all the paperwork. That way you'll be able to sign off on his training record."

"Fuck it. Fine." Youngblood waved Tia off dismissively and turned to his trainee. "Listen up, Thing. I'm going back to the PD and crash out in the break room. Come find me when you're done. And remember, I got a flight outta here in a few hours. Don't go trying to play detective. Just hang out for the MEI, then wrap this shit up."

"Yes, sir."

With no further acknowledgment of Tia, Youngblood trudged off, headed back toward the patrol car. When he was safely out of earshot, Tia turned to the trainee.

"Seriously? *Thing?*"

Puller stared with contempt at the dark figure disappearing into the night. "Yeah. That's one of his nicknames for me. It's actually one of the least offensive ones."

His diction was precise and Tia got the impression the kid was pretty book smart. She knew that wouldn't sit well with Youngblood. "Well, what should I call you?"

He managed a smile and shrugged. "Rich is good."

"Fine." Tia gave a wave with a gloved hand, then it hit her. "Wait. You said Rich?"

"Yeah." His tone was one of knowing dread.

"So, like Richard?"

"I prefer Rich."

"Richard Puller?" Tia paused and couldn't help but smile. "So your name is Dick Puller?"

It was clear he'd been through the same scenario a thousand times before. "Like I said, I go by Rich."

"I imagine you do." Tia felt bad for bringing it up. "I'm Detective Suarez. Call me Tia."

Puller's voice now carried a bit of friendly sarcasm. "Yeah. I think I've heard of you somewhere."

Tia brushed off the typical reference to her reputation. Her high-profile cases over the past couple of years had gotten plenty of local notoriety.

"I'm going to get on the phone with an MEI. We'll get this thing wrapped up as quick as we can."

"What's an MEI?" Puller asked, reminding Tia just how clueless trainees could be.

"An investigator from the medical examiner's office. In the meantime, I need you to find this guy's face for me."

"Excuse me?" The voice had pitched up again, this time with a reluctant, nervous edge.

"His face." Tia aimed her flashlight at the area beyond the head end of the body. "I bet it landed somewhere between ten and fifteen feet over that way. There should be at least one or two pretty good-size pieces. Careful where you walk. If you find something, don't touch it. Just holler at me."

"Why do I need to do all that?"

The pushback made Tia wonder if Youngblood might have a point. A trainee wasn't expected to ask a lot of "why" questions. Careful not to come down too hard, Tia let Rich know the friendly banter was over.

"First, because I said so, and I'm the detective and you're the trainee. Next, the distance from the body is going to tell us a lot about the angle of the gun. That will go a long way to confirm this is exactly what it appears to be. A suicide."

Rich looked off into the dark of the woods, uneasy. "And it is, right? I mean, it's a suicide?"

"Pretty good bet, yeah. But this is somebody's kid. They might need a little more convincing. And to be honest, I'd rather not get dragged back out here next week when some soccer mom on a family nature hike calls to report she found a rotting chunk of Mr. Hairy Cranium. So, consider it housecleaning."

He stood unmoving for several seconds, staring into the woods.

"Rich?" Tia said, unamused by his hesitancy.

He sounded lost in thought. "Yes?"

"His face, dude." Tia gave him a push toward the darkness. "Go find his face."

Tia watched him walk away, his flashlight scanning the ground directly at his feet, each step a bit more cautious than the last. Pulling her cell phone from her pocket, she scrolled through her contacts until she found the right number. After two rings, the familiar voice came across, tired but pleasant.

"Hey, Tia. I don't guess this is a social call, huh?"

"Morning, sunshine. It's your week on callout rotation, right?"

Tia could hear the woman stretching herself more awake. "Yeah. What's up?"

"I'm afraid you're going to have to crawl out of that nice warm bed and come join me in the woods. I got one I need you to take a look at."

"Okay. Where are you?"

"Oh my God!"

Tia looked in the direction of the panicked voice and saw Rich frantically checking the bottom of his boots with his flashlight.

"Tia? You still there?"

It looked like Rich had found what she'd sent him looking for. "I'm in Skeel's Woods, off County Twelve. I'll text you the GPS coordinates. And hey, can you bring me a coffee? Wouldn't you know it, I dumped mine getting out of the car."

THREE

The jagged fragment of human anatomy included a cheek, the entire left eye, and most of the forehead. Discounting the dozen or so strands of veins and shredded skin, Tia figured the chunk of flesh was about five or six inches across at the widest point. She estimated the distance to the body as twelve to fourteen feet, but she'd wait for an exact measurement until the MEI arrived. Tia knew once she wrote it down it was official and she didn't want to risk recording two different distances. She used her cell phone camera to take a few shots of the overall scene as well as the location and position of the body. All of this would be repeated by the investigator, with more advanced equipment, but Tia always liked to have her own reference material.

"So what're you thinking?"

Still on her knees, Tia looked at the trainee—who was now apparently *her* trainee. Rich stood back, keeping distance between himself and the remnant of human face. She couldn't blame him. The wide-open, disembodied eye was pointed directly up, creating the optical illusion of following her wherever she stood. The close-up examination had been a bit unsettling.

"About trajectory," she replied, directing her conversation at the eye. "Definitely upward. Hell of a load. I'm guessing double-ought buck for sure."

She stood, careful not to disturb the evidence. "Whichever, I bet a few pieces of this fella damn near took flight for a second or two."

"Seriously?"

"Considering the velocity of a shotgun round? Twenty, thirty feet in the air, I'll bet." She motioned toward a stand of nearby trees. "Go on and climb that maple right there. Wouldn't surprise me if you found a few more chunks of skull and hair in some of the lower branches."

His response was immediate and stern. "Wait a minute. I don't think I can—"

"Relax, Rich. I'm kidding."

His relief was obvious even as his eyes went to the branches overhead. "You really think? In the trees?"

She heard the inexperience in his voice, a tone that separated veterans from rookies. At some point, he would harden and be less impacted by the darkest aspects of police work. Then again, Tia knew the best cops never lost their sense of morbid curiosity. When they did, when curiosity was replaced by dull routine, crimes went unsolved and crooks went unpunished. Complacency among beat cops was the single biggest flaw in most police departments.

Jimmy Youngblood was a perfect example of a career lost to slothful bad habits. Even investigating a headless body in the woods, although inherently intriguing, was work to be avoided. Tia saw it as a mind-set that could eventually lead a cop to wind up staring down the barrel of a crook's gun, his last earthly thought being, *Ah, shit. Never saw that coming.*

A flash of lightning was followed by a low rumble of thunder.

The smell of imminent rain hung in the air and Tia hoped the investigator would arrive soon. She gave another thought to calling Dispatch to request someone bring out a pop-up shelter to protect the scene. Puller's next inquiry interrupted her thoughts.

"If we already know he shot himself then why all this, this—work? Seems excessive to me."

Tia shook her head at the trainee. "Man, I can tell who's been training you."

"Well, yeah, but maybe Youngblood has a point. If it's just a suicide, why worry about the details?"

"A few hours ago, 'it' was a 'him,' and like I said, he belongs to someone."

"Well, that's fine, but I'm throwing these boots away as soon as I get home."

"Then you're going to go through a lot of boots. You might want to give some more thought to your career choice."

Before Rich could reply, a wave of light passed high through the trees, accompanied by the distant thrum of an engine.

"Great," Tia said, getting to her feet as she felt the first light drops of rain. "That'll be the MEI. Let's get finished up and get out of here."

A moment later the familiar pickup truck of the Waukesha County Medical Examiner's Office rolled up and stopped at the yellow tape. The engine of the raised truck revved then went silent except for the random heat pings of the contracting metal. A moment later, the driver's door opened and Investigator Olivia Sorensen stepped out.

"Hey, Tia. Okay if I walk in?"

Olivia "Livy" Sorensen had joined the Waukesha County Medical Examiner's Office around the time Tia had gotten jammed up in a high-profile, officer-involved shooting. It had been straight-up self-defense against an armed suspect, but some federal outfit had tried to hijack the case. A U.S. Attorney working out of Milwaukee empaneled a grand jury and Tia found herself in the crosshairs of a federal witch hunt. When the feds kept sniffing around, Livy So-rensen, the newly appointed but highly experienced Waukesha County investigator, who had processed the shooting scene, shut them out. Tia hadn't known any of that at the time, but her boss, Ben Sawyer, had filled her in later. He let her know this Livy Sorensen woman definitely had her back.

Tia went wide around the body, signaling Rich to follow. Stand-ing at the tape, dressed in a gray jumpsuit, Livy had already begun jotting notes. Big-boned and just over six and a half feet tall, Livy towered over most of the cops she dealt with. Her imposing figure was literally topped off by bright red hair cut in a Lucille Ball poodle style.

Around the PD and other county departments Livy was known as "the Amazon." No one said it around Tia because they knew she would have their ass for it, but in the end, it didn't matter. It never took anyone long to figure out that not only was Livy Sorensen a top-notch forensic investigator, she also wasn't the type to worry about other people's opinions. It was an attribute that made Tia proud of her friend . . . as well as a little envious.

"Hey." Tia smiled, lifting the tape as high as she could so Livy could duck under. "Thanks for rolling out. Shouldn't take long."

Once past the flimsy barrier, Livy offered Tia a steaming cup. The aroma was clean—no vanilla, gingersnaps, spice, or other adul-terations. Just the smell of pure coffee.

"Italian roast. Black." Livy winked. "And I made it at home. No Starbucks."

"Thanks, but you didn't have to do that. 7-Eleven would've been fine."

"What? And listen to you carry on about what real coffee is supposed to taste like?"

Tia sipped from the cup and her craving subsided. Coffee was the one liquid pleasure left in her life and she took it seriously. "It's supposed to taste like this. Brewed, not cooked. Thanks."

The two women shared more than an appreciation for good coffee. They were soul mates of a sort: two small-town Wisconsin women who'd run off to have big-world experiences. Tia had served four years in the Marines, three of them attached to a recon unit in Afghanistan, working as an interrogator-translator. Livy had spent five years with the Cook County Medical Examiner's Office in Chicago, Illinois. Both women eventually returned to their hometown, only to be treated like misbehaving schoolgirls. Now, they worked in environments dominated by men who liked to be treated as unwavering authorities.

They each developed strategies to get the job done, usually by working around and outpacing their male counterparts—and doing all that without offending the men too deeply. At least Tia had the good fortune of working for a boss who got it. Police Chief Ben Sawyer didn't buy into the mentality that police work was for men only. Over at the ME's office, Livy didn't have it so good.

"So what've you got?" Livy asked.

A flash of lightning was followed by the loudest thunder roll of the night so far. Both women looked to the sky and Tia sped up, speaking quickly and without emotion.

"Deceased male, around sixteen to eighteen years of age, time of death is probably pushing about three hours, maybe a bit longer. Mechanism of death is a shotgun and the weapon is on scene. Blast beneath the chin, I'd guess somewhere between a fifty- or sixty-degree angle. Some good-size remnants recovered from nearby. Pretty sure death was instant."

She took a deep breath and shrugged. "All indications are suicide, but I figured someone from your office should take a look before we bag him up."

"Pretty sad story, already," Livy said.

"Yeah," Tia said. "No real upside."

That was one of the many things Tia admired about Livy. After logging hundreds of crime scenes with agencies throughout Cook

County, it was safe to say she'd seen just about every way a human life could end. But she hadn't become cold or callused.

Rich walked over to join the conversation and Tia was glad to see he was managing to get around without the need of a flashlight.

"Youngblood texted me. He's wondering how much longer we'll be out here."

"I'll bet he is," Tia said. "Rich, this is Livy Sorensen. Livy, Rich just hired on with us."

Livy smiled and extended her hand. "Hey, Rich."

"Hi." Rich made eye contact and accepted the handshake. Tia was glad to see that other than a slight raising of the eyebrows, Rich showed no reaction to a woman who was a good eight inches taller and outweighed him by a hundred pounds. "So what, you're like a doctor, then?"

Livy shook her head. "No, but I get that a lot. I'm an investigator and I work for the deputy medical examiner, Mortimer Kowalski. He's the doctor. I respond to crime scenes with suspicious deaths. Suicides, occasional homicides. Most of the time I'm out on farming accidents."

"Really?"

"Yeah. OSHA always wants to know why a worker fell out of a barn or how a farmer got run over by their own combine. Worker safety. Product liability. Pretty routine."

Noting the stiffening breeze, Tia said, "Well, safe bet this was no farming accident. We'd better hurry. Ready to walk in?"

"Sure. Let me gear up." Livy ducked back under the tape and went to the bed of her pickup. She hefted a canvas backpack onto her shoulder and, with the same arm, effortlessly lifted out a tackle box the size of a medium suitcase. From a metal storage bin, she pulled a camera mounted on a tripod, balancing the long metal legs on her other shoulder. Rejoining Tia and Puller, Livy nodded, indicating she was ready to go.

"Here, Livy," Rich said, "let me help you with some of that."

Tia couldn't help but notice he seemed much more personable with Livy than he had been with her.

"Thanks, Rich." Livy smiled, handing him the tackle box and tripod. Tia watched him struggle under the weight of the equipment as he led the way to the body. Tia stepped off to follow until Livy touched her lightly on the elbow.

"Did his name tag say Puller?" Livy asked.

"Yep."

"So his name is—"

"Let it go, Livy."

"Poor guy." They followed in Puller's wake, stopping about fifteen feet away from the body.

"Here's our boy," Tia said. "Like I said, he did a hell of a number on himself."

Tia took a long sip of her coffee while Livy began making her own assessment of the scene. Livy pulled a Mini Mag from a cargo pocket of her jumpsuit and lit the area. "I don't see an inner perimeter."

"Uh . . . yeah. That's a bit of a story. See, the first off—"

"Forget it. Not now." Livy shook her head, all business. "Anything been moved?"

"Nope. Just like we found it." Tia stopped. "I mean him. Found him."

"You touch anything?"

Tia tried not to be put off by the interrogation-like tone. She knew when Livy got in work mode, there was no joking around.

"Yes. His crotch to confirm gender. The T-shirt with two fingers." Tia held up her right hand. "And my palm against his abdomen. For all of it, I was gloved. I also tweaked his chest."

"And?"

"He was cool to the touch and supple."

"All right. Wait here, please. Don't come any closer."

Jesus. Tia smiled. *Like Jekyll and Hyde.*

Livy pointed her flashlight at the ground and took three large, carefully placed steps until she stood between the body and the shotgun. She lit up the weapon and bent at the waist for a closer look at the gun's barrel. With her feet planted, she twisted her hips to turn toward the body, moving the beam of light as she did. Back to the shotgun. Back to the body. Tia couldn't help but be impressed by Livy's flexibility. Finally Livy stood still, face and red hair lit by the indirect glow of the Maglite.

"Um . . . Tia?"

The officious tone was gone, replaced by something that fell between confusion and deep concern. Tia's coffee cup stopped halfway to her mouth.

"Yeah?"

Livy turned back for one last look at the gun, then pointed her light to the upper torso. Several seconds passed until finally Livy extinguished the Maglite and stood tall. Tia had kept her distance, so all she could make out was Livy's bear-size shadowy figure among the surrounding trees. When Livy spoke her voice was low and came from the dark.

"We got a problem."

Thunder struck overhead and a hard rain began to fall.

FOUR

The first rays of the rising sun broke through the trees, turning the air humid and warm, indicating a muggy Midwestern morning lay ahead. The wet ground was spongy under her feet and the waterlogged tree branches hung low, still heavy from the rain. She made no effort to hide the mounting frustration over a callout assignment that could now be officially categorized as a Newberg Cluster Fuck.

"Oh, sure. Of course." Tia looked up to acknowledge the bluing sky, accented by billowing white clouds. "*Now* the sun comes out."

The brief storm had been nothing more than a good summer drenching, but it had been enough to compromise the entire crime scene, which was what Livy was now calling it. More specifically, a homicide crime scene. Despite Livy's expertise, Tia wondered if the woman was overreacting. Tia had called Livy to follow protocol. Nothing more than a professional courtesy. But to her, this still felt like a straight-up suicide. She was beginning to regret that decision.

"Get him loaded up and wait for me, okay, Gina?" Livy scratched out a signature and handed a metal clipboard back to the latest arrival, a woman dressed in a gray jumpsuit that matched hers, with the letters *ME* stenciled in red on the back. "We'll head straight to the morgue. He's going to be first up today."

"You got it, Livy." She laid the clipboard on the black rubber body bag atop the metal gurney. A heavy-duty brass zipper ran the length of the bag; a large plastic tag marked "JOHN DOE" was looped through the eyelet. The body bag contained not only the near-headless corpse but also a Hefty kitchen trash bag filled with a dozen or so various-size pieces of skull, skin, and scalp.

Gina's partner in body recovery was also a woman, trim and attractive, dressed in matching overalls. The two women had worked as a team during the packing-up stage, appearing indifferent to their close contact with a body in a state of moderate rigor mortis. Tia had been impressed with the ability of both the ladies to forcefully push, pull, and contort the stiffening corpse into the body bag.

Livy turned to Tia. "You probably ought to show up at the morgue by ten. We'll sit down with Mort and brief him on the exact circumstances."

Tia looked at her watch: 7:45. "Geez."

"What?" Livy said. "You got a date?"

"Sure do. With my pillow. I'm beat."

"Yeah? Well, so am I, but it can't be helped. The cut goes this morning and I need you there."

Tia saw the hard look on Livy's face and heard what she thought might be a hint of anger in the woman's voice—misplaced, in Tia's opinion. She took a deep breath. "Look, Livy. I know you're pissed but—"

Livy gave Tia a "not now" sort of headshake and turned back to the body snatchers.

"Thanks, Gina. Like I said, wait for me, all right? I need to be there when we break him out."

"You got it, Liv."

Gina and her partner, stationed at opposite ends of the gurney, began a synchronized routine that always reminded Tia of a military drill. Gina nodded her head three times and the two female body snatchers simultaneously kicked low metal plates at the base of the gurney. The steel of the hinged legs whined like a screen door, tucking up under the thin mattress. Just when it looked as though the bed would completely collapse and the bag would roll off into the mud, the morgue attendants smoothly lifted the now-legless contraption into the air, holding it at waist height. Gina gave one final nod and the two stepped off in near perfect unison, heading for their nondescript white van parked on the road. The only thing missing was the roll of a snare drum.

As soon as the pair were out of earshot, Livy started in. "The blood pattern is all wrong, Tia. One look should've told you that."

"Come on, Livy. It's a shotgun. It's not an exact science. I've seen plenty of cases where there's no blood on the hands."

Livy took a deep breath and rolled her eyes. Her response sounded more than a bit condescending. "There's blood spatter on the barrel all the way to the trigger assembly, but nothing on the arms or hands. That is *not* indicative of a self-inflicted wound."

"'Not indicative' is not absolute," Tia said. "And I sure don't see how it gets us all the way to homicide." She had to tilt her head way back to engage Livy in a stare-off and she couldn't help but think that the two of them, standing toe-to-toe on the muddy road, probably looked a bit cartoonish, given the foot-and-a-half difference in their heights.

Listening to Livy, Tia wondered if she hadn't been too quick to assume the mortal head wound had been fired from directly under the chin. It hadn't seemed like an unreasonable conclusion. Of course, the destructive nature of a close-contact shotgun blast didn't provide the telltale burn mark of a pistol. That much, Tia and Livy agreed on. What was present was a high-velocity blood spatter pattern visible on both the victim's shirt and the barrel of the shotgun. Just where it should be when the explosive force of a shotgun blast collided with human flesh. The problem was that there was no blood on the victim's hands or arms. None. Tia knew she should've picked up on that, but she still wasn't convinced it was a deal breaker for suicide.

"You don't think that gets us to homicide?" Livy wasn't backing down. "We have forensic findings that indicate the victim was not holding the gun when it discharged, but you don't see a concern?"

Tia spouted Livy's own words right back at her. "*Indicates*. Not *proves*. Everything else about this case says suicide."

"Everything else," Livy said, "is anecdotal. Conjecture. The blood spatter is real."

"Yeah, but—"

Livy wasn't having it and she raised a hand to cut Tia off. "Yeah, but nothing. I've checked the chamber. The round was a Winchester Super-X magnum double-ought buck. Those rounds have a velocity of somewhere around twelve-to-fifteen hundred feet per second. If it was a fifteen-pellet load? That shot could have been taken from as far back as three, maybe even four feet and still had the same level of destruction."

Tia couldn't help but be impressed with the knowledge the woman carried around in her head, but she still wanted to defend her own assessment. "Or, it could've been zero contact. But unless you want to line up a couple of gelatin test dummies . . ."

Livy leaned in a little closer to make her final point. "Test dummies? How about a thirty pound block of cement? One of those rounds would turn it to dust and it wouldn't have to be zero contact."

"What are you suggesting, Livy?" Tia stood her ground. "A homicide staged to look like a suicide?"

"Thatta girl, Tia. Now you get it." Livy turned flippant before going right back to righteously pissed off. "That's *exactly* what I am suggesting."

"Jesus, Livy. You don't have to be a—"

Livy cut her off for the second time in a minute. "Why did you call me out here?"

"What do you mean?" Things were getting a bit heated and indignation crept into Tia's voice. "I was following standard protocol. You know that."

"You don't need me. You're authorized. If you were so sure it was a suicide, you could have called it. Had the body bagged up and sent to the mortuary. Right about now, some undertaker would be draining the body over breakfast while he reads the sports section. If all you want to do is save this broke-ass county another dollar or two, you should have gone with the KISS rule and left me out of it."

True enough. Tia could have ruled the death a suicide. Then it would've been a funeral home that scooped up the remains and there would have been no autopsy or follow-up investigation. Tia couldn't help but think at this point she might be okay with that. There was something to be said for the age-old KISS philosophy of policing: "Keep it simple, stupid." If she'd followed that rule, Tia thought, she'd be home in her nice warm bed, not standing in the woods, soaking wet and arguing with her friend.

"All right, Livy, I'm sorry. The body was fresh, and there were some issues about the initial response. I just thought it best you roll out so there wouldn't be any problem with the family."

"I don't believe that."

"Excuse me?"

The taller woman's voice softened as she continued, "If you were so sure this was a suicide, you wouldn't have called me. Your gut is telling you something else." Livy shrugged. "I think you should listen."

Right. That's all I need. Listen to the little voices. That worked so well the last time.

"And maybe," Livy said, sounding motherly, "in the future,

could you just secure the damn scene? Set up an inner perimeter? They teach that at the academy, right? And, I don't know . . . maybe give some thought to the weather?"

Tia was ready to respond but Livy surveyed the scene and just didn't let up. "Patrol cops tramped all over the place. All the boot prints have been degraded by the rain, so no way I'll be able to eliminate all of them."

She turned back to Tia. "You got pictures, right? I mean before the storm?"

"Yeah." Since Livy wanted to beat her up like she was some kind of malingering flatfoot, Tia figured she might as well play the part. "With my cell. Probably not worth much."

"Well, if all we have is cell phone pictures before the scene was compromised by the elements, then we'll just have to make do."

"Nice." Tia smirked. "Before it was compromised? Don't be shy, Livy. You can just say, 'before you totally screwed up the crime scene, Suarez.' No need to hold back."

"You're right." Tia heard a trace of the woman's usual good humor in her voice. "I need to work on my cop-speak. How's this? I need all the worthless pictures you took with your piece-of-shit cell phone before you compromised *and* totally screwed up the crime scene. Is that better?"

"Much." Tia took out her phone and pulled up the first picture to text it to Livy.

"Uh-uh." Livy put her hand on top of the phone to stop her. "Download the photos onto your computer and e-mail them to me. The pictures are evidence now. I don't want them on my phone."

"What's the big deal?"

"Chain of custody, maybe?" Livy said, looking at the cell phone still in Tia's hand. "I don't want my cell getting seized as evidence."

"Ah, shit." Tia understood the implication. "All right. As soon as I get to my computer, I'll download them and send them over. Definitely before nine."

"Hey, guys." Sergeant Travis "TJ" Jackson walked over. "Looks like we're about finished."

When Livy had identified the inconsistency in the blood spatter, the area had been upgraded to a felony crime scene. Travis had responded to supervise the processing of the scene. Tia knew she'd be doing most of the grunt work, but it was always good to have Travis around.

Tia and Travis had been in the same graduating class of Newberg High School. Tia had known Travis's wife, Molly, since both of them were fifth graders. During the summer of their freshman year in high school, she and Molly had been hanging out at the Dairy Queen in Newberg when Travis rode up on his BMX bike, with his blond hair and tan skin. Tia still teased Molly about the fact Travis had swept her off her feet while a Dilly Bar dripped chocolate on her chin. Tia would have been Molly's maid of honor if she hadn't been a little busy on a foreign deployment.

"Yeah, Sarge," Tia answered. "I think we're ready to wrap it up."

"I notified Dispatch and they've made a copy of the original call from the RP," Travis said. "Since this Henry guy didn't stick around, we need to find him. Maybe we'll catch a break and he'll be our shooter."

"*If* we have a shooter," Tia said, giving Livy a sideways glance and making sure to speak loudly enough for her to hear. She was surprised when Livy didn't even look up from her notes.

"Well, until we definitively rule out homicide," Travis said calmly, "that's how we'll treat it."

"Fair enough." Exhausted, at this point Tia just let it go.

"So what's your theory, Livy?" Travis asked. "Got any ideas?"

Livy finally looked up from her notetaking and spoke directly to Travis. Tia felt dismissed and she was pretty sure it was intentional.

"A shotgun blast from a distance of zero to three feet, upward trajectory that impacted in lower portion of the face. Other than that?" Livy shrugged. "I suppose the victim might have been handcuffed or restrained somehow? Then again it could have just been a struggle over the gun and it went off at just the right time. Lots of possibilities."

"What about the shotgun?" Travis looked to Tia. "Did the rain get to it?"

"Nah," Tia answered. "I think we're good. As soon as it started coming down, I got it into the trunk of my car, wrapped it in butcher paper. Any prints, fibers, or DNA should still be there."

"But the body?"

Tia could feel Livy's stare. Tia sighed, shaking her head. "Couldn't very well throw him in the trunk."

"It's an issue," Livy said. "I ran back to my truck and grabbed a tarp. I had him covered within a minute or two, but by then it was a downpour. He was pretty much soaked."

Travis looked at Tia. "You got photos before the rain, right?"

"Just cell phone. A few close-ups. A couple of overalls." Tia shrugged. "It's not like I was documenting evidence."

Travis looked back at Tia. At a little over six feet tall, crew-cut-blond and lean, he couldn't help the fact he was always a little intimidating. "Well, did you notice any blood? On the hands, I mean?"

"Can't say I did, Sarge." Tia sounded apologetic. "But like I said, I was just taking a few flicks that I could use when it came time to write my paper."

"All right." Travis looked thoughtful, taking it all in. "Well, first thing we need to do is figure out who this kid is. Hopefully he's local."

It seemed odd to think that it would be a bonus if the dead kid was a hometown boy, but Tia understood the implication.

"Yeah, that'd be nice. I could do without any interagency bullshit." Tia turned to Livy, realizing her comment might have been misunderstood. "'Course I'm not talking about you."

Livy answered without looking up from her notes and Tia heard the offense in her voice. "Oh, of course you weren't."

Travis seemed to finally pick up on the tension. "You two okay?"

"Fine," Tia said.

Livy followed immediately with, "Great . . . I need to make some calls. A few notifications." She leaned closer to Tia. "You know. *Protocol.*"

Travis watched Livy walk away, then said, "What's that about?"

Tia shook it off. "Nothing. We'll work it out."

"All right." Travis moved on. "Well, for now, get the physical description out to all statewide agencies. He looked pretty young so you might as well check the county runaway log. That tattoo oughta help."

"Can you take care of that, Sarge?" Tia nodded her head toward Livy. "I need to be at the ME's office by ten and I still have to download the photos from my phone. Depending on the mood of that boat anchor shaped like a computer, it could take a while."

"Yeah, okay, don't worry about it," Travis said. "I'll find someone to do it."

"What?" Tia pushed her shoulder against his chest. "Can't be bothered with the grunt work, boss man?"

Travis shook his head. "Got an appointment. Can't break it."

"Must be pretty important."

Travis looked thoughtful and Tia could see uncertainty in his eyes. He seemed like he was ready to say more but was distracted by the sound of a revving engine.

A Newberg squad car barreled around the bend, nearly colliding with the ME's van, idling in the roadway. The driver locked the brakes and stopped within a few feet of the yellow tape. The door opened and Jimmy Youngblood stepped out, wearing sweatpants and a hooded sweatshirt. Even from a distance, Tia could see the scowl on the man's face. Youngblood scanned the area until he saw his trainee.

"What the hell are you still doing out here, Puller?" Youngblood marched more than walked toward the terrified trainee, yelling the whole time. "I've been waiting around the station for five hours."

Rich began a stammering response but Tia jumped in: "Hey, Jimmy. Calm down. I can explain."

Youngblood turned to her. "This is none of your business, Suarez. Stay out of it."

Travis retorted, "It's sure as hell my business. Get over here, Jimmy."

Looking surprised to see the detective sergeant, Youngblood pointed a finger toward Puller. "Wait there. Don't move."

Tia stared at Youngblood as he walked the few feet toward them. She saw Livy, still talking on her phone near the road, looking over with some interest.

"What are you doing out here, TJ?" Youngblood asked, glaring at Tia.

"This case you pegged as a suicide?" Travis said. "We can't rule out homicide, so we went with a full callout."

"Bullshit." Indignant, Youngblood turned to Tia. "Who came up with that? You? Maybe one too many Shirley Temples last night?"

"Good one, Jimmy. Keep it up. You're killing it."

Livy joined the group. "Excuse me, Officer Youngblood. Couldn't help but overhear. I've done a thorough forensic assessment. There are some pretty strong indicators the fatal wound was not self-inflicted."

Youngblood looked at the woman with complete disinterest. He turned back to Travis as if he were the only other person who should be talking.

"TJ, I looked the scene over. Believe me. This was a straight-up suicide. No doubt. They dragged you out here and got you all spun up for nothing."

Livy stepped close enough to look directly down on Youngblood. She was smiling but her words were clipped. "That will be for the pathologist to determine. The medical examiner's office has taken custody of the body. The autopsy is being scheduled for later this morning."

"An autopsy? Are you joking?" Youngblood threw his head back in frustration. He went on, sounding as if he were dealing with third graders. "I should've just stayed out here and taken care of this myself."

Travis looked at Youngblood. "Well, that's over and done with. Like I said, we're going to treat this as a homicide until proven otherwise. I'll need a report from you covering initial response. I want it on my desk this morning."

"My trainee will handle it."

"Yeah," Travis said. "He'll handle his report and you'll handle yours. Like I said, we're approaching this as a probable homicide. That means everybody writes their own paper."

"Be sure to cover the time of call, arrival on scene, all that stuff." Tia winked, knowing Youngblood would have a hard time explaining his near-half-hour response time.

Ignoring her, the FTO said, "Fine. I'll e-mail you tonight from Vegas."

"No, forget that," Travis said. "You'll be a .20 before you even get off the plane. Write it this morning and put it on my desk."

"I can't believe this." Youngblood turned to Tia. "Please tell me it wasn't some little voice in your head that told you this was a homicide."

That was more than she was ready to put up with. Tia took a step toward the man, who was three times her size, but Travis blocked her path. Tia could hear the anger in his voice. "Shut it down, Youngblood. We're done here."

"Nice, TJ. Taking care of the Chief's girl, right? I hear that's like your number-one priority. Any fringe benefits to that assignment?"

Travis stepped closer. "You know, Jimmy, for a guy who's in such a hurry, you stand around and run your mouth a lot."

The two men squared off and stared each other down. Tia silently placed her bet on Travis and he didn't disappoint. "Write your damn paper. Then you can get on the plane."

The sound of another engine drew everyone's attention to a full-size van with a periscope antenna on the roof. The driver's door was marked with the logo of a Milwaukee TV station.

"I guess they were bound to show up," Travis said. "I'll deal with them. The rest of you, break it down and get out of here."

Travis headed for the media van, still staring at Jimmy as he walked away. "I want your report on my desk this morning. Do not disappoint me."

Once the sergeant was out of earshot, Youngblood said, "Seriously, Suarez. What is it with you? That boy blew his damn face off and any cop with half a brain can see it."

Tia took a deep breath, ready to respond, when Livy cut in: "It's not quite that simple."

Jimmy was clearly annoyed by the interruption. "Is that right? Tell me something, Amazon. How much time have you spent in a patrol car?"

"Zero." Livy closed the distance between them until she was all up in his personal space. "But I've been called out on more than four hundred dead bodies. Hangings, shootings, stabbings, bludgeonings, decapitations, drownings, immolations. Hell, I worked a death by stoning. You name it, I've worked it. And that includes more than one or two homicides staged to look like suicides. How about you? How many does this make?"

Jimmy took a step away from his antagonist. He turned to Rich, and Tia could hear the quiver in his voice. Could be anger or maybe fear, but either way, Livy had definitely shut him down.

"Come on, Puller. We're going to the station. We'll write this bullshit up from the patrol squad room."

He stomped toward the tape line, Livy's cold stare on his back. Before following him, Rich walked over and handed Tia the clipboard with the attached crime scene log. Not trying to hide his amusement, he looked at both women and said, "Definitely the most interesting night I've had so far."

"I'm glad to hear it," Livy said. "Sorry if I got you all jammed up with your FTO."

"Don't even worry about it. I learned a ton hanging around watching you work. Thanks."

"Hang in there, Rich," Tia said. "It won't last forever. You'll be out on your own soon enough."

A minute later the patrol car pulled away, Jimmy's continuing tirade audible until the vehicle was out of sight. She wondered again how Chief Sawyer had let the biggest asshole in the department become the gatekeeper for new cops. She turned to Livy.

"See you at ten o'clock?"

Livy was still looking down the road.

"Livy? You okay?"

"Yeah. I just can't . . ." She shook her head, turning back to Tia. "*Dick Puller?* Really? I mean, what were his parents thinking? Can you imagine what he's had to put up with?"

Tia smiled at her friend, touched by the sympathetic view coming from a woman six and a half feet tall with flaming neon hair. The animosity and frustration from the past few hours faded away. "Yeah, Livy. You gotta wonder."

"Ten o'clock then," Livy said and Tia heard her tone lighten as well. "You bring the coffee this time, okay?"

"I'll be there. And those pictures will be in your e-mail box in an hour." Tia paused and looked her friend in the eye. "I could have done a better job on this, Liv. I'm sorry."

"Stop. We're moving on." Livy headed for her truck, still talking. "Bring a cup for Mort, too. Three sugars and extra cream. And oh, yeah, grab a pack of Pall Malls. We're going to need him in a good mood."

FIVE

Tia watched the white panel van follow Livy's pickup truck down the tree-lined road, negotiating rain-filled ruts and potholes. The tires lost traction in the mud and the van fishtailed, kicking up slush and dirt, then righted itself and kept moving. Tia couldn't help but picture the bouncing corpse inside. Six hours ago, the young boy would no doubt have had strong objections to being zipped inside an airtight bag and strapped down to a gurney, but as things stood now, he'd be none the wiser.

As she often did when a young life came to a sudden and violent end, Tia engaged in a bit of magical thinking. What bloodline had been extinguished? What children wouldn't be born? What minor twist of fate would have allowed for a different end? She kept at it until the fading sound of the engine was replaced by the faint but steady beat of a bass guitar, accompanied by voices singing. Tia looked up and tried to pinpoint the direction from which it was coming, confused by the intrusion.

"Copper Lake," Travis said, rejoining her. The media van was also leaving and Tia saw that she and the sergeant were the only ones left at the scene. At her look of confusion, he continued, "You know, the campground?"

He pointed away from town. "It's about a mile or so down that way. The Church of the Rock annual retreat is this week."

"It is, huh?" Unimpressed, Tia began to clear away the crime scene tape. Beaded with raindrops, the yellow tape stretched as she pulled on it until it finally snapped, sending up a quick shower of water. She pulled it in like fishing line, wrapping it up in a wet, neon-colored ball. She headed for her squad, Travis beside her.

"A couple of hundred kids," he explained. "It keeps getting bigger every year. I'm surprised you haven't heard about it."

"Oh, I've heard about it. It's just . . ." Tia hesitated. She didn't really want to get into it with him.

"What?"

"Well . . . when it comes to the Rock, let's just say I don't think I'm part of the target audience."

"Why's that?" Travis stood next to Tia. She opened the trunk of the Crown Vic and shoved the ball of yellow tape under the spare tire. An order had come down from city hall that all crime scene tape should be recycled, as in reused. The shotgun, double wrapped in butcher paper and marked "PRESERVE FOR PRINTS/DNA," was tucked away in the rear.

"Seriously, TJ?" she said. "Can you see me at the Church of the Rock?"

Travis shrugged, leaning against the hood of his black SUV. Seven years old, it was the newest vehicle in the PD fleet and was assigned to the detective sergeant, a mild form of RHIP. "Sure. Why not?"

He's baiting me, she thought, seeing his familiar, feigned-quizzical expression. Finding hot-button topics to argue about was nothing new for them; usually the banter was spirited but friendly. Tia shook her head and figured, what the hell.

"Let's just say, Sarge, I think the Church of the Rock Kool-Aid is meant for folks with a bit lighter complexion than mine."

"There it is." Travis sounded practically victorious. He had been lying in wait and Tia knew it.

"Don't even say I'm playing the race card, white boy. I'll—"

"You are and you know it." Travis waved her off. "They get families from all over. Milwaukee, Rockford, Chicago, Minneapolis. All backgrounds and, yeah, all colors, too."

"Right. Families. And there's the other obvious disqualifier."

"Excuse me?"

"I'm not like you and Molly. I'm not trying to repopulate the earth with my seed. So—"

Travis cut her off, laughing. "Four kids is not that unusual, Tia."

"I don't have a flock of little souls—"

"Flock of souls?" Travis laughed even harder. "Where do you come up with this stuff?"

Relaxed and on a roll, Tia kept going, deciding to raise the stakes a bit. "And even if I did, I sure the hell wouldn't hand them over to that wingnut Ezekiel Mills."

His grin faltered, "Well, that *wingnut* has about five thousand committed followers."

"'Followers'? Is that what you call them?" Tia let her mouth go slack and put on a vacant stare. She topped it off with a little zombie walk and was glad to see Travis roll his eyes, but he allowed himself to smile a bit. Still, she was only half kidding.

Seven years ago, the Church of the Rock had held its first Sunday morning service in a single classroom at Newberg High School—the church had been allowed to rent the space for one dollar. Soon, Saturday evening services were added and the standing-room-only crowds forced a move to the school gymnasium. Before long, the weekly congregation outgrew the school, and the church moved to rented space in a local strip mall. Three years later, the Rock broke ground on a sleek, mostly glass, modern sanctuary and extended campus that Tia was pretty sure could be seen from space. Each week several thousand worshippers came from throughout Waukesha County and beyond, all drawn to the prosperity message of Reverend Ezekiel Mills.

"Families sign their kids up for the annual retreat months in advance," Travis said. "I've thought about trying to get on the waiting list."

"I have to say, Sarge . . . I mean, I know you're a bit of a Bible thumper, but . . ." Tia wanted to choose her words carefully. Not go too far. "Ezekiel Mills? Doesn't he, like, cast spells?"

"Ouch." Travis laughed and Tia was glad he saw the humor. "Nice, Suarez. If you don't mind, I'll stand back a bit. That lightning storm isn't that far away."

Looking at the sky, Tia yelled mockingly, "No offense."

"You'd better hope none taken," Travis said. "All I'm saying is, these days? It's nice for a family to find a place where the message is about doing the right thing. Raising kids to be good people. Successful families. That's what Mills talks about. What's so sinister about that?"

The conversation was taking a personal turn and Tia figured it was time to back off. She tilted her head slightly and nodded, doing her best to give Travis a polite look of understanding. The truth was, Tia knew all she needed to know about the renowned leader of the Church of the Rock.

Reverend Ezekiel Mills wasn't the typical Old Testament fire-and-brimstone preacher most Wisconsin Lutherans grew up listening to, bored as stiff as the wooden pews they dozed on. The man was a nondenominational firebrand and anything but stoic. Pushing sixty, he projected thirty. Tall and trim, he was blessed with a full head of wavy blond hair and skin that remained tan twelve months a year. He preached in blue jeans and white oxford shirts open at the neck, prowling around an elevated stage. Movie screens allowed even the people in the nosebleed seats to get a good look.

His appeal was his homespun values, coupled with a larger-than-life personality, all delivered to an ever-growing audience. Young families felt connected to his message of self-fulfillment, achievement, and personal happiness. Older folks appreciated his commitment to fundamental values.

Tia wasn't a convert or even a fan. She had come to resent the good reverend's coded message of exclusivity, which was now broadcast on his own syndicated radio show. Every week it was the same thing: America's current spiritual course was sending the country down the tubes. America had lost her sense of morality. America needed to find herself again and return to the good old days of yesteryear.

The problem was, for many people who also laid claim to America, those days hadn't been so good. That group included Tia, but she didn't want to have that fight with Travis. He wasn't the enemy and she knew his heart was in the right place.

"Fair enough." Tia changed the subject. "But like you said, the camp is only about a mile down the road. We probably ought to pay a visit. See if maybe anyone heard a shot or saw anything. Could be the kid was part of the retreat, right?"

Travis looked at his watch.

"What is this appointment of yours?"

"Just something I can't get out of." He looked back and his tone said he wasn't going to reveal any more. "It's personal."

"Yeah? All right. I'll go by the camp, but I'd better get moving," she said, looking at the time on her cell phone. "I still got those pics to download and Livy wants me at the morgue for the cut. Pretty sure Kowalski is going to want to take some time to chew my ass before he digs in."

"Don't worry about Kowalski. It'll be fine. Sorry about all that grief with Youngblood. I'll save his chewing-out for private."

"Don't sweat it. I figure while he's in Vegas I'll slip a dead trout under his driver's seat. Should be nice and ripe by the time he gets back from his little bromance road trip."

"I'll pretend I didn't hear that," Travis said. "But I want to be there when he opens the car door."

"And by the way," Tia rolled her eyes to give the impression the next words were tough to get out, "thanks for sticking up for me. I appreciate it. But really, you don't have to do that."

"Well, that part, Youngblood got right. I do look out for you, but it's got nothing to do with the Chief. You know that."

Her tone turned serious. "I know we go way back and all, but I put myself in the position to have to take crap off of mopes like Youngblood. I can deal with it."

"Is that how you see it? Youngblood has a right to bust on you like that?"

"That's how it is." Tia winked. "My cross to bear, right? Ain't that what your people say?"

"And what is it you heathens always say? Guys like Youngblood just need to have a big old cup of shut-the-fuck-up."

Tia laughed. "That's the damn truth." She looked her boss and friend in the eye. "But seriously. Thanks. Now get out of here. Go to your whatever appointment."

Travis opened the door to his SUV.

"Hey, TJ?" Tia called, closing the trunk of her car. He paused and looked at her. "Everything's okay, right?" Amusement gone, she added, "I mean you and Molly? The kids?"

Travis said, getting into his vehicle, "Never better. I'll tell you more when I can. Sorry you have to go to church camp alone."

"It's fine, but if they start putting their hands on me, I'm calling for cover."

"It's called *laying* their hands on you and it might do you some good." From the driver's seat he said, "But if they start speaking in tongues? Get out of there."

"Thanks for the advice." Tia turned to walk away.

"And hey, Suarez." His voice turned practically solemn. "Thanks for calling me out on this—the body, I mean. It's always good working a scene with you. Like old times, right?"

Alarmed, Tia took a step back his way. "All right, Jackson. What is going on with you? You better not have cancer or some shit."

Travis laughed and fired up the engine. "You kill me, Suarez. I'm just paying you a damn compliment. Can't a boss support his troops?"

"Whatever." She shook her head. "I'll see you in Sawyer's office. One o'clock, right?"

"Yeah." He dropped the car into gear. "Assuming the Rapture doesn't come. Cuz after that, girl, we won't be seeing much of each other." ·

Travis pulled away and Tia watched until the car was out of sight. Alone and feeling it, Tia pushed back against her never-too-distant self-doubt. For all her bluster, a strong sense of inadequacy lurked within her, never very far beneath the surface. Youngblood's comments had gotten to her, mostly because she knew he was right. Other cops did question her judgment and they had every right to. That wasn't going to change anytime soon. Not in 38 days or even 138 days.

But for all the tribulations of her life, most of them self-inflicted, she loved her job, and for the most part, she figured she was pretty damn good at it. She thought back to what Livy had said: *Listen to your gut.* If only Livy knew how risky that could be. And then there was Travis. Great boss. Better friend. If working with people like Livy and Travis meant she had to put up with the Jimmy Youngbloods of the world, so be it.

The music from the camp grew louder. Tia got into her car; it took several attempts and a good number of curse words to get the engine to turn over. Once it did, she mashed the accelerator and headed toward Copper Lake.

SIX

After a two-minute drive that took her deeper into the forest, Tia pulled through the open gate of Copper Lake Campground. She drove along a winding dirt road, made shady by the maples mixed with ash towering on each side. She passed a dozen or so small wood cabins tucked back in the trees and saw the shoreline of Copper Lake. The sun was now well above the horizon and the light reflected off the water in a way that made it clear where the name had come from.

The music had grown closer and louder and now filled the woods—guitar, piano, and percussion, sounding something like rock but without the edge. The chorus of voices were joyful and the lyrics nothing short of inspirational. Tia found it damn near nauseating.

Tia drove into a parking lot filled with buses and vans, all marked with names of different churches, mostly from Wisconsin, but she also saw license plates from Michigan, Minnesota, and Illinois. She found a parking spot near the same TV van that had come to the crime scene. No surprise, really. Reporters often had the same sort of instincts as cops. The only problem was they weren't bound by insignificant details like the truth and the law. Their mission was to do whatever was necessary to spin up a story, any story, that would capture viewers and sell airtime.

When Tia stepped from her car, the van door swung open. The same perky female reporter who had interviewed Travis at the crime scene hopped out wearing a lace blouse under a dark blazer. Her hair and makeup made her look like she was ready for a night on the town—but only from the waist up. Below, she wore sweatpants and tennis shoes. The reporter smiled and waved hopefully. Tia glared back and shook her head, doing her best to wordlessly convey "not a chance." The reporter's shoulders dropped in disappointment and she climbed back into the van.

Tia headed for a nearby building marked as the camp office, adorned with an American flag flying on one side of the door, and on the other side, a second flag marked with some sort of crest that Tia didn't recognize. She navigated her way around the puddles and mud until she came in view of a large clearing, finally finding the source of the music. A crowd of young people stood in a circle around a raised stage, their linked hands in the air, bodies swaying in unison. Tia estimated there were at least a hundred fifty, maybe even two hundred kids, all of whom looked to be around high school age. She saw they were divided into groups, wearing brightly colored T-shirts. There was a red group, a blue group, and a few others. When no one so much as glanced her way, it confirmed Tia's suspicion.

I knew it. They cast spells at these things.

The band was actually pretty good and the music had an odd sort of evangelical pull. She made it to the office building just as the song wrapped up and a cheer rose from the crowd. Tia looked back over her shoulder to see a man jockeying his way toward the stage, pumping his fist above his head. The cheers grew louder as he climbed onto the platform. Tia found the frenzy a bit unsettling. She hustled up the office stairs and across the wooden porch.

The unlocked screen door let her into a reception area that looked more like a cabin than an office. Rough wood walls cut from logs gave the room an authentically rustic feel and the raised floor rang hollow under her feet. A wood counter ran across the middle of the room, reminding Tia of a bar scene in an old spaghetti western. Or maybe a general store. Sure enough, there was a bell sitting on the counter. Tia dinged it twice. After a few seconds, a curtain behind the counter space pulled back and a woman emerged.

"Oh, good. Kitchen supplies, right?"

"No." Annoyed by the slight, even though it was a common occurrence, Tia paused, making sure she had the woman's attention before holding up her badge on its chain around her neck. "Detective Suarez, Newberg PD. I need to speak to the camp director. Or whoever's in charge. Is that you?"

"Oh no," the woman said. "I'm just waiting for a delivery. I'm Eva. Camp cook. We're going to have a lot of mouths to feed this week."

"That's nice." Tia nodded. "Like I said, I can't help you with that. Who can I talk to about your . . . what are they? Campers?"

The woman, near exactly Tia's height but twice as wide, beamed and nodded. "That's our youth corps. Wasn't that last song just wonderful?"

"Yeah. It was something. So who can I talk to?"

"May I ask what this is about?" The woman calmly laced her hands on the counter and tilted her head, sending the message that Tia shouldn't expect anything to happen too fast. Her round face was bright red, her breaths were short and labored. She looked as if she'd been exercising but Tia suspected the workout hadn't involved anything more than walking to the counter. Thick glasses with oversize frames magnified the size of her eyes; long mousy-brown hair hung down past her waist. She wore a loose-fitting dress that went all the way to the floor. The entire look struck Tia as odd for a woman who appeared to be well into her fifties.

"Well, it's not about their diet, so why don't you just let me talk to whoever's running the show."

The smile disappeared and the voice lost its lighthearted tone. "Reverend Mills is the retreat director and he's with the youth corps right now."

"Reverend Mills? That's him outside onstage?" Somehow Tia hadn't expected the big boss to be present at the campground. The woman gave a single curt nod of superiority.

"Then, I need to see him," Tia said. "It's important."

"He's giving morning motivation and wouldn't want to be interrupted. I'm afraid you'll have to wait."

"Yeah? Is that what you call it?" Tia nodded in acknowledgment, then turned to the door, ignoring the woman's protest.

"Wait. You can't go out there." Tia walked out of the office, taking some satisfaction in Eva's complete exasperation. "Just who the heck do you think you are?"

Outside again, Tia saw that most of the campers were now seated on the grass—and sure enough, on the stage was the man himself, Ezekiel Mills. He spoke into a microphone, his familiar voice amplified through a pair of eight-foot speakers, his audience as rapt as if they were hypnotized.

"Today is a day for you to once again express the power of youth. To join together in a joyful celebration of our great land. *You* are the legacy of this nation. The future is yours and you are the future!"

A cheer rose from the audience; some jumped to their feet, hands in the air.

Right on cue, the band began to play a song about lifting voices and loving life. Mills set the microphone on top of a speaker and hopped off the stage, moving through the audience exchanging high fives. He neared Tia but paid her no mind until she reached out and took hold of his arm.

"Reverend Mills?"

"Yes," Mills said, looking at Tia's hand on his arm; she could see he wasn't sure what to make of her. Young, but not young enough to be one of his drones, and a bit more assertive than he was probably comfortable with.

"Who are you?"

Tia lifted her badge into view and pitched her voice to be heard above the noise.

"Detective Suarez, Newberg PD. Is there someplace we can talk?"

Mills, slightly out of breath and looking a bit off his mark, swiped a long lock of hair from his forehead. His voice turned challenging. "Talk? What about?"

"Please, sir. Someplace private? I'll try not to take too much of your time."

Mills scanned the area and Tia knew he couldn't help but notice several of the young people were listening to their exchange. A murmur began to move through the crowd: *The cops are here.* He pushed past Tia, heading for the office. "This way."

Tia followed him back to the building, where they were met at the door by Eva the cook. She'd gone from calm and collected to damn near hostile.

"I'm sorry, Reverend," she said to Mills, glaring at Tia. "I told her she needed to wait."

"That's okay, Eva. There's nothing to be concerned about." He turned to Tia, back on his game and in control. "Please, Detective. Come with me."

Tia followed Mills behind the curtain into a small but comfortable office. Tia took the visitor's chair as Mills settled in behind the desk.

"Sorry, it's not much," Mills said, looking around the cramped space. "But we're supposed to be roughing it, right?"

The man smiled, and Tia took notice of the brightness of his teeth, offset by the tan glow of his skin. His hair wasn't the white blond she remembered from her brief glimpses of him on TV when she was channel surfing, but it did appear to be unnaturally lightened and the wave was definitely from a salon.

"So what brings you to our retreat, Detective? I must say, we've never been visited by law enforcement."

"Sir, I need to know if any of your . . ." Tia paused, wondering again about terminology. ". . . if any of the young people are missing. Do you check morning attendance? Anything like that?"

"The youth corps has two hundred and fifty members. They're divided into ten spirit tribes with twenty-five disciples. Each spirit tribe has a leader." Mills spoke with assurance. "No one is missing."

Tia wasn't at all sure if he had answered her question. "So yes or no? Do you have some sort of daily head count?"

Mills shifted in his seat behind the desk. "We don't *count heads* but I can assure you, if a young person was missing, I would have been informed. Why are you asking?"

"How do you know that, sir?" Tia sat up straight in her chair, her hands draped over each arm and her legs crossed. "I mean, if you haven't counted?"

Mills looked to the clock on the wall and his voice grew impatient. "What is your concern, Detective?"

"Sir, a young boy, probably a teenager, was found dead in the woods early this morning, about a mile from here."

The color drained from his face and Mills leaned forward in his chair. "My God, why didn't you just say so? I had no idea. Who is he?"

Tia, glad to hear the concern, decided to give him a bit more information. "We don't know who he is. From what I can tell, he was—"

"From what you can tell?" His raised voice approached panic.

"Please, Reverend, let me finish. From what I can tell he was in his teens. He had black hair past his collar. I'm fairly certain he was Native American. He had a tattoo on his—"

"Oh well, that is definitely not any of our young people." The relief in his voice was obvious, leaving Tia irritated.

"How can you be so certain, Reverend? Not much in the way of brown folks in your group?"

Mills smiled but didn't take the bait.

"Tattoos are a disqualifier." The man's disinterest had returned in force. "The Church of the Rock does not condone that sort of self-mutilation."

"Really? Where's that in the Bible?"

"I don't mean to sound boastful, Detective, but in addition to my ministerial training, I have a doctorate in psychology. I must say you project a great deal of hostility. Perhaps you should join us at the church one Sunday. Or maybe you'd be more comfortable at a Saturday night service—it's more casual but still very uplifting. I think you could benefit from some positive energy."

"My energy is fine where it's at." Tia moved on. "I'd still like to speak with your campers. Staff, too. Whoever found the body didn't stick around for the cops to show up. We're wondering if someone from your group called it in."

Mills shook his head. "I'm afraid I can't allow that. We adhere to a strict schedule of events. And besides, that sort of distressing message would have a terribly negative effect on our young people."

Tia was genuinely thrown off. "Say what now?"

"The parents of these children have trusted us with their care. I couldn't allow them to be subject to . . . I don't know . . . what sounds like a police interrogation of some sort."

"It would hardly be an interrogation. We just want to find out if anyone heard anything out of the ordinary. Maybe even saw something." Tia thought Reverend Mills might be worried about some sort of liability so she tried to ease his mind. "State law is pretty clear. Teenagers can be interviewed by the police without parental consent."

"I don't care what the law says," Mill replied with a tone of defiance. "You will not question these young people while they are in my care."

Tia leaned forward in her chair, speechless, and Mills went on, "I can assure you, Detective, the boy you found will be in our prayers but he's not associated with our retreat."

"I see." Tia gave a slow nod. "So you're saying no, then?"

"I'm afraid so, Detective." Mills stood. "I'm sorry I couldn't be of more help."

"Well, then." Tia did her best to appear helpless. "I guess if you can't allow it, we're done talking, right?"

Mills gave a toothy grin as he came around the desk, directing Tia to the office door.

"Reverend Mills." Tia stood. "I appreciate your time."

"Not at all. And again, I'm sorry I couldn't be of more assistance. It would be great to see you at one of our services."

Mills stood with his hand extended but Tia was already moving. She walked out of the office, through the lobby, and back out the front door. She glided down the steps and directly toward the crowd, still listening to the musicians. Jogging the last few steps, she easily made a running leap onto the stage. Startled, the members of the band came to a ragged halt. The last guy to give up was the drummer, and by then the singing had stopped.

She picked up the microphone Mills had left behind and tapped it twice with her finger. A loud, thumping sound boomed through the man-size speakers.

"Is this thing on?" Tia said, hearing her voice reverberate through the woods. All eyes turned her way and Tia waved. "Good morning, everyone. Sorry to interrupt your . . . concert, I guess? But this is important."

In her peripheral vision, Tia saw the office screen door fly open, banging against the log wall. Mills jumped from the porch without touching a step. He began to speed walk with arms pumping directly to where Tia stood on center stage. She ignored him and continued with her announcement.

"My name is Detective Suarez. I'm with the Newberg Police Department. I think it might be possible that one of you made a nine-one-one call last night."

The audience stared back silently, the only sound coming from Mills as he huffed through the crowd and then climbed back onto the stage. He moved to the amplifier where the microphone cord was plugged. Tia held a hand up to the audience and turned toward Mills, who now stood just a few feet away, his hand reaching for a power cord.

"Reverend Mills." It was Tia's turn to sound like the condescending authority. "If you're thinking of unplugging me, don't."

"I most certainly will." His voice was loud enough to be picked up by the microphone. "Now, I told you, Detective—"

"I know what you told me. And now I'm telling you: pull that cord and you'll be arrested."

Mills glared back at her from across the stage. "You can't do that."

Tia turned to face him and did her best to convey a patience she didn't feel. "Yes, sir, I can and I will. For interfering with the duties of a police officer."

"You wouldn't dare." Mills's voice echoed off the tall pines. Tia looked out at the captivated audience and couldn't help but think they were finding this much more entertaining than the concert. She turned back to Mills.

"Really? Are we going to go there?"

"This is a religious retreat. The police have no right to barge in here and harass these young people."

"This campground is state property. I'd be happy to discuss the finer points of the law with you in a few minutes. But for now, sir"—

she looked directly at his hand poised on the microphone cord and spoke as if she was trying to give good advice—"don't do it."

Mills's voice took on a childish quality. "Well, it's my microphone."

Tia conceded with a gracious nod. "Good point. Consider it commandeered for the moment. I won't warn you again."

Tia returned Mills's cold stare with a look of indifference. Although he remained poised to disconnect her, Tia could see the man had lost his nerve. She saw no harm in allowing him to stand in some meaningless display of defiance. She turned to the audience of young people, and found two hundred sets of unblinking eyes looking back.

"Like I was saying. Someone called the police last night. If it was you, it's important we talk."

Tia stood and looked over the crowd. "No takers?"

The silence was deafening. "All right. Well, like I said, I'm Detective Suarez. Newberg PD. I'm pretty easy to find. Call me anytime. Day or night."

Tia turned to look at Reverend Mills, who hadn't moved. He still gripped the cord with a shaking hand, his chest rising and falling with angry breaths. Tia smiled and winked. "Okay, Rev, go ahead. Give it a pull."

SEVEN

Tia drove to the Newberg field office of the county medical examiner and parked near the loading dock. Already twenty minutes late and frustrated, she pulled herself from the car and hustled inside. Tia knew she had only herself to blame. She'd spent far too much time arguing with the righteously offended Reverend Mills, who clearly believed that the spiritual bliss of his campers took precedence over a death investigation.

Not only was Tia late to the autopsy, she hadn't sent Livy the crime scene photographs from her cell phone, and on top of all that, she was showing up without the promised coffee. Safe to say, Livy was going to be unhappy.

A college-age intern Tia didn't recognize sat at the front counter and barely looked up from his computer screen. "Need something?"

Tia held up her badge. "Detective Suarez. Here to see Livy Sorensen."

With half-open eyes, he glanced toward her badge, then turned back to the sports highlights show on his screen. Sounding as though he were talking in his sleep, he said, "She's in an autopsy. You can wait if you want but those things drag on sometimes."

"Yo, slick." Tia smacked the counter twice with her palm and finally managed to get his attention and make eye contact. "I'm here for the autopsy. Buzz me through."

He jerked upright, dropping his feet to the floor, and pushed the entry button. "Take it easy. Geez. They, like, started already." Tia was happy to hear a trace of fear in his voice.

Pushing through the door that led to the secured portion of the building, Tia headed down the familiar hallway and into the cutting room. The flash of Livy's thirty-five-millimeter digital camera glared off the chrome examination table where the now naked body of the teenager was unceremoniously displayed. The remains of the head were hidden under the plain brown grocery bag that Livy had hastily applied at the crime scene as the downpour had begun. Duct tape encircled the throat like a tight blue turtleneck. The hands were bagged and taped as well. Tia couldn't help but notice the bags were still damp and dotted with water spots from the rain.

"Sorry I'm late," Tia said, relieved Livy was alone and still in the early stages of the autopsy, taking overall, head-to-toe shots. She hadn't missed much. "Find anything when you stripped him? A note? ID? Where's Mort?"

"Mort is right here, but I prefer 'Dr. Kowalski.'" Tia turned to see Mortimer Kowalski standing nearby, gowned, gloved, and ready for work. A fireplug of a man with a mop of gray hair tinged dull yellow from nicotine, he wore a plastic face shield in the up position. A lit cigarette bobbed at the corner of his mouth. "For a person with so many questions, perhaps you should try to be on time."

Pushing seventy, Dr. Kowalski had been a Waukesha County deputy medical examiner since the inception of the position over thirty years ago. The story was that he had been a country doctor, eking out a living as a general practitioner in a town full of hearty Scandinavians, who considered a visit to the doctor an insult to one's character and fortitude. Kowalski had been the only applicant for the position of county deputy medical examiner, which came with a guaranteed salary, twenty days paid vacation, and a pension that would make any cop or firefighter green with envy. He'd held the job ever since and there were no signs he planned to leave anytime soon.

There was no love lost between Tia and Dr. Kowalski. She'd been the center of more than one high-profile case that resulted in scrutiny being brought to bear not only on the police department, but allied agencies as well. That included the office of the medical examiner— and Dr. Kowalski did not respond well to scrutiny.

"The autopsy was scheduled to begin at ten and that is exactly what time we started," Kowalski said. Tia knew he was happy to get in a few early-morning personal jabs. "You missed the removal of clothing and personal inventory."

"Sorry, Doctor," Tia said, causing Livy to look up from her camera. Tia saw what might have been a trace of sympathy on her friend's face, but nothing more than that. "There was a development at the crime scene. Thought I might be able to identify the reporting party. Maybe even a witness."

She could tell she now had Livy's interest, but the doctor was the one who spoke up. "Oh yes. I heard you managed to get things off to a pretty rough start."

"Yes, sir, I did. But turns out the campground up the road is hosting a retreat. Couple of hundred young people. I was hoping I might locate the person who made the nine-one-one call."

"And?"

"It didn't pan out as much as I hoped, but I did get a chance to speak to the entire group. We might still get a lead out of it." Tia decided to leave it at that. "Anyway, I apologize for being late."

"Hm." He looked down at the body, his gloved palms resting

along the raised trough of the smooth, chrome table. "Well, as I said, Ms. Sorensen completed the inventory. I suppose she can catch you up."

Livy took the cue. "We cut the bag tag and broke him out. No issues there. I stripped him. I figured you'd want the shirt, so I photographed it and preserved it for you. It's in the drying chamber."

Livy kept talking as she worked her way around to the other side of the long table, continuing with her photography. "I thoroughly searched all items of clothing. He's got no ID but he did have a thousand dollars in his right front trouser pocket in a plain, stock white envelope, folded in half. Ten one-hundred-dollar bills. New, sequential, and uncirculated."

"Wow." Tia was surprised. "So from a bank, then, right?"

"Probably." Livy went on, "I bagged the bills and the envelope as one item but separate from the clothing. There were no other items of personal property. I bagged the trousers, underwear, and shoes. I'll impound everything in the ME's evidence room. We can discuss further processing after the autopsy."

Livy took one last picture. The flash filled the large room, which was the size of a small auditorium. She looked up, sounding tired. "That's where we're at. You're all caught up."

"So just the money?"

"Like I said." Livy was all business. "No other items of personal property."

Tia had hoped for a suicide note or at least some form of identification.

Dr. Kowalski took a last, hard pull on his cigarette, then dropped it onto the floor, grinding it into the tile with his shoe. "Now, Detective, if you feel sufficiently updated, can we move along?"

He pushed the "record" button, activating the microphone that hung above the table. After providing time, date, case number, and identifying himself, he turned to Tia. "Detective, your name and position."

"Detective Tia Suarez, badge number 4-5-6. Newberg Police Department."

Dr. Kowalski had Livy complete the same ritual and then moved on to the next procedural issue. "Ms. Sorensen, overall description, please."

Without further prompting, Livy pulled a measuring tape alongside the body and clicked on the scale built into the table. "Decedent male is currently a John Doe, five feet three and a half inches tall, weighing one hundred thirty-eight pounds. Complexion is brown, skin is relatively clear. I will now remove preservation measures that were applied on scene prior to taking custody of the body."

Livy used a pair of tactical scissors to slice the duct tape and remove the bags covering the hands and head. Tia saw that much of the head wound had crusted over and solidified, although there were still large areas of semi-coagulated blood with a syrup-like consistency. Dr. Kowalski pursed his lips and nodded—his only acknowledgment of a wound rare in its level of destructiveness. Livy continued with her on the record description.

"The decedent has sustained a gunshot wound in the area of the head and neck. A twelve-gauge shotgun with an expended shell casing in the chamber was recovered from the scene. Trauma to the face, brain, and skull was severe. The entire frontal lobe and a significant portion of the temporal lobe are gone, as well as all facial features beginning at the lower mandible and extending past the supraorbital ridge. The remaining facial muscular structure, including the mentalis, septi nasi, and nasalis has been . . ."

Livy paused, as if searching for the appropriate scientific term to describe what she was seeing, then settled for the obvious. ". . . shredded. Preliminary indications are that the wound was inflicted with a single round fired from the aforementioned firearm. It is highly probable this wound was instantaneously fatal. There are no other remarkable indicators of injury or illness.

"Doctor?" Livy looked at Kowalski and nodded, signifying she was finished with the initial on-the-record assessment of the body.

Dr. Kowalski lowered his plastic face shield and rolled the instrument tray to within easy reach. The array of tools included a bone saw and forceps alongside such common household objects as a baster and soup ladle. He picked up a scalpel that gleamed under the bright light hanging above the table.

"All right, Ms. Sorenson, let's get started. Detective, your role is strictly to observe. Please remember that."

Tia stepped back and watched as the doctor leaned in over the body. He centered his blade between the nipples, stretched back the skin with two fingers, and began the initial incision.

EIGHT

Bleary-eyed, Tia watched as Livy used both gloved hands to scoop and lift the large intestines out of the bowl of the hanging scale. Long tubular sections slipped from the tall woman's grip, forcing her to raise the mass higher to get it clear of the scale before dropping it into the five-gallon orange bucket positioned at the end of the examination table, where it landed on top of the heart, stomach, and spleen.

The digital clock on the nearby wall read 1:12 P.M. Doing the math in her head, Tia figured out she'd been awake for most of the last twenty-four hours. She'd spent the last three on her feet, watching the slow dismemberment of her John Doe. The haze of exhaustion felt a bit like getting a good load on, minus the euphoria . . . and the guilt and self-loathing that inevitably followed.

Kowalski had cut out each organ and examined the tissue for signs of injury or disease. After slicing off a small section for toxicology testing, he'd handed the body parts to Livy for weighing and disposal. Kowalski prattled on as he used a chrome soup ladle to scoop the puddle of fluids from the hollowed-out torso that had taken on the look of something like a human canoe.

"I'm not sure what it is you have in mind here, Ms. Sorensen. There are no indications of a struggle. Fingernails are clean. No defensive wounds of any sort. The fatal wound pattern is consistent with a self-inflicted and quite intentional discharge from a shotgun. Lividity strongly suggests that the body was not moved or tampered with. A shotgun was recovered from the scene. There are no indicators of second-party involvement. Is that your assessment, Detective?"

Tia looked down at the head. What was left of the traumatically damaged brain had been removed and made its way to the chum bucket. All loose organic material had been washed off, revealing the top and back of the empty, bowl-like skull, scrubbed clean and smooth.

The last thing Tia wanted was to side against Livy, but the autopsy had not changed her opinion. In fact, she was now convinced. She didn't look up when she answered, "Yes, Doctor. I'm comfortable with suicide."

"All right, then." Kowalski stepped back, seeming to signal his mind was made up. "Let's close him up, shall we?"

"Yes, Doctor." Livy lifted the plastic trash bag liner from the bucket and shook it, settling the contents to the bottom. She gave the fattest part of the bag a slap of her hand to twirl it shut, then tied a knot at the top. Livy nestled the bag down into the empty chest cavity, a standard procedure that always left Tia thinking of a gizzard bag in a Thanksgiving turkey.

Flattening the bag, Livy retrieved the two sections of rib cage that had been cut away early in the autopsy. She fit the skinless ribs back into position as if they were a matching set of giant puzzle pieces. Kowalski picked up his Hagedorn needle and loaded it with a thick black thread. He pulled the flaps of skin over the rib cage, like he was closing a set of drapes, then went to work sewing up the

Y-shaped incision that ran from both shoulders clear down to the pubic bone. His work was sloppy and inexact but the patient was unlikely to complain. The fast movement of his hands matched the cadence of his speech.

"In the future, Ms. Sorensen, if you intend to be taken seriously in this field, I would suggest you put more effort into the fundamentals. In this case, that would be protecting and preserving your death scene and then documenting your observations in a manner that can be independently verified by a higher authority."

Livy ignored him in her response. "Am I clear to print him, Doctor?"

Kowalski snipped off the thread and stepped away. "I'm finished. Go ahead."

Livy reached out and gripped the cadaver by the right hand as if she were about to introduce herself. It was coming up on ten hours since time of death and rigor was advanced. Setting her other hand at the shoulder joint to brace the body, she lifted the board-like arm straight up, then out and away from the torso.

The crack of the now-stiffened muscles echoed through the exam room, like the dry trunk of a long dead tree as it falls to the ground. Livy began to work the whole arm, back and forth and up and down, until she had completely broken down the rigor-hardened muscle enzymes. Shifting to the elbow, she applied the same technique, and when it was flexible, she moved on to the wrist, where she spent extra time getting the joint good and loose. Once the entire arm was completely pliable, she twisted and broke each finger one at a time in her fist.

Livy talked as she pressed the first limp finger against a black ink pad. "As I said before the autopsy, Doctor, I consider the lack of any blood spatter on either arm or hand to be an issue."

"Oh, do you now?" Dr. Kowalski stripped off his smock and dumped it into the nearby linen basket. He pulled off his latex gloves—originally blue, now bright red with blood—and tossed them into the wastebasket marked BIOHAZARD. His voice was dismissive. "I know you love to show off your extensive vocational training, but the lack of a splatter pattern is not unusual."

Livy rolled the last fingerprint onto an index card and spoke without looking up. "It's 'spatter.'"

"Excuse me?" The doctor was already fumbling for a cigarette.

"You said 'splatter.'" It was Livy's turn to be condescending. "The blood pattern is referred to as 'spatter.'"

"Whichever, it isn't significant under these circumstances. Once you allowed the entire body to be exposed to the elements, you created a perfectly plausible and, I might add, non-criminal explanation for why there's no blood on the hands." Kowalski sounded like he enjoyed pointing out the obvious screw-up. "Any blood was probably washed away by the rain."

Dr. Kowalski lit his cigarette and took what looked to be a long-awaited drag. He leaned his head back and blew a cloud of smoke toward the high ceiling. "But we'll never know for certain, will we?"

Tia spoke up. Agree or disagree, she wasn't going to stand by while Kowalski heaped all the blame on her friend. "That's on me, sir. I was responsible for protecting the crime scene. But Livy did make her observation prior to the rain."

"Too bad I wasn't there to see it for myself." Kowalski, short and round in stature, held his cigarette by his face, reminding Tia of Philip Seymour Hoffman playing Capote. "Unless of course, Ms. Sorensen, all your community college training qualifies you to sign a death certificate?"

Rounding the body, Livy looked directly at her boss and jerked hard on the left arm. A resounding thwack filled the air and Tia was pretty sure it wasn't the sound of hardened muscle fibers breaking, but bone cracking. "No, sir. That calls for your expertise."

"Precisely." He walked to the door leading to his office. "Finish up here and vault him. Detective, you'll have my report in seven to ten days."

When the door shut behind him, Tia waited a moment before speaking up. "What a dick."

Livy said nothing, but just continued to work the second arm, her gaze locked on the door.

"So, Liv." Tia felt a bit sheepish, realizing she had played a major role in the problem Livy was having with her boss. "Anything I can do to help finish up?"

"No, I'm good." Livy didn't look up from her work. "I'll get the prints in the system for you. The evidence will be booked here in our locker."

"Cool. I appreciate it. I'm going back to the station right now. You'll have the pictures by two o'clock."

Livy pressed her lips into a straight, thin line and shook her head. She started to roll the second thumb. "Don't bother. I won't need them."

"Look, Livy. This call has been a cluster-fuck from the minute Youngblood got his fat ass on scene. But I didn't do much better.

"Good thing is," she continued, "turns out it is a suicide and we can just chalk it up as a learning opportunity, right? Kind of like a training exercise."

Tia waited for a reply but none came. "Right, Liv?"

Livy took the four fingers on the left hand and held them flat against the bottom of the card, the last step in the printing. "You must be beat. Go on and get out of here."

"Yeah, okay then." Tia pulled off her latex gloves. They were barely flecked with blood, showing that her involvement in the almost-four-hour process had been limited to the sidelines. "Let's grab lunch this week, all right?"

Livy laid the hand gently down on the table and finally looked up, her eyes moist behind the plastic face shield. "Yeah. That'd be nice. Call me."

She turned and walked away, leaving Tia with the body of a dead boy who had most definitely come between them.

NINE

Tia paused in the entrance to the cramped office, knuckles ready to rap on the doorframe. Instead she stood straight up and said, sarcastically, "Well, take a look at you. Is that the big mystery? Sawyer kicked your ass back to patrol?"

Travis was wearing his full dress uniform complete with a clip-on necktie, basket-weave duty belt, and well-polished boots. Tia had to admit that even after two years of riding a desk as a detective sergeant, the man still looked great in uniform.

Maneuvering around the gray metal desk that dominated the small space, Travis brushed past her and headed out the door. "I told you I had a thing. You ready to brief Sawyer? He's waiting in his office."

"What kind of thing?" Tia continued to pester him as he walked by. "Let me guess. Guest speaker at the Senior Citizen Center? Or, no, wait. You're the Culver's Officer of the Month again. They're going to name a flavor after you, right?"

Her levity was wasted on an empty room and she followed him across the hallway into the administration wing of Newberg PD, where the Chief kept an office just past a small reception area. Tia nodded as they passed the Chief's secretary.

"Sorry to barge in, Carrie. Sarge here tells me we got an appointment."

"No problem, Tia." The young woman smiled. "The Chief's waiting for you."

By the time Tia got into the office, Travis was already taking a seat at one end of the couch. Chief of Police Ben Sawyer got to his feet, behind his desk.

"Hey, Tia. How you been?"

"Hello, sir. I'm good, thanks."

It had been a week or so since they'd last crossed paths, but Tia made sure to speak with formality, mindful of the fact she and the Chief were not alone. She and Ben Sawyer had a relationship that went far beyond the typical boss-subordinate dynamic. Both had grown up in Newberg, but fifteen years and a couple of social worlds apart. A shared wanderlust had sent each on their own worldly adventures and put Newberg in the rearview mirror.

A month after graduating from Newberg High School, Tia joined the Marines, where it was discovered she was a genius when it came to languages. The Department of Defense put her through a twenty-four-week crash course in Farsi, followed by a three-month immersion in Saudi Arabia. After two tours in Afghanistan as an interrogator/translator with a counterintelligence unit, Tia had been ready to come back to the much more predictable and less chaotic world of Newberg. She applied for the local PD on a whim and soon came to realize it was the work she'd been born to do. Her first boss had been Sergeant Ben Sawyer.

When Tia met Ben he had just returned from fifteen years with the Oakland PD in California. He was a celebrity of sorts, but not the kind any cop wanted to be. Ben had been forced to resign from Oakland after cell-phone video footage of him shoving the barrel of his gun into the mouth of a wanted felon went viral. Even though the action had been out of character, it had—rightfully—ended Ben's career in California.

The road to redemption hadn't been easy, but through the darkest days of his tribulation until he pinned on his stars as Newberg police chief, Tia Suarez had stood by his side. Their friendship was a bond as strong as blood but Tia tried not to flaunt it when other cops were around.

"Grab a seat." Ben looked relaxed, dressed in his dark blue, command BDU's. The cotton material of the battle dress uniform was embroidered with cloth stars, a badge, and a name tag, allowing for a more casual look than that of the traditional uniform. Instead of a fully kitted gun belt, he wore a belt holster with just his sidearm and cuffs. Like Travis, Ben had stayed fit, but he couldn't stop the graying of his close-cropped hair. The well-earned scar that ran jagged across his face stood out as his most defining feature.

Ben turned to Travis. "You're looking sharp, TJ. Everything go well? Still on track?"

Sawyer's in on it? Tia kept quiet.

"Uh, yes, sir," Travis said, looking at Tia out of the corner of his eye then back to his boss. It came to her like an epiphany, but before she could give it any more thought, Ben turned her way.

"TJ told me about your callout last night. A body in Skeel's Woods?"

Tia took a seat at the opposite end of the couch from Travis. She couldn't help but feel a bit self-conscious in her blue jeans and coffee-stained windbreaker. "Yes, sir. Victim took a shotgun round to the head. Fatal. Still no ID. Weapon recovered on scene."

"And?" Ben wanted an answer to the obvious question.

"We're pretty much settled on suicide, Chief. Still waiting for the final report from the ME. That and we've got a few loose ends to clean up."

"Is there a chance it wasn't suicide?"

"Like I said, we're pretty sure. Just want to rule out a staged job."

"'Staged'?" Ben stopped halfway down to his chair. "That sounds a bit Hollywood."

"It's just that there's an issue with the blood spatter."

When Ben only stared back, Tia went on, "There's blood on the shotgun barrel as well as the victim's clothing, and we're comfortable that the shotgun recovered from the scene is the murder weapon."

"So what's the issue?" Ben, now seated, leaned back in his chair.

"The hands and arms are clean, Chief. No spatter. None at all."

Ben furrowed his brow; when he spoke, his voice was respectful but tentative: "Did I come up with a couple of thousand bucks in the training budget or something?"

Tia knew where he was headed, but asked anyway. "How's that, sir?"

"I'm just wondering if I sent you off to some hotshot blood spatter class. That's a pretty keen observation."

Tia took the ribbing in stride. "Not all that complicated, Chief, but I won't lie. I missed it. It was Livy Sorensen who picked up on it. She noticed it right off."

"Sorensen? The MEI, right? Kinda tall? Big-boned?"

"Kinda, yeah."

"She worked your shooting scene last year, right?"

"That's her."

"All right, so we got a blood pattern issue to deal with. We'll come back to that. What about witnesses? Who called it in?"

Tia looked to Travis, who still said nothing, so she went on, "We don't know. The RP split before the first officers arrived on scene."

"The hell you say," Ben said. "No RP on a body? They just left? Who does that?"

Tia shrugged. "Well, a shooter would for sure. But more likely, just a freaked-out citizen who's seen one too many movies about headless bodies in the woods."

Tia couldn't help herself: "Anyway. Uniforms *eventually* showed up. Found the scene."

" 'Eventually'?"

Perfect. Screw you, Jimmy.

"Yeah, well, the first cops . . ." Tia suddenly felt hesitant about throwing anyone, even an arrogant jerk like Jimmy Youngblood, under the bus. She stopped talking and looked at Travis, letting him know this was his job. He didn't hesitate. Travis got behind the wheel and put the bitch in drive.

"It was Youngblood's call, Chief," Travis said "And his trainee, that new guy. Puller. They were twenty-seven minutes getting to the scene. Apparently a good bit of time after that looking for the body. I've told both of them to cover that in their reports."

"Twenty-seven . . ." Ben leaned way back and turned his face up to the ceiling. "At two o'clock in the morning? I could drive to Madison and back in twenty-seven minutes. What the hell, TJ?"

"Like I said, sir, I told Youngblood to document it. I haven't seen his report yet."

Tia could see, little by little, the Chief was becoming less comfortable with the direction of the briefing. He turned to Tia. "I hope Dispatch has something for us to go on, at least?"

"Yep," Tia said. "TJ ordered up a copy of the nine-one-one call. No worries, Chief. I'll run it down."

Tia watched as Ben mentally worked through the information. Spatter issue, late response, a disappearing RP. When he'd been supervisor of the gang unit in Oakland, he'd worked more homicides in a typical month than all the cops in Newberg combined would see in their entire career. The man knew his way around a crime scene.

"Barrel in the mouth?" The question was almost a statement.

Tia shook her head. "My guess is under the chin. Took off his entire face."

"His whole face? I take it that's the source of our ID problem?"

"Yeah. Plus no wallet or cell phone, but he did have a good bit of cash."

"How much?"

"Thousand bucks. All hundreds. Sequential, uncirculated bills."

"Bank money." Ben nodded. "Pretty obvious robbery wasn't a motive."

"Right," Tia agreed. "Which is what I think gets us pretty far down the road to suicide."

"Let's go back to this spatter issue." Ben came around his desk. He stretched his arms out and down, tipping his head back as if putting the barrel of a long weapon under his chin. Tia could see he had his finger working an imaginary trigger. "On a shotgun blast the hands and arms are going to be extended like this, right? Straight down. It's not like a pistol to the head. Couldn't he have come out of it clean? His hands, I mean?"

"That's my thought. But like I said, Livy sees it differently. And she makes a good case for it. I mean, the barrel has blood all up and down it. That means the boy's arms and maybe even his hands ought to be at least dotted with blood."

"So she's calling that a deal breaker?" Ben sounded hesitant. "We go all in on a homicide? What did Dr. Kowalski have to say about it?"

"He hasn't ruled yet, but it's pretty obvious he's leaning suicide."

"Well okay, then. So if you're good with suicide, and the ME is good with suicide, what's the problem? Can't you get Livy to come around?"

"Maybe, but we've got this one other issue," Tia said.

Ben closed his eyes for a long moment. "Of course you do."

It was clear he was getting more exasperated with the growing list of problems. After a few seconds of silence, Ben put his hands up and wagged his fingers as if asking for more. "Pile it on. What issue?"

Travis took the lead. "Out at the crime scene, Chief. We had a bit of a . . . of a . . . snafu."

Sawyer looked back and forth between both cops. 'Snafu'?"

"Yeah. Snafu," Tia said. "You know. Like a fuckup."

"I know what it means, Tia. Just tell me what you're talking about."

"We had a pretty heavy downpour last night," Travis said. "Only lasted a few minutes, but you know how the skies can open up this time of year. The crime scene got pretty well drenched."

"The body got soaked, Chief," Tia chimed in. "We got a tarp over him as quick as we could and Livy bagged the hands, but by then the scene was compromised."

"So?"

"So," Tia said, "Livy made her observation of the lack of blood on the hands before it rained, but Kowalski isn't buying it. He figures the blood was there but must have been washed away."

"So the spatter and rain issue? That's your snafu?" Ben asked.

Tia shrugged. "Or fuckup. Take your choice."

"So Mort is using our less-than-stellar performance at the crime scene to overrule his MEI? Is that fair to say?"

"Exactly."

"Who else was at the scene? Before the rain, I mean."

"Just Jimmy and his trainee," Tia said.

Travis jumped in. "I talked to Officer Youngblood, Chief. He's all in on suicide. He didn't pick up anything suspicious."

"Excuse me, Chief?" Carrie spoke from the doorway. At Ben's nod, she said, "There's an attorney on the phone. Says he represents the Church of the Rock. Says it's important he talk to you right away."

"Get outta here." Tia laughed. "You mean to tell me the church lawyered-up?"

Carrie looked at Tia, then back to her boss. "He said you should take a look at the Channel Eight website."

Ben looked at Tia. "What's this going to be about?"

"Channel Eight?" Remembering the media truck, she stopped laughing and felt an immediate sense of dread. She did her best to sound innocent and answered, at least somewhat honestly, "I couldn't tell you."

Ben got busy on his keyboard, and Tia saw Travis sit up straight and look her way. She hadn't had a chance to tell him how things went at the retreat so this would be news to him as well.

She figured she'd better start explaining. "I mean, I went by the campground to check for witnesses. Seemed appropriate. That Reverend Mills guy was there. We had a bit of . . ." She waved a hand through the air, waiting for the right words to come to mind. "I don't know. A run-in, I guess?"

"A run-in?" Ben looked up from the computer screen. "So, what, Tia? Is that kind of like a snafu?"

Tia heard the exasperation in his voice and knew she was pushing his patience. "Yeah, kinda."

"Oh shit," Ben said, leaning closer to his screen.

Tia moved her head enough to see what had his attention. The website displayed a bold headline:

NEWBERG POLICE DETECTIVE THREATENS
ARREST OF REVEREND EZEKIEL MILLS
OVER DEAD BODY IN WOODS

"What the hell?" Tia came around the desk to be sure she got it right. Below the headline was the frozen image of the reporter Tia had seen trolling the camp that morning. Ben clicked on the picture and it came to life.

"This is Lucy Lee-Jones, reporting live from Copper Falls Campground. Earlier this morning, a gruesome discovery was made a mile up the road from here."

Standing along the wood line, the microphone held to her lipstick-caked mouth, the reporter did her best to convey breathless anticipation. She began to take quick steps in the direction of the forest. "In the dark of the night Newberg Police discovered a body of what we believe was a young boy, *dead*."

The scene cut away to footage of Travis at the crime scene. He provided a brief statement confirming the fact that an investigation was being initiated into a suspicious death but gave no further information. The video returned to the live shot of the reporter, and Tia recognized the empty stage in the background. So far so good.

The reporter went on, "As documented in our exclusive Channel Eight video, we have just witnessed a volatile confrontation between a Newberg Police detective and Reverend Ezekiel Mills of the world-famous Church of the Rock. During the confrontation, Reverend Mills was threatened with arrest if he failed to cooperate with local authorities."

Tia swallowed hard and felt her heart begin to thump. She knew when it came to police-media relations, the phrase "exclusive video" was never a good thing. Again the live feed cut away and Tia saw herself on the stage with Reverend Mills. The video jiggled and bounced at first as if the cameraman had been running for a better position. Then it zoomed in on a close-up of Tia and Mills facing off. She cringed at the sound of her own voice: *"Pull that cord and you'll be arrested."*

The reporter came back on the screen and her voice hung clearly in the room.

"All attempts to obtain a statement from the Newberg detective were unsuccessful, but it is worth noting the officer involved was Detective Tia Suarez. Detective Suarez played a major role in the arrest of serial killer Harlan Lee and was also in an officer-involved shooting that took place last year. It was obvious to this reporter that Detective Suarez and the Newberg Police are going to be taking a very close look at any possible connection between the body and the hundreds of young people attending the Church of the Rock summer retreat. We will be following up on this story as it continues to develop. This is Lucy Lee-Jones, reporting live for Channel Eight, from Copper Lake Campground."

The image froze at the starting point and the office went quiet. Figuring there wasn't much for her to say, Tia kept her mouth shut and returned to her seat.

Ben sat back. After nearly a minute, he spoke. "How did it go again? 'Pull that cord and you'll be arrested'? Really, Tia? Ezekiel Mills?"

Beside Tia, Travis was staring right at the Chief, waiting for the chewing-out they both knew was coming. Tia didn't blame the Chief when he directed it all her way.

"So, let me see if I've got this straight." Ben held up a fist so he could count off each point. He started with his thumb. "You lost the RP on a dead body call. You've got an extended and unexplained response time by Patrol. The evidence indicates suicide but the crime scene is compromised and that has created a major problem with the ME's office. The only pictures you got are 'shit,' according to you, *and* somewhere in there you had the time to threaten a nationally recognized public figure, a preacher, no less, with arrest and get it broadcast on the morning news. Does that about cover it?"

Tia hid her frustration by doing her best to be flippant. She pursed her lip and scratched the back of her head. She nodded. "Yeah, Chief. I think you hit all the major points."

Travis finally spoke up. "Sir, I should—"

Ben silenced Travis by holding up the palm of his hand. Still glaring at Tia, he said, "Get a number, Carrie. Tell the lawyer I'm in a meeting. I'll call back in fifteen minutes."

As the secretary turned to leave, Ben called out, "Shut the door, please." With a nod, the young woman grasped the knob and closed the door behind her.

The office went quiet again.

"Sergeant Jackson?" Ben said, his voice quiet and firm.

"Yes, sir."

"Do the two of you need a few minutes? Confer in private, maybe? If not, I have a few more questions."

Travis looked her way and Tia shrugged in surrender.

"Now's as good a time as any, Chief," Travis said.

Ben pulled a yellow legal pad from his drawer and dropped it dramatically on his desk. He poised a pen over the paper and looked at Tia. "Just go ahead and start over from the beginning. I'm listening."

TEN

Tia got through the door first and into the hallway. She looked back toward the Chief's office and saw Travis had not walked out behind her. She leaned her back against the wall and kept her eye on the office door. By the end of the briefing it had become obvious to her that she and Ben would be having a conversation offline.

Fine with me, she thought. She figured she'd start that conversation on the subject of how does the most incompetent piece of shit on the entire PD end up training the new cops?

Travis emerged from the office and Tia stood up straight. She pushed aside her issues with Ben for a more immediate concern. Watching Ben and Travis interact at the beginning of the briefing, it had suddenly dawned on her: she knew exactly what was going on. When Travis made it to the hallway, he shook his head but smiled.

"That was a kick in the ass, right? Don't worry, though. I think I got him calmed down."

Tia ignored the comment and instead went for the jugular.

"So where are you going?"

"Now? My office. You're probably beat, so take the rest of the day off. I can't authorize any overtime for the callout, but you can adjust the time off. When you get in tomorrow, come see me and we'll get a game plan together."

"No, Travis," she said, locking her gaze on him. "I mean, where are you going? What PD? Milwaukee? Madison? County Sheriff?"

When he stared back without replying, whatever doubt she had vanished.

"I knew it." Her voice was full of betrayal and anger; her words came rapid fire: "What did you tell me? 'I gotta thing,' you said. Yeah, you got a thing. All dressed up in uniform, sneaking off. I can't believe it. You're jumping ship. Sawyer knows?"

Travis grabbed her by the elbow, pulled her across the hall into his office, and shut the door.

"TJ, what the hell—"

He put up a hand and cut her off. "Just listen."

Tia fell silent, panting. Her heart pounded in her ears.

"I wanted to tell you, Tia. I did. But it doesn't work that way. And nothing is for sure yet, so why bring it up?"

She could see he was looking for understanding. Some kind of support. She wasn't even close to giving it. "I asked you, where?"

TJ blew out a long breath and his face softened.

"San Diego County Sheriff's Office. They sent out a background investigator. We had a meeting set for this morning. Sorry. I couldn't get out of it."

"What the—?" Tia thought she must have heard wrong. "California? You're moving your family to California? Is Molly okay with this? Have you really thought this through?"

"Okay with it?" Tia heard anger creep into his voice. "Are you kidding me? This place is killing us. I've got four kids. We rent a two-bedroom house with one bathroom."

He moved behind his desk and threw down his notebook. "Do you know we're eligible for food stamps? 'Course they don't call it that anymore, they give you some bullshit plastic card, but it's the same damn thing. Fricking government handout for people who can't afford to feed their kids."

"But, TJ, you—"

"I don't want to hear it, Tia. Molly and the kids . . ." His voice went up an octave. "They deserve better than this. Hell, *I* deserve better than this."

They both went quiet and Tia knew enough to wait him out. He had more to say.

"We're practically hand to mouth. Fifty-, sixty-hour workweeks, calls in the middle of the night, and for what? Did you know our pay is the lowest in the state? Zero overtime. And our benefits?"

"But, Travis, things will—"

"Molly took Leo to the doctor last week. His fever was almost a hundred and two. He'd been sick for two days before she took him." His voice cracked. "You know why she waited?"

Tia only shook her head, silenced by his raw emotion.

"Because we didn't have the hundred-dollar co-pay. Turns out it was an ear infection. He needed antibiotics and that was another hundred bucks we didn't have.

"We waited two days." Tia stood silent and Travis glared back. She picked up on a slight quiver in his chin. "My boy was sick. He needed a doctor and we waited *two days*."

"But TJ, starting over? It's a big transition. You'll have to go through the academy again, ride patrol."

He dropped into the chair behind his desk, dejected. "Molly's sister lives out there. Big house in the suburbs. We'll stay with her while I'm in training. After that we can rent something. We won't be able to buy a house for a few years but still, the pay raise is huge. And guess what? If you work more than forty hours a week, or you get called out in the middle of the night, they actually pay you for it. Hell, they even got a pension plan. What a concept, right?"

Tia took a deep breath, embarrassed that she had been sounding like some kind of jealous girlfriend. She knew her sense of betrayal had actually been a feeling of great loss. She wanted him to know that's what it was and nothing else.

"You should have told me, Travis. I mean I get it, but man. San Diego, dude?"

"It's not just about the money. I want to be a cop, Tia." She could see the emotion on his face, knew he was struggling to find the right words.

"I didn't get to go off and join the Marines like you did," he said. "See the world and all that. Molly was two months' pregnant when we graduated high school. I swear, sometimes it feels like she's been pregnant ever since."

Tia couldn't help but smile. She knew how much Travis loved his family but she also knew he felt the weight of the never-ending responsibilities.

"Truth is, I was lucky to get this job, and it turns out I'm pretty good at it. Now? I want to do something more."

"'Lucky'? 'Pretty good'? Travis, you're the best damn sergeant in the county. Not just Newberg, the *county*. You got a future here, man. You could run this place someday. Sawyer has told me that himself."

Travis didn't seem impressed. "Did you hear what I said? I want more than Newberg."

"I know that feeling, Travis. I lived it. But believe me, there's a reason I came back."

"Well, I see it differently. Molly does, too. So if this works out, we're gone." Tia could see by the look on his face he was dug in. "And, full disclosure, I listed you as a reference. The background investigator will be reaching out to you. You all right with that?"

"Do I have a choice?"

"No. And by the way, heads-up. He seems like kind of a player. Might want to keep your legs crossed, maybe wear a turtleneck."

"Oh, great. Thanks." Tia looked at the man who was like a

brother to her. "Well, I'm going to tell him you go around here with your head so far up your ass you don't know whether you should shit or just go blind. 'Course that's only when you're not busy sexually harassing all the women in the building or doing lines of coke in the bathroom."

"Great. Thanks for the vote of confidence."

Tia knew what she'd really say to the investigator. And she knew what Ben and everyone else on the PD would say. Travis was as good as gone.

"Sorry for the hissy fit. I'm just a little blown away. I'll get used to it," she said. "Believe it or not, I like working with you. And honestly? This place is going to suck without you."

"Bullshit. It already sucks and you know it."

"Well, now it'll suck more. It'll suck like—"

"I'm not gone yet," he said. "I mean, we might have a murder to work, right?"

"Trust me." She smiled. "It's a suicide."

"Hey, you never know." He got up from his desk and came over to open the door. "Go home. Get some rest. I told Sawyer you and I would head out to the lake in the morning. Smooth things over with the church folks. Take another shot at doing the canvass interviews."

"Oh, yeah. See?" She remembered she hadn't said anything about being sent alone into the lion's den. "You go off and leave me alone and what happens? In five minutes, I'm pissing off the pope or whatever. And why the hell does a church have a lawyer?"

"You're right. I'm sorry." Travis was serious. "I shouldn't have left you hanging like that. We'll fix it tomorrow. Go get some sleep."

Halfway through the door, her shoulders dropped. "San Diego? Damn, Travis."

He smiled, his voice soft: "You can come see us every January."

Tia headed into the hallway thinking back to marines she had served with overseas. Foreign soldiers she had fought alongside. All good friends, but she hadn't spoken to any of them in years. She knew it would be the same with Travis and Molly. In a few months' time their friendship would be nothing more than warm memories. Maybe a Christmas card. And yeah, she thought. Without him around, this place is going to suck a little bit more than it already does.

ELEVEN

Tia pulled off the county two-lane and turned down the long, familiar driveway. She passed under the shaded canopy of tall, slender birch trees, following the bends and curves of the road instinctively. She'd lived on the land since she was five years old. For many of those years she and her family were the hired help and stayed in a small trailer out behind the milking shed. The time came when Tia bought the property and now she lived in the century-old clapboard farmhouse. Until recently, she had lived there alone.

The sight of the beat-up, yellow pickup parked near the house caused just the slightest elevation of her pulse. Nothing too significant, but Tia noticed. Sometimes it was hard to figure out whether she was happy to know he was home or not. Her eyes naturally went to the two-acre field where the corn had grown to nearly six feet and the bush beans were thick with pods. A row of tomato plants were thick with plump fruit, and along the border of the garden a dozen vines were loaded with pumpkins and squash. In the middle of it all, tending to the crops with the loving care of a parent, stood the tall, lean figure of Connor Anderson. As soon as she caught a glimpse of his face, her question was answered. She would always be glad he was home, but at the same time she knew he might feel differently. Couldn't blame him for that.

Tia pulled the Crown Vic alongside the pickup just as the farm-house screen door banged against the wood siding of the porch. Ringo, her Labrador-mastiff mix, had long since learned to open the door and he bounded down the three porch steps. Arriving just as she opened the car door and started to stand up, he pressed his front paws against her with all his weight, pushing her back into the car.

"Get off me, you old mouth breather," Tia said even as she hugged his neck with affection. "Let me get out, at least."

Half in her lap, mouth hanging open, and a canine grin plastered on his face, Ringo didn't move except to furiously wag his tail. She looked past his massive head toward the field. Connor waved one hand, acknowledging her, but keeping on with his work. She returned the gesture, then used both hands to push off the 140-pound dog. When Connor didn't look away she decided to take that as a good sign and headed for the cornfield with Ringo following.

Reaching Connor, Tia smiled. "That corn is amazing. You sure you didn't shoot it full of some kind of freaky hormones?"

"It's organic and you know it. Nothing but compost and TLC."

Tia looked around the garden. "It all looks great. Pick us a couple of ears. We can roast them on the grill, throw on some steaks."

"So you're home tonight?"

"Yeah. I'm done for the day. The dead body call got a little complicated. Young victim, probably sixteen, seventeen, most likely suicide, but Livy Sorensen didn't like the looks of it. Blood pattern stuff. We're doing a bunch of interviews tomorrow. We should be able to wrap things up pretty quick."

"Local kid?" Connor gave her his full attention.

"Not sure. No ID on him. Used a shotgun." Tia shook her head and made a face that said *don't ask*. "Livy is getting his prints in the system and we're sending notices to all agencies in a hundred-mile radius. Hopefully he'll get matched up with a runaway somewhere."

"And you're okay? I mean, no issues with any of it?"

She couldn't help but be a little put off by the implication and tension draped itself over the conversation. "It's a dead body, Connor. Pretty routine. I'm fine."

He held her gaze for a few seconds longer than it felt like he should before he turned back to his crops. Tia watched as he took hold of an ear of corn and pulled back on the husk to get a closer look. She tried to lighten things up.

"Damn. Wish I could get you to do that to me."

"What?" He turned to face her with something between mild annoyance and indifference.

"Come inside and lay down with me for a bit. Twenty-minute power nap, then I'll cook dinner."

"No, you've been up all night. Get some rest. I'll eat something later. I need to check the rest of the corn for silkworm."

He'd already turned back to his work, and Tia stood by, watching him. His thick blond hair poked out from under his ball cap and she saw tiny beads of sweat above his upper lip and on the smooth skin of his neck. A summer of tending crops in the sun had turned his skin a deeper brown than her own.

"So, how's it looking?" she asked, stepping closer. "The corn, I mean. Good crop?"

He answered with a shrug and it became clear he was done talking. Feeling ignored, she eventually turned to walk away.

On the porch, she took a seat in the Adirondack chair and kept watching as Connor moved between the rows of corn. She never doubted that Connor loved her, but was he going to question her ability every time she went to work? Then again, she knew it wasn't her ability he was questioning. It was her *stability*. For good reason. Even now she had to keep herself grounded in reality.

This is our field, she reminded herself. Our home. The afternoon sun was well above the horizon and the sky a brilliant blue. Still, with her mind literally buzzing from exhaustion, she had no problem imagining herself in another field. Surrounded by darkness, the rain pounding, the wind playing havoc on row after row of tall corn. The outline of a shed up ahead.

Tia closed her eyes. The voice was gone now, but the guilt would never leave. Some nights, it got to be more than she could take. But, she told herself, tonight would not be one of those nights. *It just won't.*

Nearly a year had passed since that night, but it had only been thirty-eight days since she had last been beaten by it. Connor had come home from his shift at the grocery store and found Tia crumpled on the floor, unconscious, an empty tequila bottle close to hand. He'd been about to call 911 when Tia came around, screaming back at a voice no one else could hear.

He'd stayed with her that night, then packed his clothes the following day, telling her that he'd had enough. A week later, she'd gone to his work, finding him stocking the canned goods aisle. She bared her soul. She made promises, begged forgiveness. He'd come home that night and together they'd purged the house of everything with any alcoholic content, including the nighttime cold medicine. She found a new therapist and began weekly sessions.

Drowsy, she leaned her head against the wooden back of the chair. Her mind began to fade; her eyes drifted shut and she dozed, chin falling against her chest.

The sudden buzz in her pocket startled her. Sitting up, she fumbled for her phone. The call number was blocked and her first instinct was to let it go to voicemail, but she answered anyway.

"Suarez."

"Detective Suarez? Newberg PD?"

The voice was unfamiliar. "Yeah. Who's this?"

"Deputy Jensen, Rock County Sheriff's Office. Catching you at an okay time?"

"Depends on why you're calling."

"Yeah, all right, then." The deputy was definitely native Wisconsin and the nasal twang was Fargo-strong. "You're listed as the point of contact for an unidentified decedent. Body found in Waukesha County? You got him listed as sixteen to eighteen, male, possibly Hispanic or Native American?"

"That's right. What do you got?"

"I took a report on a runaway this afternoon. Seventeen-year-old Indian boy. Well, half, anyway. Lives here in Rock County outside Milton. You familiar with us down here?"

"Sure. Fifty miles southeast, right?"

"That's us. Anyway, yah, I took a report here about an hour ago. A mom reporting her son as a runaway. Last seen yesterday morning. Never came home. She waited a day, said it wasn't the first time he'd run off. But when he didn't show up today, she gave us a call."

"And you think he's my DB?"

"So yah. The physical description is a match, down to the clothing. And this tattoo you listed got my attention." Tia could tell the deputy was reading from the teletype. "Web of right hand, letters *HTH*."

"That's right."

"Well, my missing is named Henry Tyler Hayes and Mom confirms he had a tattoo of his initials. Got prior contacts for some local shenanigans, so I went ahead and pushed his ten print. It's a match on your body."

"No shit?"

"Yah. He's your guy, all right. Any chance a shotgun plays into your scenario?"

"Yeah. An eight-seventy. How did you know?"

"Mom says a long gun is missing from the home. She don't know guns so good but sure sounds to me like she's describing a single-barrel pump-action shotgun."

"Great work, Deputy." Tia looked at her watch. It was pushing four. "I'll be there in an hour."

"Yah, okay, then. I'll be waiting for you."

Tia was ready to click off but then heard: "And, oh, by the way?"

"Yeah?" Tia looked toward the field to see Connor walking her way.

"I gotta say that was a hell of a case you ran last year. The fella you took out in the cornfield? Some good shooting, from what I hear."

Tia didn't acknowledge the attempted compliment. "I'm leaving now. See you in an hour."

His attention drawn to the one end of the phone conversation, Connor stopped at the bottom of the steps. When he spoke she heard an edge in his voice: "Leaving for where?"

"Rock County. We got an ID on the body."

"You just got home."

"Yeah, you know how it goes." She stood up. "I'll make the next-of-kin notification and get back as quick as I can."

Connor stared at her and then climbed the three steps leading to the front door. He whistled for Ringo, who was stretched out on the cool wood of the porch. The old dog pulled himself to his feet and sauntered inside. Connor followed him in and the screen door slammed shut behind them, with neither man nor dog offering any show of affection.

TWELVE

With the convertible top down and the windows wide open, warm air blew hard in her face. She cranked the radio loud and music poured from all six speakers while she sang along with Los Lobos' "*Ya Se Va*." The country roads allowed her to avoid the interstate, and afternoon commuters headed out of Milwaukee and Madison, the closest Wisconsin ever came to a traffic jam. She maneuvered through the constant curves and finessed the car up and down the dips and hills of the two-lane highway.

Twenty miles out of Newberg, she came to a one-mile stretch of blacktop, straight and flat as a runway, bracketed by tall corn on both sides. The road ahead was clear, so she shifted from third to fourth, mashed down on the accelerator, and felt the smooth jump of the RPMs. She settled back against the tuck-and-roll upholstery, and the car responded by seeming to take flight into air that was nothing but a blur of green and blue.

The thought of a one-hour drive in the run-down department vehicle with a top speed of sixty had been too much, so Tia took her own car, a restored '64 GTO convertible. The loud music and stiff breeze would help her to stay alert, and she figured she could probably shave twenty minutes off the drive. She told herself the decision was nothing more than a matter of personal preference.

She had to believe that. Otherwise this could be the first of a series of subtle rationalizations she knew were already lining up not so deep in her subconscious. The next would have something to do with pulling off the road to fight the fatigue from the eighteen-hour workday—a chance to stretch her legs or grab a bite to eat. By the end of the long string of seemingly inconsequential decisions, she'd find herself sitting alone in some dark restaurant, staring at a bottle. Thinking, *It'll just be this one.*

That was a definite risk, untethered as she was from an official police car. With sixty miles of open highway between her and her destination, Tia would pass by more than a few out-of-the-way, shit-kicker bars and honky-tonks. Places where anonymity was listed on the menu just above the selections of bourbon and scotch. The kind of joints that reached out to snatch cars driven by the Tias of the world, no matter how fast they might try to fly by. She was already feeling the pull. Her unpleasant departure from home only made it worse.

She'd followed Connor into the house to find him standing at the sink, his back to her. She'd turned him around and held both his hands. "I just want to get this ID confirmed and make notification to the next of kin. I'll interview the mom and come home. The deputy tells me the weapon was family owned, so that pretty much clinches manner of death as suicide."

"So why the rush?" He had made no effort to hide his suspicion and doubt. "Handle it tomorrow."

"Connor," Tia said. "The woman's looking for her son. We know he's dead. You're okay with leaving her staring at the door all night, waiting for him to walk in?"

"Well then, let the locals make notification."

"And say what?" Tia gave him an example of how that might

go. " 'Hello, ma'am. Just want to let you know your son was found dead in the woods fifty miles from here. Call this number for details.' Come on, Connie."

Tia knew Connor had no comeback. A combat veteran, he had lost too many friends and had been very near death himself at one time. He was more than a little familiar with the grief and suffering endured by families who'd lost a son or daughter on the cusp of adulthood. Just because this boy took his own life didn't mean his people didn't deserve compassion and support.

"Look. I'm dead tired," she said. "Believe me, I'm not going to need any help getting to sleep. I'll drive straight there and back, no pit stops. Then I'll turn off the cell until tomorrow. I promise."

"Don't you see?" Connor shook his head. "This is the pattern. This is what you do."

"What do you mean?" The question sounded ridiculous, even to her. She knew exactly what he meant.

"You're getting yourself all wrapped up, drawn into this case. You'll just keep heaping it on until finall—"

"That's not going to happen this time." There was some anger in her voice. "It's a suicide. I think I can handle it."

"You said yourself, he was just a kid."

"Look, I do the interview with the mom, tie up a few other loose ends, and I'm done, case closed. At least it will be for me," Tia added, wondering about Livy's potential reaction to this development.

"Loose ends, huh?" It came out cruel whether he meant it to or not. She dropped his hands and turned her back.

"It's my job, Connor." A job they both knew she had come very close to losing.

It had only been a month, thirty-nine days, to be exact, that Tia had been tying up another loose end on a case. A neighboring agency had needed a Spanish translator to interview migrant workers about a sexual assault on a fifteen-year-old girl. The crime scene had been a barn but Tia had to walk through a cornfield to get to

it. When she arrived on scene, the victim had already been trans-
ported to the hospital in Madison. All Tia needed to do was interview a few peripheral witnesses. She never met the victim, never
even saw her.

Her new private shrink, a nice woman with a practice out of Milwaukee, called it a "trigger," which had struck Tia right away as a
screwed-up label to lay on a cop trying to come back from a pretty
nasty shooting. But whatever it was called, the case sent her reel-
ing. She'd slipped and in a big way.

"Fine, Tia. Go." She heard doubt in Connor's voice, and maybe
a touch of cynicism. "But when you come up on one of those loose
ends that you just can't manage to tie off, make sure you don't pull
on the rope too hard."

As predicted, the trip took less than an hour. After Deputy Jensen spent ten minutes admiring her ride and walking her down his
personal teenage hot-rod memory lane, Tia managed to get the
vitals on mother and son.

Apparently both were frequent flyers with the sheriff's office.
Mom, a well-known local hype, had numerous priors for under the
influence, petty theft, and solicitation. The boy had been hooked
up for an auto theft that had been knocked down to joyriding, then
followed that up with a couple of assaults.

"His last beef was assault with great bodily harm. That landed
him in Lincoln Hills up in Irma. According to his sheet he got out
a little over three months ago. They must have got his attention,
because he's been laying pretty low."

On paper at least the kid struck Tia as one of those hardhead
cases that got offered a second chance, then came back for a third
and a fourth. It seemed to her that the combination of addict parent and shithead kid was quick becoming the new nuclear family
of the rural poor. The deputy offered to tag along but Tia cut him
loose, promising to text when she cleared his town.

Tia followed the deputy's directions to a single-wide set off a county road five miles outside of Milton. The trailer, not much more than a tin hotbox on cement blocks, sat perched on the edge of a plowed-up field of cracked dirt that Tia guessed hadn't seen a crop in five years. The driveway was about a quarter-mile long and as Tia got close, a woman in short, cut-off jeans and a tube top came out to stand on a tiny landing that the trailer manufacturer probably promoted as a porch.

A dark-skinned little girl with a head of kinky brown hair, somewhere around four or five, followed the woman out and stood at her side. A few seconds after that a toddler wearing nothing but a diaper emerged. Tia couldn't be sure if the littler one, who was as pale as the mother, was a boy or a girl.

The woman cocked her head and looked suspiciously at Tia out of the corner of one clear eye, the other being creamed over with a buttery yellow glaze. She hugged two bony arms across her body, a cigarette smoldering between fingers she had wrapped around a red plastic cup.

"That don't look like no county car I've ever seen," she said as Tia parked and got out of the GTO.

"Excuse me, ma'am?"

"Ain't you Social Services?" Her voice was lazy with phlegm and her lips looked cotton dry. She raised the cup and slurped off the rim, but it sounded as if she had to settle for mostly ice. "Your surprise monthly visit, right?"

"I don't know anything about that, ma'am." Tia held back on identifying herself. "Are you Carla Hayes?"

The woman's expression and voice turned wary. "Who's asking?"

"I'm a police detective, ma'am."

"Driving that?" She pointed a finger at the GTO, still looking at Tia.

Not about to explain, Tia held up her badge. "Detective Suarez from Newberg. Are you Mrs. Hayes?"

The woman gave a bit of a snort. "Say it all fancy. *Mrs.* Hayes."

"Carla Hayes." Tia said it sharply, letting the woman know she was running out of patience. "Yes or no?"

"I'm Carla but ain't never been a Mrs. anybody. I guess by looking at all this you'd think so, huh?" She leaned over the railing, looking down on Tia, and gave a sweep of her hand. "Me and all my fine things. These here beautiful children."

Tia took a look around and saw an AMC Gremlin sat parked at the end of the trailer, the distinctive rear end poking out from under a canvas tarp. What she could see of the car was layered in an inch of dust and sat on two flat tires. The only green things growing in the hard dirt were tall weeds and random patches of scrub grass. A rusty swing set and a couple of overturned trikes stood as markers of rural poverty. Tia figured Carla spent most afternoons self-medicated, anesthetized against the squalor of what looked to be a pretty damn meager life.

Judging by her loose gestures and slurred speech, Tia figured Carla would blow around a one-five. Maybe even a little higher, but over the years she'd obviously developed some resilience, and she seemed to be functioning well enough. She was standing rock steady and had no problems being conversational.

"So now tell me." Carla kept up with her role-playing. "Why is there a Newberg detective in my courtyard?"

Tia took a deep breath. Time to get it over with. "I understand from the Rock County sheriff you reported your son, Henry, as a runaway?"

The playacting stopped and the woman's voice turned angry. "Well, shit. What now? Goddamn that boy."

Tia walked to the bottom of the two steps so her head was right at the woman's waist. Here it comes, she thought. She looked up to make direct eye contact. "Can we go inside, ma'am?"

"Why? What's he gone and done?"

The woman was slower than most. "Maybe it would be better if we talk inside." Tia looked at the children, then back at their mother. "In private, I think."

That line seemed to do the trick. Carla finally flipped from anger to borderline panic. "Wait. Where is he? Why are you here?"

"Let's step inside, Carla. Is it okay if I call you Carla?"

The woman dropped to the tin porch as if someone had swept her legs out from under her, suddenly face-to-face with Tia, the porch rails separating them like the bars of a jail cell. She pulled the toddler roughly into her lap; the child tried to break away and began to cry. The older girl studied Tia, her face calm with fascination.

At some point, Tia knew, there would be shrieking. There was always shrieking. When it came, Tia wondered if the truckers passing by on the highway heard Carla scream.

"Tell me, goddamn it. Just tell me where my Henry is."

Tia figured that notifying this pathetic woman about the death of her son while they were clustered around the stairway of a rundown mobile home was no better or worse than doing it inside. When parents learned they'd just become lifetime members of the world's worst social club, it never went as planned.

"I'm afraid he's dead, ma'am." Tia forced herself to take the woman's shaking hand. "Henry is dead."

THIRTEEN

Tia sat next to Carla on a floral-print couch in a room so small that if she stretched out her arms, she'd be able to touch both of the thin metal walls. It had taken several minutes to get a histrionic Carla into the trailer; she'd sobbed inconsolably for fifteen minutes after that. Tia had managed to settle the children in front of a television, spreading a dingy bedsheet over a brittle, threadbare carpet that crunched under her boots. She figured out the ancient top-loading VCR and stuck in a copy of *Finding Nemo*. Both children dropped down and stared with vacuous attention at the bleary picture on the twenty-inch screen. Tia was pretty certain the same distraction strategy had been used on these two before.

Carla Hayes was slumped on the couch, exhausted and spent, head lolling back, eyes closed, dull brown hair lifeless against her bony shoulders. She was that indeterminate age, anywhere between thirty-five and sixty—years of drug abuse had taken a hard toll, leaving her with the sucked-in look found mostly on POW's or hard-core addicts. Her cut-off jeans extended just past her crotch, exposing ghost-white legs dimpled with cellulite. A frilly orange tube top lay nearly flat against her sunken chest. Her paper-thin skin was the color of paste, dotted with blotches of dried blood on her arms and legs, several oozing a yellowish pus.

"How much are you using?" Tia asked. "I'm guessing heroin?"

Carla moaned and wordlessly waved her off, scratching in slow motion at one of the many scabs on her face.

"Are you sick right now?" Tia knew the answer. She was sure the woman had been using the alcohol to hold off the pain of physical withdrawal but the sudden stress of the moment had brought on the early pains of detoxification.

Carla gave a weak nod. Tia could see her gray, chipped teeth when she spoke. "Henry was supposed to re-up. But he left yesterday and now . . ."

Her voice trailed off but she was done crying over him. "How could he leave me like this?"

"What do you mean, 're-up'? Henry was an addict?"

"No." Her head turned back and forth against the couch, eyes closed. "Henry takes care of me is all."

"Henry's your hook-up?" Tia couldn't keep the judgment from her voice.

"Never mind all that," Carla snapped back. "Where is he? I want to see him."

Tia pulled her cell phone from her pocket and swiped to the close-up photo of the hand. "Do you recognize this tattoo, Carla?"

Carla took the phone from Tia and held it inches from her face with a look of bleary-eyed concentration. Slowly her face contorted and she forced out her words: "That's Henry. That's his hand. He did that to himself. It was just his initials is all."

With the identity confirmed by next of kin, Tia went to take her phone back but not before Carla swiped the screen. The next picture showed the entire body.

"Jesus-fucking-A-Christ!" Carla threw the phone across the

room and put her hands to her face. Her breath came in large ragged gulps, growing in intensity. Tia knew what was coming. She moved back just as Carla turned her head and leaned over the side of the couch, her shoulders hunched. Typical of addicts, there was no actual projection, but a weak heave produced a stream of brown liquid mixed with gray chunks that dribbled onto the carpet, creating a new stain pattern over an old one. The baby looked their way for a moment, then turned back to the screen. The older girl took no notice at all.

Cursing under her breath, Tia retrieved her phone. It had hit the wall and landed on a relatively nontoxic section of the carpet. She held it up and gave it a close look before reluctantly putting it back in her pocket. She'd de-con it when she got back to the car. She waited impatiently for Carla to finish heaving. She had no sense of fraternal kinship with drunks and addicts. When Tia slipped, she was a "leave me the hell alone" drunk. She never went looking for sympathy and rarely handed it out. Surveying the room, Tia found a moist rag on a lamp table and threw it in Carla's general direction.

"Here. Clean yourself up."

Ignoring the rag, Carla pulled herself to her feet. She staggered through a nearby doorway and Tia heard more retching followed by the flush of a toilet. A glance at the kids made Tia wonder just what it would take to get a reaction out of them. Anger set up at the edge of her mind, but it was better than despair.

"This is just great," Tia mumbled to herself. The summer heat had pushed the temperature in the trailer to somewhere around eighty-plus. She looked around at the space crammed with furniture, junk, and trash. Pizza boxes. Fast-food wrappers. Near the door, a dozen or so shiny green blowflies chowed down on dried-up cat food in a plastic dish. The only other sign of a cat was the lingering stench of urine. Rickety particleboard cabinets hung from the low, eight-foot ceiling and served to partition the kitchen from the living room. Yellowed tape held a number of photographs to a wall of fake wood paneling.

Tia stepped over for a closer look. One showed a young woman, maybe in her early twenties, standing alongside a mountain of a man with dark skin and jet black hair that hung down past his broad shoulders. Tall and well built, he stood shirtless, his arm draped possessively around the woman's neck, glaring into the camera. Tia looked close, and concluded the woman was a younger and healthy version of Carla. Her body curvy and full, thick blond hair falling halfway down her back. Her eyes were bright and blue if not a bit tainted with boredom. No doubt about it, the years and the dope had hollowed the woman out.

Another image was a wallet-size school photo that showed a young boy, eight or nine years old, also with deep brown skin and shiny dark hair, but cut in a choppy, home-done style. He wore a shy smile that showed off the sort of dimples that might eventually open a lot of doors and maybe even break some hearts. Cute kid, she thought, then picked up on a sorrowful look in his near-black eyes. Another photo showed the same boy in his early teens. Carla, still attractive but looking more worn, stood alongside him. Tia could see in her the first signs of the hard life that lay ahead.

The boy was shorter than his mother, and with a body that seemed out of proportion. His posture was hunched in a way that made him appear smaller still. A cigarette hung from his lips and he held a bottle of Jack Daniel's down low by his hip. He stood with his weight on one foot and looked into the camera in a way that told the photographer to just get it over with. Tia looked close at the hand around the whiskey bottle and saw the blurred image of a tattoo.

"Well, hey there, Henry."

"Who would do that to him? Kill him like that?" Tia turned and saw Carla standing in the doorway of the bathroom, eyelids drooping. "Who killed my son?"

Tia zeroed right in on the fresh needle track in the fold of the woman's left arm and the skin burn from the tie-off still visible as a faded red line encircling her scrawny bicep.

"Goddamn it, Carla!" Tia shouted, rushing forward. Both kids looked up. She grabbed Carla by the chin and looked into her pinpoint pupils. Shoving past her into the bathroom, Tia found a half-dozen dirty, orange-tinted cotton balls, a syringe, lighter, and spoon. No sign of actual product. No doubt the woman needed a fix but by the look of things, all she'd been able to do was chip at it.

Returning to the living room, Tia found Carla starting to nod off on the couch, a chunk of vomit still stuck like jelly to her chin. The kids had checked out again, staring at a school of cartoon fish pursued by a shark.

To counteract the little bit of dope, Tia forced Carla to sit up and drink some warm, watered-down Coke from a Big Gulp cup left out on a table. She scrounged around on a bookshelf and found a cellophane bag of candy corn. When Carla tried to turn her head away, Tia shoved them into her mouth two at a time and ordered her to chew.

"Carla, you can't be slamming dope with kids in the house."

"I ain't slamming nothin'," Carla said, chunks of candy dribbling from her mouth. "Don't you get it? That's the problem. I'm sick."

"Cotton shooters count, Carla. You say Social Services comes over? Do you know what they're going to do to you if they show up now?"

"What happened to Henry?" Her voice was a raspy whine. "Where is he?"

Tia asked the obvious question: "Carla, did Henry ever talk about wanting to hurt himself?"

"What? Henry? Suicide?" Carla managed to sit up on the couch and flipped yet another emotional switch. "Never. He'd never do that. I can't believe you think that."

You bet, Tia thought, looking around. What a crazy leap that would be.

Tia imagined a boy, growing to be a man, living in this trailer with this woman. She wanted to lash out, to scream, *What else would anyone think?* She breathed in deep to control her anger.

"You told the deputy a gun is missing from the house, right?"

Carla's voice became less certain. "It was his father's. But that doesn't mean—"

Tia swiped through the pictures on her phone until she came to the shotgun. Gripping the phone firmly, she held it inches from Carla's face. Carla reached for the device and Tia pulled it away.

"Just look," Tia said flatly, with no trace of sympathy. "Does that look like the gun?"

Carla leaned in, squinting at the phone. "It looks the same, but what does that mean? Who killed Henry?"

Tia put the phone back in a pocket of her jeans. "When Henry left, he took the shotgun with him. And that's the gun that killed him, Carla. Do you think maybe, just maybe, Henry was . . . I don't know. Hurting? Upset about something you didn't know about?"

"Henry? Hurting?" Carla scoffed at the thought. Tia watched as she pulled her withered body to her feet with the effort expected from a person who weighed three hundred pounds not ninety-five. She pushed and stumbled her way past Tia, took three steps from the couch to the kitchen, and scooped an open pack of Newports off the counter. "Believe me. Henry don't hurt. Him and all his bad-ass Chippewa blood."

Carla dug her finger into the crumpled cellophane and came out with a mangled cigarette. She tossed the empty pack on the floor and held the last smoke up to her face, caressing and stroking it back into shape. She pulled back her stringy hair and leaned over the gas stove to fire up. In the second before the blue flame flicked to life, Tia pictured a small explosion, but no luck. Carla straightened and took a deep pull on the cigarette, staring at the pictures taped to the wall.

"Henry had royal blood. He was Indian. His people were all chiefs and warriors. He knew all about that. Was proud of it." She pointed in the direction of Tia's phone. "He'd never do that to himself. Never."

Carla blew out hard; smoke climbed the wall, clouding the photographs. She stood quiet, staring ahead.

For an instant her gaze settled on the image where she and Henry stood side by side but then she snatched a different picture from the wall—the one where she stood next to the handsome, shirtless man. She returned to the couch, clutching the picture, and spoke with the cigarette bobbing in her mouth. "Henry was like his father. 'All in for Indian,' they'd say."

She held the picture up for Tia to see as smoke continued to billow from her mouth. "Pretty back then, huh? All the boys wanted to get with me. And I mean all of 'em."

Tia felt disgust but not surprise that Carla was going to make the death of her son all about her. She knew enough to let the woman talk. Useful information that would paint a picture of Henry's life would soon begin to trickle out.

Carla kept staring at her younger, prettier self. When she spoke again, the tone of longing and nostalgia had disappeared, replaced by anger and resentment.

"Henry would never kill himself. Too much of his father in him. Full-blooded Chippewa. Big-shot Indian chief. Always carrying on about the Chippewa way. Like I gave a shit. But look at me," she said, tapping the picture. "Beautiful, right?"

Tia didn't figure Carla was done so she stayed quiet and waited. Carla stared at the image of her younger self for nearly a minute before she went on.

"When I got pregnant, Jerome, Henry's father, moved us onto

the reservation. Way up north in Minnesota, near the Canadian border. Jesus, those winters, you wouldn't believe."

The sugar from the soda and candy seemed to have kicked in and she kept talking. "'Course he didn't ask my opinion, right? One Deer, they called him, like he was all something special. Said he knew I was going to have a boy. He was certain of it. Some kind of Indian spiritual bullshit. Said no son of his would be raised by white people. Big man. So off we went to live in the woods like some sort of damn savages."

Carla stopped talking. The silence stretched on so long that Tia decided to prompt her. "So he was right, wasn't he?"

Startled by the interruption, the woman stared at Tia, confused, as if she'd suddenly appeared out of nowhere. Tia reoriented her. "I mean, you had a boy? You had Henry?"

"Well, so what? I mean, fifty-fifty chance, right? Anyway, Henry turned out to be . . . well, different, not all big and tough like his father, the bad-ass Indian. Pretty soon, Jerome lost interest in both of us."

"Where is he now? Jerome, I mean."

"Dead," Carla blurted out with a laugh, as though the memory amused her. "Ice fishing, drunk as hell and on thin ice in April. Dumb ass."

She took another drag and kept talking. "No way I was going to live way the hell out there. Henry and I bounced around for a couple of years. It was just the two of us at first. Before long I met some guy. Well, a couple of guys, I guess."

Her voice went flat as she continued, pointing at each of the children in turn. "I had that there older one when I was staying in Beloit. Little one was born over in Racine. Landed here a year ago."

"And Henry?" Tia asked. "He lived here with you?"

"He came and went. Always has, but none of that matters a damn bit." She spoke with conviction. "I'm telling you, lady, Henry would not kill himself. No way in hell."

"Do you know why Henry was in Newberg, Carla? Why he'd be out in the woods?"

"How would I know? He don't tell me nothin'. I told you. He was like his father. Come and go as he pleased."

"Well, is there someone who might know?" Tia asked. "Friends, maybe? Coworkers?"

"Didn't have no job. Not much in the way of friends, neither."

"How about at school?" Tia asked.

"Dropped out last year. Then the law sent him up to that Lincoln School. You know the place I'm talking about? That juvenile hall kinda place?"

Tia nodded her head. "Once he got out of there, he just never went back to regular school. Said he didn't need it, but I know other boys were always giving him a rough time on account of his size and all. He's always been a little funny-looking."

Carla shrugged. "But he was right. He didn't need that shit. Henry was smart. He was always good at figuring out ways to make it in the world. He was all kinds of resourceful, ya know? He didn't have no patience for schoolwork or punching a clock."

"Did any of his business involve, say, drugs? Maybe he supplied other people, not just you?"

"I don't know nothing about that. Henry took care of me. But he did his own thing. Sometimes he'd be gone for a few days and I'd have to get the sheriff to bring him back."

"Where would he go?"

"Just carousing. He was still a boy. A kid, really. He did what he wanted to." Carla spoke with a trace of pride. "Tell ya this, though, he'd always come back flush with cash."

Tia said, ready to wrap things up, "We're going to need to positively confirm ID. Something like a driver's license, social security documents. Medical records would be best. Do you have anything like that?"

"Medical records? Nah." She gestured at her other children.

"These ones I do, 'cause Social Services is always up my ass about it. But Henry? He never seen a doctor except for a few times up near Bemidji. His father took him. Told the doctors to fix him."

"What's that mean?" Tia asked. " 'Fix him'?"

Carla took another drag and looked down at the photo again. "I don't know. Turned out he had some bone thing."

"Bone thing?"

"I said I don't know." Exasperated by the questions, Carla's undeveloped maternal extinct came through loud and clear. "He just—they called it something. It was a bone thing. Said there weren't no fix for it. He's just different is all."

Tia had reached her limit. She stood. "That'll be it for now, Carla. I'm going to head back to Newberg. We'll do our best to figure out what happened."

"I told you what happened." She blew out a last cloud of smoke and jabbed her cigarette hard into an ashtray on the table. "Somebody killed him and I want to know who."

"I know, Carla. You said that already." Tia reached into her pocket and pulled out a business card. "This is my name and phone number. On the back I'm writing down the number of the medical examiner's office. The autopsy was done this morning and—"

Carla sat up straighter. "Autopsy? You cut him up? You cut him all up without even telling me nothing?"

"It's not up to you or me, Carla." Tia realized she was enjoying the opportunity to remind Carla of her place in the world. "It's the law. It's part of the investigation. You said you wanted to know what happened, right?"

"No." The woman could sound like a three-year-old. "I told you, I know what happened. Somebody—"

Tia cut her off. "Whatever happened, to figure it out, there needs to be an investigation. Part of that is the medical procedures."

"What about his stuff?"

"Stuff?"

"Money, maybe? What about that?"

"His property has been seized. You'll be able to petition for it later."

Carla's voice went from sorrow to desperation. "So he had money, then? How much? I need it."

"Like I said. After the investigation is complete you can go to court."

"How much?"

"A thousand dollars."

Carla cracked a slight smile. "That's my Henry. Like I said, always flush with cash. How long do you think it will be before I can get it?"

Tia didn't need to hear any more. She knew what Carla was after. She stood and looked down at the woman on the couch. "It'll be a while. You probably ought to get over to the methadone clinic in Janesville."

Suddenly looking afraid, the dead boy's mother grabbed at Tia's hand.

"Can you help out? Just a few dollars? It's for the kids. I mean, they gotta eat."

Beyond exhausted, Tia couldn't take any more of Carla's histrionic, self-involved bullshit. She'd done her job and was ready to go. The baby had fallen asleep, lying on the sheet on the filthy floor, and Tia could see dirt caked in the folds of the child's neck and arms. The older one stared at Tia in a way that seemed to say, *Take me with you.*

"Sure, Carla, I'll help you out," Tia said. "Sit tight for a minute."

Tia stepped back outside and found the night had turned as dark and black as her mood. She walked past the GTO and halfway down the drive before she took a deep, cleansing breath. The stench of the trailer seemed to follow her, clinging to her hair and clothes. She pulled out her phone and hit "redial" and pressed it to her ear. Too late she remembered the contact with the carpet and cursed under her breath, moving the phone away from her face. A voice came through and she recognized the twang, with the sounds of a ball game in the background. Her head buzzed with anger and resentment, and she had to remind herself that her feelings had nothing to do with the man on the other end of the phone.

"Hey, Deputy," she said, putting on her professional-cop attitude and concealing her emotions. "It's Suarez again. Sorry to bother you, but I need you to send some of your people out here to the Hayes place. And bring Social Services. Got a couple of kids who need to be taken into protective custody."

The deputy said Dispatch would get a patrol unit out to her right away. Walking back toward the trailer, Tia wondered if taking the kids away from Carla was too much. The woman had just lost her son. Then she heard Carla on the phone, her voice desperate and playful all at once.

"Come on over, then. You can stay for a while, right? We should party."

Tia leaned against the hood of her car and stared up at the evening's first few stars. She'd wait out here. She'd had more than her fill of Mrs. Carla Hayes and she was starting to think there was only one way to get free of it.

FOURTEEN

Tia opened the door and hoisted herself into the SUV. She plopped down in the seat, turned to the driver, and smiled. "Morning, you rat bastard, turncoat piece of shit."

Travis smiled back and raised a cup printed with the image of a green mermaid. "Good morning to you, too. Want a sip?"

"I'd rather be waterboarded." Tia knew he was messing with her. "Why you buy that nasty shit? Tastes like microwaved motor oil. You ought to go by Alex's place."

He shrugged. "I passed four of them on the way here. Just easier is all."

"I thought you'd be in sunny California by now."

"It doesn't work that way and you know it." Still holding a coffee cup, Travis made a sloppy, one-handed three-point turn in the driveway, nodding toward Connor's pickup. "Where's Connor?"

"Sleeping." Tia strapped on her seat belt. "He's back on night shift at the Pig."

Connor worked at the local Piggly Wiggly grocery store. He didn't like his disability checks being his only income and he sure as hell wasn't going to let Tia be the only real breadwinner. Or what she liked to call "crumbwinner." Tia knew it had been hard for Connor to go from marine sniper to gimpy grocery clerk, but the sad fact was, they needed the money. He'd been taking his organically grown vegetables to sell at the farmers market at the state capital in Madison on the weekends, but once he paid for his space and gas money, he just barely covered his costs.

Travis pulled back out onto the highway, heading for Copper Lake.

"You sure we have to do this?" he asked. "I mean, if we got this thing all dialed in for suicide, we could just write it up with an anonymous RP."

"What?" Tia said. "You scared to go out there? Afraid I might ruffle some more godly feathers?"

"Not a bit." Travis drove with a hand draped over the steering wheel and his elbow resting on the open window. He wore a white cotton shirt stylish enough that Tia figured Molly must have picked it out.

"I think we should at least make the effort," Tia said, turning serious. "Figure out who found him to begin with and called it in. Even if we strike out, we can say we tried."

"Sounds reasonable," Travis said. "But what say I do the talking? You good with that?"

Tia looked out the window. "Okay by me. You speak that Holy Roller bullshit better than I do."

"Because you don't speak it at all."

She could hear the judgment in his voice and turned to face him. "Come on, now. That's not fair." Tia broke into a muddled version of the Lord's Prayer meant to be stunning in its irreverence. Travis shook his head and looked away. Mission accomplished.

The morning sun was bright but the air was still cool and crisp. Tia put the window down to enjoy the fresh breeze, proud of herself for resisting last night's stronger-than-usual temptation. She didn't want to admit, even to herself, how hard it had been. Truth was, only the knowledge that Connor was at home and probably waiting up kept the car headed down the road without any stops. But even when he left for the graveyard shift an hour later, she managed to control the urge.

"So tell me again: Who was this kid?" Travis asked.

Tia had called Travis on the way home to fill him in on the development out of Rock County and the interview of Carla. By the end of their conversation both were feeling even more comfortable with the suicide assessment.

She reached for the radio dial and turned from his country music station to Latin. "Name is Henry Tyler Hayes. Like I said on the phone, seventeen, living in a single-wide down in Rock County. Dad's dead. Mom's a hype."

"Nice way to be seventeen."

"Oh, and get this. I forgot to tell you. The thing Mom is most busted up about?"

Travis looked at her, waiting, and she went on, "Losing her hook-up."

He turned off the radio. "How's that?"

"Henry kept her in H. She looks to have a pretty good habit."

"So he's a dope dealer, then?"

"Well, at some level, I suppose."

"So what are you thinking?" Travis asked. "He was buying? Selling?"

"Hard to say. And then you come back to the suicide thing, right? I mean, who kills themselves with a thousand bucks in their pocket?"

"What, then?" Travis sounded a bit exasperated. "Now you're with Livy?"

"Just keeping an open mind. But one thing's for sure: the kid had a miserable life. That mother? Shithole of a trailer? If he did off himself, it was a pretty reasonable decision."

"You talk to Livy? Catch her up?"

"Not yet." Tia wanted to clear the air with Livy, but she wasn't looking forward to the conversation. "I'll get with her today."

"Yeah, make sure you do. We all need to get back on the same page." Travis said it like an order then his tone changed to something more personal. "Everything else go okay? You good?"

Tia went back to looking out the window. She understood that Travis felt like he needed to ask. He was a boss. He needed to make sure the department's resident alcoholic and occasional basket case wasn't feeling too much pressure. She understood but it didn't change the fact she resented the hell out of it. She reminded herself, once again, it was a well-earned reputation that she had bought and paid for.

"Yeah, man." She kept her voice humble. "We're good. I appreciate your asking."

"No, you don't." He gave her a sideways glance before turning back to the roadway. "Just be sure you get with Livy."

The truth was, the interview of Carla had been bad enough, but the drama with the kids had been nearly more than she could stand. It didn't matter how bad life might be, children would typically cling to their parents. Better to hang on to the misery they knew than face the fear and uncertainty of the unknown. But when Tia had spoken to the four-year-old, who said her name was Rae, about leaving her mom and going away with two strangers, the girl calmly posed a simple question.

"Will there be food there?"

Taken aback, Tia answered, "Yeah. Of course, Rae. Good food. You can eat as much as you want."

The girl had taken her little brother by the hand and looked Tia in the eye. "Okay. We'll go."

Carla, no doubt realizing the removal of the kids would have an immediate impact on her income, had pitched a major fit when Social Services showed up. Tia had pulled her off to the side and quietly reminded Carla what a search of the trailer by the Rock County deputies might reveal. The woman had immediately stopped complaining and instead tried to display some care and concern in front of the social workers.

"I know, babies. I know you'll miss Mommy, but it won't be for long."

The drive back to Newberg had taken less than forty-five minutes—Tia had been afraid to go any slower. After a hot shower and a mug of chamomile tea, she went to bed exhausted. Connor left for his night shift and even though she had not slept in nearly twenty-four hours she tossed and turned most of the night. But by God, she'd made it. *Thirty-nine.*

They passed a few minutes talking about Molly and the kids until Travis changed the subject. "The background investigator from San Diego Sheriff's? He roamed the hallways yesterday. Did he find you yet?"

Tia didn't want to talk about it. "Nope."

"Well, he hit up a bunch of guys. I'm pretty much the talk of the PD."

"I'll bet you are." Tia did her best to sound upbeat but she still wasn't used to the idea. She tried to play it off. "By the way, can you take Youngblood with you?"

"I knew you'd ask, but Molly said no way. She figures you'll come around eventually. You two are perfect for each other. She thinks you'll have beautiful kids."

"Oh, bullshit." Tia shivered in disgust. "She did not say that."

Travis laughed out loud as he turned into the campground entrance.

Unlike the previous day, the place was quiet. No one was in sight. The only sounds came from a flock of crows that took off, agitated by their arrival. Somewhere in the distance a chain saw buzzed, probably working hard on a tree trunk, but other than that, it was graveyard quiet.

"Where did everyone go? Yesterday there were, like, twenty church buses. Couple of hundred kids floating around."

"Floating?" Travis sounded defensive, as if he figured Tia was still taking cheap shots.

"Relax. I just mean that yesterday there were kids all over the place. Now it feels deserted."

She watched as Travis looked around, ready to agree with her. She grabbed his arm, feigned panic. "Oh my God, TJ. We've been left behind."

He shook his head and she laughed. "'Left behind,' get it? That's what you guys call it, right?"

Ignoring her, Travis drove up to the door of the office cabin. The kids might have left but Tia gave a good visual scan for the media truck. She was glad to see no sign of Lucy Lee-Jones anywhere.

They walked in and found the same woman Tia had spoken to the previous day standing at the counter, with the regional news section of the *Capital Times* spread out in front of her. Reading upside down, Tia saw a headline about the discovery of the body and a still photograph showing her and Mills facing off on the stage of the campground.

Great. The print media were following the lead of the television coverage and connecting the dead body to the church retreat. That would make Ben's day. Tia knew they needed to get ahead of this thing, to put out the flames of hysteria before the media hype sent it completely off the rails. Tia wasn't one of those cops who hated the media. She understood the role they played. Even appreciated it. But just because it was a slow news day, which was just about every day in Waukesha County, wasn't a reason to create a bunch of commotion about a damn suicide.

The woman looked up as the police officers entered. Her expression shifted rapidly from mild politeness to a tight-lipped scowl that dug a deep crevice between her eyebrows. She stared at Tia then turned pointedly to Travis.

"Can I help you?"

Tia touched Travis lightly on the arm, a signal that she'd handle the conversation. She did her best to work up a genuine smile. "Eve, right?"

"Ev-*a*," she said. If eyes could really shoot daggers, Tia thought, she would be a bloody mess on the floor. Travis cleared his throat, enjoying her obvious popularity. Without looking his way, Tia pressed ahead.

"Right, right. Sorry. Eva. So, is Reverend Mills in?"

"No, he's not." Eva looked back down at the newspaper. "No one's here, just me."

"What about the, uh . . . youth brigade?"

Eva scoffed. Obviously offended she looked up from her paper and practically shouted, "Youth *corps*."

"Oh, sorry. Youth corps. Where are they?"

"Everyone is gone, Detective. After your visit and the television broadcast, well, parents started calling, coming to get their kids. Everyone left."

"No shit?" Tia blurted out. "Sorry. I mean, really?"

"Yes, really." The camp cook turned to Travis and was no more friendly to him. "You're together, I take it?"

"Yes, ma'am. I'm afraid we are." Travis pulled his wallet badge from his pocket. "I'm Sergeant Jackson, Newberg PD. Detective Suarez and I need to meet with Reverend Mills and maybe work out a way we could speak to—"

"Like I just told you," Eva said. "Everyone has left."

Tia heard a noise behind her.

"Reverend Mills?" Eva said, looking past Tia and Travis. "When did you come in?"

Tia turned, ready to face off with the Reverend, but was surprised to see a man who looked to be in his mid-thirties smiling in the office doorway. Handsome and well built, he was dressed casually in jeans and a T-shirt. His smile conveyed an easy-going personality.

"Hey, Eva. Just picking up a few things for my dad." He came out to stand by the counter. "I'm Sam Mills. Can I help you with something?"

Travis took the lead. "Sergeant Travis Jackson. Detective Tia Suarez. We're with Newberg PD. Are you part of the retreat?"

"Not officially, but after all the excitement last night, I came to help get the kids all reconnected with their parents. Come on into the office."

Following the men, Tia shot Eva a last smile. The cook didn't smile back.

"I'm sorry. Did she say Reverend Mills?" Travis walked into the office ahead of Tia.

"Yes, but my father is *the* Reverend Mills," Sam said. "I'm the mere-mortal other guy."

Sam motioned to one chair and pulled another from along the wall. He kept talking as he stood behind the desk stacked with boxes full of books and papers. "I usually don't have much to do with the retreat. I mean, I used to, as a kid, but not anymore."

"As a kid?" Tia asked, taking a seat.

"When Dad's church was up in Chippewa Falls. We had a summer retreat back then, too. Nice campground in Chippewa County."

Tia nodded. "Oh, I see."

"But anyway, when things got a little nuts yesterday, I volunteered to come by, help everyone get checked out. I'm just packing up a few things for Dad. He's pretty upset, didn't feel like coming in." There was sadness in his voice as he went on. "He loves this place. Practically moves in every summer."

"So then I take it you know everything that went on?" Travis asked. "All about the body?"

"Oh, yeah. It's all everyone's talked about. Some of the parents . . ." He shook his head. "But that's not important. It's just so tragic. Even a bit scary."

"That's why we're here," Travis said. "We've got some follow-up to do."

Dropping a few more books into a box, Sam said, "I'm sure you do. How can I help?"

"There's a problem about the discovery of the body," Travis said. "We, the police that is, didn't find him on our own. Someone called nine-one-one, but we don't know who."

Tia couldn't resist chiming in. "There's a good chance the call came from someone at the camp, but I didn't get a chance to find out yesterday. Now everyone is gone."

Sam smiled and nodded. "Yeah. Dad filled me in on all that."

"Too bad he couldn't have been more helpful," Tia said. "Might have been able to clear this all up nice and quiet. Without all the media drama."

"You're probably right," Sam said with a shrug. When he went on, his tone was disarming. "But then again, you might have figured out some way to get your message across without threatening to arrest him."

"Good point." Tia stared at him. "I probably went there a bit too quickly."

"Would you really have done it?" he asked. "Arrested him, I mean."

Tia ignored the question. "So you don't have a formal role at the camp?"

"No. Why do you ask?"

"Nothing, really. Just seems odd," Tia said.

"How so?"

"I don't know." Tia pushed back in her chair, raising it slightly up onto two legs. "Just seems like, you know, you'd be heir apparent and all."

Tia felt daggers for the second time in less than five minutes, this time from her boss.

Sam laughed it off. "You live up to your billing, Detective."

Tia couldn't help but like this guy. His manner was relaxed and unflappable. He reminded her of Connor back in simpler times.

"You didn't answer my question. Would you really have arrested him?"

"You preach with your dad?" Tia wasn't going to answer him, maybe because she wasn't sure what the answer was.

"No, I have my own church in Milwaukee."

"Milwaukee, huh?" Tia raised her eyebrows. "Bet you can really pull in the crowd down there, right?"

Travis smacked her on the arm.

"It's all right." Sam waved it off again. "I get about fifty folks in for services on most Sundays, but our real emphasis is outreach. We run a food bank, drug counseling center, day care. A shelter in the winter. So, no. I'm not . . . what did you say? 'Pulling them in.' As far as preachers go, my dad is the big dog in the family."

"Reverend—" Travis said, clearly ready to refocus the conversation.

"Please, call me Sam."

"All right, Sam. As Detective Suarez was saying, it seems likely the nine-one-one call came from someone here at the campgrounds. Or if not, someone may have heard or seen something. We, the police department, that is, would like to conduct canvass interviews of all the young people that were here last night."

"Canvass interviews?"

"Yes," Travis said. "A nonintrusive, noncustodial interview. Very limited in scope. An officer would meet with each participant, one on one. Then we'd use a list of predetermined questions intended to identify any possible witnesses. Can you help us out with that?"

"To be honest, we canceled the retreat to avoid just that."

"I'm not following you," Travis said.

"After the news broadcast, we were flooded with calls from parents. Some just showed up unannounced and took their kids home. Quite a few of them were concerned the kids were going to be questioned by the police. In the end, the church elders conferred with legal counsel and it seemed best to cancel this year's retreat."

"Okay, then how about this." Tia was glad to hear Travis challenge the Reverend. "Give us addresses and phone numbers. Now that the kids are back with their parents, we'll take it from there."

Sam shook his head. "Every one of the retreat participants is under the age of eighteen. Our legal team is uncomfortable releasing their personal data to the police."

Travis persisted. "Sam, we're conducting a legitimate investigation into the death of a seventeen-year-old kid. Why would anyone not want to answer a few questions?"

Sam shook his head and his body language signified to Tia he might agree with them, but he had to stick to the party line. "I'm sorry, Sergeant, but like I said, it's on advice of legal counsel."

"How about staff?" Tia asked. "Can we talk to them? Get their names and addresses?"

Sam mulled it over for a moment, still reluctant, then said, "I don't see why not. They're adults. They all signed waivers. You know, for background checks, so they could volunteer and be around the kids. I guess that's reasonable."

Travis and Tia nodded at each other, then Travis said, "Good. We'll start with that."

Sam called Eva's name. There was a pause while they waited, then she appeared in the doorway. Tia noticed she was out of breath again.

"Yes?" she asked.

"Eva, do we have a list of all the adult volunteers, counselors, everyone on staff this week?"

"Yes. I have it. I had to make the meal cards."

"Great. Can you print that out for me?" The young reverend smiled at the cook.

"And phone numbers," Tia said. "Home addresses, too."

Eva looked to Tia and back to Sam. "May I ask what this is for?"

"Just trying to help the detectives." Sam's voice took on a new, businesslike tone that Tia was glad to hear. "And do be sure it includes everyone's contact information. How long will that take?"

"Well, I don't know." Tia heard the woman's reluctance. "I'll have to go through files and . . . well, it could take a while."

Tia turned in her chair and faced the woman. She made it as clear as she could that any initial attempts to resurrect their relationship had come and gone. "But you just said you have it, right?"

Eva threw a quick glare toward Tia then looked back to Sam. "It's going to take some time."

"All right, Eva. But let's make it a priority, okay? Get it done as soon as you can," he said, dismissing her. When she turned to leave, her long hair swung out far enough to swish against the frame of the door. "No sense in you guys hanging around here. I'll stay on her about it and let you know when it's ready."

The detectives stood and Travis stuck out his hand. "Thanks for your help." The two men shook while Tia watched, feeling like a spectator at some male bonding ritual. Sam spoke but only to Travis. "Not a problem. Happy to help. So anyway, how's it going? Any ideas?"

"What? On the body?" Travis said. "We're leaning toward suicide."

Watching Sam's face, Tia saw what she thought to be genuine sorrow.

"That's rough," he said. "Especially him being so young."

"So you'll get a hold of me when the list is ready?" Tia interjected, pulling a business card from her pocket and laying it on the desk.

An awkward moment passed until Sam spoke. "Sure. I'll give you a call or text you or something."

Back in the car, Travis turned to Tia. "Sorry about that. Didn't mean to step on your case."

Tia knew what he meant. She wished he hadn't given up the suicide angle but it was over and done with. "No worries. He seems legit. No reason not to tell him."

"What about Livy?" Travis started the car. "You going to be able to bring her around? Get her onboard with suicide?"

"Definitely on my to-do list for today. Convince the forensic expert she's got it all wrong," Tia added, pointing down the road. "But for now, just Holy Roll my ass outta here. I think I'm starting to have visions."

Travis shook his head. "You never stop, do you?"

Tia tuned the radio to the Latin station and cranked the volume. "Never."

FIFTEEN

"Hey, Livy, you remember about a year ago, that case we had? The guy with the arrow through his chest?"

Tia sat on the corner of the smooth wood countertop in the closet-turned-evidence-processing-room of Newberg PD, her feet dangling a foot above the cement floor. She watched as Livy finished up her print work on the Remington shotgun.

"It wasn't through the chest," Livy answered without looking up. "It entered through the duodenum and traveled upward to pierce his spleen. It never entered the chest cavity."

Typically, in a case of suicide, Tia would process her own evidence, but she'd asked Livy to come by the station and handle the shotgun. She wanted a chance to talk with Livy and hopefully come to some kind of understanding.

"Yeah, okay, whatever," Tia said. "But you remember the case, right? The guy who gut-shot himself through and through with a crossbow? You were pretty damn sure that was murder."

"Is that what this little charade is about?" Livy said, stopping to look up. "Having me come over here to process your evidence for you?"

Tia stayed on point. "Scene had some crazy blood spatter, right? Looked like the guy had been in a fight for his life. I was just about to jump the shit of that poor schmuck who called it in, remember? I started leaning all over him about 'where were you?' and 'who were you with?' Then it dawned on me."

Livy went back to work. "That case was entirely different."

"That's right, dumb-ass detective me posed the obvious question: If he went and got himself murdered, who dead-bolted the door from the inside?"

It had been a gruesome scene. A twenty-three-year-old man, dead in a hotel room. A carbon-shafted hunting arrow with a steel broad-head tip buried in his body right up to the fletching. All four walls of the small room were smeared and spattered with blood. At first glance, it looked as though there'd been a significant struggle and the scene had the feel of a homicide. Then Tia noticed the damage to the door. The hotel manager had forced the door open because it was bolted from the inside with a three-quarter-inch steel rod. The windows were all barred. They found the compound crossbow, still on scene, half hidden under the bed.

"Every bloody smear of a print came back to him. Probably thrashed around for an hour before he finally died. We never figured out if it was intentional or not, but yeah. Poor bastard somehow managed to shoot himself with a bow and arrow."

Livy finally looked up but refused to engage in any argument. "Completely different."

"I don't see how it's so different," Tia said cautiously. "Sometimes the answers are right in front of you. Common sense, you know?"

"Oh really?" That got Livy a bit more riled. "Common sense is one thing. Taking the easy way out is another."

"Think about this case, Livy. Here you got a boy with a miserable fricking life. He loses his dad. He's a supply mule for his junkie mom. He quits high school because all the other kids make fun of him for looking like a damn elf. He gets shipped off to juvie, where he gets his ass handed to him a time or two. I mean, he brought the gun with him. You think, what? He's going on a turkey shoot?"

Glaring at Tia, Livy finally seemed ready to fully engage when the door opened and Rich Puller walked in.

"Hey, Detective . . . Sorry. I mean Tia." He turned to Livy and his toned changed to something that struck Tia as a bit friendlier. Intimate, even. "Hey, Livy."

Livy blushed a bit as she replied, "Hi, Rich."

Tia looked back and forth between them, smiling. "Well, hey, Rich. What brings you by?"

Rich held what Tia recognized as a department supplemental report, typed and completed. "My report from the crime scene. Sergeant Jackson approved it. Said you would want a copy. Told me you were down here in the evidence room."

"Give." Tia waggled her fingers and Rich handed her the report. Sure enough Travis's initials and badge number were at the bottom. Still seated on the table, she started to skim through it, glad to see that Rich could write. The way hiring had been going lately, some of the reports coming across her desk struck Tia as the work of fifth graders.

"How about Youngblood?" she asked, still reading. "Did he turn his in yet?"

"Uh, I'm not sure." His uncertainty drew her attention and she looked up to see that he had that same expression of conflict she'd seen at the crime scene. She knew Youngblood had a reputation of being a hard-ass with his trainees, but something more seemed to be bothering the rookie. Tia kept reading then stopped.

"You were just coming from Taft Street? That's, like, ten minutes from the crime scene. What took so long?"

"I'm done here." Livy stripped off her latex gloves, picked up the shotgun by its stock, and offered it to Tia. "All yours. You can take it back to the evidence locker."

Rich stepped in. "I can take care of that, Livy."

"Thanks, Rich," Livy said, handing him the weapon. "I'm finished with it. No need to glove up."

Taking the weapon, Rich looked it up and down. "Nice gun, but I think I like the one at the range better."

Tia stopped reading and exchanged a look with Livy. They both smiled at Rich's comment. Tia turned to Rich.

"Is that right? Pretty particular about your eight-seventies, huh?"

He held the gun higher. "Just doesn't feel like it would be as easy to handle."

Tia looked down her nose at the rookie. "It's the same gun, Rich. It's a Remington eight-seventy."

"No, this one's different." Both women looked at him. He went on, sounding matter of fact. "Definitely heavier."

"What the hell are you talking about?" Tia jumped off the table.

"I don't know, I can just tell. It doesn't have the same balance." Rich held the gun out in front of his body and looked at it lengthwise. "Longer barrel, I think."

Tia turned to Livy and saw a quizzical look on her face.

"Give me that," Tia said, taking the weapon.

She brought the butt to her shoulder and pointed the muzzle at the wall. With her cheek against the breech, she sighted in on one of the cement blocks. She bounced it a bit in her hands to judge the weight. Rich was right. She turned back to Livy and saw they were both coming to the same conclusion. "I'll be damned."

The MEI quickly threw her brushes and powders into the tackle box she used to carry her gear and latched it shut. "The funeral home is coming by this morning for pickup. The mother authorized cremation."

Both women hustled past Rich to get out the door, Livy leading the way. Tia, still carrying the shotgun, yelled ahead, "Well then, we'd better haul ass. Can you drive?"

Livy held up her keys, already in the hallway and headed for the exit.

"Where are you guys going?" Rich sounded confused.

Tia stopped long enough to give instructions. "The morgue, but don't worry about that. Go find Sergeant Jackson. Tell him to stick around. I'll be back to brief him. Tell him it looks like we're back to homicide."

It came to her, and Tia stopped abruptly. She turned back to Rich, shaking her head.

"What?" he asked, still in the dark. "What is it?"

Tia smiled. "She is *never* going to let me live this down."

SIXTEEN

The three miles to the medical examiner's office was all farm-land, so Livy took advantage of the near-empty street and drove the county pickup truck like she'd stolen it. Strapped into the passenger seat, Tia pulled out her phone and banged out a quick Google search, amazed how easily she found what she was look-ing for.

"*Bone thing,* huh?"

"What?" Livy glanced at her, still speeding up. "What are you talking about?"

"Something Carla Hayes said during her interview. About Henry." Tia held the unloaded 870 between her knees, with the stock resting on the floor. Even at a seventy-degree angle, the bar-rel almost touched the roof. She couldn't believe her oversight.

"I'm just so used to the police model," Tia went on, thinking out loud. "If it hadn't been for the rain . . . if we hadn't had to scramble to preserve the scene . . . I think I would've picked up on the differ-ence."

She shook her head, defeated. "Anyway. I got it coming. Go ahead."

"Forget it," Livy said, staring straight ahead. "I should've noticed."

A wooden-sided delivery truck, piled high with produce, lumbered out from a dirt road, pulling in front of Livy's truck. Livy swerved and blasted the horn. Tia braced for impact and turned to look out her passenger window at the other terrified driver, who also swerved to avoid a collision. What seemed like a dozen ears of corn launched out of the delivery truck and smacked against Tia's window. Livy cut back into her lane and didn't even slow down.

"Damn, Livy." Tia pushed back in her seat. "If you want, I can drive."

"I'm mad at myself, too." Livy didn't even acknowledge the near crash. "Mort's always blowing through autopsies. Ignoring protocol and procedures. He does that all the time and now—" Her voice tightened. "Oh, shit. They're here. Hang on."

Livy had nearly reached highway speed as she came up the narrow straightaway that led to the parking lot of the ME's office. They hit a dip in the road and Tia felt a brief sensation of flight, followed by the two front tires slamming into the pavement. The undercarriage dug into the road and Tia grabbed the shotgun by the barrel to keep it from smacking against her face. She made a mental note to go back later, curious to see just how big a divot they had taken out of the blacktop.

A cream-colored hearse was parked at the loading dock, and two men in dark suits were wheeling a gurney and body bag down the ramp. Dr. Kowalski, the usual cigarette burning in his hand, stood nearby with an older, dignified-looking man also dressed in a dark suit. He was tall and thin with a full head of gray hair combed back. Even from a distance, Tia could see the man's suit was of fine quality and tailored to perfection. Kowalski and the dapper dresser looked to be talking between themselves while the grunts did the heavy lifting.

Pulling into the lot, Livy finally let up on the gas, but waited until the last second to hit the brakes. The tires locked up and the truck skidded to a stop. Kowalski stepped back with alarm, and Tia whipped open the door and jumped from the truck before it even stopped moving. Livy was right behind her. The acrid smell of burned rubber and hot oil floated through the air. Tia saw Kowalski's expression go from alarm to annoyance at the sight of them.

"Ms. Sorensen, what is this all about? You nearly ran me over."

Livy ignored the gross exaggeration. "Doctor, there's been a development with the evidence. We need to reexamine the body. Can we please take him back inside? I'll explain everything."

Kowalski looked over his shoulder at the tall gentleman and smiled, his voice dismissive, if not a bit embarrassed. "Go on, Jacob. I'll take care of this."

Jacob, who Tia figured had to be the mortician, nodded at his two lackeys, who resumed pushing the gurney toward the hearse. Livy stepped in front of them. "Dr. Kowalski, really, we need to—"

"Ms. Sorensen." Kowalski pointed his cigarette at the trio of men and put the other hand on his hip. "Mr. Taschner is from the funeral home. He has taken custody of the body. There is no need for any further exam. I have all the information I need to make my determination."

"No, sir, you don't," Tia said. Kowalski could fire Livy, but he couldn't fire her. "Livy's right. You need to do a more thorough exam of the body."

"More thorough?" Sounding offended, Kowalski wheeled around to face Tia directly. "What exactly are you implying, Detective?"

Tia turned to the man she assumed to be Mr. Taschner: probably pushing seventy, his hair actually more silver than gray and accented by an ashen complexion. He held his hands at chest level in front of him, his fingers tented together. The man had a horse-like face, long enough that Tia was pretty certain he could turn on a look of grief whenever necessary.

"Sir, I'm Detective Suarez, Newberg PD. If you could have these men return the body to the exam room, we'll explain inside."

"Don't bother, Jacob," Kowalski retorted, sounding entirely exasperated. "Detective, I'll say it again. My exam is complete and the body is now the property of Taschner Funeral Home, per the family's request. I'll speak to both you and Ms. Sorensen in my office. Go there and wait for me."

"Sorry, Doctor, but I can't do that." Tia reached inside Livy's truck and came out holding the shotgun. Other than Livy, everyone had what struck Tia as a comical reaction. The two men at the stretcher instinctively put their hands in the air and their jaws on the pavement. The gurney began to roll away and only Livy's quick reaction saved it. Taschner gave out a squeal that could've come from a teenage girl.

"Good God, Detective," Kowalski said. "Have you lost your mind? What—"

"We'll just do it here. Unzip him, fellas." Tia walked over to the gurney, shotgun in hand. The two men looked at each other, arms still raised, and did some sort of mental drawing of straws. Eventually one of them reached out with a shaking hand and pulled on the zipper. When it didn't move, Tia pushed his hand aside. "Let me help you."

Setting the shotgun across the bottom half of the body bag, Tia yanked hard on the zipper, pulling it down the whole length of the corpse. When she pulled back the sides of the bag, a blast of refrigerated air hit her in the face. Before her lay the headless, naked remains of Henry Hayes. The mortal head wound had the look of an empty bowl, stained with brown and black paint. The ears had begun to wrinkle, and much of the hair had fallen out and was scattered in the bag. The only smell coming off the body was clean and antiseptic.

"Mother Mary." The attendant standing next to her staggered and Tia felt a pang of guilt. The man probably hadn't realized what he had been pushing down the ramp.

"Sorry," Tia said, reaching out to keep him from falling. "Hey, Livy, can you give me a hand?"

Livy took the man by the arm and led him to the open hatch of the hearse. "Sit for a minute."

"Detective Suarez." Kowalski looked around the parking lot and then down to the open body bag. His voice shook with anger when he spoke. "This is an abomination. I have no idea what's gotten into you. But you will zip up that bag and step away or I swear I'll have your badge."

Tia grabbed Henry's cold right hand. The rigor mortis had run its course, so the arm was limp, pliable, and easy to manipulate. The mottled skin had the feel of heavy rubber, and the fingernails had turned gray and become almost concave. Feeling a little uneasy, part of her wanted to glove up, but she had momentum and knew she just needed to tough it out. She pulled on the arm so it was at full length.

"Livy, you want to go ahead and line it up?"

Stepping up to the other side of the gurney, Livy picked up the shotgun. Grasping the dead boy's forefinger, she inserted it into the trigger assembly. Tia laid the barrel along the area of the missing face.

"Can't be certain," Tia said, looking at the placement of the tip of the barrel, "but I'd say that's about where Henry's nose would've been."

Holding the finger in place, Livy shifted the rifle about, trying different angles, but the muzzle never came close to falling under the area that would have been the chin.

Kowalski couldn't help himself and leaned in. "What are you getting at?"

Tia let go of the arm and took the shotgun from Livy. "The

barrel length of this shotgun is too long, Doctor. Henry could not have placed the barrel under his chin and still been able to pull the trigger."

The ME stared at the body, then at the shotgun. His lips moved but no sound emerged. Tia continued to explain while Livy tucked the arm back inside the body bag and zipped the bag shut.

"Henry's mom, Carla, told me he'd been diagnosed with some sort of bone disorder. I'm willing to bet if you get a hold of his medical records you'll find out the condition was something called hypochondroplasia."

Kowalski shot her a blank look and Tia laughed. "Yeah, I'm with you. Believe me. All I know is on the way over here, on a hunch, I Googled 'short arm disease' and there it was."

Tia held up her phone, showing the ME the Web page she'd called up. She repeated the name of the condition, emphasizing each syllable. "Hypo-chon-dro-plasia."

Dr. Kowalski took the phone and started reading while Tia kept talking. "No offense, sir, but we didn't actually record Henry's over-all size or proportions. I think if we measure his arm span, we're going to see he couldn't have used this gun to kill himself."

Tia shrugged and shook her head as if they'd all fallen for some sort of low-brow magic trick. "His arms are just too short."

Tia turned to Mr. Taschner. "Sir, could you ask your men to wheel the body back inside? We're not quite ready to give up custody."

Looking up from Tia's phone, Kowalski interjected, "Hold on, Detective. I haven't authorized any—"

"Fine. Break him out again. I'll get a tape measure."

"Oh, for—" Kowalski gave in. "Jacob, please take the body back inside. I'll be sure to move things along."

Taschner huddled with his two men for a moment. The one that had gotten a good look at the remains not only appeared reluctant to approach the gurney, Tia was pretty sure he was giving some thought to just quitting on the spot. Taschner talked to him quietly, at one point laying his hand gently on the man's shoulder. His partner patted him on the back, and within a minute they were pushing the gurney back up the loading ramp, followed by Taschner and Kowalski.

Tia watched the men with the gurney disappear inside. Kowalski followed along, the last in line. He looked back over his shoulder at both women, his face practically contorted with disgust. Tia gave him a wave.

"I don't say this very often, Livy," Tia said, standing beside her friend, "but I'll be damned. That was a first."

"Yep," the tall woman said. "Postmortem exam in a public parking lot? That's one for the ages."

Tia went all business. "I think we should be able to get good enough measurements to rule out self-inflicted. I need to get TJ and Chief Sawyer up to speed. Obviously, this changes everything. Let's get inside."

Tia only took a single step before Livy grabbed her lightly by the arm and pulled her back.

"Tia Suarez." Livy's voice was nothing short of giddy and Tia knew what was coming. She didn't blame her a bit. "I damn sure told you so."

SEVENTEEN

B en stared out his office window and Tia could see the muscle
in his jaw working in time with the clenching of his fist. At
the other end of the couch, Travis gave her a tight shake of his head
and put his finger to his lips, signaling her to let the man stew. The
day had heated up but not to the point where the city budget allowed for the air-conditioning to kick in. The cramped office was
uncomfortably warm.

"What did you call it again?" Ben asked. She could see beads of
sweat just beneath his close-clipped sideburns.

"Hypochondroplasia," Tia said, the pronunciation coming easier each time she said it. "It's a bone disorder, a mild form of dwarf-
ism. People who have it generally stay pretty small and they have
short arms and legs. Henry was diagnosed when he was eleven. The
medical records in Bemidji confirm it."

"You got that already?" Ben sounded impressed.

"Just over the phone, on the down low. A records clerk helped
me out. To get them formally, I'll need to write a warrant or get
Carla to sign a release. But yeah. He had short arm disease."

"Nice work." Ben looked at her, his face earnest with respect.

Tia shrugged.

"Give me the figures again." He was back to staring out the window, which, Tia knew from past experience, meant she had his undivided attention. He was concentrating. "Overall length and such."

"It's not the police tactical model we're all used to. It's a Remington 870 American Classic with a twenty-eight-inch barrel." Tia was reading from her notebook. "This model has an overall length of forty-eight and a half inches, with a length of pull of fourteen inches. That means that with the barrel touching his chin, Henry had to deal with a distance of thirty-four inches to the trigger. Based on his wingspan, he wouldn't have been able to reach more than twenty-nine. And even then we'd be talking the very tip of his finger."

"Length of pull?" Ben asked, but then answered his own question. "That's from butt stock to trigger, right?"

"Exactly. And like I said, that leaves Henry with damn near three feet of gun to get up under his chin. Just no way he could do that."

"What does Kowalski say?"

"I imagine you'll be hearing from him." Tia didn't want to say any more than necessary but she didn't want her boss getting caught flatfooted either. "I guess you could say Livy and I took matters into our own hands. Kowalski's being kind of a dick about it."

"How's that?"

"He says he can't go with suicide because he can't get an exact measurement from chin to tip of extended finger. I mean, with the victim's face being blown off and all, but it's not even close. I'm telling you, Chief, this boy did not shoot himself with *that* gun."

"I don't know, maybe Kowalski's got a point," Ben said, doubt in his voice. "I had a guy in Oakland, put a flintlock rifle in his mouth. You know, like a Daniel Boone sort of thing. Long-ass gun.

Used his toe to pull the trigger. I don't know if he had this hypo-chon-whatever you call it. But, yeah. Used his *toe*."

"Hypo-chon-dro-plasia," Tia beat back the counterargument, saying, "And forget about it. Henry had his shoes on."

"Okay then, what about a stick?" Ben swiveled his chair around to face both Tia and Travis. "I mean, he was in the woods. What if he used a twig or something to reach the trigger?"

"Wha—? 'A twig or something'?" Tia grew exasperated. "Look, Chief, the barrel length and Henry's medical condition prove Henry couldn't have shot himself with the gun recovered from the scene. And that's supported by the lack of blood spatter that Livy documented. All that adds up to homicide. In my opinion, con-clusively."

"The rain, remember?" Ben said. "That could have washed away the blood on the hands—"

Tia cut him off. "I saw the hands, Chief. I got pictures. There's no blood."

"You yourself said those pictures are shit. Cell phone camera in the dark with no flash." Ben didn't give up. "Or what if the spatter was super-high velocity? Microscopic? Maybe your camera just didn't pick it up."

"Excuse me?" Tia couldn't believe what she was hearing. "Super-high . . . what are you even talking about?"

Finally opening his mouth, Travis said, "Or how about this? What if—"

"Jesus, enough already!" Tia chopped the air with her hand and raised her voice. She needed to get these guys back on point. "What's with all the damn what-ifs?"

The Chief and the sergeant both stared at her, silent. She said what she knew to be the obvious truth. "*What if* somebody put the gun under his chin and pulled the damn trigger?"

After a long silence, Ben spoke, sounding as if he was mostly talking to himself.

"Occam's razor."

"Exactly," Tia answered, relieved that he seemed to be coming around. "Right up there with 'keep it simple, stupid.'"

"Okay. I'll bite," Travis chimed in. "What razor you talking about?"

"Occam's razor," Ben repeated.

"Who's Occam?" Travis asked, looking confused.

"Some dead guy. It's not important." Ben explained, "Occam's razor is the idea . . . the principle, really, that when you're trying to solve a problem or figure out an occurrence, and you've got different possible solutions, pick the simplest one. The fewer assumptions, the better odds you have of being right."

"Really?" Tia looked across the desk, doing her best to come off dull-witted. "So, like, don't assume he took his shoes off and put a stick between his toes? Or somehow created invisible, microscopic blood spatter with a twelve gauge?"

Ben and Travis exchanged a look of respectful exasperation that Tia was more than familiar with. She liked it when she could shut them down.

"Bottom line," Tia leaned back on the couch and did her best to convey the argument was over, "Henry's stature and the dimensions of the gun add up to an indisputable physical obstacle to suicide."

"Okay," Ben said. "But I'm getting calls from city hall. I've got to tell the mayor something. What I hear you guys saying is that this is murder. A well-crafted and staged one at that. Is that what we're going with?"

Tia looked at Travis and gave a deferential sort of shrug, but said nothing. She looked back to Ben. "That's where we're at, Chief."

"Fine," Ben said. "Then we best kick this thing into gear. What's the plan?"

"We're getting a list today of all staffers and volunteers who were at the retreat," Travis explained. "So far, they're pushing back on giving up the names of the attendees. I get that. I mean, they're all minors, so the church has parents all up in their grill about it. Eventually we're going to need those names, too."

"I can start with the staff list," Tia said, checking her phone for missed calls or texts. "Reverend Mills is supposed to call when he has it ready."

"Ezekiel Mills?" Ben sounded intrigued by the idea. "He still talking to you?"

"No," Tia said, "he's not. But his son is. Sam Mills."

"There's another Reverend Mills?" The Chief sounded surprised.

"He's a preacher at a smaller church in Milwaukee. Seems like a reasonable guy—more than his old man, at least. I guess you could say he's our emissary. That's a religious thing, right, TJ?"

"Yeah, and we need one." Travis looked at Ben. "Somehow that whole 'do what I say or I'll arrest you' thing plays hell on a man's spirit of cooperation."

Ben moved on to a new issue. "So what all do we know about our victim? Known associates? Priors?"

Tia nodded. "He definitely had some run-ins with the law down in Rock County. Mostly nickel-and-dime stuff. Spent some time up at the Lincoln School. According to the deputy I talked to, he'd only been out a few months. I'll follow up on it."

"What about next of kin?"

"Not a pretty picture. Dad's dead. Mom's got a heroin habit. Looks like Henry was her hook-up. Kept her in H."

"I swear," Ben said. "If you had told me ten years ago that there would be a heroin epidemic in Wisconsin farm towns, I never would have believed it. It's like Oakland in the early nineties, just with cows, corn, and white people."

The room went quiet with the stark reality, until Ben spoke again. "Well, if you need to, reinterview her. But we're going to need a full profile on our victim."

"I have to give it to the woman," Tia said. "She wasn't buying suicide. Screaming murder all the way."

Ben nodded, then asked, "What about the nine-one-one call?"

"I've listened to the recording," Tia said. "I'm guessing white male adult, but it sounded like he was trying to disguise his voice. Low tone, muffled. Called himself Henry, which tells me he knows our victim."

Ben nodded. "Didn't want to give his own name, so he panicked and used the victim's."

"That's what I'm thinking." Tia looked down to her notebook. "Phone is dead. Doesn't even go to voicemail."

"Burner outta minutes?" Chief asked.

"Most likely," Tia said. "But it was two o'clock in the morning in the middle of the woods. Only one tower to ping off of out there."

Travis spoke up. "We'll write a warrant for a tower dump. See if the caller made calls to any other numbers. Even without subscriber info, we can work it backwards from there."

"Makes sense," Ben said.

"I'd like to get at least a week's worth of data. Track the activity for the days leading up to the shooting."

Travis nodded. "Only problem is judges don't like us getting our hands on a lot of personal data that isn't crime related."

Ben looked to Tia. "You know a friendly judge?"

"I know a few. And if I can't get a judge to sign off, I know some black hats. I can get the info one way or another."

Ben shook his head. "Don't go there."

"Didn't bother you when it was your ass in a sling," Tia said, smiling.

"Yeah, it did, you just never bothered to ask. Keep it legal. Write the warrant and get it signed."

"You got it, boss." Tia wasn't going to argue the point. She was pretty sure that based on the latest developments indicating homicide, she could justify a legitimate search warrant for a tower dump. That way, if whoever dialed 911 used the phone to make any other calls, those numbers would be listed.

Ben stood up, his way of signaling it was time for them to get at it. "All right. Sounds like you guys have plenty to do. Get the list from Mills, go at the mom again, get the medical records confirmed, and write paper for the cell records."

The detectives got up and Travis opened the door just as Mortimer Kowalski reached for the doorknob from the other side. The ME practically fell into the office.

Carrie was right behind him. "Sorry to interrupt, Chief, but Dr. Kowalski said it was urgent."

With a nod to Carrie, Ben said, already looking at Tia, "Hello, Mort. What brings you over?"

"I need to meet with you, Chief." Kowalski looked at Tia. "Privately."

Tia smiled at the doctor then turned to her boss. "I can stay if you want."

"I said privately." Kowalski glared and Tia then turned back to Ben. "Please, Chief."

"If this is about the Hayes boy, I'll need Sergeant Jackson in here. He's supervising the investigation."

"Fine." Kowalski glanced Tia's way and she saw his look of satisfaction. "Perhaps it would be best if the sergeant stayed."

The Chief nodded his head toward the door. "Tia, you know what needs to be done. Get started. We'll brief again soon."

Tia stopped in the doorway and turned, not at all certain she liked the idea of the doctor being allowed to tell one side of what had been a dicey situation. She took a step back toward the office, ready to object to the arrangement.

Travis looked sheepish but Ben seemed to read her mind. His tone left no room for discussion. "Close the door on your way out, Tia."

EIGHTEEN

Tia sat alone at her desk in the bullpen office she shared with the three other Newberg PD detectives. She'd been trying to work on the search warrant for nearly an hour, but her mind kept wandering down the hall. She wanted to walk down to the Chief's office and find out firsthand what sort of bullshit Kowalski was peddling. If one thing made her crazy about working in this hick town, it was the good old white boys' club. Every politician, every city department head, every mover and shaker of any sort was part of the clique. A clique that Tia was excluded from by more than one obvious disqualifier. Ben wasn't exactly an active member, but there were times he benefited from the network. Then again, she reminded herself, he had never disrespected her and he sure as hell had never stabbed her in the back.

"But still," she said out loud. "This is *bullshit*."

Her mind made up and ready for a fight, Tia was halfway out of her chair when her phone chimed with a text from Sam Mills. He had her list and was offering to drop it off at the PD. Tia had a better idea.

Some fresh air and time away from the building would do her good. After a quick back and forth, Tia headed out, making sure to pass by the admin wing on the way. The door to the Chief's office was still closed. Her slow burn went up a few degrees but she kept walking.

On the sidewalk, headed for downtown, Tia forced herself to reassess. There were times she was ready to say the hell with it and walk away. But the obvious question was, then what? Tia knew the truth. She was no Travis Jackson, a great catch for a more prosperous department. After two high-profile shootings, a well-documented psychiatric breakdown, and a department-wide reputation for hitting the bottle, Tia Suarez was damaged goods. Skills or no skills, no PD would even think about bringing her on. In some ways, when it came to the law enforcement job market, Rich Puller had better prospects. If she wanted to be a cop, the only place for her was Newberg PD under the watchful but protective eye of Ben Sawyer.

So, what then?

The hell with Kowalski. The disclosure of Henry's condition, plus the physical measurements of the gun, sealed the deal. Livy had been right all along. Henry was murdered and the killer was devious enough to stage the scene as a suicide. There was no denying it. It was time to stop talking, stop analyzing, and find out who killed him.

The coffeehouse was filled with the usual midday crowd, drawn by the aroma of the daily roast. Tia scanned the room and saw Alex Sawyer near the back of the shop, where several shelves were stocked with collectible hardcover books.

Tia walked up behind Alex, who was sorting through a box of new arrivals. "Hey, you. Anything good?"

Alex was already smiling when she turned and gave Tia a hug. "Hey, stranger. Where've you been?"

The two women embraced. The Chief's wife, Alex, was Tia's closest female friend and Tia typically stopped in at the shop every morning before heading to work. It had been several days since she'd last visited. "Sorry. I've been a little busy."

"Yeah, I heard." Alex smiled. "I caught your onstage performance on the news. Nice job."

"Oh, you saw that?" Tia scrunched her face and waited.

"Sure did. I thought you handled the good Reverend very well. He's a pompous ass, from everything I hear."

Tia laughed. "I wish you were chief, because that's not how your husband feels about it."

Alex laughed in return. "Because when it comes to dealing with the press, he should talk, right?"

Tia smiled. This was why she'd told Sam to meet her at Books and Java. She and Alex shared a bond no one else could fully appreciate. When Alex had been accused of murder and faced the possibility of spending her life in prison, Tia had stepped up and helped set things right, nearly getting shot to death in the process.

More than that, she and Alex shared another level of intimacy, one that flowed from the relationship each of them had with Ben Sawyer. For all his flaws, they knew he was a good and honest man. Seeing Alex now reminded Tia that while Ben was her boss, he was also her friend. The bitterness she'd carried into the store faded away.

"Definitely." Tia spoke with warmth. "Ben Sawyer. King of media relations."

Before she could say anything else, Alex looked past her. The smile on her face shifted to one Tia called her "professional hostess look" and she said, "Hi. Can I help you with something?"

Turning, Tia found Sam Mills standing immediately behind her, a thin manila envelope in his hand. Sam nodded toward Alex but spoke to Tia, extending the envelope toward her.

"Hi, Detective. I didn't mean to interrupt, but I've got that list for you."

"I told you, Sam. It's Tia." She took the envelope and gestured at Alex. "This is my friend Alex Sawyer. Alex, Sam Mills."

"Hi, Sam."

"Nice to meet you, Alex. Any relation to the police chief?"

"Which one?"

Sam looked confused. "I don't follow."

"My husband, Ben, is the current chief. My dad, Lars Norgaard, is the former chief."

"Really?" Sam sounded genuinely interested.

"Sam's got the legacy thing going on in his family, too," Tia said. She figured she'd better let Alex in on the relationship. "His father is Ezekiel Mills."

"Oh." Alex nodded politely. "Are you a pastor?"

"Yep. Like father, like son." Sam seemed anxious to leave the subject and nodded his head toward the envelope. "So anyway, Detective, you've got your list."

"Great." Tia looked inside the envelope and saw several sheets of typewritten names, addresses, and phone numbers. "Thanks. This is really helpful. I appreciate it."

"Don't thank me. Eva put it together."

"Uh, sure." Tia laughed. "I'll drive right over to the campground. Thank her in person."

"Yeah, you did leave an impression with her, too. But we're all moved out of the campground." Sam gave a polite smile to both women. "Anyway, I should probably head back down to the city."

"Where's your church, Sam?" Alex asked.

"First Friendship Church of Milwaukee." He seemed almost embarrassed. "Little place on the north side."

"You're *that* Pastor Mills?" Alex's face lit up in response. "First Friendship? Isn't that the church spearheading the social enterprise project, 53206?"

Sam seemed pleased by the recognition. "Yeah, that's us."

"I've heard great things about that, Sam. Really exciting." Tia could hear the admiration in her friend's voice. "Listen, if there is ever anything I can do . . . maybe some job training or just donate some free-trade coffee? I'd love to get involved."

"Wow, Alex. That's really cool of you," Sam said, sincerity apparent in his voice. "I might just take you up on that. A coffeehouse like this? That would be a great fit. But like I said, we're still getting things off the ground."

"Just let me know when you're ready."

Sam turned to Tia and offered his hand. "Well, I guess I'll be taking off."

"Thanks again, Sam." They shook. "And seriously, I didn't mean to rock the boat with your dad or even Eva, for that matter. I was probably out of line with both of them."

"We all could have handled this better. But no real harm done." Sam stopped and shook his head. "No, I don't mean that. The boy . . ."

"It's okay," Tia said. "I get what you're saying."

The minister nodded, said goodbye again, and left. As soon as the door closed behind him, Tia turned to her friend. "Damn, Alex. You're practically swooning. Good thing your husband wasn't here."

"Oh, stop." Alex turned her attention back to the box of books. "Do you know about the First Friendship Church?"

"Never heard of it. Anything like his dad's church?"

Alex rolled her eyes. "Are you kidding? First Friendship is all about community outreach and urban renewal. They're heading up this crazy-ambitious social enterprise project, the 53206 Transformation Project."

"Come again? 'Social enterprise'?"

"Geez, Tia. Don't you read the paper?"

"Mostly I read crime reports," she said with a shrug.

"You should branch out. I saw an article about a year ago in a coffee free-trade magazine." Alex looked Tia up and down. "Lefty rag. Cops probably would never pick it up."

Tia laughed and took a seat. "Yeah, probably not. What did it say?"

"The church is sponsoring what amounts to a micro-version of Amazon, except all the products are made by people in the community. Everything would be made locally and shipped from the 53206 zip code."

"Impressive." Tia nodded. "To bad it has to be in Kil-town. It's a dying city."

"You're a cynic."

"No. I'm a cop."

"Same thing." Alex shelved two of the books. "Personally, I think he's on to something. We all know that local is the way to go. Does he have something to do with your case?"

"Not really." Tia looked out the door and saw Sam getting into a beat-up Toyota Corolla that made her Crown Vic look high end. "Just helping us ferret out a few leads. ID some witnesses."

"So now you're thinking it's not suicide?"

"Still up in the air, but in my opinion? It's a homicide."

Alex stopped shelving the books. She spoke as someone who was an expert on Ben Sawyer, "Well, just remember, your opinion is the one that counts."

"Right." Tia nodded and grinned. "In theory, at least."

The noise level in the shop had grown; Tia and Alex both looked toward the counter and saw the line had grown longer. Alex sighed and said, "I'd better help out. Come by tomorrow morning before the rush. Let's talk."

"I'll try, Alex. Good to see you."

As Tia headed back toward the PD, a task list formed in her mind. First thing was to finish up the warrant and get over to the courthouse. With any luck she'd find a friendly judge and get it signed before close of business. Once that was handled, she'd get started drilling down on every name on the list of retreat staff to see if that turned up anything. The planning made her feel energized and she quickened her step.

NINETEEN

J ust as she reached the PD, her phone chimed with a text. It was
from Ben.

MY OFFICE ASAP

No doubt he had a few things to say to her after meeting with
Kowalski. Fine, Tia thought. The direct approach. She should have
been included in the meeting to begin with and she'd let the Chief
know it.

Taking the back steps of the two-story building—the ones that
led directly to the Chief's office—Tia walked into the waiting area.
She was surprised to find Rich Puller sitting outside Ben's closed
office door.

"Rich? What're you doing here?" Dressed in civilian attire, the
rookie looked even younger than he did in uniform. He shrugged
his shoulders, appearing despondent, but offered no explanation.
The office door opened and Jimmy Youngblood walked out. His
face flushed and set in a hard scowl, he stopped short when he
saw Tia.

"Hey, Jimmy." Tia was confused. "I thought you were in Vegas?"

"Change of plans." The FTO glared at Tia. "I guess I should've figured you'd be in the middle of this."

"Middle of what?" Tia looked at Rich, then back at Youngblood. "What's going on?"

"Like you don't know," Youngblood said, then turned to his trainee, who had gotten to his feet. "Your turn, Puller."

Jimmy walked up until he was face-to-face with Rich. He spoke in a low voice, but Tia was only a few feet away and heard every word. "Shoulda listened to me, dumb shit. Now? Your ass is fried."

Behind him, Travis emerged from the Chief's office and nodded at Tia. "Let's go, Jimmy. We need to stop by the armory."

The men walked off, Jimmy casting a last look over his shoulder at Rich and Tia.

"Officer Puller, sit tight." Ben Sawyer stood in the doorway of his office. "Let me meet with Detective Suarez first."

"Yes, sir." Tia could hear the dejection in Rich's response as the younger officer sat down again, shoulders sagging.

Stepping into Ben's office, Tia closed the door behind her. "I guess I'm not here to talk about your meeting with Kowalski?"

"What?" Ben sounded genuinely confused, but only for a moment. He shook his head. "You mean your public postmortem examination? Jesus, Tia. This time did you at least make sure you weren't on camera?"

"No promises, but hopefully not." Tia couldn't help but feel relieved that he seemed to be making light of it.

He moved to his desk then stopped and turned, his hands on his hips. "Really, Tia? The parking lot?"

"It wasn't like that, Chief. Livy and I tried to—"

"Not now." He raised his hand to stop her. "You did what you had to do at the moment. I get it."

Another pang of guilt ran through her, this time for having ever doubted him. "Exactly, sir."

"Well, I can handle Kowalski. It's not the first time he and I have disagreed. I didn't call you here for that."

"Okay. Then, what?"

Ben motioned Tia to the couch. "I just put Jimmy Youngblood on suspension, effective immediately."

"What?" she said, stunned. "Say that again, Chief?"

"He's suspended from all duties. Travis is collecting his gun and badge right now." He took a deep breath. "Good chance he ends up getting terminated."

"Damn, Ben." Tia didn't hide her shock. "What the hell did he do?"

"The one thing that'll get a cop fired every time," Ben said. "He lied."

Tia thought of Rich in the hallway and the comments Youngblood had made on his way out the door. She remembered her conversation with Youngblood at the crime scene about the response time.

"This is about the DB call, isn't it?" she asked, finally taking a seat.

Ben turned a bit more officious. "You know something or are you guessing?"

"I know it doesn't take thirty minutes to get anywhere in this town at two A.M."

Ben nodded. "Unless you have to get dressed."

"Seriously?" She couldn't help but laugh. "Please tell me he was with some other guy."

"Knock it off, this is serious." Tia could see the situation pained him. "As soon as Travis brought me their reports, I got both Youngblood and Puller in here. Talked to each of them. I'm not going to go into details, but . . ."

Ben looked at the ceiling, then closed his eyes. "Of all the calls, right? I mean, here we are, already at odds with the ME's findings.

We've got a half-dozen significant issues to overcome in what is looking more and more like a homicide, and now I've got to deal with the fact the first officer on scene was coming from his girl-friend's house."

He returned his attention to Tia.

"Honestly, I could've dealt with that. Hell, it's no secret I've done worse. But Youngblood tried to cover himself and filed a false re-port. Then he doubled down on that and tried to get his trainee to lie. He took what might have been an ass-chewing and turned it into a cause for termination."

"He dragged Rich into it?" That was a step too far even for Tia, who had been known to bend a rule or two in her time.

"Yeah, but the kid didn't bite. Straight shooter." Ben nodded his head toward the closed door. "Rich told the truth, but that pretty much burns Youngblood to the ground, and I don't doubt for a mo-ment Jimmy is going to get the word out to all the patrol dogs. Put his own spin on it."

"That puts the kid in a pretty lousy spot," Tia said.

"Exactly," Ben said. "That's where you come in."

"Me?" Tia didn't like the sound of that. "How so?"

"I'm temporarily assigning Puller to Investigations." Ben paused. "Until further notice, he works for you."

"Excuse me?" Tia was not the least bit interested in having to babysit a trainee.

"It's just until things cool off. A few days, tops," Ben said. "I'll hit all the briefings. I can't say much because it's a personnel matter, but I'll make it plain that Youngblood burned himself. His predic-ament has got nothing to do with Rich Puller."

"Just put out an email."

"That won't do it and besides, emails always seem to end up in the wrong hands. I'm already going to get enough crap from the union. I don't need the press or any other outside forces involved."

"Well, what do you want me to do with a trainee?"

"Whatever, Tia. Just keep him out of the crosshairs. I know Jimmy's got friends on the graveyard shift. I don't doubt some of them will want to make things difficult for the kid."

Tia held up the envelope containing the list Sam Mills had given her. "Ben, I've got work to do. I just picked up the list of every staff member who worked at the retreat. There are over fifty names. Plus, I still need to finish the search warrant for the tower dump, and walk it over to the DA's office."

"Great. You're always bitching about how short staffed we are. Now you've got some help."

"From a probie? Seriously, Ben, the last thing I need is to be dragging around a clueless trainee."

"Like I said, it'll only be for a few days."

Before Tia could argue any further, Ben put up a hand and shouted, "Puller, get in here!"

Rich Puller opened the door and walked in. He stood in front of the Chief's desk like he was getting ready to face a firing squad. "Reporting as ordered, sir."

"Until further notice you're assigned to Investigations. You'll work under the supervision of Detective Suarez. Understood?"

Puller stared at his feet for several seconds before looking up, his face a mask of confusion, his voice incredulous. "What?"

"I said, you'll answer to Detective Suarez." Tia could hear Ben's impatience. "You got a problem with that?"

"No, sir. Not at all." The beginning of relief edged into Rich's voice. "I figured I was . . . I just thought . . . No, no problem at all. Thank you, sir."

It dawned on Tia that Rich had been sitting in the hallway waiting to be fired. In some departments, that might have happened—probationary trainees were always expendable. Realizing she'd been in similar situations herself, she felt her anger melt away. Through no fault of his own, the rookie had been dealt a pretty lousy hand and it wasn't over yet.

Tia reluctantly decided to go along with Ben's plan.

"You heard the Chief, Puller." Still sitting in her chair, she looked him up and down. "You work for me now."

Relief flooded his voice, filling the office. "Yes, ma'am. I'm ready."

"Is that it, Chief?" She smiled at her boss and did her best to let him know he'd get no further resistance. "We got plenty of work to do."

"Good." His expression and voice softened a touch. "I'll let you guys get to it."

"What about your meeting with Mort?" Tia asked as she stood. "Are we good? You and me, I mean."

"We're always good, Suarez," he said. "Your methods, sometimes? Those, I might have a problem with. But yeah. We're good."

TWENTY

"So, you want to tell me about it?"

Tia and Rich sat alone in the detective bullpen, Tia behind her desk and Rich in the chair usually reserved for victims or witnesses.

"What's to tell? Sergeant Jackson told me to write a thorough report, so I did. Then Chief Sawyer called me in, started asking questions. Wanted to know why it took so long for us to get on scene." Rich shrugged. "So I told him."

"It's all right, Rich." Tia wasn't going to push him. "You don't have to—"

"Look," Rich said firmly. "All I know is, usually around one in the morning, Officer Youngblood tells me to drive to a house over on Taft. He goes inside, I stay in the car. If a call comes over the radio, I answer. He hears the call on his portable and usually comes right out."

"Usually? How often does this happen?"

"Every night."

"Every night? Holy . . ."* Tia's voice faded and she wondered how Ben would handle this mess.

"Yeah, pretty much," Rich said. "But honestly? I never cared. Meant less time for him to be crawling up my ass about one thing or another. Or talking about all the girls he slept with in high school."

"Ah, yeah. I imagine that gets old."

"You have no idea." Rich took a deep breath. "So, what? I'm a rat now?"

"What do you mean?"

"I mean, I told Chief Sawyer the truth. About Youngblood, that is." Rich looked at Tia with as much insight as a cop with six weeks of experience can muster. "I might not know much about police work, but I know that makes me a rat."

"That's Hollywood crap, Rich." Tia leaned toward him. "All that 'blue wall' stuff? It's true. You're damn right cops stand together, but there's a limit. Most cops I know, any decent cop, that is, they don't expect you to lie to cover up for somebody. All that dumb-ass Youngblood had to do was tell the truth. He definitely would have gotten chewed out. Probably even suspended for a few days. Now? He'll be lucky if he keeps his job."

"Seriously?" Rich said. "That seems pretty harsh."

"Think about it." Tia figured she might as well start his training. "You're a cop who's got a documented reprimand for lying. Filing a false report."

"Yeah. So?"

"So now, every time a defense lawyer files a Pitchess motion to get a look at your internal affairs file, they're going to see that you've been untruthful in the past."

"A what motion?"

"Never mind, that's not the point." Tia wanted Rich to get it. "Let's just say that by some miracle Youngblood actually ends up doing some actual police work. Say he trips over a key piece of evidence in a major case. But his personnel record shows that he's got a prior for dishonesty. How's that going to go over with a jury? Think OJ, you know what I mean?"

Rich stared back, his face blank, and Tia tried again. "You know, Mark Fuhrman?"

"Who?"

Tia shook her head and started to wonder if she'd make much of an FTO. "Bottom line, Rich. Juries don't trust cops as it is. Put one on the stand who's a known liar? A documented bullshit artist? Forget about it."

Rich nodded as if it was starting to make sense. "I guess I didn't think of it like that."

"You should. You're a cop now. You have to think like that," Tia said. "And just remember, this isn't on you. Youngblood's an asshole for putting you in this position. That's how most anyone is going to see it. You'll come out of this fine."

"Then why am I working for you? Why can't I finish up my training? I only had three days to go."

"Chief's just playing it safe. You'll be back on patrol in no time." Tia pushed back her chair. "But for now, like the man said, you work for me."

"All right," Rich said. "I'm ready."

"I hope so, because our suicide? Looks more like a homicide."

That got Rich's attention. "Seriously? Somebody murdered him?"

"Yep, but we've got a lot of catching up to do."

"What do you need from me?"

Tia handed him the manila envelope. "This is a list of all the staff members who were at the church retreat. I need you to run every name. Have you done anything like that?"

"Yeah." Rich took the list out of the envelope and began studying the three pages. "My first week of training was in the records division. I learned about all the different databases. At least the basic ones. Pretty simple."

"Oh, was it? Well, let's see how you do. First you should check CHRIS, the Criminal History Records Information System. That'll give you any previous arrests, crime reports, traffic tickets, any police contacts. That's what I'm looking for, all right? Prior contacts with police. Anything at all. Got it?"

Rich nodded. "Got it."

"Might as well run the names through the sex offenders registry, too." Tia pointed to an empty desk. "Use Bruno's desk. He's on vacation until next week."

Rich nodded and moved to the workspace. "I'm on it, Detec— sorry. *Tia.*"

"Great." Tia moved to her own desk. "I'm going to finish up a search warrant for cell tower info. I want to try to get a judge to sign off on it today."

Rich looked up from where he was sitting. "And thanks, by the way."

"How's that?" Tia asked.

"I don't know." He shrugged, looking self-conscious. "For listening. For not calling me a rat or anything."

"Are you kidding me?" Tia looked up from her keyboard. "With a name like Dick Puller? Hell, boy. Rat would be an improvement."

TWENTY-ONE

Tia stood over the sink and scraped a plate of grease, corncob, and bits of fat and gristle into a large bowl, all under Ringo's watchful eye. The dog stood almost as tall as Tia, his front paws on the kitchen counter, his tail smacking the wall with the steady beat of a metronome. The smell of grilled meat lingered in the farmhouse where Connor and Tia had sat at the small dining room table, enjoying their first meal together in nearly a week. Tia had saved a few prime pieces of steak for the dog, and judging by the stream of drool, he had obviously figured out what was coming. She tossed a chunk of meat in his general direction and Ringo snatched the food in midair, practically inhaling it. Just as quickly as the meat disappeared, he stared at Tia, focused and ready for the next bite.

"Atta boy." She figured this feeling was the closest she'd ever come to maternal pride.

She used her shoulder and upper body to shove the dog back onto all fours. After a few minutes of playful torture, she put the bowl on the kitchen floor.

"There you go, killer. It's all yours." He plunged his muzzle into the bowl and Tia knew it would be a while before he looked up.

Standing at the sink, finishing the dishes, Tia was glad to have Ringo for company. Connor had gone to work an extra shift—a double tractor trailer was due in and the store's shelves had to be fully stocked when the doors opened at 6:00 A.M. The job paid a buck over minimum wage, and the hours of heavy lifting would play hell on his legs, but with the PD's salary freeze and no overtime pay, there was no convincing Connor to give up his grocery store paycheck. Tonight's steak dinner had been a luxury, but one they both thought was worth it.

She thought back to their conversation before he'd left for work. They'd been sitting on the bed and she was working on snapping the last buckle on his prosthetics. He had his legs draped across her lap, his voice relaxed and full of contentment. He reached out his hand and stroked her cheek.

"We need to do that more often. Sit, I mean. Together. Talk."

She'd leaned in and kissed him, then whispered in his ear, "We need to do *this* more often."

Tia walked into the living room, stepping around Ringo, who was pushing the empty bowl across the floor with the power of his tongue. "It's empty, boy. Let it go already."

Tia was still amped up from her crazy but productive day. The fiasco in the parking lot felt like it happened weeks ago, but it had just been that morning. As tragic as the case might be, working a homicide was a consuming and invigorating experience, a break from the routine of bar fights and the occasional street robbery. She also realized how close she'd come to putting the boy in the ground without concern. Just another tragic case of a Native American suicide.

She'd written the warrant for the tower dump requesting ten days' worth of data from the single tower in the vicinity and driven to the county courthouse in Waukesha. She struck out on locating a friendly judge and had to shop it around, eventually finding herself in the chambers of the duty judge, Andrea Jacoby. Known as a no-nonsense civil libertarian, Judge Jacoby gave Tia even more judicial pushback than she had anticipated. Judge Jacoby made it clear she was not keen on the idea of police gaining access to a cache of unrelated cell phone information. During a lengthy discussion, Tia explained that few calls would likely be part of the dump, given the cell tower's location and the time period covered by the request. She also assured the judge that there were no less-intrusive means by which to gain the needed information. In the end, Judge Jacoby said she would allow access to the data from the night of the shooting. No more. Frustrated but feeling fortunate to leave with something Tia took the signed search warrant and swung by the post office. She overnighted copies of the warrant to all major service providers, asking for an exigent handling.

Tomorrow would be another full day, she thought, settling onto the couch and picking up the remote. First order of business would be to reinterview Carla Hayes. Get more of a read on Henry's lifestyle. And she really needed to get started on the church interviews. Rich could help with that. But all that could wait. Like Connor was always telling her, sometimes she just needed to take her pack off and chill. She clicked the remote, figuring she'd catch the last couple of innings of the Brewers game. Falling asleep on the couch until Connor came home sounded like a nice evening. The screen came to life and what she heard and saw was so unexpected she spoke loud enough to draw the attention of Ringo, who'd finally given up on the bowl.

"What the hell . . ."

On the TV screen, Mortimer Kowalski stood at a podium that Tia recognized as the one at city hall, used for occasional press briefings. Behind Kowalski stood Dietrich Andreasen, mayor of Newberg, along with the Reverend Ezekiel Mills. Off to one side stood Sam Mills and Carla Hayes. Whatever was going on couldn't be good. She pulled her cell phone from her pocket, checking to be sure she hadn't missed a call or text from the department. The screen was blank. Nothing from Ben or Travis.

Kowalski read from notes. "Based on my analysis of the evidence collected at the crime scene along with the results of the autopsy, I've concluded that the manner of death in the case of Henry Hayes was suicide. I've conveyed my findings to the victim's family along with the condolences of the Waukesha County Medical Examiner's Office. I will be forwarding my report to the Newberg Police Department and I anticipate this will conclude any investigative proceedings."

Kowalski fumbled with his papers and remained behind the podium looking awkward and out of place. Mayor Andreasen stepped forward, pulling Kowalski by the arm and away from the podium, allowing the mayor to take center stage.

Tia didn't know much about Mayor Dietrich Andreasen other than what she had witnessed since he took office less than a year ago. A Swedish immigrant who came to America on a temporary college visa, Andreasen married his way into permanent citizenship. A mere twenty-year resident of Newberg, he was a bit sensitive to his shallow local roots, but ran for mayor nonetheless and surprised everyone, winning by less than 1 percent on a 20 percent voter turnout. He'd run on a platform of fiscal conservancy that he quickly turned into nothing short of scorched-earth austerity. Known to be an avid tennis player, the mayor made sure the public courts near his home were maintained, but all other city parks had fallen into disrepair. Then came the closure of the library, which the mayor pointed out was an obsolete institution in a day when most people read books on electronic devices. When a group of concerned citizens objected, pointing out that not all families with children were so fortunate to have such luxuries, the mayor said, "Those kids can't read anyway."

"This tragic situation has been a shock to our community."

Mayor Andreasen spoke with solemn self-importance. His Nordic accent was still thick and at times made him hard to understand. "I'd like to thank Dr. Kowalski for his quick determination in this case and I, too, offer condolences, on behalf of the entire Newberg community, to the Hayes family." He nodded toward Carla Hayes, who appeared tiny in the row of men. Her hands were knotted together in front of her, and at the sound of her name her eyes went from staring into the camera to the floor.

"I'd also like to extend a formal apology to Reverend Ezekiel Mills," Mayor Andreasen continued, "for the impact this incident had on his church and its annual retreat, a summer highlight for hundreds of young people from around the region. It is regretful Reverend Mills was left with no alternative but to cancel the festivities."

The mayor turned slightly to face the Reverend. "And of course, we deeply regret any initial misunderstandings with members of our police department."

"Seriously?" Tia shouted and stood up from the couch. Ringo, using his canine instincts, clearly sensed her anger and hunkered down. He pressed his head against the floor, and his tail went flat and still. The mayor droned on:

"Every citizen of Newberg greatly appreciates the role Reverend Mills plays as the spiritual leader of our community. I know it will come as no surprise to anyone to learn that Reverend Mills and his congregation have reached out to assist the Hayes family during this very difficult time.

"Now I'd like to invite Reverend Mills to say a few words, to provide us with his perspective on this tragic event."

Tia scoffed aloud as Ezekiel Mills stepped to the microphone. His tan skin glowed under the lights and his hair was coifed to perfection. Tia hadn't picked up on it before, but with Sam Mills still visible in the background, she saw the subtle resemblance between father and son.

"This indeed is a tragic and senseless loss of a human life," Mills began in his clear, well-practiced evangelical delivery. "A heartbreaking reminder not of the failing of any one person, but instead a failing that we all must share. But I do see God's hand at work, for when young Henry committed his desperate act in so public a way, it demands we take notice of the suffering of others.

"Suicide among young people of Henry's generation, particularly in the Native American community, is at an all-time high. It speaks to a sense of despair and hopelessness that permeates our society. But that is a larger issue, one that we must address over a long period of time. For now, we at the Church of the Rock will do all we can to help Henry's mother, Ms. Carla Hayes, and her surviving children work through their grief and loss." The senior Reverend Mills turned to look over his shoulder. "Now, I've been told that Ms. Hayes would like to say a few words."

Tia's voice was venomous. "Oh, don't you even . . ."

Tia watched as Sam Mills escorted Carla to the microphone, his hand lightly touching her elbow. The grieving mother wore a modest, long-sleeve, navy-blue dress straight off the rack at JCPenney. The collar went all the way to her throat, and her face was chalky white, thanks to a thick layer of foundation and cover-up heavy enough to fill in and smooth over the pockmarks and speed bumps. The makeup was miracle enough, but Carla had clearly spent some time in a salon—Tia wondered if the Church of the Rock had paid for the work. Her hair, which had been filthy, oily, and lank less than twenty-four hours before, was now washed, brushed, and pulled neatly back off her shoulders. It was quite a transition from the half-conscious woman on the couch and Tia figured the average viewer would be sucked right in at the sight of this grieving mother.

"I—I just want to say thanks to Preacher Mills," Carla stammered, her gaze darting from the camera to the row of men behind her. She looked down at the podium where, Tia assumed, her comments were scripted out. Sure enough, Carla fell into a cadence of reading. "I mean, Reverend Mills, for all his help. His son, too. I know my boy Henry had problems. I only wish he would have come to me. I wish I could have been there for him. I don't like thinking of him all alone in the woods."

Carla stopped and looked up, sounding as though she had gone off script. "Dyin' that way. He was a good boy and this is gonna be a hard time—"

The woman buried her face in her hands and Sam Mills stepped forward to offer comfort, putting his arms around her. Tia didn't buy any of it. Her feelings hardening, she yelled at the screen, "What a crock of shit!"

The cop in Tia watched Sam Mills guide Carla away from the podium, assessing the woman's current state. The street-grade heroin, she guessed, had been replaced by something more sophisticated, a smoother balm. Methadone. Maybe even Oxy. Enough to make her functional without destroying her shot at earning the public's sympathy.

The mayor returned to the podium. "Thank you very much. That concludes our press conference. Out of respect for the Hayes family, we will not be taking any questions."

Tia shouted, "No shit, you won't!"

The men huddled together and shielded Carla until the camera panned away from the now empty podium. Tia saw that several camera crews from Madison and Milwaukee were in the room. The familiar face of Lucy Lee-Jones came on screen and she began a recap of the story. The reporter spoke with the usual mix of high anxiety, unease, and groundless innuendo.

"Well, there you have it, folks. The story that we originally broke on Channel Eight Action News has now been officially ruled a suicide."

The reporter's image disappeared from the screen, replaced by the video of Tia and Mills on the stage at the campground.

"Oh for—not again." Tia had seen the video a dozen times. Just about every cop in the county had emailed her a link along with smart-ass commentary. Some good-natured. Some not so much. The video had a roadkill sort of pull to it and as much as Tia wanted to turn away she felt herself sucked in. The reporter's voiceover continued to provide details.

"This investigation, marred from the beginning with oversteps by local police, now appears to be drawing to a close, but conflict may be brewing within the walls of Newberg PD. An anonymous but reliable source familiar with the investigation has told me that while most officers with knowledge of this incident concluded the death was a case of suicide, apparently one individual detective insisted that the death of Henry Hayes was the result of foul play. This appears to have exposed a rift within the organization that my source says is an ongoing problem at the Newberg Police Department. This is Lucy Lee-Jones, reporting from Newberg City Hall."

Tia sat down hard on the couch, resisting the temptation to throw the remote at the screen. Instead, she stabbed at the television with the device, and the picture on the screen collapsed in on itself, along with the mood that had been so promising just minutes earlier. *Oversteps by local police. An individual detective. Ongoing problem.*

Anonymous but reliable source, Tia thought. No way that's anyone other than Youngblood. Tia could accept that; she expected no less from him. But another conclusion left her feeling like she'd been sucker-punched.

What was Ben's role in all this? And what about Travis? They'd both met with Kowalski behind closed doors. Kicked her out of the office. They must have known what was coming. Hell, she thought. Maybe one of them was the anonymous source.

Anger and a sense of isolation overtook her. She felt a tightness in her throat and she swallowed hard to fight the tears she knew were coming. Why does any of this surprise you? she thought. When are you going to learn? You're alone. You're a fraud. An imposter. You aren't even the person you pretend to be. You will never be part of the club.

Tia took a deep breath and exhaled, the air coming out loud, ragged, and full of emotion. She looked at Ringo, who was still plastered against the floor. His eyes met hers, and he halfway rose up off the floor and low-crawled toward her. He nudged his head under her hand and she knew exactly what he was trying to communicate: *Don't do it. I'm here.*

She gave the dog a single pat on the head and looked at her phone. Still early. Plenty of time. The solution was obvious and she grabbed her keys off the wall. The overwhelming sense of surrender was in and of itself intoxicating. A minute later she was in the GTO, top down and at high speed, already feeling the euphoria of the first drink.

TWENTY-TWO

When Tia pulled up in front of the trailer, the bright colors of the new plastic jungle gym stood out in the early morning sun and got her immediate attention. The Gremlin was out from under the tarp, washed clean and sitting on four good tires. A pink bicycle with training wheels and purple banana seat sat next to what looked to be a brand-new trike. The trailer itself appeared to have been power-washed and the weeds were gone. The surrounding hard-packed dirt had been raked smooth and dotted with potted plants. A rust-colored pickup truck, raised up high on four knobby tires, was pulled up close to the trailer. Tia saw a "Make America Great Again" sticker plastered in the back windshield.

Tia climbed the short steps, still debating the wisdom of her plan. As soon as she had woken up, she'd decided to drive to Carla's trailer alone, without first checking in at the PD. As far as she was concerned, the Henry Hayes case was still an open homicide and she wasn't going to take the chance of being shut down. She didn't need anyone's permission to do her job and if she had to work it alone, then so be it. Alone wasn't so bad. It had worked the night before.

After watching the press conference, Tia left the farmhouse and drove south on State Highway 83 to a roadside tavern, ten miles past the county line. The place was dark and dank, lacking in any of the typical fanfare that encouraged socializing or casual conversation. She took a seat at the end of the bar and ordered up a double shot of well tequila, glad to see the one other patron paid her no mind. She stared at the glass and mentally threw it back over and over again, imagining the glorious burn of the cheap liquor that would start on her lips, move to her throat, past her lungs, and then settle in her gut. When the bartender announced last call she was the only one left, still staring at the untouched glass of clear liquid. When the lights went up, he came over to stand in front of her, his hands resting flat against the bar, a dishrag thrown over his shoulder.

"So, what did you decide?" He looked to be a bit gruff but his voice carried the keen insight of a man who'd seen this act before. "You gonna drink it or not?"

Tia pulled a ten-dollar bill from her shirt pocket. She picked up the still-full shot glass, placed it on top of the bill, and slid it across the bar. The bartender took the ten spot and went to the cash register to make change.

"Keep it. Rent for the barstool," Tia said, nodding her head in appreciation for his patience. She stood and walked to the door. When the bartender called out she heard no judgment in his voice.

"Come on back if you change your mind."

Tia had driven home to find Connor sitting with his elbows on the kitchen table, staring ahead, both fists in a tight ball covering his mouth. His prosthetics were off and on the floor next to him. She sat down in the chair across the table, filled with love for the man and personal pride for herself. It would have been easy to toss back that two-dollar shot, but she knew it would have been the most expensive drink of her life. Then again, sitting on a barstool at one o'clock in the morning, she knew, it's easy to wonder who really needs work, friends, and self-respect. But Tia also knew the only thing that had kept her from giving in was this moment. The chance to look straight into the eyes of Connor Anderson, and know she had not let him down.

She told him everything. The press conference. The sense of betrayal. The overwhelming feeling of self-doubt. Her life as an imposter. All of it on a night when she was alone and on the edge. But most important was one simple fact: he was the one thing in her life worth living for. If that required sober living, so be it. They made love for the first time in six weeks. When she'd left the house he was still asleep.

Tia put her ear against the trailer door and heard nothing. She banged hard against the thin metal and stood back. She waited a half minute, then cop-knocked it, and the door shook under her fist. Still no response.

Tia leaned over the railing and used her fist to pound against the metal siding. "Carla, open the door."

A few seconds went by before Tia heard the shuffle of footsteps. The door opened six inches, revealing Carla's face, still caked with makeup that didn't hide the dark circles under her eyes. She was wearing a Spotted Cow beer T-shirt that came down to the middle of her thighs. Her hair was matted and flat on one side, and Tia picked up on the smell of bourbon when the woman spoke. "I ain't supposed to talk to you."

Tia knew she should try to cajole Carla into being more cooperative. Show sympathy and try to regain the woman's trust, but it just wasn't in her. "Oh yeah? And who told you that?"

"My lawyer." Carla said the two words defiantly and Tia got it. For the first time in a long time—maybe for the first time ever—Carla felt like she had the upper hand on somebody. Like she counted for something.

"You mean the church lawyer?" Tia tossed her head back toward the car and new toys. "Is that all it took, Carla? Couple of tires and some toys for kids you don't have? Now you're going to take advice from a bunch of people who don't care about you or what happened to your son?"

"You don't know anything," the woman said. "They's good people. They all came out and fixed up my place. Took up a collection and everything. Said they'd help me get my kids back, bought 'em toys. They're even going to help me find a job and stuff. That's more than any cop ever done for me."

"That's just what you want, right, Carla? A job." Tia laughed. "What happened to 'Henry would never kill himself'? Isn't that what you told me? You sounded pretty damn sure of yourself."

"I talked to the doctor. He explained everything." Carla's voice cracked with what sounded like sincere emotion. "Henry killed his self."

"Kowalski? Is that who you mean?"

Carla shook her head. "I don't want to talk to you. They said you'd try and trick me. I want you to leave."

Before Tia could answer, the door opened wide and a man filled the doorway—more than filled it, in fact. Dressed in nothing but boxer shorts and a tank top, his face was beefy and red. Tia picked up on the same strong smell of alcohol, along with sweat and drugstore cologne.

"Come back to bed, baby," he said, towering over both women and pulling Carla back through the door. He gave Tia a yellow smile. "You can come along, too, if you want."

Tia held up her badge. "Actually, you probably oughta hit the road, pal. Me and Carla have some things to talk about."

"He don't have to leave and I already told ya," Carla leaned in toward Tia. *"I ain't talking to you."*

"You heard the woman." The man took two steps onto the porch toward Tia until his massive stomach pushed against her. Considering the mood she was in, that was all she needed.

Tia grabbed his groin and squeezed. Even as he folded at the waist, he came around with a drunken and sloppy haymaker that she easily avoided. She hooked him under the arm and he stumbled farther forward on the porch. Tia allowed his own momentum and three hundred pounds of body weight to carry him over the short railing and onto the hard dirt below. He landed in a heap.

Easily vaulting the railing, she picked up a shovel leaning against the trailer. He managed to pull himself to all fours, cursing. She didn't wait for him to come toward her before she swung the flat metal head of the shovel at full strength, striking him in the meatiest portion of his back fat. No doubt it stung like hell, but other than a nasty bruise, he'd be none the worse for it. He howled out anyway.

"Bitch! What kinda cop are you?"

"Get your fat ass up and in that truck or the next one, I swear, I'll put it right in your ear."

It was obvious the man wasn't one to take orders from women, even ones armed with a shovel. "Fuck you. I ain't leavin'."

Irritated that he'd call her bluff, she walloped him again in the same spot.

"Goddamn!" he yelled. "All right. Just let me get my clothes. I'll go."

"Forget it." There was no way Tia was letting the man back inside the trailer, where he could easily arm himself. "Carla, go get this man his clothes and car keys. He's decided to leave."

"I told you, he don't have to. You do."

Tia kept her guard up and shouted back over her shoulder, "I swear, Carla, you ever want to get your kids back, you better help me out here. Give the man his clothes."

Carla huffed and disappeared inside the trailer. When she came back she threw a wad of dirty clothes at the man, along with a wallet and keys. She looked at him with disgust, clearly disappointed he couldn't even defend her against a woman cop a third his size.

Tia nudged him with the business end of the shovel. "Now get in your truck and head down the road."

The man pulled himself to his feet and stumbled to his pickup, still carrying his crumpled up shirt and jeans. Tia waited until the truck turned onto the main road before she threw down the shovel and turned back to the trailer. Carla was no longer in sight. Tia jumped back up onto the porch and went through the door.

Wide-eyed, Carla stood holding her cell phone and Tia grabbed it away.

"Not yet. First, you and I are going to have a talk. Then you can call whoever you want."

"I told you, I want you to leave."

Winded from the scuffle, Tia took a deep breath. "Look, Carla, I just want to talk to you. Can we just sit? Five minutes?"

The woman shook her head and held out her skeletal hand. "Give me that phone."

Looking around, Tia noticed the floral-print couch had been re-placed by one of blue cloth that looked brand new. The filth-covered carpet was now a low-pile, stain-free Berber. A flat-screen television was showing *Jerry Springer*. Tia shook her head and tossed Carla the phone.

"Fine. Call your lawyer. But you should know—you were right. Henry didn't kill himself."

"The doctor said nobody else was there." Tia heard the doubt in Carla's response. "He said Henry was all alone and he killed his self. Why would he lie to me?"

"I don't know, Carla. He could be lying. Or maybe he's just wrong. Maybe he's not very good at his job. But, I'm telling you"— Tia pointed a finger at Carla and spoke as if to give credit where credit was due—"*you* were right."

"I was?" Carla still held the phone but showed no interest in using it.

Tia sat down on the couch and patted the cushion next to her.

Carla took a step back, crossed her arms in front of her, and shook her head. Tia didn't force the issue.

"Do you remember when you told me Henry had a bone thing?"

Tia was encouraged by Carla's quick nod.

"His condition was called hypochondroplasia. Basically, it meant his arms were too short for his body."

Carla's face brightened. "That's it. That's what the doctor in Bemidji called it. Hypo-something."

"Right," Tia said. "And because he had that condition, he couldn't use that shotgun to kill himself. His arms just weren't long enough."

Carla dropped onto the far end of the couch, as far from Tia as she could get. Her voice was low. "Then how did he die?"

"Someone else used the gun to kill him. And they used it in a way that would make people believe Henry killed himself." Tia paused. "That's the truth, Carla."

The dead boy's mother stared blankly ahead. The woman would either tell her to leave or start asking questions. There was nothing more Tia could do. A silent minute stretched by.

"Then who?" Her voice was nothing more than a whisper. "Why?"

Tia surprised herself by leaning over and taking Carla's hand. "I don't know, but I want to try and find out. For that, I'll need your help."

Carla scanned the trailer, gazing at each of her new possessions. Tia forced herself not to judge the woman too harshly. She spoke quietly. "No one needs to know you talked to me."

"I told you," Carla said, her anger replaced by a helplessness that Tia sensed was very much a part of her life. "I don't know nothin'. I didn't think Henry would do that but . . . I just don't know anymore."

"Do you know why Henry went to the woods that night?" Carla looked at her lap and shook her head. "How about how he might have gotten there?"

"He hitched a lot. Sometimes he'd take the bus. He had some friends who had cars." Carla smiled, looking proud of her son. "I told you. Henry was smart. He just knew how to make his way in the world."

Tia imagined a dark-skinned teenage boy standing on the side of the highway with a shotgun on his shoulder, trying to hitch a ride or jump on a bus. Even in rural Wisconsin that would be a stretch. "What about his friends, Carla?"

"He didn't have much in the way of friends, but there was one fella. Somebody he called Kimo. They was in that juvenile school together. I know Henry's seen him a bunch of times lately, since they both got out. Kimo always be pullin' up in a big black truck and they'd go off."

"Kimo?" Tia didn't want to write the name down just yet, worried that might spook Carla into going quiet. "What about a last name?"

"I don't know. That's all I knowed him by."

"Could Kimo have gone to Newberg with Henry? Did you see him around that day, before Henry left?"

"I don't remember. Maybe he was here." Carla shook her head. "Lots a times I don't remember things so well."

Tia got the impression Carla was really trying, but the woman's limitations were obvious. But the name could be helpful.

The Rock County Sheriff's Office had told Tia that Henry had spent some time in Lincoln Hills, the correctional facility for Wisconsin juvenile offenders. If Henry and this "Kimo" were at Lincoln Hills together, it should be easy enough to determine the boy's identity. She moved closer to the woman.

"Carla, Henry had a thousand dollars in his pocket when he died. It was brand-new money. The serial numbers were sequential. Do you know what that means, 'sequential'?"

"Like in a row? One, two, three? Like that?"

"Exactly." Tia nodded. "Numbers in a row and brand-new bills.

That means the money most likely came right from a bank. Does that make any sense to you?"

"Well, Henry always had money, but I never heard about no bank. He just had it is all."

"You say he always had money? But he didn't have a job, did he?"

"He didn't need no job. I told you, Henry was smart that way."

The well was going dry and it was time to back off. Tia put as much warmth as she could into her voice.

"Thanks for talking to me, Carla," she said. "You know, when I first met you, I thought Henry killed himself and you said you knew he'd never do that. Well, I was wrong and you were right."

"I know. I know I was. But that doctor saying he did . . . I mean, how am I supposed to tell a doctor what he don't know? I didn't think much of him, but he is a doctor. I mean, who am I?"

Tia nodded, imagining how Kowalski must have come across. "You're Henry's mother, Carla. That's who."

"Yeah?" Carla almost smiled. "That doctor don't care nothing about that. He don't know anything about living like this."

"I'm going to go now, Carla. Do you still have my card with my phone number?"

The woman nodded.

"You call me if you think of anything else. Or if you need anything."

Tia got back to her car and banged out a quick text. The news conference had made it clear this case wouldn't be solved through conventional means. But that was no problem for Tia. She was at her best when she was ad-libbing. Before she got to the end of the driveway she got a reply to her text and the answer she wanted. No surprise there, she thought. There were certain people Tia knew she could always depend on.

TWENTY-THREE

"So, what? We're like spies now?" Tia leaned her elbows against the metal pipe railing, sure to speak loudly enough to be heard over the rushing water below.

"You wanted to talk," Livy said. "What did you think? I'd say, sure, come on down to the office. We'll chat."

"Something like that, yeah," Tia said. "But hey, this is fine. Very scenic."

It was Livy that Tia had texted when she left Carla's trailer. Now the two women were standing on the walkway over the Nagawicka Dam, just outside Newberg. The location for the meet struck Tia as a bit melodramatic, but she'd agreed. The thousand-acre Lake Nagawicka, affectionately known by the locals as Nag, was one of fifteen thousand documented lakes in Wisconsin, which in the mind of most Wisconsinites made their state the real Land of Lakes.

Driving in, Tia had passed a dozen or so shoreline properties owned by the Milwaukee elite and rarely occupied, other than for weekends and holidays. She'd parked and walked in from the beach, where a couple of teenagers sat at a picnic table smoking a blunt.

Half a dozen old men sat in lawn chairs on the boat dock; they looked more interested in drowning worms and swapping stories than catching the largemouth bass and pikes Nag was famous for. Come the weekend, Nag would play host to families from a hundred miles around, but on a mid-week sunny afternoon, all was peaceful.

If Livy was looking for a place they could talk unnoticed, Nag was a good choice.

"So how's Mort?" Tia asked. "Still all spun up?"

Livy wordlessly nodded, staring into the white foam of the mini-waterfall. Tia followed Livy's gaze to a disoriented walleye, about twenty inches long, swimming in tight circles in the pool just beneath the dam. Tia figured the yellow fish must have gotten caught in the spillway from Nag. Once he got his bearings, he'd spend some days in the cool waters of the Bark River. From there, he'd likely swim with the current as far south as Fort Atkinson. Then it would be on to the Mississippi and the world would lay wide open before him. Tia thought to herself a fish could do worse.

"Mort's not exactly thrilled with me right now," Livy said.

"What do you mean?"

Livy straightened up and grabbed a piece of the pipe railing in each fist. She stretched her back and cast a long shadow on the water below. "He's pulled me off the callout rotation and all current death investigations, including the Hayes case."

"But that's your job, Livy."

"Not anymore." Livy smiled but her voice broke and Tia saw a glisten in her eyes. "You're now looking at the new director of postmortem property control."

Tia stared at her, dumbfounded, so Livy continued, "Current assignment? Inventory of all nonevidentiary unclaimed property recovered from decedents. I guess he wants to make sure nobody makes off with an old pocketknife or anything."

She finally looked up from the water and smiled at Tia. "You'd be amazed how many guys die with a condom in their wallet."

"Damn, Livy." Tia was at a loss. "How long is this going to last?"

"Well, we got stuff going back about ten years, so that should keep me busy for pretty much the rest of my career."

"What about the Hayes case? Who's going to process the evidence?"

"Kowalski filed his report with the state DOJ this morning. Manner of death, suicide. End of story. That means no DNA analysis. No gunshot residue testing. No evidentiary processing of any sort by the state crime lab. Forensically, we're dead in the water."

"But what about the gun length? We proved it. Henry couldn't have shot himself."

"The man with *MD* after his name disagrees and that's how he wrote it."

"Then we'll go to the county medical examiner. Get a second opinion."

Livy shook her head. "Henry was cremated about three hours ago. There won't be any second opinion. Just Mort's word."

Tia was stunned. There were always hurdles in a major investigation, but this was different. In this case, the obstacles were being set up by the very people who were supposed to help clear the path.

"So how's your boss taking it?" Livy asked. "The press conference, I mean. Mort's findings."

"Sawyer? Haven't seen him. Travis either. But when I do, if either of them knew about that bullshit?" Tia thought about the possible confrontation. "Safe to say I might end up with a new job assignment myself. Maybe no job at all."

"Well then, what?" Livy asked. "Any ideas?"

"Yeah. Good old-fashioned police work," Tia said. "And you know what that means, right?"

Livy raised an inquiring eyebrow.

"Follow the money," Tia said.

"Sounds good." Livy looked up. "How do we do that?"

"The thousand dollars in Henry's pocket. It was in an envelope, right? Uncirculated, sequential bills?"

"Yeah."

"So it's not robbery," Tia said, staring into the water. "And I'm pretty sure it's not dope-related either."

"I agree on no robbery. The shooter would've taken the money. But you don't see a possible dope angle?"

"Nah." Tia talked it through: "Even if Henry was slinging a bit of dope, he wasn't big-time. He was just taking care of his mom. So if he was doing some nickel-and-dime deals, I don't see any of his customers paying for their shit with uncirculated Franklins."

"Good point." Livy nodded.

"That money was a payoff." Tia spoke with certainty.

"Come again?"

"Someone brought him a grand in brand-new bills. Someone owed Henry for something."

"But if you were paying him off, then why kill him?" Tia could hear the interest in Livy's voice and she wasn't surprised by it. Tia knew Livy wouldn't be able to just let the case go. "And if for some reason you did kill him, why not take your money back?"

"Haven't quite figured that out yet."

"I guess that's why you get paid the big bucks, right, Detective?"

Tia smiled. "Actually, Liv, this is where you come in."

Livy narrowed her eyes and her voice was suspicious. "I'm afraid to ask but, how's that?"

"The money is impounded in the ME evidence locker, right?"

"So?"

"So," Tia leaned one elbow against the metal railing and turned to her friend, "we might not be able to get any DNA work done by the state lab, but we can still use good old-fashioned fingerprints."

Livy stared back in silence and Tia went on, "Everyone knows you do the best print-comparison work in the state. You already pulled some great prints off the shotgun. Maybe you'll find some on the money too."

Livy shook her head. "Slow down, Tia. Quite a few problems there. Number one, what exactly would I be looking for? Comparison-wise, I mean."

"Who knows?" Tia said. "I've got a list of every staff member from the retreat. Rich is working on that, so maybe—"

"Rich?" Livy perked up.

Tia didn't want to explain Youngblood's suspension. "Yeah. He's assisting me while he finishes his training. But the point is, if you work up any latents on the envelope and bills, maybe we can come up with someone to match them to."

"Okay," Livy said. "Do I get to move in with you? Maybe live in your garage?"

"What are you talking about?"

"I just told you," Livy said. "I'm cut off. I don't have access to the case or the evidence. If I start checking things out of the evidence locker? Working up a latent-print report? Like I said, it will be a real test of our friendship because when Mort finds out, I'll be fired."

"Look, Livy. You could have signed off on suicide, but you didn't. You put in the effort, processed the shotgun, and now look where we are."

"That was dumb luck. If Rich hadn't been there, we probably both would have missed it."

"Exactly." Tia lightly swatted Livy on the arm. "And who says we can't get lucky one more time? Maybe with a little print work?"

Livy shook her head, but Tia could sense her slow surrender. "All right. I'll look for a chance to process the evidence for latent prints. But you have to bring me something to compare them to. No promises. And for the record, as far as your typical schemes go? This is pretty weak."

"It's all we got, Liv."

"So, really," Livy said. "Rich is working with you on this case?"

"Yeah, he is," Tia said. "I guess I should've brought him along. Something tells me he could have softened you up a whole lot quicker on the print idea."

Livy blushed. "Oh, stop it."

"Sorry," Tia said. "But seriously, he's got some good instincts. Might turn out to be a pretty good cop. I'm starting to like the kid."

It was obvious Livy wanted to change the subject. "So, you heading back to Newberg?"

Still thinking about the press conference, Tia said, "Not yet. I've got one more stop to make."

They figured it would be best if they didn't leave together, so Livy headed out alone. Tia lingered for a few minutes, taking a last look into the water. The walleye had recovered from his dizzy fall and she watched him glide away, allowing the current to carry him slowly south.

TWENTY-FOUR

The Crown Vic was made right off as a PD ride so the whistles and "Five-0" catcalls started before Tia even pulled to the curb. Across the street, a corner boy dressed in baggie shorts to his knees and a tank top—a kid she figured couldn't be older than nine or ten—looked Tia's way and broke into a dead run. Tia couldn't help but be impressed by the display of agility considering his tomato red Nike Lebron's were loosely tied and at least two sizes too big. About halfway down the block, he turned back, looking over his shoulder. When Tia showed no interest in giving chase, he dropped down onto the cement porch step of the nearest house, breathing hard. He sat with his elbows on his knees, doing his best to appear uninterested in her arrival. Across the street a group of young men loitered under a McDonald's sign so heavily tagged with graffiti the Golden Arches were mostly red and blue. They all gave Tia a hard look, but were way too cool to run.

The traffic on the 94 had been light, so she'd made the drive from the lake to the north side of Milwaukee in less than an hour. She'd found the church easily enough. The two-story structure had a steep-pitched roof that was topped by a tall steeple and a bell tower that Tia could see had no bell. Most of the windows were boarded over except for one all the way at the top. There, a pane of stained glass showed a levitating Jesus with arms outstretched and eyes cast down to the street. Tia wondered if the glass remained intact out of respect or because it was beyond rock-throwing distance.

After seeing him at the news conference, Tia remembered how Alex had gushed over Sam Mills and she had decided to do some online research of the preacher. She hadn't found the trade magazine Alex had mentioned, instead coming across a year-old piece from the Milwaukee *Journal Sentinel*. The lengthy article, titled "Father and Son," was a human-interest story, contrasting the professional careers of Ezekiel and Sam Mills.

After seminary, the younger Mills had spent two years in Africa as part of a humanitarian outreach effort. In the article he was portrayed more as the voice of the downtrodden than as a preacher. A realistic purveyor of modern social issues, his statements attempted to explain the public health benefits of needle exchange programs and free condoms for teenagers.

Apparently, Ezekiel Mills had declined to be interviewed, for all quotes attributed to him were taken from other interviews, press releases, and sermons.

It seemed pretty obvious the reporter had slanted the article to emphasize the philosophical differences between Sam and his father. One man was serving the lowliest members of one of the poorest cities in the country. The other preached a message on the glory of wealth to an audience of a thousand people whose idea of human suffering was the Packers losing to the Bears.

The sign outside the church read, FIRST FRIENDSHIP CHURCH OF MILWAUKEE, PASTOR SAM MILLS, EVERYONE WELCOME. We'll see about that, Tia thought.

She pulled on the heavy, ten-foot-tall wooden door and walked into a building bustling with energy. The laughter of children came from all directions. The walls of the long hallway were covered with art made by kids, mostly from paint, colored felt, sparkles, and glue. Tia walked slowly down the hall, studying the bright images, until she came to a door marked OFFICE.

Inside Tia found an African-American woman sitting at a desk with a Bible open in front of her. The woman's sand-colored hair was pulled back in a ponytail of long, tightly wound sister locks that fell past her shoulders. Looking up from her reading, she flashed a smile so genuine Tia could only smile back.

"Hi, welcome to First Friendship. I don't recognize you, do I?"

"Probably not," Tia said. Dressed down in jeans and a collared shirt that she wore untucked to conceal her gun, she had every intention of withholding her identity as a cop. "I was looking for Pastor Mills."

"Oh, he's around here somewhere. Let me find him." She needed both hands to heft a bulky walkie-talkie not unlike the type carried by Newberg PD officers, which meant it was about ten years behind the times in terms of technology. "What did you say your name was?"

"Oh, sorry." Tia already liked the woman and her answer felt deceitful. "Tia. He knows me."

The woman held the radio awkwardly near her face and pushed the "talk" button. Tia noticed the simple gold band on her left ring finger. She spoke louder than necessary into the radio. "Hey, Pastor Sam. You there?"

After a few seconds of dead air, his reply crackled through: "What's up, Darby?"

Darby hunched her shoulders and smiled. Tia was pretty sure the room got brighter. Darby winked as she spoke into the radio. "Tia is here to see you."

"Tia?" Even through the static, Tia could hear his surprise. There was a long pause followed by, "Be right there."

The receptionist said, "You want to sit? Can I get you anything?"

"No, I'm fine. Darby, is it? That's a pretty name."

"Thanks. I like your name, too. *Tia.*" Darby nodded in approval. "You look like a Tia. How you know Pastor Sam?"

Tia decided to come clean and tell the truth just as the outer door opened. Sam Mills walked in. "Detective? What brings you all the way into the city?"

"Detective?" Darby said and Tia picked up on her disappointment and apprehension.

Apparently so did Mills, for he spoke reassuringly. "Yeah, Darby. Tia is a detective in Newberg. She's a friend."

The woman's smile had been replaced with a look of suspicion. Tia was pretty sure Darby wished she'd been less helpful.

"I'm not here for work," Tia said. "Well, I mean, it *is* work, but it's not got anything to do with folks down here."

"Yeah?" Darby said, unsatisfied. "Okay. You just didn't seem like no cop to me is all."

Tia smiled. "I get that a lot."

"Come on in my office," Sam said. "Thanks, Darby."

"Yes, thank you," Tia said, meaning it. "Nice to meet you."

Darby didn't look up from her Bible. "Okay, then."

"Sorry about that." Tia followed Sam into his small office, which was lined with full bookshelves. It had a single window, covered on the outside with thick security bars. He took a folding chair from the wall and offered her a seat. "I didn't mean to—"

"You mean Darby? No worries, but yeah, she's a little skittish around the police. I don't think you'd blame her."

"How's that?"

"Her dad's been in prison for sixteen years."

"That's rough," Tia said. "What was it?"

"Twenty-five years for cultivation."

Confused, Tia said, "Cultivation of what?"

"Marijuana." His tone was clipped.

"Then it couldn't have been local cops. It had to be a federal thing, right?"

Sam shrugged. "Yeah, not that it matters much to the guy doing time. Apparently he had a pretty good indoor grow and a really lousy lawyer."

Tia wasn't surprised. Back in the day, when the War on Drugs was in full operation, if a person got in the crosshairs of the DEA, it wasn't all that unusual to get locked away for the long haul. Even for growing pot in your basement.

"So," Tia said. "He's in a federal pen?"

"Yeah. He used to be in Marion, and Darby got to visit him once a month or so. She could take the first Greyhound down there in the morning and the last one home at night. But then about two years ago they transferred him to a prison out in Arizona and she hasn't seen him since."

"How come?"

"What's she going to do? Buy a plane ticket? Book a hotel?"

Tia was struck by the emotion in his voice, which sounded a bit like anger. He went on, "It doesn't work that way. For the Darbys of the world, a trip to Arizona may as well be a trip to the moon."

"That sucks."

"Yeah," Sam said. "It's always seemed odd to me that the government doesn't give some consideration to keeping an inmate close to their family. Seems like that would go a long way in terms of prisoner morale. Not to mention it's the decent thing to do. At least her husband is closer."

"Her husband?"

"Dale," Sam explained. "He's doing time for a local thing. Officially, it's commercial burglary, which is a felony. Personally, I call it petty shoplifting. He got a year. He was almost finished, about thirty days to release, when he got into a fight with another inmate. Ended up getting another seven years tacked on for assault."

"Damn. He must have messed the guy up, huh?"

Sam shrugged. "That's what the guards said, but I know Dale. He told me it was self-defense. He's in Waupun. He should be out in three to four years if he can stay off the radar."

"Sounds rough." Tia couldn't think of what else to say. She'd long since come to realize prison could be an all-in-the-family-type experience. She knew of plenty of fathers and sons who were locked up at the same time.

"Their son, Robbie, turns eighteen in a few months. She's afraid to let him out of the house." Sam shook his head. "Darby's a great woman but she's got some trust issues when it comes to the system. So anyway, what brings you to the city?"

"Honestly, I just came down . . ." Tia's mind was still on Darby and it took her a moment to mentally change topics. She was careful not to come off too strong. "Uh . . . I was surprised to see you on television. The press conference?"

"Oh yeah. Dad asked me to help out with the boy's mom. She's kind of a mess." He looked at her closely. "She said you came by and told her about her son's suicide."

"I did." Tia nodded. "She was pretty adamant that her son was murdered. And now I agree with her."

"Really?" Sam was taken aback. "But the ME? He's ruled it suicide."

"I won't get into that," Tia said with a shrug. "Call it a professional disagreement. It happens on occasion."

"And this is one of those occasions?" Now she picked up on his hesitancy.

"Looks that way." She nodded. "There's pretty strong evidence, irrefutable, actually, that Henry's wound was not self-inflicted."

Still standing, Sam leaned back against his metal desk. "Well, no offense but I think I'll go with the scientific community."

Tia tilted her head and wondered where the conversation was headed. "What's that supposed to mean?"

"Well, again, no disrespect, but a medical doctor declared the case a suicide. That sounds pretty conclusive to me."

Tia was starting to feel a bit testy and it came through. "Just because he's got *MD* after his name doesn't mean he can't blow the call."

Sam crossed his arms over his chest and cocked his head to one side. "And that's what you think happened? This Dr. Walkoski got it wrong?"

"Kowalski, and yeah," Tia said. "He spit the bit on this one."

Sam stared ahead for several seconds, then shook his head and went to take a seat at his desk. "Do you really want to put the family through this, Tia?"

"Meaning?"

"Meaning this is already a very emotional and difficult situation. And now you're talking about . . . I don't know, adding all this suspicion and innuendo." He stopped and stared at her. "We're talking about murder, Tia."

"Yes, we are." Tia finally took a seat in the chair Sam had offered. She leaned forward with her elbows on her knees. "And I plan on solving it."

"Is that what this is?" It was Sam's turn to get testy. "Some chance to play cop?"

"I'm not playing anything." Tia didn't move and her voice was calm but stern. "I am a cop and this is a murder. But the only reason I came by is to ask you to not be turning Carla against me."

"What do you mean?"

"This attorney you have for the church told her not to talk to me."

"Come again?"

"I went by to see Carla this morning. She was very . . . well, I don't know what to call it but the bottom line is she was told by an attorney not to speak with me. I'm assuming it was the attorney who represents Church of the Rock."

"I had no idea. I'm sorry that happened, Tia. I'll have a word with Mr. Myers." Sam's tone softened. "And I'm sorry about the 'play cop' comment. I was out of line. This is just coming as a bit of a shock. I know you have a job to do."

"Exactly," Tia said. "So let me do my job and you do yours."

"And what exactly is my job?"

Tia leaned back in the chair and tried to lower the tension. "I think it's great that your church has reached out to Carla. I hope you can help her. But honestly? I think it's a little over the top."

"Sorry, Tia," Sam said. "Again, I don't follow you."

"The makeover at the trailer." Tia paused and when Sam only stared back she went on, "Flat-screen? New couch?"

Sam closed his eyes and nodded. "That sounds like my father's doing. I'm talking about my earthly one."

"Ah." Tia allowed herself to smile. "Guess I got my do-gooders mixed up."

"If it ever involves luxury items and bundles of cash," Sam hooked his thumb in the general direction of Newberg, "head west to the glass cathedral. The best I can do for anyone is a bag of canned goods and maybe a voucher for a night at the Super 8."

"I'll keep that in mind," Tia said.

"But seriously," Sam said. "If anything I've said or done has somehow interfered or made your job harder . . . well, I apologize. It wasn't my intent. And I'd like to think I can speak for my father as well. I'll have a talk with him. But again, I just have to say: it seems to me like the family has been through enough."

"I appreciate your honesty, Sam." Tia stood to leave. "Sorry again if I upset Darby. She seems really great."

"She is," Sam said. "She's a tough lady."

"Sounds like she has to be," Tia said, closing that part of the conversation. "I should be getting back to Newberg. Need to check in with my boss. Can you point me to a drive-through? Maybe something just a little better than that Mickey-D's across the street?"

"I know a great place. Five minutes from here. My treat."

Tia looked at her watch. It was pushing noon and she still hadn't checked in at the PD. She was sure Travis and maybe even the Chief were looking for her, but Sam was her best avenue to maintaining open relations with the church, which meant access to Carla and the long list of still to be contacted staff members from the retreat.

"Sure, Sam," she said. "But I'll buy my own, all right?"

"Great." He hesitated. "You mind driving? My car leaves a lot to be desired. It's pretty much on its last leg."

Tia laughed. "Sure, we can take my ride. You're going to love it."

TWENTY-FIVE

Tia followed Sam's directions through the city streets. They enjoyed a good laugh about the condition of Tia's car, and she explained the draconian budget cuts at Newberg PD. He wanted to take a picture of her sitting on the phone book but she refused. He pulled out his cell phone and took it anyway.

"I better not see that on Facebook or anything," Tia said.

"No promises," he replied, smiling. He pointed through the windshield. "Just about another mile or so, straight up this road. It'll be on the right."

As they drove past boarded-up storefronts and run-down apartment buildings, the conversation shifted to more serious topics. Tia asked Sam about his life as a minister, not tipping her hand that she had already done a bit of her own research. He surprised her when he opened up about it so quickly. Looking casually out the windshield, he talked about his time trapped in the middle of the Sudanese civil war.

"Seemed like one day we went from worrying about potable water and malaria to running from a rebel faction that had never heard of the Geneva Convention. I was there with half a dozen other missionaries. I ended up getting separated from my group so I hid out with a family of Copts."

"Copts?" Tia asked, drawn in by the story and already quietly comparing it to some of her own combat experiences.

"Coptic Christians. There's a long history of Christianity in Africa. Persecution. Genocide. But anyway, it was ten days before I saw an opening to escape across the northern border into Egypt, so I took it. Found my group at the American embassy. They'd written me off. We were another three months getting stateside. A few weeks after we got back I learned through the embassy that the family had been picked up by a group of rebels. The men, a father and his three sons, were tortured. Burned alive. The women. Well no one knows for sure."

"Jesus, Sam." Tia forgot for the moment she was talking to a preacher. "Sorry, I just mean, that's awful."

"No worries and believe me, I've taken his name in vain a few times myself. I look back and think of what I could've done. What I *should* have done."

Tia heard the anger in his voice and it was anger she understood. "That's a lot to carry around. Trust me. I speak from experience. You gotta let it go."

The car went quiet for a few minutes and it was Sam who redirected the conversation. She could hear the different tone in his voice, as if he was anxious to change the subject. "Not looking for an argument, but can I ask you something?"

"Go for it."

"Do you . . ." He hesitated. "Do police officers rather . . ."

When he stopped again, Tia looked his way. "Go ahead, Sam. Just ask. Do police officers what?"

"I just wonder, do they ever stop and think about the impact they have on communities? Communities like this one, I mean. North side of Milwaukee."

"'Course we do." Tia had been ready for a challenging topic and was surprised how easy his question was. "We're pretty damn proud of what we do. Keep people safe. Take bad guys off the street."

"Bad guys. Right." He nodded. "I figured that's how you'd see it."

"What other way would there be to see it?"

Tia looked his way but Sam ignored the question and seemed to be lost in his own thoughts. He tapped the passenger-side window with his finger.

"About six miles in that direction," he said, "just down the Ninety-four, there used to be an Allis-Chalmers plant. In its heyday, it employed over fifteen thousand workers. Machinists, welders, skilled assembly workers. The kind of jobs that let people live in good neighborhoods. Be part of healthy communities. This part of Milwaukee was solid middle class. Good families. Schools. It was the kind of place where the police just didn't see any need to get all that involved. People took care of themselves."

She wasn't sure where he was going with it, so she stayed quiet. He went on, "That's all gone now. That whole world is gone. The jobs. The communities. The *life*. Nowadays, this part of Milwaukee has one of the highest unemployment rates in the country. And it's not just the unemployment. Drug addiction, eviction, school dropout rates, single-parent households. All the things that pull communities apart are right here. And the only thing society has done about it? I mean the *only* thing? Is to send in the police."

Tia had been down this road plenty of times. In fact to her it was like a broken record that blamed the cops for all the social ills that plagued America. "Okay, but all the things you're talking about. Lost jobs, no opportunity. How is that the fault of the police?"

He smiled. "Exactly. It's not your fault, so why involve you? The cops, I mean."

"Sorry, Sam. I'm not following you."

He turned to her and his face was serious. "The police didn't create the problem but they've been sent in to fix it. Or at least contain it somehow. How does that make sense?"

Tia stopped at a red light and saw that on three corners of the intersection were boarded-up businesses. The fourth corner was a check-cashing store with an armed guard stationed at the front door.

"Well then, tell me," she asked. "Who are you going to send in to handle the drug problem? Social workers?"

"In some cases, yeah."

"No offense, Sam, but I don't think you have a realistic view of the problem."

"I live in this neighborhood, Tia. I think I have a very realistic view."

Tia looked out her window and saw a lanky teenage boy giving her the hard look, practically bouncing on his toes. Tia figured on taking the preacher to school.

"Watch this."

Tia hit the brakes and opened her car door. She put one foot on the street and the boy took off at a dead run. He whistled in a way distinctive enough to stand for something. Some sort of warning.

Tia shut the car door and looked back across the seat. "They probably aren't actually flushing the dope yet, but they're at least getting ready to. No doubt barricading the door. You think what? You could talk your way in? Reason with the homies?"

"Cheap cop parlor trick." Sam waved her off. "I'm not talking corner boys and dealers. I'm talking about the other ninety-eight percent of the people that live in this ten-block area. Those people? They watch the cops come and go every day. And all they see is their neighbors, husbands, and sons getting chased down, cuffed, and hauled away."

"That's not all we do, Sam. We don't just try to put as many people in jail as we can, all right?"

"Really, Tia?" Sam looked directly at her. "Don't tell people in this neighborhood that's not what cops do. Because it is."

"How's that?" She knew she was sounding defensive but she couldn't help it.

"Tia, you're now driving through the neighborhood with the highest per capita incarceration rate on the planet." He stopped to let it sink in. "Not the state. Not the country, mind you. *The planet.*"

Tia had no comeback.

"And we're not talking about major dope dealers, or killers, or rapists. More like shoplifters and pot dealers." He shook his head and she heard a bit of disgust in his voice. "Justice system? I swear, Tia, call it whatever you want, but it's anything but *just.*"

Before Tia could think to respond, Sam pointed out the window. "Turn in here."

She pulled into a large lot in front of a three-story brick building that stretched out over the entire city block. A dozen or more cars and trucks sat parked in front, and Tia could see men unloading lumber and Sheetrock. A banner hung across the tall windows of the second floor. It looked to be at least fifty feet long and in bright yellow letters against a black background it read:

53206 TRANSFORMATION PROJECT

"Hopefully, you like good home cooking," Sam said, his voice back to its lighter tone and filled with enthusiasm.

Tia followed Sam as he walked toward the building, waving to the workmen, calling them by name.

"So far, we're just employing about fifty men on the construction project. Getting the building back up to code. It's been empty for almost thirty years. All the workers are local from right here in the neighborhood."

Tia looked down the block at the imposing structure. She could barely see where the building ended. The red brick was turned mostly black with a half-dozen smokestacks jutting into the blue sky, imposing but silent, as if lying in wait, ready to churn back to life. The building made Tia feel as if she'd walked onto a movie set depicting a world gone by.

"What's the story on this place? Looks like it's got some history."

"When it was first built just before the Civil War it was a tannery," Sam said. "After that, it had a pretty good run as a textile mill. Wasn't nearly as big back then. Around the time of the Second World War it was expanded and outfitted as a tire plant. Employed over five thousand men, running twenty-four hours a day. Closed down about twenty-five years ago."

Tia saw that even Sam was awestruck, like he was meeting the building for the first time. She felt it, too. It was one thing to look down from the interstate onto the shuttered factories that dotted the Milwaukee skyline. It was another thing to stand in their shadow and sense the power they once possessed.

"We should be able to house a few dozen small businesses," Sam said. "We've already got on-site day care. We hold NA and AA meetings two nights a week. Pretty soon, we'll have a community center, job training. Neighborhood clinic. All under one roof. After that, we'll start opening up for-profit businesses and ship the merchandise all over the country."

She heard the excitement in his voice, and even though it sounded like pie in the sky, she didn't want to come off rude. "Hell of a project, Sam. Really something."

Tia followed Sam inside the building, where the smell of hickory barbecue caused her stomach to come to life with pangs of hunger. A large collection of tables and chairs, mostly occupied, were set up on the first two levels, just inside the entrance. Tia figured the large, open space, which took up the first and second floors, was once the lobby for a business, or maybe a showroom of some sort. The high ceilings had been painted flat black, leaving the original ventilation piping exposed. The walls were redbrick and decorated with large black-and-white photos that looked to be pictures of nineteenth-century Milwaukee. There were other color photographs of people and places of the current neighborhood.

Tia couldn't help but notice the mixed crowd of people. Some looked to be from north Milwaukee, but several tables were occupied by men and women in business attire whom she guessed had come from the south side.

"A member of my congregation had a rib joint just a few blocks from here. He'd been robbed three times in a month and was ready to give up. I convinced him to set up in here. Says he's done more business in two weeks than he did in the last six months at his old place. He's going to need to hire a couple of more cooks and waitstaff, too. And with the crowd of people always around, well . . . the *bad guys,* as you call them, have stayed away."

Sam introduced Tia to the owner, and some of the young people waiting on the crowd and busing tables. A few minutes later Tia and Sam were seated on the upper balcony, in front of a floor-to-ceiling window that looked out over the city. A biracial woman wearing a shirt marked 53206 brought over a plate full of baby back ribs covered in barbecue sauce along with sides of baked beans and cornbread.

"Here y'all go. Dig in." She smiled at Tia and winked at Sam before hustling away.

"I said a burger, Sam." Tia stared at the mounds of food. "I'll sleep for a week if I eat all this."

"No worries. I can take it back to the church. It'll be gone in five minutes. Just try it."

Tia helped herself and found it hard to hold back. "I'm no authority on soul food, Sam, but this is amazing."

She could hear the pride in his voice. "I'm trying to get the *Journal Sentinel* to come do a review, but really, I think word of mouth is all we need. It gets busier every day."

The talked while they ate, and once again the conversation turned personal. She found herself opening up more than she typically did in work situations. She told Sam about her time in the Marines. She talked about Connor and his long recovery after stepping on an IED. She even mentioned her own on-duty injury, a near fatal shooting, and the difficult months of recovery. She gave her family history a light pass, mentioning that her dad was a dairy worker, but staying away from the early years she spent in migrant camps, when her family had followed the picking season from state to state. But what she did tell him left an impression.

"Sounds like you've overcome a few obstacles of your own." His voice was respectful. "I hope I didn't sound all preachy before. Giving you some kind of sermon."

Tia picked up a short rib and bit into the meat. She winked. "Maybe a little, but hey. You are a preacher."

Sam looked back across the table like he was sizing her up. Drawing some sort of conclusion. "You're what I call the Abraham Lincoln factor."

Tia laughed. "Oh man. Here we go again. Sermon number two."

Sam smiled. "No, seriously. People like you pulled yourself up by your bootstraps. Overcame adversity. Took the bull by the horns. All that jazz."

Tia used the almost clean rib bone for a pointer. "Exactly. Seems like everyone ought to do that."

"Don't you see? That's the problem." Sam leaned across the table and squeezed her hand. She felt his excitement, not anger. "You think since it worked for you, why doesn't everybody do it, right?"

"Yep." Tia nodded her head. "And not just me. What about Darby? Dad locked up, husband, too. Doesn't look to me like she's hitting the crack pipe or getting loaded on Mad Dog 20/20 every night crying 'woe is me.'"

"Well, Tia, I wish I could take what you and Darby have running through your veins and inject it into that boy back on the corner. I wish I could give every young father in this zip code the kind of internal fortitude that your dad must have. I wish it was that simple. But unfortunately, the human spirit doesn't work that way."

"No?" Tia asked. "Then how does it work, Sam?"

He smiled. "Mysteriously, Tia. Very mysteriously."

Tia sat for several seconds and stared at him. "I like sermon number two better. Abraham Lincoln? That's pretty damn inspiring."

He waved a hand at her and turned away smiling. She laughed to let him know it was all in fun.

"I need to get back, Sam." Tia pulled a twenty from her wallet, knowing it was her last one until payday. She put it on the table.

"Hey, this was on the house," he said. "Seriously."

"That's okay." It didn't matter if it was her last few bucks. Tia didn't take free meals. "I'll be back and I'll bring some friends. That was amazing food."

They both stood to leave and Sam said as he led the way out, "Come back in a couple of weeks. Big celebration."

"How's that?"

"We're closing escrow. After that, we can really start getting this place in operation."

"Place like this? That check is going to have some zeroes."

"We've got donors and philanthropists lined up. We're depending on the generosity of a lot of people but it's all finally coming together."

They walked outside and the sun was warm on her face. She looked over to see the construction crew was still hard at work. "How about your dad's congregation?"

"Oh yeah," Sam said. "They're a big part of this. But the way I see it, they damn sure ought to be."

"How so?"

Sam kept walking and looked toward the men still unloading the truck. "They live an hour from here, Tia. But it may as well be . . ."

He stopped and shook his head in frustration, his hands on his hips. "You ever think about how much of life comes down to the womb you fall out of and the zip code you land in?"

Tia smiled, thinking of her own life. "That's an interesting way of putting it but, yeah. I know what you're saying."

Sam nodded and smiled. "Well, like I said. The ribbon cutting is in a couple of weeks. Should really be something. You should come."

Tia nodded once. "Count me in, Sam."

Tia's phone buzzed. She pulled it out and saw a text message from Travis that was nothing but a row of question marks.

"I better get back to Newberg," Tia said, punching out a quick reply to her boss.

"All right, Tia," Sam said. "Thanks for coming by. Sorry if I stepped on your case but I'm glad you came to see me about it. Always better to talk things through, right?"

Tia nodded in agreement. "Thanks for the tour. You want a lift back to the church?"

He was already walking away, headed for the building. "No thanks. I'll hang out here for a while and help out. I'll find a ride back."

Tia got back to her car and as she pulled out she saw Sam helping to unload twelve-foot two-by-fours. He stood out as the only white face among a dozen young men, mostly black but one or two who looked mixed. She even saw a couple of older Latino men. The whole crowd worked together, smiling and laughing, but no one more than Sam.

TWENTY-SIX

Tia drove the Crown Vic hard on the eastbound 94 and headed straight to the PD. Tempted to use the grill-mounted blue light, she realized her lousy time management didn't actually constitute an emergency. It wouldn't have made much difference anyway. Her squad already had trouble keeping up with the other cars on the freeway. She parked and double-timed it up to Travis's office, knowing he was probably not going to be particularly happy with her arrival time.

He had every reason to be angry. Whatever his role in the press conference may or may not have been, Tia knew she was out of line for not checking in first thing in the morning. The PD was in the middle of a controversial death investigation that had the department under a great deal of media scrutiny. She had no right to pull some disappearing act. She was out of breath when she arrived in Travis's empty office. She texted his cell and he responded immediately: *Chief's Office NOW*

Great. She reminded herself again, she had it coming.

Tia walked to the admin wing and saw a BACK IN FIVE MINUTES

sign on Carrie's desk. The Chief's door was closed so Tia gave it a soft knock and walked in.

Ben looked up from behind his desk. Travis was seated alone on the couch. Two chairs had been pulled up to complete a circle, occupied by Mayor Dietrich Andreasen and Reverend Ezekiel Mills. Taken aback by the makeup of the group, Tia gave the situation a quick assessment. She recognized it would be important to maintain an appropriate level of decorum, but she didn't intend to kiss anyone's ass. She'd pay her respects to the Chief, complete any business with her immediate boss, and make her exit as quickly as possible. As for the other two in the room, they were of no consequence.

"Sorry to interrupt, sir." Tia nodded to the Chief then turned to Travis. "Hey, Sarge. Did you want to—"

"Good afternoon, Detective. Have a seat." The terse direction came from behind the desk, where the Chief sat dressed in his full dark blue uniform that included his gold-plated collar stars, metal badge, and nameplate. "I asked Sergeant Jackson to hunt you down. I'd been hoping to meet with you this morning. Go over a few . . . recent developments?"

"Sorry, sir," Tia said. She braced herself for the order to shut down the investigation. "I've been out running down some leads."

"Is that right?" Ben's voice held no anger. In fact, Tia felt that strange connection between them taking place and the most significant emotion she picked up on was his disappointment. She was certain he knew the disappearing act had been deliberate. "I'm assuming you saw the mayor's press conference last night."

Tia finally acknowledged Mayor Andreasen's presence by briefly looking in his direction, but when she spoke she turned back to the Chief. "I caught most of it."

"Well, we were just—"

"If I may, Ben," Mayor Andreasen said, cutting the Chief off. The mayor was dressed in his typical dark business suit, red tie, and American flag lapel pin. His black oxfords were buffed to a high shine. The mayor wore his wispy brown hair plastered into a bad oily comb-over that did nothing to hide a significant case of pattern baldness. "The purpose of this meeting was not to initiate a discussion or seek input. I merely stopped by out of respect to your office, and to explain my reasoning."

"I appreciate that, Mr. Mayor," the Chief said. "I would have appreciated it even more if you had told me in advance of your press conference."

Ben shot a quick look at Tia, then turned back to the mayor. "I really believe that was premature."

Tia immediately deduced two things. Number one, Ben had been caught flatfooted by the press conference, and second, he knew that Tia had doubted him. Her thoughts of self-recrimination were interrupted.

"Well, I'll take the blame for that, Chief." Reverend Mills threw an insincere smile Tia's way, before looking back to Ben. In contrast to the mayor's attire and somewhat stuffy presentation, Mills appeared completely at ease. Leaning back in his chair, his legs comfortably crossed at the knees, he was dressed in his typical denim jeans ironed with a crease and deck shoes with no socks. He wore a well-fitting light-salmon-colored polo shirt and Tia had to give him credit for that. Not just any man could pull off pink. Before continuing, he took a sip from a can of organic beet juice. Tia assumed he'd brought it with him since the vending machines at the PD offered nothing so exotic. She listened as he went on.

"The press conference was my idea. After I met with the mayor and Dr. Kowalski, I just felt it was important for the entire community to come together. As tragic as it is, it's time for us to wrap our arms around the Hayes family. The last thing we want to do is complicate the issue by having the good people of Newberg out there thinking there's a killer on the loose."

"But there may well be, Reverend," Ben said, giving no ground.

"Now, now, Ben." The mayor spoke as if he were scolding a child, while at the same time wanting to impress the other parent in the room. "The Reverend is absolutely right. You heard Dr. Kowalski's statement. This is a suicide, plain and simple."

Ben turned to Travis. "Sergeant Jackson, where are we with our investigation?"

Travis sat up straight on the couch and Tia watched as he turned his attention to the Reverend and the mayor. "We believe the physical evidence from the scene conclusively proves that the wound could not have been self-inflicted. We're in the process of attempting to identify witnesses. Other persons that may have been in the woods that night. The obvious place for us to begin is with those who were attending the youth retreat."

"I'm afraid I'll have to stop you right there, Sergeant," Reverend Mills said, putting up a hand. "We will not be providing any information to the police department about our attendees. In good conscious, we just can't."

"We already have it, sir," Travis said. "Your son provided us a list of all the adult staff members. He was understandably reluctant to provide any information about minors. We all agreed that would be something to discuss in the future, if it becomes necessary. But for now, we'll be contacting adult staff members only."

Reverend Mills, who had just taken another drink of juice, was clearly caught off guard. He swallowed hard, nearly choking, and his face flushed with anger. He sat forward in his chair, and both feet went flat against the floor. "Sam gave you that? When?"

Travis nodded to Tia and she spoke up. Based on their recent history, she took care to be exceptionally respectful. "Yesterday, sir. We're currently in the process of evaluating the list for witness potential."

Reverend Mills initially looked to Ben but then appeared to think better of it. His voice lost the smooth, almost hypnotic tone he was famous for. Instead, he was practically sputtering. "Dietrich, what is going on here? How can the police department justify harassing the people who volunteered their time, only to find out they'll now be questioned by the police? This is outrageous."

The mayor turned to Ben, only slightly calmer than the Reverend. In his excitement his accent became more pronounced. "Chief Sawyer, I have to agree with Reverend Mills. I don't think it was appropriate for your officers to—"

"Detectives," Tia said.

The mayor turned toward Tia, annoyed. "Excuse me?"

"Sergeant Jackson and I are both detectives." Tia smiled and held eye contact. Mayor Andreasen stared at Tia a moment longer then turned back to Ben.

"I don't think it is appropriate for your people to . . . to . . . *pressure* Sam Mills into handing over information about . . . who was it again? Staff members? I must say, this does sound a bit heavy-handed."

"Not at all, sir." Tia turned to Reverend Mills. "I just left a meeting with Sam and we had no issues. In fact, I appreciate his cooperation. You'll be happy to know we left on very good terms. He actually showed me around his church and the urban renewal project he's working on. It's really something."

"Oh yes." Reverend Mills rolled his eyes. "My son. Out to save the downtrodden of the world."

Regaining his composure, Reverend Mills once again turned his attention to the mayor. "I'm very disappointed that our police department is insisting on pursuing a case that is clearly nothing more than a personal tragedy. It seems to me that the church is in a much stronger position to help heal this community, not to mention the Hayes family, than the police force."

The mayor was quick to respond. "I agree. Chief, I think it's time to put an end to this waste of time and taxpayer money."

"Thank you, Mayor," Ben said. "Your concerns are duly noted."

"What does that mean?" Tia could hear the offense in the mayor's response. "'Duly noted'?"

"That means we will continue our investigation and I can assure you when we have gathered all the facts we will document our findings," Ben replied, his tone professional. "And the concerns you've expressed here today, along with Reverend Mills, will be documented and . . . *duly noted*."

The room went silent for several seconds. Tia was surprised when it was Reverend Mills who spoke up and not the mayor. "That is very disappointing, Chief Sawyer. I had hoped you would be reasonable about this delicate situation."

Ben pursed his lips and nodded. "Well, Reverend, I don't ever like to disappoint any of the residents of Newberg, but in police work that pretty much comes with the territory."

"If I were you, Chief," Reverend Mills said, "I would be most concerned with disappointing *certain* residents. Residents who have the ear of all five members of the city council. Not to mention their home addresses and cell phone numbers."

Ben stared at the Reverend long enough for everyone in the room to become uncomfortable. When he spoke his words were slow and measured. "Since you barely tried to conceal your threat, Reverend, let me put it to you another way. I'm not the least bit concerned about your ability to rattle the cage of local politicians. You're right. There are five members of the council and if you get three of them to agree that I need to go, then that's that. But in the meantime this is my department. These people work for me and we will pursue investigations as we deem appropriate."

Reverend Mills and Ben stared at each other for several seconds and it was Mills who blinked first. He took a last swallow of juice, then lightly tossed the can across the room where it landed neatly in the trash. "I think we're done here, Dietrich."

"Yes, Reverend Mills. I believe we are." The mayor stood,

pushed back his shoulders and stared at Ben, still sitting calmly behind his desk. "I completely agree with the Reverend. Perhaps it is time for the council to reevaluate your performance."

"You know where to find me, sir."

Ben stood, while Tia and Travis remained seated. Tia couldn't resist giving Ezekiel Mills a hard look as he left the office. He'd made it clear he was gunning for her boss. It was official. He'd drawn a line in the sand. Both men left the office and Tia leaned over and kicked the door shut with her boot.

"Sorry, Chief," Travis said, looking at his phone. "I didn't want to interrupt, but I got a phone call from California. You mind if I take a few minutes?"

"Yeah, sure." Ben looked at Tia. "Can you stick around?"

Travis hightailed it out of the office, already dialing his phone. Tia stayed in her seat.

Ben didn't waste any time. "Where were you all morning?"

"Working, Chief. I thought it was important to reconnect with Carla as soon as possible. I also met with Livy. Discussed some ideas that, candidly, I think you'd rather not know about. And I really did drive to Milwaukee and spent some time with Sam Mills. I wouldn't say he's exactly in our camp but I think he'll stay out of our way. Can't speak for his dad."

"Well then, I guess you have been busy." The disappointment was still there.

"Yeah. But I should have checked in. And to be honest, I was a little peeved."

"About what?"

"The press conference. The meeting you and Travis had with Kowalski yesterday. I thought you might be ready to shut this down. Sorry if it seems like I doubted you."

" 'Seems like'?" Ben smiled. "Well, if we're making true confessions, you weren't the only one who was a little worried."

"How's that?" Tia asked but she already knew.

"It's been a rough couple of days. Just figured you might've slipped. Couldn't blame you if you had. Spent the better part of the morning worried you might be in rough shape somewhere. Afraid to reach out."

"I get it. It was close. But no . . . I'm good."

"I'm glad to hear it. You know I'd be there for you, right?" Ben said. "And not as the Chief. As your friend."

"No worries, Ben. I'm good." She saw that her answer didn't satisfy him. "But yeah. I know."

"Thing is, Suarez, you and I are in the same boat. Based on our histories, we got no place else to go. So for the time being, at least, Newberg is stuck with us and we are stuck with each other."

"I could do worse, Chief."

"Likewise, Tia. Likewise."

She stood and headed for the door. "Hold tight, boss. This case is going to turn soon. We'll get through it."

"Yeah," Ben said. "One way or another, we definitely will."

TWENTY-SEVEN

R obert Horatio Gosforth."

"Hey to you, too, Rich." Tia walked into the bullpen, where Rich Puller sat at a computer. Tia wasn't used to working with a partner and she sure wasn't used to having a trainee. Probably not what the Chief had had in mind, but she'd left Rich on his own for the day. She hoped he'd made good use of the time. "So who's Robert Horatio Goforth?"

"Not Goforth. Gosforth." Rich leaned back from the desk and held up several sheets of computer printouts. "The list you gave me yesterday? He's one of the staff members."

"Okay. What about him?"

"Well, it so happens he was the only person on the list with a Rock County address, like our victim. So I figured that might be a good place to start."

Tia nodded in approval. "Did he pan out?"

"Sort of." Rich referred to one of the printouts. "I did like you told me and entered his name into CHRIS. I got a hit out of Grant County for a disorderly conduct conviction three years ago."

Tia took a seat at her desk and turned to face him. "Go on."

"I dug a little deeper. Turns out the conviction is related to an arrest out of Platteville." Rich's expression was all too familiar to Tia. When cops started to run down leads, it never took long for it to turn into a game of cat and mouse. When it was a homicide case, it was more like a big game hunt. Now Rich had the look of the hunter. "He pled out to disorderly conduct, but the actual arrest was for 944.2."

"Really? How did you get that?"

Rich shrugged, nonchalant. "Called Platteville PD. Had a records clerk scan the report and email me a PDF."

Tia was impressed. "Nice job." Rich smiled at the praise. She mused, "An indecent exposure charge means one of two things. Either he was having sex in a public place or he was letting his crank hang out for some fresh air."

"The first one and get this. Turns out, Gosforth wasn't alone when he got hooked." Rich handed Tia a printed copy of the police report.

Scanning the printout, Tia looked at the arrestee block, where Gosforth was listed along with . . . "Charles Stevenson? Gosforth got arrested with another dude?"

Rich smiled and raised his eyebrows. "Read the narrative."

Tia read on and laughed. "Damn. Sounds like they were having a time." Tia turned to the next page and kept reading. "Holy shit. Get a room, fellas."

"I figured you'd want to know a little bit more about him, so I did some social media excavation. With a name like Robert Horatio Gosforth, I knew he'd be pretty easy to mine."

She had definitely underestimated Rich Puller, Tia thought. Leaning back in her chair, she put her boots up on the corner of her desk. "I can't wait to hear it."

"Pretty basic stuff. Public record site shows he's been paying a mortgage in Evansville for the last eleven years."

"Evansville? That's Rock County, right? Like our victim?"

"Yep. His Facebook is wide open. He lists his employer as the local public school district. Looks like he's a teacher. Wife. Twin daughters, probably nine or ten years old."

Tia shook her head. Ten years ago, everything Rich had just told her would have required dozens of phone calls, hundreds of miles of travel and probably more than a few hours of surveillance. He'd done it in less than a day without leaving the office. On top of that, the employment history might have even required a search warrant, but since it had been left in plain view on the internet, any person on the planet with access to a computer could have at it. All reasons that Tia would never involve herself in online social media.

Rich wasn't done.

"He looks to be pretty heavily involved in his church. Place called New Hope. It's nondenominational."

Tia nodded. "Just like Church of the Rock."

"Exactly."

"Well damn, son. Anything else?"

Rich smiled, clearly pleased with himself. He leaned back in the swivel chair. "He fancies himself a fly fisherman."

"Nice work, man." Tia was impressed. "Really well done."

"Thanks. So what now?"

Tia thought back on her conversation with Livy. Someone in Henry's last hours had been willing to part with a good bit of money. Someone who had enough of a life to be able to walk into a bank and walk back out with ten brand-new hundred-dollar bills. Not that public schoolteachers were rolling in it, but it's possible, she thought. Especially if that schoolteacher was married, with kids . . . even though he had once been arrested for orally copulating another man in a public park. Tia didn't want to get too far ahead of herself, but yeah. This could pan out.

"Get your coat." She brought her feet down off the desk and stood. "We're taking a drive."

TWENTY-EIGHT

amn, Tia. Your squad car is a real piece of shit."

"And you're telling me that because I didn't already know?"

Having tossed the phone book in the trunk, Rich adjusted himself in the lumpy driver's seat, his foot mashing the gas pedal against the floorboard. Tia craned her neck to get a look at the odometer and saw the needle was creeping just past sixty miles per hour.

"Go easy on her. If we have to call a tow in another jurisdiction, that's going to be damn humiliating."

Rich shot her a smile. "More humiliating than the phone book?"

Tia cocked her head, speechless. The boy was starting to show some spunk.

It was just an hour to Evansville; Rich was driving so Tia could continue to work up the intel on Robert Gosforth. Via her smart phone, she got the address for the one and only elementary school. Searching a few more social media sites told her that his online presence showed regular involvement with the New Hope Church, also located in Evansville.

It seemed likely that Gosforth's attendance at the Copper Lake retreat was associated with his church. If that was the case, it stood to reason that perhaps other church members, including some teenagers, might have attended as well. Tia couldn't figure at this point if the man represented a real lead or not, but it definitely needed to be fleshed out.

They pulled to the front of the one-story brick school building that was on a tree-lined street of single-family homes. The school was set in a deep expanse of green grass. Getting out of the car, Tia could see the playground was surrounded by tall trees that provided thick shade from the sun. She imagined most of the kids who attended the school walked in from the surrounding neighborhoods.

Just inside the main entrance Tia spotted a directory listing all the teachers and their assigned classrooms—and right beside it, a notice politely asking visitors to check in at the office. Tia knew in today's world that just didn't cut it. The door to the school should have been locked and the list of classrooms was a major security breach. She checked the ceiling and saw no sign of security cameras monitoring the entrance. Chief Sawyer had long since buttoned down the school safety issues in Newberg. For now, Tia thought, she'd take advantage of the school's lapse in security, but at some point she might stop back by and tell them they needed to get their act together.

"Come on," Tia said, lightly tapping Rich's arm to get his attention, having found the number of Gosforth's classroom.

"Aren't we going to check in?" the rookie asked.

"Not yet and hopefully not at all," she replied.

She led the way to the classroom, happy to find that it was near the end of the building, far from the office. Looking through the slender pane of glass, she saw a white man standing in front of a classroom filled with twenty-five white children. Tia thought back on all her years of public school in Newberg, where she was the only brown face in a pale sea. Shaking off the memory, she tapped on the door, then poked her head inside.

"Mr. Gosforth?"

"Yes?" His voice was guarded and he glanced quickly at the push-button phone on his desk. She pulled her badge out just far enough for him to see.

"Could you step out in the hallway for just a moment, sir?"

"What's this about?" he asked, his voice full of doubt. "Does the office know you're here?"

"Please, sir." Tia looked at the twenty-five faces staring back at her. "It will just take a moment."

Gosforth stared back for several seconds before turning to his students. "Class, take out your journals. Practice this week's spelling words."

He joined Tia and Rich in the hall, looking nervous.

"What on earth is this about?" He looked back and forth between Tia and Rich. Tia wasn't surprised when he settled his eyes on Rich. "I asked if you checked in at the office."

Rich seemed ready to respond and Tia stepped in front of him so that Gosforth would redirect his focus.

"Good afternoon, sir," Tia said. "I'm Detective Tia Suarez, Newberg PD. This is Officer Puller." Though Tia kept her voice low, it still seemed to echo down the empty hallway. "I wonder if there might be someplace we could go to talk? Just for a few minutes."

"Ah, Detective Suarez." Gosforth nodded knowingly. "Now it makes sense. I was told I might hear from you. I was also told you could be a bit pushy."

Tia was thrown off, but only for a moment. "How so?"

"I received an email from Reverend Mills." He hesitated. "Well, I'm not sure it was actually from Reverend Mills, but someone at the Church of the Rock."

"Really? I'm curious what it said."

"Just that my name, everyone's name, I suppose, had been released to the Newberg Police Department as part of an investigation of some sort. About that body found in the woods. Turns out he killed himself, isn't that right?"

"Still investigating, but like I said," Tia looked up and down the hallway lined with miniature lockers, "is there someplace we can talk?"

"I don't think that will be necessary, Detective. I'm afraid I can't help you. I was at the campground for less than two days before the retreat was canceled. I certainly don't have any knowledge of that boy."

"He was from Rock County, sir. Lived just about twenty miles from here. Were you aware of that?"

"Well, yes, I did hear that, actually. But I'm afraid I still can't help you."

"You'd be surprised, sir. Sometimes very small pieces of information that don't seem to be related lead to things that are."

"I'm sorry, Detective. But if I do think of anything, perhaps you could leave me with a card?"

"I really think we should talk, sir." Tia didn't want to play her whole card. At least not this early and right here in the middle of the man's workplace. "Is there a better time for you?"

"I'm going back to my students. Have a good day, Detective."

Oh well, Tia thought. I tried.

"Mr. Gosforth, about your arrest in Platteville." He wheeled around like a spinning top, and Tia watched as the blood immediately drained from his face. She couldn't help but feel a tinge of guilt. "I wonder if you could tell me the exact circumstances of the offense. That was, what? Three years ago?"

Gosforth looked up and down the empty hallway before replying, and when he spoke, his voice was low and his mouth barely opened. "How did you know about that?"

"Sir," Tia lowered her voice as well, "we're police officers. It wasn't hard. Now really, can we just find someplace that's private? I'm sure this can all be cleared up."

"There's nothing to clear up." Gosforth looked back at Tia, his chin quivering but his voice steady. "I told you, Detective. I can't help you."

Tia looked at Rich. She didn't like the idea of teaching the trainee how to twist the knife so early in his career but then again, he'd have to learn at some point. "Well, Mr. Gosforth, that's too bad, because I'll bet you have gone through a lot of effort to keep that situation in Platteville quiet. I'm guessing your wife doesn't know anything about it. Probably not those cute little girls of yours either. What are they? Eight? Nine? Twins, right?"

"How did you—"

"By the way, pleading to disorderly? That was smart." Tia nodded, maintaining a cool stare. "Situation like that, you could have ended up a sex offender. There'd be no hiding that, would there? That could have played hell on a teaching career."

Gosforth looked at his wristwatch and Tia saw that his hands were shaking. "I can't leave campus right now. I have to finish the day. I'll meet you at the Cracker Barrel in one hour."

"Is that here in town?"

"God, no." He came off desperate. "This is a small town, Detective. If anyone sees me talking to you . . ." He looked up and down the hallway again. "Take the 14N six miles past the city limits. Like I said, I'll be there in an hour."

"Great, Mr. Gosforth. We'll get this cleared up." Tia offered her hand. "I really appreciate your cooperation."

The teacher looked at her hand as if ready to spit on it. "I'm not cooperating. You're blackmailing me and I don't appreciate it." He drew himself up, turned away, and walked back into his classroom.

Rich hadn't said a word through the entire exchange, just watched, wide-eyed.

"I know that wasn't cool," Tia said. "But sometimes you have to help people along a bit."

"So now what?"

Tia looked at her watch. "We got an hour. Let's do some recon work."

TWENTY-NINE

Making productive use of their downtime, Tia had Rich drive to both addresses that might be listed as target locations for future search warrants.

"I don't get it," Rich said as he followed Tia's directions to Gosforth's house. "Aren't we getting a little ahead of ourselves? I mean, the guy has an interesting prior and seemed a little evasive, but a search warrant? At his house?"

Tia looked back and forth between the street signs and the directions on her phone. She was really starting to warm up to Rich and she liked the fact that he asked good questions. "You're right," she said. "We're a long way from crashing his door or anything like that, but we've got some downtime, so why not use it? And, if things heat up and all of a sudden we're looking to hang paper on him, we've got our description and flicks ready to go. Beats having to do a hasty scout on the fly when the bad guy's already hinked."

Rich looked across the seat. "What the hell did you just say?"

Tia laughed. "Slow down. Here's the house."

Tia had Rich pass by slowly while she used her cell phone to take pictures of the cookie-cutter single-story ranch-style home. She scribbled out notes for the physical description that would be part of the potential warrant. She noted the shingle roof, location, and construction of the front door and the prominent numbers affixed to the house that identified the street address. After that, they swung by the New Hope Church and did the same thing. Tia had trouble imagining circumstances that would lead to the church being listed in a warrant, but it was good to know where it was.

They stopped in at the Evansville PD out of professional courtesy, to let the watch commander know they were in his town on follow-up, but not expecting any problems or a need for assistance. The WC was a thirty-year career cop out of Rockford working on a second pension. As Tia spoke, he barely looked up from his copy of *Maxim,* wise enough not to ask for any more details than the out-of-town cops willingly provided. Tia had always figured that strategies to maintain plausible deniability was a mandatory course of instruction in most police commander training courses.

They pulled into the Cracker Barrel parking lot fifteen minutes early and walked in to find Gosforth already sitting in a booth deep in the back corner of the restaurant.

"What the hell?" Tia stood in the gift shop with the faux–log cabin decor. The restaurant was about half full of mostly senior citizens enjoying an early dinner. "Come on, Rich. Let's go see what this is about."

With his back to the wall, Robert Gosforth stared straight ahead. His hands looked clammy with sweat, knotted together like a nervous ball of energy on the table. Next to him was a second man, who was talking directly into Gosforth's ear. Balding and wearing a rumpled suit, the man was pushing sixty, Tia figured. A leather satchel sagged on the floor at his feet. He stopped talking and sat up straight as the Newberg cops approached.

"Hey, Mr. Gosforth. What gives?" Tia said, playing innocent though she knew exactly what was up.

The lawyer did his best to take charge, pointing to the empty side of the booth. "Have a seat, Detective."

"You got a name, Counselor?"

"Have a seat."

"Funny name." Tia slid into the booth and nodded for Rich to do the same. She looked at Gosforth. "I would've thought you'd want to keep this just between us, Robert."

Gosforth swallowed hard; his gaze darted around the restaurant, but he said nothing.

The older man responded, "Phillip Myers, attorney at law. I represent Mr. Gosforth. What is it you wish to discuss with my client?"

"Well, Mr. Myers," Tia said, remembering the name that Sam had provided. "You get around, don't you? I think you actually represent Church of the Rock, right?"

When Myers didn't bite, she looked across the booth and did her best to sound disappointed. "Really Robert? A lawyer? For what?"

Myers put his hand on his client's arm. "Mr. Gosforth will not be answering any questions. The reason I'm here, Detective, is to inform you that if you capriciously divulge this man's criminal history to anyone I will see to it that you're held to answer for it."

"How's that?" Tia knew exactly what the attorney was talking about, but she was going to make him spell it out. She listened to Myers but stared at Gosforth, who refused to look back.

"If Mr. Gosforth's criminal history becomes public knowledge, he will no doubt suffer significant damages. Not only personal and professional embarrassment, but very real financial damages. If that happens, I will see to it that you're held liable." He paused and Tia saw his mouth turn up in a bit of a smirk. "Well, perhaps not you personally. I don't think you'd be able to afford the amount. But your department has deep pockets."

"Not as deep as you probably think."

"Deep enough, Detective, but trust me when I say you don't want to find out."

Tia pushed back, still staring across the table at Gosforth: "So it's my fault if, say, the school principal decides to do a random criminal history check on all teachers?"

Gosforth let out a small gasp and leaned in as if to speak. Myers squeezed his arm. "Be quiet, Robert."

He stared at Tia. "Yes. That would be your responsibility, because it would not be random. And, based on what Mr. Gosforth has told me about your hallway threats, I'm comfortable that I could prove that in a courtroom."

"Threats?" Tia clicked her tongue and looked across the table. "Robert, did you actually feel threatened?"

Myers leaned in closer, raising his voice. "You talk to me, Detective."

Tia finally looked at him. "I didn't threaten Mr. Gosforth. I'm conducting an investigation into the death of a young man from Rock County. Mr. Gosforth was in the vicinity at the time of death and he's from Rock County. It's not complicated. It's called an investigative lead."

"First off, it's my understanding that case has been ruled a suicide. And secondly, for the record, Mr. Gosforth is under no obligation to answer your questions, nor is he required to explain a long-ago misdemeanor conviction. He has a right to privacy."

"It's public record, sir," Rich said. Tia started to kick him under the table but stopped herself. He'd earned his seat.

"And," Tia said, "it really wasn't that long ago. Three years, right, Robert? How old were your girls then? Seven? Eight, maybe?"

Gosforth seemed close to becoming physically ill. He turned to his attorney. "Oh my God, Phillip, maybe we should—"

"Robert, shut up." He locked his gaze on Tia. "Public record or not, if that information comes into the possession of his employer or any member of Mr. Gosforth's family, I will assume that happened through your actions and that your intent was retribution.

We'll let the court decide the propriety of it. Now, I'm not sure what kind of fishing expedition you're on, but it will not involve my client. Am I making myself clear?"

"Mr. Gosforth," Tia said. "This is unnecessary. I just have a few—"

Myers pulled himself to his feet. "Come with me, Robert."

"Robert," Tia said, freezing the teacher in place halfway out of the booth. He looked at her, his expression fearful and uncertain. "We'll see you again another time."

Myers drove his finger closer to Tia's face than she liked. "This man is represented by counsel, Detective. You'll be wise to remember that."

"Knock it off, Myers," Tia said, still seated and basically trapped in the booth. She knocked his hand away. "Mr. Gosforth is not accused of a crime, so you know as well as I do that right to counsel doesn't attach. And when it does, he's the only one who can invoke. Not you."

Tia looked at Gosforth, who was now standing. "And if you do decide to hide behind a lawyer, Robert? You'll need a better one than this mouthpiece."

Taking Gosforth by the elbow, Myers steered him away. "We're done here."

"You're right," Tia said. "For now."

Attorney and client walked away. Tia sat in silence for a moment. She felt the weight of Rich beside her; they were sitting close enough that she sensed the rise and fall of his breathing.

"Hey, Rich?"

"Yeah?"

"Do you think this is weird?"

Rich laughed, then slid out of the booth and moved to the other bench. Tia smiled. "Much better. Thanks."

"I guess I got us all spun up for nothing," Rich said. "I thought this might pan out."

"Are you kidding? We rattled his cage, big-time. He didn't lawyer up for nothing."

"Okay," Rich said. "So now what?"

Tia pulled out her phone and banged out a quick text to Livy, thinking back on their recent conversation. Livy replied immediately with a thumbs-up emoji.

"We follow the money, Rich," Tia said. "Come on, let's go home."

THIRTY

B ack at Newberg PD, Tia cut Rich loose in the parking lot. Before they parted, she told him not to feel bad about the fact that Gosforth had lawyered up. He'd done some great police work and his background intel on Gosforth was their best lead so far. The guy was hinked up about something. He might just turn out to be the nervous type around cops, but Tia had a good feeling about it.

At her desk, Tia wrote up a report covering the day's activity and emailed it to Travis for approval. She checked her email inbox and saw an incoming message from one of the cell service providers. She opened it hoping it was a quick response to the warrant. It was.

The body of the email was filled with references to privacy issues, non-disclosure warnings and other legal-ese. Tia skimmed the email but knew from prior experience, what she wanted to see would be in the attached document. She clicked on it and opened the one-page excel spreadsheet. As she'd anticipated there had been very limited cell activity at that particular time and location. Since the judge had only authorized a single night of activity, the spreadsheet listed fewer than a dozen calls. She immediately scanned the document for the phone number that had made the 911 call, but it wasn't there. Tia did recognize Jimmy Youngblood's number, which appeared several times. She also saw calls from Livy's phone. There were a few other numbers Tia didn't recognize, which were most likely passing motorists or maybe someone from the campground. Running the calls down would be good training for Rich. She double-checked her email to make sure no other providers had responded. Nothing yet.

It was coming up on five but she figured she could justify an early exit. If she left now, she and Connor could have a couple of hours together before he went to work at the Pig. It had been a long day but she felt energized by what she thought was good progress. Even after the bullshit press conference, she had managed to stay in the good graces of both Carla and Sam Mills. She figured that could prove useful down the road. The hell with the senior Mills and she wasn't the least bit concerned with what the little minion of a mayor might think. Most of all, Tia was confident the Gosforth lead had legs. The case was moving forward and her chief had her back. Yeah, she thought. A good day's work.

Not to mention, she thought, congratulating herself, you turned forty. It was the longest streak of complete sobriety Tia could remember since the shooting that killed one cop and nearly killed her.

Passing the desk Rich had been using, she noticed the list of retreat staff, along with several pages of printouts—the computer background checks that Rich had completed. Tia perched herself on the corner of the desk and flipped through the sheets.

Once again, she found herself impressed with his thorough work. Rich had run every name through the CHRIS database, the Wisconsin DMV, and a few public record sites. He'd turned up plenty of traffic violations and even two DUI's. Several of the retreat staffers had financial troubles, including foreclosures and bankruptcies. Tia laughed out loud when she saw that Eva Davis had a prior arrest for shoplifting at the Walmart in Sheboygan. The pious camp cook had a rap sheet.

Tia had to give Eva credit, though—she'd included her own name on the list. That thought got Tia looking for two other names, but neither appeared. Curious, she returned to her own desk, sat down, and pulled up the criminal history screen.

She typed in the name Sam Mills, and added a few other parameters to try to zero in on what was a pretty common name. Listing his race and estimated age, and giving Milwaukee as his city of residence, still left her with more than fifty possibilities. A few had significant arrests, but their physical descriptions and ages weren't close to the Sam Mills she was interested in.

Tia expected the other name would be a bit easier: Ezekiel Mills. She knew that Mills maintained a home in the most exclusive neighborhood in Newberg, so she entered that as city of residence. She hit "send," expecting to see a return of "no record on file," but up popped a crime report out of Chippewa Falls. The report was over eight years old and was listed as ORO—"officer's report only." That designator indicated a noncriminal report of some kind—someone reporting suspicious activity, lost property, or some other trivial matter. Tia clicked on the case number for details.

Ezekiel Mills was fully identified with his height, weight, date of birth, and home of record, which at the time of the report was in Chippewa Falls. That struck Tia as odd; identifying data for noncriminal reports was typically limited to name, address, and phone number. What really caught Tia's attention was the designation after Mills's name: POI. Why, she wondered, would Mills be listed as a person of interest in a report that wasn't even categorized as criminal?

Tia looked at the name of the reporting officer, a Chippewa Falls PD detective named Andrew Coleman. Pulling up the website for CFPD, Tia easily found the phone directory. She dialed the number for the investigations bureau and a receptionist picked up on the third ring.

"Hello, this is Detective Suarez, Newberg PD, down in Waukesha County. I was calling for Detective Andrew Coleman. I don't know if he—"

"Hold, please."

The phone clicked over to elevator music and Tia wondered if she'd really get that lucky. Her question was answered before the end of the first song.

"Coleman."

Tia couldn't keep the surprise out of her voice. "Andrew Coleman?"

"Andy, actually, but yeah. What can I do for you?"

"I'll be damned," she said with a laugh. "That was a shot in the dark. I just pulled up an eight-year-old case, saw your name on it, and figured why not?"

The Chippewa Falls detective laughed good-naturedly as well. "It happens like that sometimes, huh? Who is this again?"

"Yeah, sorry," Tia said. "Detective Suarez, Newberg PD. Tia Suarez."

"Well, what can I do for you, Tia?"

"I'm working a case down here, doing some background work on persons known to be in the area of a possible homicide."

"Oh yeah? Caught a good one, huh? Beats the car burglary stuff, right?"

"For sure, but this one's kind of odd. Seventeen-year-old kid, found dead in the woods. We're going back and forth with the ME on suicide or homicide."

"Oh, man, that's rough. Sorry if I popped off."

"What do you mean?"

"Just, you know, saying good case. I mean, I got a seventeen-year-old son myself." The phone went quiet for a moment. When Andy spoke again, his voice was serious. "How can I help?"

"Like I said, Andy, I'm looking at an eight-year-old officer's report. No crime indicated, but you've got a man listed as a person of interest."

"Really? On an ORO? Strange." Tia picked up Andy's curiosity and she could hear him begin to tap a keyboard. "Give me the info. Case number, name."

"Sure," Tia said. "You may even have heard of him. Ezekiel Mills?"

The phone went silent and the tapping stopped. Tia waited but there was no response.

"Hello?" Tia said. "Andy?"

"What's this about?" He suddenly sounded like a different person—wary, guarded. Gone was the sense of cooperation.

"Just routine checks." Tia did her best to sound casual. "Like I said, just doing general background work on persons known to be in the area."

"And you're digging into Ezekiel Mills?"

"Well, I wouldn't say digging. But I guess you have heard of him, huh?"

"Yeah, well, I don't really think I can be of much help. Like you said, case was eight years ago. Doesn't really ring any bells."

Bullshit, she thought. "No sweat, Andy. If you could just pull a hard copy of the report and send it over? Fax or PDF, whichever's easiest."

"I don't know if we'll have a copy of something that old. You should probably call somebody in the records division."

"Yeah, okay then. So no memory of it, huh?" Tia went fishing. "I mean, this was before Mills hit the big-time and all, so maybe—"

"Like I said, Detective, it doesn't ring any bells. Now, if that's all you needed, it's getting late."

"Right." Tia was already clicking on the report to pull up whatever else might be available. "Thanks for your help, Andy. Last thing. Could I get the number for your records—"

The line went dead. "What the hell was that about?" Tia said as she hung up the phone.

Tia scrolled through the screen and found there was no narrative or other detail on the report. She did find the name of the reporting party. Owen Allen Vickers had been twenty-two years old at the time and living in Chippewa Falls. She printed the report.

"Why not?" Tia said to herself. "I'm on a roll."

Pulling up the white pages for Chippewa Falls, she punched in Vickers's full name but got nothing. She tried the same thing for Eau Claire, which was twenty miles south of Chippewa Falls; still nothing. Tia was thinking of other communities in the Chippewa Falls vicinity when it dawned on her. She smacked her palm against her forehead and rolled her eyes, realizing she was letting the excitement get to her.

"DMV, dumb ass." Tia punched the full name and date of birth listed in the police report into the Wisconsin DMV computer. The curser blinked for a few seconds then came back with the driver's license information for an Owen Allen Vickers in Rice Lake, Wisconsin. The date of birth was an exact match. She went back to her white pages search and the Rice Lake listing popped up with a phone number.

"Yes!" Tia quickly dialed the number. On the second ring, she hung up.

She needed to slow down. It was pretty obvious to Tia that Detective Coleman had been holding back. There was something about the officer's report that he had decided not to share. As the reporting party, Owen Vickers would know what that was.

What if he clams up like Coleman? If he hangs up on me, I'm done. Tia knew she needed to talk to Vickers face-to-face. She needed to go to Rice Lake.

Tia punched the locations into MapQuest. Two hundred-seventy miles northwest. The route would take her right through Chippewa Falls, so she could stop at the PD and get a copy of the old police report. From there it was another fifty miles up the 53 to Rice Lake. If she took the Goat, she could make the whole circuit in less than seven or eight hours. She picked up the phone—not to call Vickers.

"Hey, Rich. It's Tia. We got another road trip tomorrow. I'll pick you up at the PD at zero-five."

Tia heard the confusion in his response. "No. It's got nothing to do with Gosforth. At least, not that I know of. But don't worry about it. Be here at zero-five."

She listened then laughed. "Yeah, Rich. That means five A.M. We're going to Chippewa Falls, then on to Rice Lake. I'll explain everything on the way."

She emailed Travis to let him know she and her trainee were hitting the road early to run down a lead. She didn't go into detail other than to say she'd be taking her own car and submitting a voucher for gas money. The way she planned on driving, the Goat would be sucking it down.

This could just be a rabbit hole, she thought. It was definitely a departure from the Gosforth lead that in her gut felt really promising. But Tia knew the worst mistake a detective can make is to have tunnel vision. She needed to see the whole playing field.

When she finally left she saw it was almost six. Connor was leaving for work in less than two hours. She turned out the lights and headed for the door.

THIRTY-ONE

Tia turned off the interstate and drove through the still-quiet downtown streets of Chippewa Falls. They pulled up to the police department at twenty minutes before eight o'clock and parked the GTO in the public lot. They'd made great time, so much so that at one point Rich had asked why he only got to drive the Crown Vic.

Her answer was simple: "Because no one drives the Goat but me."

During the drive to Chippewa Falls, Tia filled Rich in on how she'd found the eight-year-old CHRIS entry and on her odd conversation with Detective Coleman.

"So," Rich said, "maybe he really just didn't remember?"

"Could be," Tia said, thinking back on the detective's personality flip over the phone. "But I want to see the report for myself. The RP is an Owen Vickers. He's another hour north in Rice Lake. We'll take a look at the report narrative. See if it's worth reaching out to him."

A woman in civilian attire and carrying an American flag stepped out from the lobby of the two-story redbrick building. Going to the nearby pole, she clipped the flag onto the halyard and raised it to the top. She bowed her head and stood for a few moments before disappearing back into the building.

Tia looked at her phone and saw the time was 8:01. "Right on time. Let's go."

The same woman who had raised the flag was seated at the glassed-in front counter. She smiled pleasantly. "First customer of the day. How can I help you?"

Tia pulled out her badge. Caught unprepared, Rich fumbled around but eventually produced his patrol badge.

"Good morning, ma'am. I'm Detective Suarez with Newberg PD in Waukesha County. This is my partner, Ri . . ." Tia stopped herself. "Officer Puller. We need to pick up a copy of a police report."

The woman reached under her desk and came up with a pre-printed form that she slipped through an opening in the glass. "No problem, Detective. Just fill this out for me."

"The case is eight years old," Tia said, filling in the form. "Will that be a problem?"

"Shouldn't be. Nothing gets purged before ten years."

Nodding, Tia returned the form, and the receptionist took it and said she'd be right back.

"Partner, huh?" Rich said.

"Relax." Tia knew he was happy with his elevated status. "Doesn't mean you drive the Goat."

A moment later the woman returned empty-handed. "Sorry. I spoke too soon."

"How's that?"

"Well, I'm not sure." The receptionist seemed genuinely confused. "Everything else from that time period is on the shelf—just that one report is missing. What was it?"

"Just an officer's report. No crime listed."

She shrugged. "Well then, maybe it got purged early. Sorry."

"Does that ever happen?" Tia asked. "A single report gets purged?"

"No," the woman said. "Not really."

Tia wasn't happy, but that wasn't this woman's fault. She had a feeling she knew who might be responsible. "Can you tell me, is Detective Coleman in?"

She laughed. "I doubt it. Detectives don't start wandering in until after nine o'clock. They're not like civilian staff."

"All right, then. Can you do me a favor? Let him know that Detective Suarez came by. Tell him I said thanks for the help. I definitely owe him one."

"Sure will." She smiled. "And I'm sorry I couldn't be of more help."

Once they were outside, Rich said, " 'Thanks for the help'?"

"Yeah," Tia said, seething, pulling hard on the car door. "Big help. He pulled that report—I'd bet money on it."

"Now what?"

"What the hell," she said, starting the engine. "We'll spitball it. Let's go to Rice Lake."

THIRTY-TWO

R ich used the driving time to try to find a work address or employer information for Owen Vickers of Rice Lake, with no luck. Tia had the home address from the DMV, so that was where they headed. It was after nine when they pulled up to a neat, single-story home on a typical, tree-lined Wisconsin street.

"We'll cold-knock it," Tia said. "Hopefully he's home."

As they walked up to the door, Tia saw an envelope attached by a clothespin to the outside of the mailbox. The cursive writing on the envelope looked feminine. Tia knocked on the door and waited. A moment later, the door was opened by a blond woman; Tia figured she was in her late twenties.

"Mrs. Vickers?"

The woman, guarded but pleasant, dried her hands on a dish towel. "Yes?"

It had been a guess, but a good one. The more this woman thought Tia knew, the more likely she was to feel compelled to cooperate.

"Ma'am, we're police officers from Newberg PD down in

Waukesha County. We were hoping to have a chat with your husband, Owen."

Looking back over her shoulder at the stairway, the woman replied, "He's still in bed. He worked a late shift. Can I ask what this is about?"

"It would probably be better if we talked to your husband."

The woman pulled her shoulders back and Tia felt a wall go up between them. She'd miscalculated.

"Well, like I said, he's sleeping. I'm not waking him unless you tell me what it is you want."

"You're right." Tia did her best to sound conciliatory. "I apologize. I just didn't want to bother you with it. There's a police report out of Chippewa Falls from eight years ago. Your husband—"

"How do you know about that?" There was alarm in her voice now, maybe even a trace of something else. Was it fear? Anger? Tia scrambled for a new tactic.

"It came up during a records check in an investigation we're working in Newberg—a rather serious case. So, it's important we speak with Mr. Vickers."

Mrs. Vickers stepped outside and pulled the door behind her, leaving it open just a crack. On her face was a look of desperation that Tia had seen before when a person was suddenly confronted with the resurfacing of an ugly past.

"My husband is not going to talk to you about that. He can't. And even if he could, I wouldn't let him. We—" Her voice began to rise in anger and Tia watched as the woman tamped it down. "He's put that behind him. For good. Now please. I want you to leave."

"Mrs. Vickers, I know you're trying to protect your husband. But I should tell you, we're working on a murder investigation."

Startled, the woman fumbled. "Murder? Who? What do you think my husband has to do with it?"

"Nothing at all, ma'am. I don't want you to think that." As much as Tia wanted to talk to Owen Vickers, she didn't want to unnecessarily scare his wife. "But he might be able to help us in our investigation."

Tia watched the woman think. "If you don't want us to speak with him now, that's fine. We can come back another time."

"No, you won't." The firmness in her voice told Tia that Mrs. Vickers had made up her mind. "If there's one thing we learned through that whole mess, it's how not to be pushed around by the police. Now leave. And if you come back, I'll file a complaint for harassment."

With that, she went back inside. The door clicked shut, then Tia heard the deadbolt turn. Shaking her head, Tia turned to leave, Rich beside her. When he spoke, it was as though he'd read her mind.

"This is getting interesting."

THIRTY-THREE

After striking out in Chippewa Falls and Rice Lake, Tia was frustrated, staring down the barrel of a fruitless six-hundred-mile road trip. Oh for two, she thought. Not wanting to feel like the day was a complete bust, she decided on one more stop. They headed east on the 29, hitting a diner in Wausau for lunch. From there, they drove north to the town of Irma and pulled up to the locked chain-link fence, topped with looping razor wire that surrounded the Lincoln Hills School for Boys. After signing in and locking up their guns at the guard shack, they waited for an escort to take them to the main administration building.

According to Carla, Lincoln Hills was where Henry had met Kimo. She'd laid out her thoughts to Rich during the drive. "We should be able to get full ID on this Kimo kid, plus some background on both him and Henry. Maybe figure out how they would've hooked up on the outside."

Ten minutes of standing at the guard shack went by before a gray-haired man that looked more grandfather than jail guard sauntered across a large open field. Dressed in a rumpled dark green uniform he identified himself only as Jake and apologized for the long wait. "Staffing sucks" was the limit of his explanation. Tia noticed, typical of custodial guards, Jake's black belt was equipped only with Mace, handcuffs, and a baton. No guns were ever allowed in lockup facilities, including a juvenile facility like Lincoln Hills.

Seeing Tia's questioning look as they headed across the empty, eerily quiet yard, Jake explained that all the juvenile inmates were currently completing their compulsory education requirements. Tia had visited most of the adult prisons in the state, and this facility felt no different. Lincoln Hills School housed juvenile male offenders from throughout Wisconsin. At any given time, about two hundred teenage boys called the facility home. Some stayed months, some were there for years. The most serious offenders would leave the facility at eighteen—only to be transferred to an adult prison, where they'd finish their sentences.

Previous dealings with the staff of Lincoln Hills School had taught Tia that the only way to get good information was to visit the facility in person. Recent state and federal investigations had uncovered acts of misconduct ranging from inmate abuse to unauthorized release of information. There had been a round of firings at all levels of the organization and procedures had been tightened. Now, trying to get even the most basic information long distance involved formal letters of request on department letterhead and other such nonsense. Showing up with a badge still worked, and was how Tia preferred to do business anyway.

Tia and Rich were escorted to the counseling offices, where they sat for another twenty minutes in the reception area watching shackled teens being escorted in and out of the various cubicles. Eventually a tall, slender black woman emerged from behind the counter, dressed in khaki pants and a dark green polo shirt with a Wisconsin Department of Corrections embroidered logo. A star-shaped badge was clipped to a black basket-weave belt.

"I'm Trisha Washington. You the ones here about Henry?"

"Yes, that's us. Newberg PD." Tia stood and presented her badge. "Someplace we can talk?"

Trisha gave Tia's badge a close examination, then walked away, signaling them to follow. She led them down a hallway bordered by cubicle spaces on both sides and walled off by six-foot partitions. Several were occupied by counselors engaged one-on-one with juvenile inmates.

"Sorry, it's going to be a little crowded," Trisha said, ushering them into a cubicle barely big enough for a desk, a short file cabinet, and one extra chair. "We'll have to make do. But hey, I'm lucky. Most of the cubicles are doubled up."

With Trisha seated at her desk and Rich perching on top of the file cabinet, Tia took the second chair. Quarters were so tight that her knees rubbed against Trisha's pants leg. Tia got the sense that the counselor was an overworked but conscientious professional who happened to have picked a line of work that tends to wear down the soul.

Omitting pleasantries or small talk, Trisha picked up the file sitting in the center of her desk and began. "Henry Tyler Hayes. He spent ninety-seven days here and was released this spring. His sentencing offense was auto theft and assault. If it'd just been the auto theft, he probably wouldn't have been here more than a couple of weeks, but the assault was against a cop. That'll always buy you some time. He'd been scheduled for a hundred eighty, so he did pretty well, stayed out of trouble, for the most part. Few demerits for shenanigans in class. He had some hygiene issues, didn't like showering much. Probably because most of the other inmates figured he was an easy mark for taking out . . . well, frustrations and such."

"'And such'?" Tia heard the implication.

"Some of that goes on. We do our best but, you know, staffing being what it is . . . Anyway, Henry was small and he had that long hair. I imagine he got cornered more than a time or two."

"So did you know about Henry?"

"Yep." Trisha handed the file to Tia. "Suicide, right? Sorry to hear it. Bit of a knucklehead for sure, but I had hopes for him."

Tia didn't correct Trisha's assessment, just opened the file and looked at Henry's intake photo. Unsmiling and sullen, with apathy in his eyes. The date on the photograph made the picture less than six months old, the most up-to-date photo she'd seen. She couldn't help but think Henry was a pretty cute kid. A vision of his remains in the woods came to mind and she did her best to block it out. "Any suicide attempts while in custody?"

Trisha answered quickly. "No, never. Didn't see anything like that. In fact, for all the shit he had to put up with, he struck me as a tough kid. I wouldn't have thought he'd do something that desperate."

"How about cliques. Who did he hang with?"

"We've got a few Native American boys here, but Henry pretty much stayed by himself."

"What about Kimo?"

Sheila nodded. "Oh, yeah. Kevin. I forgot about him. They did end up being pretty tight."

"Kevin?" Tia asked.

Trisha reached for the file cabinet; Rich stood and stepped out of her way. She thumbed through the files until she found the one she was looking for. "Kevin Demetri Moore. He liked everybody calling him Kimo."

Rich was making notes, so Tia kept asking questions. "How do you mean that? He liked everybody calling him Kimo?"

"Well, you know how it is," Trisha said, handing over the file. "Some kids earn a nickname for something. Athletics, brains, whatever. Kevin? He's the kind of kid who comes up with his own nickname. One that sounds cool. Then he makes sure everyone uses it. Kid was always trying to come off as a player. Thought he knew all the angles."

Tia looked at the photo of Kimo, taken against the same wall as the one of Henry, with his date of birth at the bottom. "Looks like he turned eighteen a few weeks back."

"Yeah," Trisha said, sounding thankful. "Won't be seeing him again. His next screw-up will land him in the big leagues."

"Think that'll happen?"

"With that kid? Absolutely. He'll go pro for sure."

Tia looked at the file. "Grand theft? Doesn't seem that hard-core."

"No, but damn sophisticated for his age. His scam was daytime car burgs of high-end vehicles parked in front of strip joints. He'd watch for the right victim profile, hit ones he figured would never make a report. The only reason he got caught was he broke into the car of a couple of undercover vice cops working a detail. Apparently they were working out of a court-seized Corvette that caught Kimo's eye. They served paper on his house, found stolen property from a dozen unreported cases."

Tia looked at the smiling face of Kevin Moore, a good-looking redhead with broad shoulders and bright hazel eyes. Sure enough, he had the vibe of a kid who was always planning his next scam.

"So he spent a lot of time with Henry?"

"Kimo had been here a few months when Henry showed up. It was Henry's first time in real custody, and like I said, it was rough for him. His size didn't help him any. Not right off, but after a while, he and Kimo seemed to warm up to each other and the older boy started looking out for Henry."

Shaking her head, Trisha added, "Seems odd, though. Strange pair."

"How so?" Tia asked.

"Kimo was a player. One of the older boys. City kid—on the out-side and definitely in here. Pretty much a shot caller. Not sure why he bothered with Henry."

"Who got out first?"

Trisha closed her eyes and leaned her head back as if trying to recall the order of events. "Seems like Kimo got out and Henry followed after just a couple of weeks. Sorry, I can't keep them all straight. It's pretty much like an assembly line. You can check with the discharge desk to get the exact dates."

Tia made a few notes. "Would it surprise you to know they hooked up. Apparently they were hanging around quite a bit the last couple of months."

"Wouldn't surprise me at all," Trisha said. "It's a pretty regular pattern—boys leave, get together on the outside, then end up coming back together. Birds of a feather kind of thing."

Rich piped up. "What about drugs? Either of them involved in that sort of thing?"

Tia gave Rich a nod of approval. Good question.

"No shortage of dope comes through," Trisha answered. "But I don't think either of them was slinging any of it. Didn't strike me as users either." She looked closely at the two cops. "This doesn't sound like follow-up to a suicide."

"No, I don't imagine it does," Tia said. "Let's just say the jury is still out."

When Tia didn't offer anything more, the other woman nodded as if more than satisfied not to get overly involved in a couple of kids who were no longer her concern.

Trisha reached into another file in the cabinet and pulled out a single sheet of paper. "If you want to take hard copies of personnel files out of the facility, you'll have to fill out the release form. Then, I need to get it approved at a command level."

Tia took the form, looking back at Trisha. "Seriously?"

Trisha rolled her eyes. "Yep. Sorry. New rules."

Tia completed and signed the one-page form and handed it back.

"I'll push it through. Should be able to get it approved in a few days."

Trisha put the completed form in a wire basket. "If that's all you need, I got a couple of fellas locked up in solitary I should have a talk with. I swear it's like herding cats, but some of the cats are damn tigers."

"Thanks for your time, Trisha. You were a big help."

"Not a problem. Hope you clear it all up."

All three stood at once and laughed when they practically knocked each other down.

"All the money they spent investigating everybody," Trisha said, "I just wish one of them eggheads had figured out we just need some damn space." She volunteered to walk them to the discharge desk, where Tia could get information on departure dates.

Heading down the hallway, Trisha told the cops more about the housecleaning that had occurred the year before, after a sixteen-year-old inmate had tried to hang himself in his room. Several officers had lost their jobs and others were demoted.

"The whole problem is staffing. I feel bad for the new officers working night shift. Four guards for two hundred boys? And believe me, half these little shits? They *ain't* boys. Assaults on staff have gone up every year. I can tell you right now, nobody's investigating that."

At the outtake desk, they were given the exact entry and exit dates for Henry and Kimo. Tia did the math and realized that the two teenagers had spent a little over two months in custody together before Kimo was discharged. Henry followed him out twenty-six days later. Tia wrote down the last known address for Kimo and the name of his probation officer.

Twenty minutes later they were headed south, discussing the day's efforts.

"So what do you think, rook?" Tia asked. "Was the trip worth it?"

"Beats graveyard patrol, but I don't know. I guess we have to wait and see, right?"

Tia looked at the clock on the dash. She appreciated his positive attitude, but she wasn't so sure. It had been a long day and Tia couldn't help but be frustrated by the lack of progress. She did her best to put a positive spin on it. "That's all you can do sometimes, Rich. Just go out and beat the bush and wait for someone to poke their head up."

THIRTY-FOUR

By the time they reached the Newberg city limit sign it was pushing five o'clock. While an interview of Kimo was vital, it wasn't something they needed to do that day.

On the other issue, Tia was stumped by the standoff with the CFPD detective and, for that matter, Mrs. Vickers. A noncriminal police report from eight years ago? How bad could it be? She knew they'd be taking another run at Vickers or maybe she'd even have Travis shoot a call to Chippewa Falls PD. Go over the detective's head. But no doubt, the interview of Kimo was more pressing. He had a known relationship with the victim. That put him at the top of the list.

Tia talked as they drove the last mile to the station. "Might even be good if we watch him for a few hours—Kimo, that is. See what he's up to."

"What are you thinking?" Rich asked.

"Nothing specifically, just a few hours' surveillance," Tia said. "Maybe we can get a twist on him. Sometimes that . . ." Her voice trailed off. A hundred yards up the road she saw four media trucks in the Newberg PD parking lot. Several cars with media door magnets were also parked nearby.

Tia drove past the gauntlet of vehicles. Several reporters were lined up, using the station as a backdrop. Each one stood in front of a camera holding a microphone pointed in the face of Ben Sawyer.

Parking at the far end of the lot, Tia and Rich entered the building through the back door. As they passed the report writing room, they saw several uniformed officers watching the television set mounted on the wall. Tia stopped and tapped Rich on the arm to draw his attention. The reporter on the screen was none other than Lucy Lee-Jones.

". . . a conclusion of a self-inflicted gunshot wound. But apparently, despite these findings of the medical examiner's office, detectives of the Newberg Police Department have gone forward with what amounts to a covert criminal investigation that is now focused on the volunteer staff members of the Church of the Rock annual retreat. Sources with knowledge of the investigation reveal an alarming pattern of intrusive interviews and aggressive attempts to leverage information from retreat participants. It has also been reported that at least one officer has been suspended for misconduct related to this incident."

A collective groan and a few choice words went up from the officers gathered around the set. The reporter went on, "Earlier today I spoke with Phillip Myers, an attorney representing the Church of the Rock as well as individuals who attended the retreat, and he had this to say."

The picture cut to a different location and Tia recognized the man's mop of hair and rumpled suit and resisted the temptation to curse.

"It is my intent to file a formal complaint of harassment against the Newberg Police Department, specifically Detective Tia Suarez. This tragic case is being used to grandstand and harass innocent bystanders who had no involvement whatsoever in the suicide of young Henry Hayes. It is nothing more than showboating and an abuse of power."

She'd heard enough. "Let's go," she told Rich. "We need to check in with Sergeant Jackson."

At the sound of her voice, one of the uniformed officers turned and Tia saw that it was Stan Hansen, beat partner and friend of Jimmy Youngblood.

"Well, no shit," Stan said, sounding angry. Tia kept walking, then stopped when she heard Rich's voice behind her.

"Hey, Stan," the trainee said.

"'Hey, Stan?'" the officer mimicked Rich, then his voice turned disdainful. "The fuck you say, boot. Youngblood gets suspended and you go off to play detective? All because of some bullshit suicide?"

"It wasn't like that." Tia heard desperation in the young officer's voice. "I just told the Chief—"

Hansen, who was about the same height as Rich but a good forty pounds of muscle heavier, moved in closer. "Save it, Puller. You'll be back in a beat car soon enough. We'll talk about it then."

Tia stepped between them. "Go upstairs, Rich."

Rich couldn't let it go. "Stan, really. I didn't mean—"

"Upstairs, Puller." Tia pointed down the hall. "Now."

Visibly reluctant, Rich walked away, leaving Tia facing off with Hansen, who was flanked by several other patrol officers. "Knock it off, Hansen. You don't even know what you're talking about."

"I don't, huh?" Stan didn't back down. "Because we've never been here before with you, have we, Suarez? Going off half-cocked. Making the department look like shit. Do you just get off on the attention? Is that it? And now because of all your bullshit, Young-blood is—"

"Oh, lighten up, Stanley." Tia knew he hated the use of his full name and she enjoyed using it. "Youngblood made his own bed.

If he can't keep it in his pants for a whole shift that's his damn problem."

Tia stepped in on the other cop, not the least bit intimidated by his size. "Now, stay away from my trainee."

"*Your* trainee? Jesus, this place . . ."

The cop walked away shaking his head and Tia let it go. With a last glance at the television screen she saw a live shot of Ben Sawyer on the screen answering questions that came rapid-fire from a half-dozen reporters. Tia knew he was just outside the main entrance to the building and she fought the temptation to join him. Instead she headed upstairs to find out just what the hell was going on.

THIRTY-FIVE

An hour later, after giving a full briefing of the day's activity to Travis, Tia took the time to talk to Rich about what had happened with Stan Hansen. The confrontation had left the young officer shaken, but he didn't want Tia to formally report the incident. Tia agreed that was probably the best course, then made sure he got back to his car without any further harassment or run-ins with Patrol.

Back in the building she walked past the admin offices. Carrie had gone home for the day but the light was still on in the Chief's office. Tia stuck her head around the partially opened door and saw Ben behind his desk, still in uniform, watching himself on the computer. She'd caught most of the news broadcasts on the TV in Travis's office. They'd flipped from channel to channel and both agreed the Chief held up well under the grilling. Three stations out of Madison and a half-dozen out of Milwaukee had carried the story, and all from the same angle: the Newberg Police Department was engaged in some sort of wildcat investigation.

Tia walked into the office and collapsed on the couch. "How you holding up, boss?"

"It's like a walk down memory lane." He smiled and Tia had to laugh.

"Yours or mine?"

Turning serious, he said, "What's this I hear about a dust-up in the hallway? You and Puller going at it with Hansen?"

Tia smiled. "Very impressive, Chief."

"I still have my sources," Ben said. "You need anything from me?"

"Nah," Tia said. "I got it. Rich handled himself well."

"I don't want this shit spilling into the hallway." Ben pointed to his computer. "But who's talking to the media? They seem to know a lot about our business."

She blew out a long breath. "Could be just about anybody. Rich and I have rattled some cages. Then of course there's Youngblood. You gotta know he's pissed."

Tia changed the subject. "What about city hall? Now they must really be breathing down your neck."

"Strangely quiet," Ben said. "I don't know if that's good or bad. I'm guessing the mayor is waiting to see which way the wind blows with public opinion."

Tia knew even though Ben was playing it off, he had to be worried. This could be just the excuse the mayor was looking for. When this sort of public spectacle arose, the police chief was usually the first to go. She tried to reassure him.

"Hang in there, Ben. Rich and I are running down some good leads. Eventually a couple will intersect, then we'll know if we're onto something."

Ben nodded. "Couple of wires touch, you get a spark, right?"

"That's what I'm hoping for."

"Okay," Ben said and Tia knew he was probably pushing

back pangs of jealousy. The man was not one to sit behind a desk. "You're still sure this boy didn't somehow manage to shoot himself?"

Tia couldn't blame him for asking. He wanted an easier solution, with no headlines and no internal bickering. Without the political infighting that could cost him his job. Tia knew all he had to do was side with Kowalski, give in to the mayor, just write the kid off as a suicide, and his life would get a whole lot easier. But Tia knew the man better than that.

"I'm sure, Ben. Just run blocker for me for a couple more days. I'll come up with something."

"All right. Let's see how things go tomorrow," the Chief said. "Go home. Sounds like you've had a long day. Tell Connor I said hey."

"He's probably gone to work already, but I'll let him know when I see him."

"You two doing okay?" Ben asked.

"Never better," she said. "But you know how he is. Proud guy. I just wish he could do better than stock boy."

Ben nodded. "Get outta here, Suarez. You've done enough damage for one day."

Tia paused at the door. "You're right. I do seem to wield a hammer at times."

"I was kidding."

Tia took one step back into the office. "I raise a lot of hell for you, Ben, and you've always got my back. I appreciate that."

Ben waved off the compliment. "I said get out of here. But not for too long. You need to get this thing figured out for me or I might be joining Connor at the Pig."

Before heading out the door, Tia stopped by her desk to see if Livy had called or emailed. She didn't want to push it. Livy had enough going on without Tia breathing down her neck. When she saw that her desk phone was blinking with a missed call, she was hopeful until she checked the number and recognized it. Detective Coleman. She picked up the phone and dialed the number. He picked up on the third ring.

"Hey, Detective Coleman. You called?"

"Yeah, Tia. I just wanted to apologize for the way things went down."

Wondering if he was referring to their initial conversation or to pulling the report, she asked, "What are you talking about?"

"Well, I just didn't figure on Reverend Mills reacting like that. I mean, I thought he deserved a heads-up, but I never expected he'd throw you guys under the bus and go to the media like that."

"Oh, that." Tia played it off, realizing she'd found the leak: Ezekiel Mills. No surprise. "You know, civilians can be touchy."

"Well, I'd appreciate it if you'd tell your Chief I apologize."

"I'll do that." The man sounded sincere, so Tia figured she'd try one last time. "A copy of that report would go a long way in convincing him you mean it."

"I can't do it, Tia." She heard real regret in Coleman's voice. "I had to sign a nondisclosure agreement. You ever seen one of those?"

"Nah. Can't say as I've been through that."

"I mean, if I disclose anything, they can sue me, fire me. Hell, I think it even said something about cutting my prick off."

Tia heard the detective take a deep breath. "'Course, the one thing that trumps a nondisclosure agreement is a court subpoena. I mean, so I've been told."

The phone went silent as if Andy wanted his last comment to sink in.

"Anyway," he said, "I'm sorry. About all of it. I hate the fucking media and if I had anything to do with giving them a chance to screw with cops, then I take the hit."

Tia let him off the hook. "Don't sweat it."

"All right. By the way, got your message from the front desk. I take it you were being a wiseass?"

"Oh, absolutely I was, but now I'm dead serious," Tia said. "I appreciate the call and thanks for the heads-up."

Tia hung up. *A nondisclosure agreement? What the hell for?* Tia knew she needed to get a copy of that report one way or another.

Tia went by the Chief's office but Ben had left. She'd fill him in later.

THIRTY-SIX

A phone call to Adult Probation got them a work address for Kevin "Kimo" Moore. A few weeks after his discharge from Lincoln Hills, Kimo had turned eighteen and his file was transferred to Adult Services. He still owed the state twelve months of formal probation and now that he was an adult, if he wanted to stay out of custody, he had to find a job. Thanks to a state program that paid a big chunk of his hourly minimum wage, he was working at a high-end auto dealership in Sun Prairie. Tia and Rich showed up first thing Friday morning and checked in with the manager inside a glass cubicle that gave him a view over the sales floor.

"Hell, he's only worked here a month and he's already in trouble?"

"Nothing like that," Tia said. "Just need to talk to him about some of his former associates."

"Damn well better be former." The manager leaned his three-hundred-pound frame against his office chair that let out a long whine of protest. "Can you believe the owner hired this guy? The kid's got a history of boostin' cars and we got a million dollars' worth of inventory on the lot. What sense does that make?"

"Like I said, sir. Just routine. Nothing to worry about."

"He's around back." The manager went back to punching numbers into his desktop calculator. "The redhead with the mop and bucket. And while you're back there, tell him to stop standing around with his thumb up his ass and get to work."

"How do you know he's doing that?"

The man let out a loud short laugh. "Like I said, just tell him."

Tia and Rich walked through the work bays and sure enough found a tall redheaded kid with a wiry frame, squirreled away in a back corner of the garage. He stood in a lean-and-rest stance, staring out an open roll-up metal bay door. His hands were stacked at the top of his mop handle, forming a chin rest. A cigarette smoldered between two fingers and the early morning sunlight had turned his eyes as green as the distant hills.

Tia waited to address Kimo in case he decided to do what came naturally. When she got within twenty yards, she called out, "Kevin Moore?"

The cigarette stopped halfway to his mouth. The young man looked at Tia and the badge hanging from around her neck. He stood up straight and slid his hands down the mop handle, like he was ready to push it to the floor and bolt. His gaze darted to the open garage door and the street beyond.

"Don't even think about it," Tia said, ready to run herself but hoping she didn't have to. "Be cool. We just want to ask you a few questions."

"Fuuuuck." Tia could see the tension in his limbs. "That's all you guys ever want and I keep ending up in a holding cell."

"We can do it that way if you want," Tia said. "Or you can just chill. You decide, Kimo."

A sudden work ethic seemed to overtake the young man, who

began to push the mop across the oil-stained cement floor. "Can't you see I'm busy? Who are you, anyway?"

"I'm Suarez. This is Puller. Newberg PD. Need to talk to you about Henry Hayes." Tia watched for a reaction. Kimo didn't look up but seemed to push the mop a little slower.

"Heard he kilt hisself." His sheet said Kimo was born and raised in Milwaukee's Merrill Park, the historically Irish neighborhood that was slowly transitioning into an African-American community. Tia wasn't surprised to hear him use the language and speech of the inner city, but it seemed odd coming from a kid with a ruddy complexion who looked as though he'd be right at home on the streets of Belfast.

"Well, you heard wrong," Tia said. "Somebody did it for him."

Kimo stopped, looking up at the two cops. "The fuck you say?"

"You heard me." Tia studied his reaction, trying to detect genuine emotion beneath the boy's natural bluster. She saw either shock or fear, but wasn't certain which. "Henry went and got himself murdered."

Kimo recovered and threw out a dismissive hand, turning away. "Then I don't even need to be talking to you. I ain't got nothing to say about no killin'. You all just leave me the fuck outta that."

Tia took a deep breath and shook her head. "Then here's what we'll do. We'll cuff your ass up, parade you across the sales floor, throw you in the back of our squad car, and go with that holding cell idea of yours. We'll let your boss know he's going to need a new man to handle all his shit details. Your probation officer will be pleased."

While Kimo cursed her, Tia went on, "Or I can tell the boss man out there that you agreed to help us out on some bullshit, nothing case. That you're obviously a man ready to return to his civic duties. We'll get you out of here for an hour and I'll be sure he doesn't dock your pay. Hell, on top of all that, I'll buy you breakfast."

"Fuck breakfast. If I'm gonna talk to you, I want a burger."

"Fine," Tia said. "I'll buy you a breakfast burger and you'll tell us what you can about Henry."

"I told you. I don't know nothing about Henry gettin' his ass kilt, but if he did? Be just like him. Always talking all that Indian bullshit, pissing people off."

"See?" Tia smiled. "You do know Henry. Put your mop away. Let's go."

Twenty minutes later Tia and Rich sat in a corner booth across from Kimo in the Culver's on Main Street in downtown Sun Prairie. Tia let Kimo get halfway through his double butter burger with cheese before she started in. She stole a fried cheese curd off his tray and took a bite, then did her best to start the conversation off nice and casual.

"When did you first meet Henry?"

Kimo answered with his mouth full of bread and meat. "Lincoln Hills. He came in after I'd been there a month or so."

"Yeah?" Tia said. "Talk about that. How you guys hooked up and all?"

Kimo stopped. "Hooked up? What the fuck you saying? You think I'm into that gay shit? Hell, no. Not even at Lincoln. Shit, I had female staff wanting to get with me. Why would I hook up with Henry?"

"Damn, Kimo. Relax. I'm not saying that. I mean you hung out, right?"

"Yeah." Kimo nodded. "We hung out, that's all. He'd never been locked up before."

"I hear you kind of looked out for him. He was having a pretty rough time of it."

Kimo took his last bite. "I want another one."

"Not now. I said, word is you looked out for him. Is that right?"

Kimo shrugged. "Some guys was getting to him. Hard mother-fuckers just killin' time, waiting to get kicked over to Waupun. Some of 'em, they be trying to bitch Henry out. So, yeah, I looked out for him a bit."

Tia knew she'd made a mistake with the inadvertent sex talk. Apparently some of the inmates did go after Henry sexually, but Kimo wanted it to be clear, he wasn't one of them. She went at it from a different angle. "So what then? He made some enemies?"

"Nah. Nothing like that." Kimo jammed the last three curds in his mouth and slurped his Coke, looking at the menu board. "Why you thinking he was murdered?"

"Don't worry about it." Tia could feel the beginning of the rhythm. They were close to exchanging real information. "How did you hear about it, anyway?"

"Damn girl," Kimo said, sounding relaxed, "that shit all up on the news. Still is. I seen you giving that preacher all kinds of shit. That was tight."

"You watch the news?" Rich butted in, sounding surprised. His precise diction along with his youthful appearance earned a reaction.

"Fuck you mean, white boy?" Kimo leaned across the table and cocked his head. "I can't watch the news? You calling me stupid, motherfucker?"

Rich tried to fluster out a response and Tia saw Kimo's eyes light up at having found a weakling. She grabbed the half-full cup of soda off his tray and flung it back at his chest. Kimo caught it with both hands but not without a good bit splashing up onto his work shirt.

"Knock that shit off, Kimo. You keep talking to a cop like that, you're gonna get your ass tuned up."

Kimo's eyes blazed when he sat back in the booth. "So am I getting another burger? Cuz if I ain't, we done."

Burger or not, Tia knew they were done. There was no way she could let Kimo get away with disrespecting a police officer to the degree he had, but now Kimo had shut down and she hadn't gotten a damn thing out of him. She could feel Rich squirm next to her and she figured he knew he'd screwed up. She gave it another go anyway.

"Henry's mom says you've been coming around. You didn't happen to go by last Sunday? Maybe give him a lift to Newberg?"

"His ma be crazy." He shook his head. "Bitch stays high all the time."

Staying calm, Tia said, "Did you check in with Henry last Sunday?"

Kimo turned back to the weak link. "Yo, homes, what do you think? I look like I keep a fucking calendar?"

Rich knew enough not to answer.

"When did you see Henry last?" Tia asked.

"Few days ago at his trailer. That's all. I didn't give him a ride anywhere." Kimo looked hard at Tia. "I gotta get back to my job."

The noncommittal answer was close. She needed a few more minutes. "I thought you wanted another burger."

"Nah, fuck that." He stood and looked down at his wet work shirt, his pride kicking in. "I answered you-all's questions. I'll walk back."

"That's fine, Kimo," Tia said. "If we need to talk to you again, we'll have a couple of uniforms swing by. Give you a ride down to the station." Without another word, the boy stalked off.

Rich waited until Kimo was through the door. "Sorry about that."

"You sure as hell should be." She was frustrated enough not to worry about how the young cop took the criticism. "You know why he turned down a second burger? Because he had your ass for lunch." Rich stared at the tabletop and Tia went on, "Don't be popping off when I'm working somebody like that."

"You're right," Rich said. "It won't happen again."

Tia watched as Kimo reached the street and stuck his thumb out, apparently too damn lazy to walk the six blocks back to the dealership. "Be sure it doesn't."

"Yes, ma'am."

"Knock off the puppy-dog act, Rich." She stood. "You messed up, but we're still partners. But you damn sure owe me eight bucks for that little dickwad's burger and curds."

"Fair enough," Rich said. "What now?"

Tia saw Kimo hopping into the back of a pickup. He looked her way and saluted with his raised middle finger. She gave some thought to chasing the truck down and hooking the boy up. She was pretty sure he was holding back and didn't like letting him walk away. She could figure out a real charge later but for now, his wiseass mouth and middle finger could go down as contempt of cop. Good enough for a probation violation. A couple of days in an adult lockup would do the boy some good. Something told her Kimo's PO wouldn't have a problem with it. Her mind was pretty much set on hooking him up when her cell phone buzzed with a text from Livy.

nag in 30 mins?

She'd find another opportunity to deal with Kimo and his attitude. She returned his salute as the truck pulled away.

"You're a lucky little shit, Kimo." She smiled at Rich, letting him know she was already moving on. Sending a quick reply to Livy, she said, "Come on, partner. Let's go see your girlfriend."

THIRTY-SEVEN

It wasn't surprising to find the Nag parking lot more crowded than it had been earlier in the week. It was Friday and the forecast called for a stretch of hot and sunny. That meant lots of folks were getting an early start on the weekend. As Tia and Rich walked the quarter mile to the dam, they passed by several family picnics, the dock was lined with fishermen, and boats pulling skiers sped around the lake. Rich took the time to try and set the record straight for the tenth time since they'd left the restaurant.

"I'm telling you, she's not my girlfriend. Why did you say that? Did she say something to you?"

"Jesus, Rich." Tia laughed and shook her head. "Relax. I was just pulling your dick is all."

"Oh yeah, that's funny."

Livy had been leaning against the bridge's railing, but straightened as Tia and Rich approached. Tia saw a large plain envelope in her hand.

"Hey, Livy," Tia said, smiling. "Any chance that's a time-stamped picture of somebody standing beside Henry? Maybe with a long-ass shotgun at the low ready?"

"Not quite. But close."

"Seriously?" Tia asked, all humor gone from her voice.

Livy looked past Tia. "Hi, Rich. I heard you were working with Tia. How you holding up?"

"Hi, Livy. You should probably ask her, but wait until I'm not around. We had a rough morning."

"Knock off the chitchat." Tia was serious. "What's in the envelope?"

"Good news and bad news." She passed Tia the envelope.

Tia tore it open and pulled out the sheets inside. "Talk to me."

"I processed the envelope and each of the bills individually. I was actually surprised because there weren't many prints on the cash. Usually money is like a pea soup of partials. But the bills were new, so it wasn't bad. I lifted quite a few identifiable latents."

"And?" Tia was just starting to scan the report.

"Sure enough. Gosforth's fingerprints are on the money and the envelope."

"Get the hell out of here." Tia looked up. "Are you kidding me?"

After getting shut down by Gosforth's attorney, Tia had texted Livy the details on the Gosforth development. Tia was hoping Livy might figure out a way to access his record prints so she could compare them to any latent prints she was able to lift off of the money and envelope. Still, Tia never expected this kind of result. This was a home run.

"I accessed Gosforth's prints through the state DOJ database from the prior arrest you told me about." Livy pointed to a section of the written report that Tia held. "I've got him on six of the ten bills, plus a couple of really nice full fingers on the envelope. I think his hands must have been sweaty."

"This is awesome, Livy." Tia didn't try to hide her excitement. "You really nailed it."

"Don't forget, I said good news and bad news."

"What bad news?"

"It's like I already told you, Tia, you can't use any of this. None of it really does us any good."

"Come again?" Tia looked up from the three typed pages.

"All this work and my testimony will be inadmissible. Kowalski will quash it."

"We can work through all that," Tia said, sounding confident.

Livy stared back, incredulous, and, Tia thought, maybe even a little bit scared. "Tia, I removed currency from the evidence locker without authorization. I accessed a person's criminal history file for a case that isn't even open. On top of all that, even if there was an open case, I'm not cleared to work on it. If I even think about writing this up as a formal report on ME letterhead? Mort will go bat-shit crazy. For sure I'll be fired."

"Bullshit," Tia said. "We're going to find a way to work around Kowalski. I haven't said anything to Chief Sawyer yet, but if I need to I will. Livy, Gosforth's fingerprints on the money? This is huge."

"Mort's already signed off on suicide. He's not the type to change his findings, especially after all that has gone on."

"What about Henry's prints?" Rich asked, startling Tia. She'd almost forgotten he was there. But yeah, the victim's prints were important, too.

"Page three of my unauthorized report that doesn't really exist," Livy said. "His prints are only on the envelope."

"Then he probably had just gotten the money, right?" Rich said.

That made sense to Tia. Henry hadn't handled the money, just the envelope. He'd probably looked at it, but he hadn't touched it. "So there probably wasn't a lot of time between him getting the envelope and his getting killed."

"And he must have gotten the envelope from Gosforth," Livy said.

"If you're not clear to work the case," Rich asked, "how did you get away with doing all this?"

"I turned off the overhead surveillance cameras in the evidence locker while Mort was out to lunch. I processed the bills right there in the evidence room, and photographed the latents with a digital camera. Couple of close calls but I got away with it."

"Geez," Rich said and Tia wasn't sure if he was shocked or turned on by this different side of Livy's personality.

"I did the actual comparison work at home. I was up most of the night.

"Look here." Livy pointed to the last page of the report. "I also compared Gosforth's record prints to the partial latents I lifted off the gun. No matches. I did find Henry's prints on the gun, along with several other prints that don't belong to Henry or Gosforth."

"No chance for DNA analysis on the shotgun?" Tia asked.

Livy shrugged. "Not from me."

"How so?" Rich said, smiling. "I'll bet you could do it."

"Not without a degree in molecular biology and a million-dollar lab. This?" She winked, motioning to the report in Tia's hands. "Easy. I did the actual comparison work in my basement with a five-dollar magnifying glass."

The DNA evidence would be incontrovertible, Tia knew, but this work was solid evidence implicating Robert Gosforth in Henry Hayes's murder. In fact, Gosforth's prints on the money practically put him at the scene of the crime. It wasn't a slam dunk, but Tia wanted another shot at questioning Gosforth. If things went right, she'd have a signed confession to shove up the ass of his attorney. But to do that, she'd have to disclose the fingerprint report.

"This report practically gives us probable cause for arrest,"

Tia said. "What we need now is to get Kowalski to knock off his obstructionist bullshit so we can formalize your findings and get DNA analysis of the shotgun."

"Good luck with that," Livy said. "If you need me, I'll be at my desk. Sorting pocketknives."

Tia did her best to set Livy's mind at ease. She told her she'd keep the latent-print work off the books for now. They said their good-byes and Tia once again picked up on some chemistry between Rich and Livy.

Tia and Rich headed back to the car and Tia couldn't help herself. "Not your girlfriend, my ass. Why don't you just ask her out, already?"

"You really think I should?"

"Sure, Rich," Tia said, doing her best imitation of giving helpful advice. "I mean, think about it. Nowadays, sometimes the guy takes the girl's name. Play your cards right and you could finally get out from under the Dick Puller thing."

THIRTY-EIGHT

Tia headed for Travis's office with Livy's report in her hand. She'd left Rich in the bullpen, thinking that if this didn't go well, she needed to keep him clear. Tia knew the stakes. She had encouraged Livy to disregard the direction of the deputy medical examiner. To disobey the orders of her superior. Tia had no intention of letting Livy take the hit. It had been Tia's idea and she was going to let her boss know it. If Travis did what he should do, Tia figured, in about thirty minutes she'd be joining Youngblood on the couch, watching reruns of *The Price Is Right* on the Game Show Network.

Tia stood outside the office door and took a deep breath. She gave a soft knock, and not wanting to lose her nerve, walked in without waiting for a reply. Travis sat behind his desk. A man Tia didn't recognize sat in the visitor's chair. He looked her way, aiming his gaze at her chest, took a quick tour, then finally rose to make eye contact.

"Great. I was just getting ready to call you," Travis said, getting to his feet. "Tia, this is Detective O'Donnell. He's a background investigator for the San Diego County Sheriff's Office. I know you've heard I applied out there. He's got a few questions for you."

"Tia Suarez. Good to meet you." She stuck out her hand. Though O'Donnell was still slouched in his office chair, at least now his eyes were focused somewhere above her neck.

"I've heard a lot about you, Suarez." O'Donnell shook her hand, holding it longer than was polite. "Looking forward to talking with you. Do you have a few minutes now?"

"Actually, I don't," Tia said, sounding as dismissive as possible. "Travis, we need to talk. In private."

Travis glanced at O'Donnell. "Tia, Detective O'Donnell has a flight out tonight. He just needs a few minutes. We can get together later."

"I need to meet with you and the Chief about the Hayes case. It's important."

"Chief Sawyer is out of the office," Travis said. "I'll get ahold of him. By the time you and Detective O'Donnell are done, the Chief should be back. Sound good?"

Unhappy, Tia turned back to the detective. "How long's this going to take?"

O'Donnell looked at Travis and winked, then turned to Tia. "I don't know. You gonna tell me he's a wife beater? Maybe a serial rapist?"

O'Donnell laughed out loud, and Travis smiled uncomfortably and looked at Tia, silently pleading for her to just go along.

"How long, Detective?" Tia said, staring at Travis.

O'Donnell shrugged. "We can get it done in fifteen minutes or so."

"Fine." The look Tia shot Travis's way made no attempt to hide her frustration.

Travis smiled in return. "Good. Use my office. I'll go find the Chief. Come over to his office when you're done here."

Once the door closed behind him, Tia turned to O'Donnell.

"I don't mean to be rude, Detective, but can we make this quick?" She took a seat behind Travis's desk.

"Call me John," the San Diego cop said. "Sorry. I can see you've got a lot going on." O'Donnell opened a leather binder, revealing a preprinted questionnaire that, even from Tia's angle, looked lengthy.

"First, I just need to get some background on you." O'Donnell's eyebrows lifted as he added, "Everything I've heard so far is pretty impressive.

"So," he continued, "first let me get your full name, date and place of birth." Tia rattled off the information and made sure to maintain a consistent cadence and tone as she went on. "Place was Brownsville General in Texas."

"Really?" O'Donnell said. "How did you end up in Wisconsin?"

"My dad's job was here."

"What kind of work did he do?"

"Hey, John, this is about Travis, right?"

"Yeah, sure." O'Donnell's eyes went back to his notepad. "I forgot. You're in a hurry."

"Like I said, I don't mean to be rude and I don't want to blow this for Travis," Tia said. "I mean, I've known the guy since third grade and I honestly don't have a bad thing to say about him. His personal life, he's like a damn choirboy. We were partners in Patrol before he was promoted and he's an amazing cop. Didn't matter how crazy shit got, I never saw him go high and right on anything."

Tia was glad to see O'Donnell taking notes. He looked up and smiled. "So you're former military, huh?"

"Excuse me?" Again she wondered why they weren't talking about Travis.

"You said 'high and right.' Military term. What branch?"

Tia took a deep breath and smiled, remembering that Travis really wanted this job. "Marines."

"No shit? I was Air Force Reserve. Got called up and deployed to Bagram in Afghanistan. Loaded jets for bombing missions," O'Donnell said. "How about you? Stateside mostly?

"How's that?" Tia asked.

"Well, I mean, since WM's are mostly in support roles, right?"

"WM?" Tia knew the acronym. But for some reason, she just didn't like this guy using it.

"Women Marines, right?"

Tia stared at the detective long enough to wipe the smile off his face. Tension rose in the room, which was exactly the result she wanted. "I did six months at the Defense Language Institute in Monterey, crash course in Farsi. After that another six months immersed in Saudi Arabia. Once my skill level was satisfactory, I hooked up with a recon platoon in the Helmand Province. We were responsible for locating high-value targets. I was the unit interrogator/translator. Spent three years in an FOA."

O'Donnell's pen had stopped moving. Tia motioned toward his paper. "FOA. That's the acronym for 'forward operating area.' If you want to write it down, that is. Now, did you have any questions about Travis?"

The detective began to stumble through inquiries about Travis's honesty and temperament. There was a knock, then the office door opened and Rich walked in, carrying a FedEx packet.

"Excuse me, Detective Suarez?"

"Yeah, Rich."

"This just came for you." Rich looked to the man in the chair and Tia could see he was speaking carefully. "It's about that lead you put out? The search warrant?"

Tia looked to Detective O'Donnell. "We good, John? I really need to get back to work."

"Uh, sure." O'Donnell was all business. "I think I got everything I need."

Tia headed for the door. She stopped, smiled at the detective, and did her best imitation of polite. "Good meeting you, John. Truth is, you guys are nuts if you don't hire Travis. My guess is in five years, you'll all be working for him."

THIRTY-NINE

Tia and Rich left the sergeant's office and headed down the hallway. Tia took the cardboard envelope from Rich and started opening it as they walked. Most search warrants that involved the release of phone records were handled via email, but hardcopies through the mail weren't unheard of. Tia was already reading when they made it back to the bullpen.

"Who were you talking to?" Rich asked.

"Forget it. Above your pay grade."

Tia got to her desk and sat down. She pulled out the documents and again found a cover letter addressing legal issues. She turned to the sheet marked 'Captured Call, Text and Data Transmissions' and began to read. The list was two pages and contained more data than the first carrier, but still the call traffic was light and easy to sift through.

After 3:00 A.M., she saw calls she recognized—her own number, Travis's cell, and Livy's. Above them Tia found the 911 call that had been made by the burner phone at two-eleven in the morning.

"Well, what do you know," she said, "Youngblood got something right. Here it is."

With Rich looking over her shoulder, Tia pointed to the number that had been captured on the 911 call. But that didn't tell her anything she didn't already know. She began to scan the report for any other calls connected to the same number that had dialed 911. Rich beat her to it.

"Here," he said, pointing to a call made just a few minutes after midnight. "An outgoing call from that number. Two hours before the nine-one-one call. Looks like they talked for about eight minutes."

Tia was jotting down the number when Rich pointed again. "Here's another outgoing call. Just ten minutes before the nine-one-one."

Tia looked closer at the printout and saw the second outgoing call was in fact to the same number and had lasted one minute.

Tia scanned the two pages of call activity but there were no other incoming or outgoing calls associated with the phone that had made the 911 notification. She was pretty certain, that like the documents she had received via email, most of the other data listed was from the pinging cellphones of passing motorists. She couldn't help but think how enlightening it would be to track a couple of weeks of the calls between these two numbers, but that would have to wait. For now, this was all they had to work with.

"All right, so here's what we know," Tia said, pointing her pen at the precise call line. "Whoever called in the dead body also made two other phone calls. The first call was a couple of hours earlier and lasted eight minutes. Then, the second call was just ten minutes before the nine-one-one call. That call only registered for one minute, which means it was somewhere between zero and sixty seconds."

Tia looked at her partner. "Rich, you know this case as well as I do. What do you think this tells us?"

"Well, we've pretty much decided that the thousand dollars is some kind of payoff, right? So that first call, it's a discussion. Some kind of delivery instructions, maybe. That's why they talk for so long."

Impressed, Tia waved a hand. "Keep going."

"That second call, the shorter one. That was the call just before the meet. Final arrangement kind of thing."

"So what do we need to know now, Rich?"

There was no hesitation in his voice. He tapped the report with his finger. "We need to figure out who's at the other end of these calls. We need to know whose phone *that* is."

"Any suggestions?"

Rich shrugged and spoke with a new confidence. "Let's dial it up."

Tia looked at her watch. "School's not out yet. Want to bet it goes to voicemail?"

Rich grinned so broadly that Tia knew he had come to the same conclusion. If the phone number belonged to who they were both thinking, they wouldn't need to disclose Livy's unauthorized print report. Tia dialed the number and put the phone on speaker. After four rings, the familiar voice came on.

"Hello, you've reached Robert's cell phone. I'm probably in class with my kiddos or hopefully out having fun with the family, but either way, leave me a message and I'll call you back. Have a blessed day."

"'Kiddos'?" Rich said. "What a fucking tool."

Tia looked at the wall clock. Briefing the Chief and Travis would have to wait. "School's out in less than an hour. We'd better take the Goat." She gave Rich a playful push as she moved past him to the door. "And don't ask."

FORTY

At the last intersection before Evansville Elementary School, they found Robert Gosforth acting as a crossing guard, wearing a brightly colored vest and holding a stop sign up high in one hand. A dozen kids were gathered on the sidewalk, waiting to cross the street when he looked at the approaching GTO and made eye contact with Tia.

Seeing his fight-or-flight instincts kick in, she down-shifted while mashing on the accelerator. The engine's RPM's revved and the car raised up like a thoroughbred waiting for the gate to open. Gosforth's body deflated with the knowledge that there was no escape. Tia parked along the curb and told Rich to wait with the car. She knew she was going to push the legal envelope and she didn't want Rich caught up in any potential fallout. She stood at the edge of the road while Gosforth escorted the children across the street, then walked back toward her, his face a mask of dread.

"I don't know why you're here, Detective, but I want—"

Tia was certain the next words he spoke would be about his attorney. She cut him off. "It's important you stop talking right now, Robert."

Shocked, Gosforth did just that and Tia was quick to start in.

"Here's what you need to know," she said. "I have evidence detailing your cell phone calls from the night Henry was killed. With those records I can put you at the crime scene at the time of the murder. With that information, I can get a warrant for your bank records and I'm pretty sure I'll find a thousand-dollar cash withdrawal, won't I? Knowing banks these days, they probably even have high-definition video."

Tia leaned in, wanting to plant a seed she already knew would take root. "I'm even willing to bet at some point I'll find your fingerprints on the money that we found in Henry's pocket."

Tia paused for effect and saw that Robert's lips were trembling. She went for a big finish. "I'll arrest you. I'll book you. I'll collect your DNA to test against the shotgun. Then I'll send your ass to prison for murder. I can do all that, starting right now."

"It isn't like that, Detective." She knew he was trying not to cry. "You have it all wrong."

"No, I don't. I might have some of it wrong, but I don't have it all wrong. You want to help me get it all right? Then we need to talk. Just you, me, and my partner."

"What about—"

"Ah, ah, ah. Don't say it." She shook her finger. "Because if you do, you can make that call from a jail cell."

His voice conveyed his complete surrender. "What do you want me to do?"

"You finish up here. Then you meet me back at that cheesy-ass restaurant. We'll finish our discussion. If you're not alone, and if that L-word so much as crosses your lips . . ." Tia punched him lightly on the arm. "You're tomorrow's headline, baby. And I'm talking every newspaper in Wisconsin."

Another group of children were ready to cross the street. Gosforth looked at them, then at Tia. His voice rung with defeat. "I'll be there in thirty minutes. I'll come alone."

FORTY-ONE

Ten minutes after Tia and Rich seated themselves in the same corner booth they'd used before, Robert Gosforth walked into the restaurant. Alone. He looked even more nervous than usual and his bird-like eyes surveyed the entire dining area, but he walked to the booth without hesitation.

As he got closer, with his hands jammed into the pockets of his jacket, Tia felt the restaurant begin to spin. Her heart skipped and her mind flashed back to another time and place, but one that was eerily similar. A booth in a café, sitting across from another cop. A desperate man, walking toward her with his hands out of sight. The smell of fried walleye filled her nostrils, making her nauseous. Her system was flooding with adrenaline. She resisted the overpowering urge to scream a warning to her partner.

Tia instinctively pulled her nine-millimeter from her holster and held it at the low, ready in her left hand under the table. She was careful to position it so she wouldn't endanger Rich, who was sitting on the opposite bench, his back to Gosforth.

Her heart pounded; her eyes fixed on his hands. She played it out in her head: at the first twitch, the first gleam of metal, she'd start firing.

When Gosforth stopped beside the table, she reached across his waistline and grabbed his right hand with her own, trapping it in his pocket.

"Hey," Gosforth protested. "What are you doing?"

"Don't move your hands. Stand very still."

"Why? What's the matter? You told me to come here."

"Rich," her voice was calm but Tia knew she was on the verge of a panic attack. "Would you pat Mr. Gosforth down, please?"

Rich quickly slid from the booth and stood behind Gosforth, pulling both his hands out of his pockets and behind his back. Tia saw both hands were empty but she kept her weapon out and concealed under the table.

"My God," Robert whispered as if everyone in the restaurant weren't already staring. "Is this really necessary? You asked me to come here and here I am. Are you going to arrest me?"

Tia ignored him and looked to Rich, who was finishing up the pat-down.

"He's clean."

She breathed deeply and tried to refocus her mind. She saw understanding on Rich's face and nodded to let him know she was okay. She slid her gun back into its holster. "Just needed to check you for weapons, Robert."

"Well, that was completely unnecessary." He looked around the restaurant and saw all eyes were watching him. "And absolutely humiliating."

Tia was back on her game. "Scoot over, Rich. Let Mr. Gosforth sit next to you."

Gosforth took a seat next to Rich.

"Not trying to embarrass you, sir," Tia said, her heart rate returning to normal. The churning in her stomach subsided. "Thank you for coming."

"Well, once again, Detective, you've left me with little choice."

Tia couldn't help but think he wasn't the only one who was feeling like he had little choice. She didn't exactly relish the idea of trying to get a confession from a killer in the middle of a restaurant. But she knew she couldn't risk a custodial interview. If she took Gosforth to the station, that would be the equivalent of an arrest and she would have to Mirandize him. He'd lawyer-up and that would be the end of their conversation. To be able to wall off Livy's involvement, Tia needed a confession. Her only choice was to go slow. Get him talking. Pull the truth out of a man who had everything to lose. And do it right in the damn Cracker Barrel.

Tia removed a digital recorder from her pocket and placed it in plain view. She turned it on, leaned across the table, and spoke directly to him. "I want to be very clear about this. You're free to leave. You're not in custody. You're not under arrest. You don't have to talk to us. You can get up and walk out. Do you understand that?"

"And if I do that, what happens?"

Tia shook her head and spoke deliberately. "No promises. We'll continue our investigation. My gut tells me that at some point, we'll come back to arrest you."

His voice cracked and she could hear the strain in his next words: "You just think you know so much, don't you?"

"Like I told you, I know a lot, but I don't know everything. You want to help clear things up? Tell us what led you to being in the woods at two o'clock in the morning with a dead body."

"See? You're wrong." He emphasized each word by tapping a finger against the table. "I was never around a dead body."

Tia sighed, mostly for dramatic effect. "Look, if you're going to sit there and—"

"Henry Hayes was extorting me." Robert looked at the table, not meeting Tia's eyes.

Good start, Tia thought. Motive. "How's that? What did he have on you?"

"Six weeks ago, I was at a conference in Madison. Henry approached me and started a conversation."

Tia decided not to ask where this spontaneous conversation might have occurred but she didn't doubt it was somewhere that Henry made Robert as a mark, as a guy looking for some action.

"Anyway, we talked. He said he had a room." He looked around, keeping his voice low. "He also told me he was nineteen."

"So," Tia urged him along, "you went back to his room?"

"Yes, we did. And we had sex, okay? Consensual, adult sex."

"Sorry, but it doesn't matter if he said he was nineteen or a hundred nineteen. Turns out he's seventeen. That's on you, pal. It's a bitch, I know, but the law is clear on that point."

"Oh, don't I know." His voice shook with anger. "Henry made that quite clear."

From the corner of her eye, Tia saw that Rich was listening intently.

"As soon as we·. . . well . . . afterwards . . . his friend came into the room. He had a gun. A shotgun. They both made me sit on the bed while they played back the . . ."

"They'd recorded you?" Tia asked.

"Yes. All of it." He put his head in his hands. "They have everything on camera. They threatened to put it on the internet. I mean, right then, right there. They were just going to put it out there for the whole world to see it."

Tia couldn't believe that the man was willing to lay out a solid motive for murder. A schoolteacher, married, active in his church— public disclosure would ruin his life. Tia thought she might be just a few minutes away from a full confession.

He began to cry. "They took all the money I had. They made me drive to an ATM. The machine would only let me withdraw four hundred dollars, so that's what I gave them. Henry told me he'd be back, that he wanted more."

"Did you hear from him again?" Tia asked. "I mean, after that first night?"

"About two weeks ago, he called and said he wanted more money. I told him I didn't have it. He said he'd call again and I'd better be able to come up with it."

"When did he call again?"

"A few days before the retreat. He said he wanted his money. *His* money, he said. Like I owed it to him."

Tia knew the answer to her next question but she wanted to hear it from him. "How much did he want?"

His voice was quiet. Defeated. "A thousand dollars. I had to get a cash advance from my line of credit."

"So then you made arrangements to meet."

"Yes. He called me the first night of the retreat. He asked if I had the money and I told him I did. He said he would call back and tell me when to meet him."

"And?" Tia tried encouraging him.

"And nothing. He called me. I met him in the woods like he told me. He was with the same man from the hotel room. I gave him the money. Then I walked away. I swear, that's what happened."

"Wait a sec." Tia hesitated, a thought forming in her head. "Why the retreat?"

"Excuse me?"

"Why did you meet Henry there? You both live in Rock County, about twenty miles from each other. You could split the difference and it's ten miles. Why did Henry meet you in the woods outside of Newberg?"

"I don't know, Detective," he said, sounding annoyed. "I was in no position to make demands."

"That's not my point, Robert." Tia looked directly into his eyes, letting him know the question was important. "Did you ever mention to him that you would be in Newberg? That you'd be attending the retreat at Copper Lake?"

Robert paused as if suddenly realizing there might be some significance to her point. "No. I don't believe I did. In fact, I'm sure I didn't."

Tia needed to think it through. She looked at Rich and nodded, signaling for him to take over.

Rich started off slow. "Mr. Gosforth, can you describe Henry's friend?"

"Tall, thin. Red hair. Probably around the same age as Henry. Maybe a few years older."

"That's the person who was in the hotel room with the gun?"

"Yes," Gosforth answered.

"Did he bring the gun to the woods?" Rich asked.

"Yes. He was holding it the whole time. When I walked away, I could hear them both laughing and saying that they would call me again sometime."

"What did you do then?" Rich asked. "After you gave Henry the money?"

"I went back to the camp and went to my cabin. The next day I heard about the body." He looked back and forth between Tia and Rich. "That's the truth. I know I was wrong not to tell you all of this when you first came to me, but how could I? I don't know anything about how that boy died."

"I believe you," Tia said and she saw his immediate look of relief. "Don't get too excited. I'm not going to arrest you but you're a very important witness. You're not going to be able to keep this a secret."

"But my job, my family . . ." The teacher leaned forward and grabbed Tia's hand. "Please, Detective. I know I was wrong, but I thought he was . . . I didn't know I was breaking the law."

"I get it." She pulled her hand away. "But I think you need to go home and talk with your wife."

Robert sat for nearly a minute. "I should never have gone. If I had just not been there, I wouldn't be in this mess."

"Gone where?" Rich asked.

"The retreat."

"Why did you go?"

Robert looked up. "Everyone wants to be involved in the Church of the Rock retreat. To be that close to greatness? When Reverend Mills came to our church we ended up talking about the retreat. He invited me to attend as a youth counselor."

He sat in silence for nearly a minute, before he pulled himself to his feet. "When will I hear from you again?"

"Can't say for sure," Tia said indifferently. "But you will. Soon."

"Fine." He looked to Rich, ignoring Tia. "Thank you. You've been very kind and decent."

When he'd left, Rich leaned over the table and said, "So do you really believe him?"

"What?" Tia asked with a smirk. "That you're kind and decent? Sure. You're swell."

"I'm serious," Rich said. "Do you believe he didn't kill Henry?"

Tia watched through the window as Robert made his way to his car. She saw him open the door and sit in the driver's seat. He rested his head against the steering wheel, and his shoulders began to rise and fall. She regretted the fact he had been pulled so deeply into the investigation, knowing his personal life would be highly scrutinized. As far as the man's marriage went, that was between him and his wife, but Tia decided she would do what she could to help keep the rest of his life intact. She felt certain Robert Gosforth was not a killer.

"Yeah, Rich. I think I do."

FORTY-TWO

Tia sat back on the couch and looked up from her notebook to face Ben, behind his desk, and Travis, next to her on the couch. Both had been taking extensive notes over the past forty-five minutes. In her peripheral vision she could see Dr. Kowalski seated in a chair, arms across his chest, scowling in her direction. The only movement coming from the doctor had been the steady rise and fall of his chest. Rich was in a chair across from Tia and had managed to follow her explicit instructions not to say a word.

After leaving the restaurant, Tia had called Travis and told him she needed to meet with both him and the Chief, and that she wanted Dr. Kowalski there as well. During the detailed debrief, Tia had been careful to make no reference to Livy's unauthorized lab work, but everything she did report was absolutely true. The list of the adult staff members at the retreat had led to the identity of Robert Horatio Gosforth. A routine records search indicated that Gosforth had a prior arrest for public indecency. The cell phone tower dump identified Gosforth's phone as being associated with the phone that called 911. In a noncustodial interview, Gosforth admitted to being extorted by Henry and paying him a thousand dollars' cash on the night he was killed. And Gosforth described a second person who had acted as an accomplice during Henry's crime. This person was with Henry the night he was killed and the description provided by Gosforth matched a known associate by the name of Kevin "Kimo" Moore. According to Gosforth, Kimo had been armed with a shotgun.

"So do you believe Gosforth?" Ben asked. "That when he left, Henry was alive?"

"Yes, sir," Tia said. "I do. It just doesn't make any sense that Gosforth would leave behind a thousand dollars of his own money. The guy lives on a teacher's salary. But even bigger than that, I don't see a guy like Gosforth fighting Kimo for a gun. And I sure don't see him taking a close-range shot at Henry. It's just not in him."

Ben nodded in agreement. "All right, then. What now?"

"We go at Kimo," Tia said, sure of herself. "I've already put out the word to Sun Prairie PD to pick him up. For now, it's just a probation violation. Since we can put Kimo at the scene with the shotgun, I say we get him in the box and go right at him. He might not be our shooter or maybe he is, I don't know. But either way? The boy knows the whole story."

"Puller," Ben said. "What do you think?"

"Uh . . ." Rich looked back to Tia, as if surprised to be included and unsure how to respond.

"Well, answer the man," Tia said.

"Yes, sir. Seems like the next logical step."

Ben nodded at the trainee, then turned to his Sergeant. "TJ? Your thoughts?"

"Absolutely. Let's get the little shit in the box," Travis said, but his voice lacked conviction.

"Chief." Tia looked directly at her boss. It was time to throw down the gauntlet. "We need lab work."

Ben turned his attention to the doctor, who had still not said a word since the beginning of the briefing. "Well, Mort. I take it you won't object to reopening your investigation into the death of Henry Hayes?"

Kowalski looked toward Tia then back to Ben. It seemed to Tia he was working hard to maintain his composure. He made sure to direct his comments to the Chief. "In light of these most recent developments, yes, Ben. I will authorize the reopening of the investigation of the Hayes case."

"Hang on a second, Doc. As far as the PD is concerned, the case was never closed." Tia did her best to keep the attitude out of her voice. "I just want to know: Do we get lab work or not?"

Kowalski finally looked her way. "Yes, Detective. You'll get your lab work. Fingerprint work will be completed by Investigator Sorensen. Any DNA analysis will be completed by the state lab."

"Thank you, sir," Tia said, knowing she had pushed it far enough and she needed to tread lightly. "I appreciate your cooperation."

"And just so you know, Ben," Kowalski said as he stood to leave. "The press conference was all the mayor's idea. I knew it was a rush to judgment."

"I'm sure you did, Mort," Ben said.

Kowalski gave a last look around the room, stopping at Tia. "I'll let Ms. Sorensen know you will be getting in touch with her."

Tia's phone buzzed with a text. She pulled it out and began to read, glad that Kowalski took the opportunity to leave. She turned back to Travis. "My contact at Sun Prairie PD. Kimo's in custody. He's at St. Mary's Hospital in Madison."

"I'm sure there's a story behind that," Ben said, looking toward Tia and Rich. "You two get over there."

"Actually, Chief," Travis said, "may I speak to you and Tia for a moment?"

Rich said to Tia, "I'll wait for you in the bullpen."

Travis shut the door behind him. "I just got a call from Detective O'Donnell. SDSO is ready to make me a job offer."

"That's great, Travis," Ben said, sounding like he meant it. "Congratulations. I never doubted for a moment they'd hire you."

"Thank you, sir. The only problem is the academy start date has been moved up to next week. They want me to come out this Monday for swearing-in and department orientation. I know that's not fair to you, and if you want, I'll tell them I can't make it, see if they can put me off until the next class."

"No, Travis," Ben said reassuringly. "We'll make it work somehow."

After everything Travis had been through to make this job happen, Tia was surprised not to see any joy on his face or pick up any sense of elation from him.

"Thanks, Chief." Travis turned to Tia. "I hate leaving right in the middle of this."

"Don't worry about it," Tia said, moving for the door. "Rich and I have it under control. You do what you have to do."

"Tia, I want to—"

"We'll talk later." Even she heard the tension in her voice. She turned to Ben. "Chief, I'll check in with you when we get back from the hospital."

"Thanks, Tia. And good work on this," Ben said, still looking at Travis.

With a last look at her sergeant, Tia walked out the door. She headed down the hallway with her eyes stinging, wondering to herself if she could have possibly handled that any worse.

FORTY-THREE

At the hospital in Madison, Tia and Rich learned that Kevin "Kimo" Moore was in intensive care and under the guard of Sun Prairie PD. Outside the room, the officer guarding the door introduced himself as Donnie Trevino. Tia immediately picked up on Donnie's distinctive accent, a blend of big city wise guy and Canadian hockey player. Donnie said he hailed from the Cicero neighborhood of Chicago up until four years ago, when he hired on with Sun Prairie PD. Tia noticed his tumbled-dry uniform was tight across the middle, where he carried an extra twenty pounds. His duty belt hung low on his hips and instead of the collapsible-style baton that most cops had been carrying for over twenty years, Donnie sported a solid-ash twenty-four-inch nightstick with a leather strap. But she made him to be a good guy, confirmed when he began to offer his apologies for the damage done to her wanted subject.

"We went to contact him at the dealership like you asked. Took two units, covered the front and back." Tia picked up on the fact that Trevino was a bit embarrassed by how things had gone down. He launched into his story.

"I wasn't the contacting unit, all right? I was just outside, standing next to the garage bay, ya know? Watching the back when he just, like . . . *flew out*." An animated speaker, Trevino spread his arms and lunged a bit to demonstrate his point. "I mean, he was ten feet in the air when he passed by me. By the time I realized what the hell just happened, he had twenty yards on me. I took out after him and I gotta tell ya, and I'm not lying, I was closing. I woulda caught his ass; swear to God I woulda."

"Where did he take off to?" Tia asked, already enjoying the story and the enthusiasm with which it was being told.

"Son of a bitch, I mean, I'm just watching all this happen, right?" Trevino ramped the pace up even more. "I'm watching while he runs his dumb ass right out into the middle of the One fifty-one and, boom!" Trevino banged his fist hard against his palm, then put both hands out in front as if to signify the obvious end to the story. "Smacked by a Prius doing about sixty."

"How bad is he?" Tia asked, laughing.

"Scrambled up his brainpan pretty good, but I don't figure he'll notice much difference. Worse thing is a busted femur, and I'm talking like bone-poking-out, mangled-as-hell busted." Trevino smiled as if to say the injury was well deserved.

"I gotta tell ya, this guy," Donnie hooked a thumb toward the door of the hospital room, "he's all stretched out on the hood of this little bullet car when I come running up. Dog-ass tired, right? I mean, I ain't run like that since the academy. I see his leg is . . . well, it ain't where it's supposed to be, that's for sure. He looks to his right, all bleary-eyed, half-conscious, says, 'Ohhh . . . whose foot is that?' I was so pissed by then I gave it a good cuff with the back of my hand and said, 'Yours, you stupid motherfucker.' Pretty sure that's when he passed out from the pain."

"Damn, Donnie . . ." Tia laughed. "But he's going to live, right?"

"You kiddin' me?" Trevino blew it off. "You know how it is with crooks, sons of bitches got more lives than . . . Hell, if I got clipped by that golf cart of a car going half as fast? They'd already be raising a glass. Lining up the bagpipes and planning my funeral."

A few more questions assured Tia that no officers had been hurt, the only cop injury being to Trevino's pride. They laughed it off together, Tia telling him not to worry—he'd be drinking free beer for a while with that story. After thanking Trevino for the briefing, she and Rich went into Kimo's room.

Sure enough, Kimo's right leg was in an air cast that went from ankle to hip bone. Even with the bubble wrap, Tia could see a jagged section of bone jutting through the torn flesh of his thigh. It was the kind of break that meant several surgeries, months of bed rest, and years of rehab. All paid for by Wisconsin's taxpayers. Even at his age, Kimo would be lucky to ever walk without a limp.

Kimo's head was wrapped in white gauze that was moist and stained brick red across the forehead. His eyes were shut and Tia had to fight the urge to do like Trevino and smack him on the leg to wake him up.

"Not so full of spunk now, is he?" Rich sounded like he was enjoying the view.

An IV bag full of a clear liquid hung from above the bed, dripping steadily into Kimo's arm. He was breathing on his own and his eyelids were fluttering.

Tia looked around and saw a tall chrome stool on wheels, probably used by the medical personnel. She wheeled it in close to Kimo's bedside and took a seat. She leaned down next to his ear. "Open your eyes, dumb ass."

His face twitched and Tia was certain he'd heard her.

"I swear, Kimo, I will grab that leg bone of yours and use it like a Nintendo joystick if you don't open your damn eyes." Kimo's eyes half opened. "See? There you go. You're practically ready to walk out of here."

"I ain't talking to you," Kimo said in the lazy cadence of someone feeling the effect of opiates. "You tryin' to put a killin' on me."

Tia ignored the obvious invocation of his right to silence. She looked Kimo up and down. "Heard you took a nasty spill."

"I said, I ain't talking."

"You might want to reconsider. Things have changed quite a bit since we got together. I can put you in the woods with a gun and a dead body. You sure you don't want to clear up some of the details?"

She saw recognition cross his face. "That's right, Kimo. We talked to some folks. We can put you at the scene, with the murder weapon. In the high lexicon of the legal world, that's what we cops technically refer to as being fucked.

"As in," Tia leaned in a little closer with each word, "You. Are. Fucked."

When Kimo shook his head, Tia went on, "We talked to Gosforth. We know you and Henry were extorting him."

"Say what?"

"Extorting him. You know what that is, Kimo?"

Kimo shook his head in slow motion. "I just know Henry sucked his dick and we was cashing in, like anybody would."

"Exactly," Tia said. "That's extortion, dumb ass. Did you put Henry up to that?"

"Put him up to it? Shit . . . Henry didn't need no encouragement." When he looked at her, she could see that his pupils were nothing more than tiny black points. "You telling me you wouldn't suck a dick for a thousand dollars? Hell yeah, you would."

Tia scooted her stool in closer, making sure to knock up against Kimo's leg. His howl was primal. The door to the room opened and Trevino stuck his head in.

"Everything okay in here?" he asked.

Rich moved to block Trevino's view as he replied, "Yeah, we're good." Officer Trevino nodded and the door closed.

The redhead's eyes were screwed shut but tears still managed to leak out. "Goddamn you . . ."

"This conversation ain't about me, Kimo," Tia said. "Don't make that mistake again."

"I'm just saying, Henry was down with it," the injured man said, now staring at her, his face a mask of pain. "Whatever you call it. Ex-storing them dick-smokin' fuckers. He worked 'em good. I was his partner. His cover man. I was in for forty percent. Why would I kill him?"

"So you're saying this wasn't a onetime deal?"

"Hell, no. Henry told me all about his scam when we was in Lincoln."

"What scam?" Tia knew they were getting somewhere.

"Henry talked about always seeing those rich fuckers on TV. Rich old white dudes, always getting busted and shit because they couldn't resist getting with a young'un. Politicians, football coaches. Schoolteachers. Henry said he'd get with one, film the shit, and tell 'em he was gonna put it all over the internet.

"He tol' me he was making steady bank, but every once in a while someone'd get all feisty and shit. Said he needed him a partner. So when I got outta Lincoln, we started workin' together."

"So he set up Gosforth?"

"Schoolteacher?" Kimo nodded, drifting further under the influence of the narcotics. "Hell, yeah. We did that one together. Shit went smooth, too. Had him on video. We was going to clean up on that old boy. String him along, hell . . . for years. I mean, what else was the motherfucker gonna do but pay up?"

"Henry set up the meeting for the payoff?"

Kimo didn't respond so Tia asked again. He nodded loosely. The IV bag was nearly empty and Tia knew the drugs were really beginning to kick in. She hoped to get her next questions answered before he went under.

"You carried the gun, right?"

"That's how we did it," Kimo said. "Hell, man, why would I want to kill him? We was partners."

"All right," Tia said. "Who else was in the woods that night?"

"Yeah, there you go," Kimo said. "Exactly."

"What do you mean, 'exactly'? Exactly what?"

"Who else . . . exactly."

The door to the room opened again and she turned to see Officer Trevino waving his arms over his head like he was warning them of some disaster. A moment later a doctor filled the doorway, a look of exasperation and anger on his face.

"What in the world are you doing? This man is in no condition to be questioned. He is scheduled for a major surgical procedure in thirty minutes." Tia held up her badge, ready to introduce herself, but the man kept talking. "I don't care who you are or what crime you think is so important that you have to come in here and question my patient. I need you both to leave."

Tia checked on her witness and saw that he was out. Frustrated, she knew that for the second time she'd been close to getting real answers from Kimo, a guy she pretty much figured as having all the answers. But once again, she'd have to wait. Still, Kimo wasn't going anywhere. She nodded to Rich and they headed out the door.

FORTY-FOUR

The sun was beginning to settle below the horizon by the time they pulled back into the Newberg PD parking lot and drove past the line of media trucks—longer now that talk-radio and cable channels had joined the fray. All the pundits had their own opinions allowing for plenty of on-air antics, but in the end everyone agreed, the Newberg Police Department was out of control. To Tia, it all felt painfully familiar.

She dropped Rich at his car and told him to head home. Nothing else could be done until they got a clear shot at Kimo and, considering his medical condition and the attitude of his doctor, that could be days away. Further complicating the issue, once his mind was clear of the painkillers, a man of Kimo's pedigree, Tia felt pretty certain, would stick by his right to counsel.

While she hadn't gotten much from her reluctant witness, Kimo had confirmed that Henry was the textbook definition of an unsympathetic victim. The picture Kimo painted was of a first-rate con artist who preyed on the darkest secrets of vulnerable men. It was also pretty clear Gosforth had not been Henry's only target.

How many marks was he playing? Henry had turned sexual extortion into his own little cottage industry and there were still unidentified players involved. And Tia was certain, one of them killed Henry.

Giving the media trucks a wide berth, Tia headed for the back steps of the PD, realizing there was one issue hanging over her head. She wanted to see Travis, apologize for blowing him off in the Chief's office. Tell him even though she was mad as hell he was leaving, that was only because she couldn't imagine working for a better sergeant. Or finding a better friend. She put her head down and quickened her step to get inside.

"Excuse me, are you Detective Suarez?"

Tia turned to see a man standing on the grass near the back door, his hands jammed into the pockets of a light gray hoodie worn over a T-shirt and jeans. Her gut said television cameraman—at this point they all recognized her. She took a step in his direction.

"Yeah, that's me," Tia said. "You're not supposed to be back here. What station are you with?"

"Excuse me, I'm not with—"

"Look, dude, you guys have been circling like vultures for going on three days. You know I'm not going to comment on anything." Tia couldn't keep herself from cracking wise. She shook her hands as if calling up evil spirits. "Now if you'll excuse me, I got a *secret investigation* to work."

Tia made it as far as the first step.

"My name is Owen Vickers."

She spun around. "You're Owen Vickers?"

"Yes, I am. Is there someplace we can talk?"

The nearby reporters were beginning to take notice.

"Yes. I mean absolutely. Come on inside." Tia tried not to sound too anxious as she led the way into the building. "I'm embarrassed, Mr. Vickers. I apologize. I just figured you were with the herd out there."

"I get it. Looks like you got a lot going on," Vickers said, sounding reasonable and following her down the hallway.

Tia opened the door to the first-floor interview room. "Come on in. Have a seat."

Vickers stood in the doorway, staring into the small, box-like room. The only furnishing was a metal desk, two stiff-back chairs, a wall clock, and a rotary phone. "Is this a recorded room?"

Tia smiled at the man's savvy question. "Yeah, it is, but only if I hit the switch."

"Then I want you to promise me you won't." Tia heard the nervous tremor in his voice.

"You got it, sir." Tia pointed to a toggle switch partially concealed on the edge of the table. "There it is and I won't touch it."

"I've got your word on that?"

"You do. What are you worried about?"

"I'm not worried about anything. Just that I've been down that road with cops. Eight years ago. Took a long time to put it behind me."

"I understand. Come on in." She pointed out the camera in the joint of the wall and ceiling, repeating her assurance that it was turned off. Tia shut the door and took a seat. She gestured to the only other chair in the room. "Can I get you some coffee or anything? Soda?"

"My wife told me you came by our house." He sat on the edge of the chair, back straight, his hands still buried in the front pockets of his hoodie. His dark hair was chopped short, with uneven bangs that looked like he'd cut it himself. His face was thin and pale, but behind the smudged lenses of his wire-frame glasses his blue eyes were clear and penetrating. Tia picked up on the hardscrabble life of an intelligent man.

"Yeah, I did. Me and my partner. You'd already gone to bed. She didn't want to bother you." Tia went for casual conversation. "You work nights, huh?"

Owen nodded his head but wanted to move things along. "She said you were asking about a police report, from Chippewa Falls."

"That's right." Tia spoke casually, working to ease the man's nerves. "She was nice, your wife."

"How did you find out about it? The report, I mean. What's it to you?"

Tia did a quick silent assessment and decided to skip the chit-chat. The "softening up" approach wouldn't work on this guy. The best way to deal with Owen Vickers was to be upfront and honest. Something told her that the cops he'd dealt with in the past hadn't been.

"We're investigating the death of a seventeen-year-old boy found in the woods. He was shot to death a mile or so from a campground that was occupied by a church group." Tia watched for Owen's reaction as she laid out the facts. "The group included Ezekiel Mills."

Tia paused for a reaction but when Owen only stared back, she went on, "My partner and I were doing some background work. Routine stuff. Records checks on everyone who had been at the campground. That's when I came across the report from Chippewa Falls. Your name was in it, along with Mills."

"The boy was seventeen?" Tia heard what struck her as disbelief in his voice.

"Yeah. Indian kid. Name of Henry Tyler Hayes. Mean anything to you?

"No," Owen said. "Nothing."

"Initially we were thinking suicide, but turns out, he was murdered."

"My God. I can't believe . . ." Tia picked up on his mild shock before Owen went on, "I can't help you with any killings, Detective."

"Well, like I told your wife, you just never know how the pieces are going to fall into place. Sometimes things seem completely unrelated, then you put them together and everything makes sense."

"I really don't know why I came down here. I didn't even tell my wife. She doesn't want me talking to you. She . . ." Owen's voice sounded hopeless, then resigned. "Well. She just doesn't really understand."

"Doesn't understand what?"

"What it's like when no one believes you. When everyone thinks you're a liar. As if I'd make up something like that. Sometimes I don't even think *she* believes me."

"Believes what, Owen? I'm not following you."

Owen looked to the floor. "I'm not supposed to talk about it. It was all agreed to. They told me I could get sued for libel."

But he wanted to talk about it, that much was clear. He didn't drive over two hundred miles to Newberg for nothing. Tia knew she just needed to wait. He would bring himself around. The buzz from the second hand of the clock marked time and still she waited. He took a breath and looked directly at her when he spoke.

"When I was thirteen . . ." It sounded as though he pushed the words out but then he stopped and turned to stare at the door. Tia knew he was reconsidering. She wondered how she should react if he simply changed his mind and decided to leave.

"Owen?" She said and he looked back toward her. "When you were thirteen?"

He took a breath and dove in. "When I was thirteen, my parents split up. Actually, my dad just took off. Found out later he'd moved to Pittsburgh. A woman, I think. My mom, she was a wreck. There was no child support or alimony. Nothing. She got a job as a wait-ress working nights. It was pretty fucked up." Owen stopped. "Sorry."

Tia shook her head. "No worries. I agree. Sounds totally fucked up."

"At some point she, my mom, that is, decided we all needed to go to church. She thought it would be good for us."

"'Us'? You and . . ."

"My sister. She was six. She died three years ago. Car wreck in Sioux Falls."

"I'm sorry to hear that."

Owen waved off the sympathy and fell into a steady cadence. "We ended up at a little church in Chippewa Falls. That's when I met Ezekiel Mills. He didn't have one of those megachurches back then. Just, I don't know, a normal-size, regular church, I guess."

Even though her mind was already racing, Tia was careful not to jump in or appear anxious. She felt pretty confident where Owen's story was headed, but she knew it was his story to tell.

"Right off, my mom thought he was, like, some kind of prophet. We started going to services three times a week. I still remember the first time he came over to our house. Just for a visit. You know? Like pastors do. My mom freaked out, cleaning and cooking. You would've thought the pope was coming."

Tia smiled but still kept quiet. Owen finally sat back in his chair. He took his hands out of his pockets and rubbed his palms nervously across his legs.

"But don't get me wrong. I thought he was pretty great, too. I mean, at first. I don't know . . . he was just nice to me, right? He'd say hi at church. Talk to me about school. He was a great talker. And man, he could listen. He could make even a dumb kid feel pretty important. Couple of times we went out after Sunday services and got ice cream. Sometimes my sister would tag along but mostly it was just me and him. He hired me to cut the church lawn. Then I even started to cut his lawn. Paid me like twenty bucks a month and believe me, that was a fortune. After a while he started taking me to ball games. Taught me to fish."

Owen paused and Tia sensed this was it.

"I was really into stargazing back then. Sometimes we'd, I mean, me and Mills, we'd lay on a blanket in his backyard and watch for shooting stars. Or we'd just call out different constellations by name. Hours at a time . . ."

Owen stopped. When he picked up again his voice went from nostalgic to one of resignation. He swatted at the air with his hand as if shooing away the memory. "Anyway, that's when it started. I was fourteen years old and I had a relationship with Ezekiel Mills."

"A relationship?"

"Yeah." Owen's eyes never left hers. "A sexual relationship."

"Owen," Tia spoke carefully, "fourteen-year-old boys don't have sexual relationships with grown men. Fourteen-year-old boys are molested. They're victimized."

"Yeah? Well, I let it happen so . . ." Owen shrugged his shoulders and looked up toward the ceiling. He pointed to the camera. "You sure that thing's not on, right?"

"It's not on," Tia said. "Owen, you didn't let it happen. You were groomed. He picked you out because you were vulnerable."

Tia saw the glisten in his eyes and he smiled in a way that said he felt foolish. "I thought he loved me. I thought maybe I loved him. That maybe this was how I was supposed to show it. I mean, I was proud, you know? He could have chosen anyone but he chose me."

"You're right," Tia said. "He did choose you. Because he knew you were hurting. That your dad had left and that you were alone. To him, you were a mark."

Vickers looked up at the ceiling, then back at Tia. She saw the still-burning grief of a lost childhood in his eyes. She didn't doubt a single word he'd said. "How long did this go on?"

"About two years. Then it just . . . stopped. After that, he acted as if nothing had ever happened between us," Owen said. "Barely spoke to me. I thought it was something I'd done, at first. But after a while, it was like I was coming out of some kind of trance, you know? It all came clear and I was just so . . . so *ashamed*. Embarrassed. Even angry, I guess, but I sure as hell wasn't going to tell anyone. So, I just . . . I don't know . . . went on with my life . . ."

His voice trailed away and Tia tried to reassure him. "It's not unusual for boys to respond that way. They internalize. At that age they hardly ever disclose."

"Yeah," Owen said. "I can believe that."

He sighed and shook his head. "I'd always planned on going to college, but I barely made it through high school. A lot of alcohol. Drugs. Sex that I didn't even want or understand. Men and women."

"I'm guessing at some point you did talk about it?"

He gave her the slightest smile. "I met my wife. Man . . . I don't think I would have survived much longer without her. One night, I told her everything. All of it. It was like scrubbing away some nasty oil that had been on my skin for years."

Owen put his elbows against the metal desk and crossed his arms. "After we got married, we had a son. I was twenty-one years old. It had been years but I couldn't look at my boy without remembering what it felt like to be that alone. To be so desperate for someone to care about me that I would do those things. I wondered how I could have been so gullible."

Tia fought to maintain some level of professionalism, but she felt like she'd never had a more intimate conversation. She resisted the temptation to reach out to him.

"I felt like I had let Mills get away with it. I couldn't keep quiet any longer." He looked up and Tia saw his relief that the worst of the story was over. His voice went clear and matter-of-fact. "So I went to the police."

"That's the police report?"

"Yeah, eight years ago. By then it'd been almost seven years since we'd . . . well, since it had ended. I thought maybe too much time had passed, but the police said I could still press charges. So I told them I wanted to. I didn't want it to be happening to other boys."

"So was there an investigation?"

"If you want to call it that. After I gave them my statement, they asked me to call him on the phone. Get him to talk about what happened between us." Owen nodded his head toward the wall. "That was in a room almost exactly like this one."

Tia nodded. "It's called a pretext. A controlled phone call. Pretty standard tactic. What happened?"

"I did what they told me to. I confronted him. I asked him why he'd done all those things to me. He acted like he didn't know what I was talking about. Within a couple of minutes he hung up."

Owen took a deep breath before going on. "The next day, he went to the police department with a lawyer and told them about the phone call. Said he was worried that I was having some sort of breakdown. That I was unstable. 'Course he denied everything."

"Pretty slick move on his part," Tia said. "He probably figured out it was a setup call, so he turned the tables on the cops. Walked right into the PD and played it off."

"Tell me about it. The next thing I knew they were investigating *me*. Wanted to know what I had against Mills. Why I was trying to ruin his life by making things up. They threatened to arrest me. I ended up having to get a lawyer. In the end, he backed off; the cops did, too. I just wanted to forget the whole thing. All of it. That's when my wife and I moved to Rice Lake."

Owen paused and when he spoke again his voice was tired, as if he'd lived the whole nightmare all over again. "A few years later I heard that Mills had moved away. I kind of wondered about that, but to be honest, I didn't even care. I just wished I'd never said anything."

"I can understand that."

They sat in silence for a minute or two.

"I'm not sure what any of that has to do with a murder case, but . . ." He shrugged. "That's what happened."

"Well, like I said, Owen, sometimes the pieces just start to fall into place."

"All right, then. If it helps, fine. Let me know what else you need me to do. I'll deal with the fallout." He smiled. "Our house is rented, but he can sue me for my ten-year-old Hyundai."

The room went quiet and Tia watched as the smile slowly left his face. His chin quivered slightly at first then almost convulsively. He took off his glasses and tossed them down on the desk. He covered both his eyes and lowered his head. His shoulders began to shake and Tia sat still while Owen Vickers sobbed and sobbed. From past experiences in similar situations, Tia knew it would likely be several minutes before he composed himself and he could use some time alone. She leaned forward and touched him lightly on the knee.

"Take your time, Mr. Vickers. I'm going to step outside, okay? Give you a little privacy."

"Why?" She heard fear in his voice. Near panic. "What are you going to do? Are you going to call someone? Him? Are you going to call him? Is that camera still off?"

"Mr. Vickers." Tia set her hand on his shoulder and squeezed reassuringly. "Owen, trust me. I'm not going to call anyone and yes, the camera is off. And just so you know? I believe every word of what you said. Every single word."

Their eyes met and his anguish seemed to lighten. Tia stood and walked out the door.

Once in the hallway she strode quickly to the administrative offices which, as expected, were dark and empty. Stepping into the Chief's office, she clicked on the light, then picked up his trash can. *Yes!* Tia pumped her fist. The city's cut back to once a week janitorial services had paid off. Carefully extracting the juice can, she gently shook it and felt a little liquid sloshing around in the bottom.

More than enough, she thought. *More than enough.*

FORTY-FIVE

H ey, Tia, wake up. We're here."
Tia sat up, initially disoriented. She'd never actually ridden in the backseat of her GTO. When she saw Rich looking down over her, it took a few seconds to remember how she'd gotten there.

Tia had called Travis at almost 3:00 A.M. and after an awkward apology for her walk-off, she filled him in on what Owen Vickers had reported. They both agreed, there was no getting around an interview of Reverend Ezekiel Mills. They also agreed it would rock Newberg to its foundation, and it might take what had been pretty ridiculous regional media coverage and turn it national. When Travis was hesitant, Tia pointed out the connections.

"Think about Gosforth's statement. He was being exploited by a couple of young con men. These little shits Kimo and Henry. They played on men for their sexual proclivities, right? Men with a lot to lose. Now we find out that Ezekiel Mills might have the same issues. He might be someone who ended up in a situation where he was being blackmailed."

"But is that really enough to haul him in? Question him about a homicide?"

"When you think of what's at stake? Yeah, it is."

Travis sounded tired and Tia pictured him still in bed. The man was supposed to be in California in two days. She was pretty sure at this point he just wanted to check out. Her emotions and exhaustion got the best of her.

"Don't worry about it, Travis. I'll take the heat. You can just get on the plane. I got this."

That brought him fully awake. "That's not what I'm saying, Tia. Can you just slow down for a minute?"

"Then what *are* you saying?"

"You're telling me that Ezekiel Mills went out into the woods at two o'clock in the morning and blew a kid's face off. That we ought to bring him in and question him about a murder?"

"I don't know if he pulled the trigger, but yeah. He's connected." Tia's head hurt and buzzed with fatigue. "Maybe he's the shooter, or maybe not. I don't know what to think, Travis, but we can't ignore it. I mean, Mills has been cockblocking this investigation since day one. You were there when he admitted the hasty press conference was his idea. And the detective out of Chippewa Falls tells me it was Mills who leaked our interview with Gosforth to the press. Now with this Vickers thing? Come on, Travis."

"Can we at least give the Chief a heads-up first? Does he need to wake up and see it on the fricking news?"

Tia knew he was right. There was no rush at this point. The man wasn't exactly a flight risk and chances were he was still feeling pretty confident. Most importantly, Tia knew she needed to wait to interview Ezekiel Mills. She was pretty certain her best ammunition against him was still pending.

Right after she'd escorted Owen Vickers to his car, Tia had booked the nearly empty beet juice can into the PD evidence room.

She'd called Livy to brief her on the developments and Livy had promised to pick the evidence up first thing in the morning and hand deliver it to the DNA examiner at the DOJ lab in Madison. Livy said on a case of this magnitude they could get results in a matter of hours.

The dregs of juice contained Ezekiel Mills's saliva and therefore, his DNA profile. And when compared to the DNA lifted from the shotgun, Tia knew it would identify the killer. She was certain of that.

"All right, Travis," Tia said into the phone. "We'll brief Ben beforehand. In the meantime, I'm going to head back up to Lincoln School. Pick up the files I ordered on Kimo and Henry."

Travis and Tia agreed to meet with the Chief at noon in his office to break the news. That's when Tia called Rich and told him to get over to the station. When he started asking questions she repeated her orders and hung up the phone. He showed up ten minutes later and she was already asleep in her desk chair. He was wearing blue jeans and a Packers T-shirt. He had on black-framed glasses and there were sheet lines on his face.

"What's with the specs?" Tia asked.

"I wear contacts. What's going on?"

"Now you really look like an egghead." Tia held up the keys to the GTO. "We need to be in Irma in two hours. You're driving. I'm sleeping. Do not wreck my car."

A wide grin broke over his face as he snatched the keys from her hand. "I can make it in an hour and a half."

Good to his word, Rich made the drive in a little over ninety minutes. He parked the car and they walked to the guard shack. Tia was surprised to see the same person on duty. He explained shifts were twelve on, twelve off, so the odds were always pretty good. Sure enough, the old man, Jake, showed up a few minutes later to escort them in.

When they got to the admin building, Trisha Washington was

just pouring her first cup of coffee. Tia explained what had developed, that Kimo might very well be involved in the murder of Henry Hayes. Tia thought it best to leave the rest of the details out. If the Ezekiel Mills connection somehow got out, there'd be no stopping it.

"Well then," Trisha said. "I'm sure you're going to need those files. I've got the copies ready for you."

Trisha took Tia and Rich back to her cubicle, passing through a long hallway. Tia rubbed her face, doing her best to wipe away the fatigue. She looked off to the side and stopped in her tracks. What she saw brought her fully awake. She moved to a door located in the hallway for a closer look. She stood and peered through a thin, wire-mesh window into a classroom.

"I'll be damned," Tia said, still staring into the classroom.

"Hey, Tia?" Trisha said, stopping in the hallway. "You okay?"

"That's Sam Mills," Tia said, then looked at Trisha. "That's Sam Mills from Milwaukee, right?"

Trisha came back and looked through the window. "Sam? Yeah. He's been volunteering up here for a few months. Really helps out. Like I've told you, our staffing has been cut to the bone and having a volunteer who has a background in counseling helps. Why shouldn't he though, right? Damn near seventy percent of everyone who comes through here is from Milwaukee. It's hard to keep the boys from rival gangs separate."

Hearing herself, the woman laughed. "See? There I go. Calling them boys."

"What's he do?" Tia looked in at Sam sitting in a circle of metal folding chairs, along with ten boys all dressed in tan jumpsuits and black sneakers.

"You're looking at it," Trisha said. "He runs a discussion group. Mostly anger management, impulse control. The boys seem to like him. His class is strictly voluntary but he never has an empty room. Then again, they get easy points for being in his class and there's no homework. All they have to do is talk. Goes toward time off for good behavior. You know him?"

"Yeah," Tia said, still looking through the window. "We had lunch. Showed me around his church and some project he's working on."

"That transformation project?" Trisha asked.

"That's it. You've heard about it?"

Trisha smiled. "That's all Sam talks about. I have to say, I wish the state would throw some money his way. Sounds like he's on to something. For that, I might give up my fancy office.

"You want to say hi?" Trisha said, putting her hand on the door.

Tia looked at Sam sitting in a chair, leaning forward with his forearms on his knees and his hands clasped in front of him. He looked on intently as the young men in the group talked among themselves.

"No. Not right now."

"I'll tell him you stopped by."

"Actually, I'd rather you didn't, but there is one more thing you can do for me."

FORTY-SIX

They made it back in time for the noon briefing. Tia filled Travis in on the latest development and they both briefed the Chief. He was nearly floored by what he heard, but he gave Tia the go-ahead. She made the call. At precisely one o'clock Reverend Mills walked into the police department and Tia wasn't at all surprised when he arrived alone. He wasn't the sort to hide behind an attorney. If she had been talking to his father, she knew it would have been entirely different.

"Hey, Sam. Thanks for agreeing to come in." Tia walked up to where Sam had taken a seat in the small lobby. She was surprised when he stood to give her a warm hug. When he pulled away, he wore a genuine smile. "I was thinking of you today. I enjoyed our talk this week."

"Me, too, Sam."

"What's up?"

Tia walked Sam into the interview room that was connected to the lobby. It was a near-exact copy of the room she and Vickers had shared a few hours before, but it wasn't located in the secure area of the building. It was easily accessed by anyone in the lobby area, including civilians. She shut the door and said, "By the way, I want you to know, this door doesn't lock."

Sam cocked his head a bit and smiled as if perplexed. "Okay. Good to know, I guess."

"And," Tia said. "I also want you to know, Sam, you're free to leave anytime you want. You don't have to talk to me and you don't have to answer any questions."

Sam stopped smiling and his face turned serious. "What's this about, Tia?"

"It's just important, Sam, that you understand you can leave when you want and that you are here voluntarily. Do you understand?"

Tia didn't want to put Sam on guard by having to advise him of his Miranda rights, so she had intentionally created the circumstances where that wouldn't be legally required. She merely needed to confirm that Sam felt free to leave.

"I understand what you're saying, Tia. But really, why am I here?"

Tia motioned to one of the two chairs in the room and Sam took a seat. She saw his eyes go to the thin manila folder she had intentionally left on the desktop. The folder was clearly marked with the logo of the Wisconsin DOJ Laboratory. Tia took the other chair.

"I'd like to discuss a couple of issues related to our homicide investigation."

"Oh that?" He smiled and his voice was no different from when they had met in his office just a few short days ago. "The press has been pretty rough on you guys. Can't be easy. I have to say I admire your tenacity."

"How so?"

"The ME ruled the death a suicide. To a lot of people it seems like the police are way off base." Sam spoke like he was talking about some rambunctious kids. "But you guys just keep plowing ahead."

"Actually, Dr. Kowalski has decided to reopen the ME's investigation. He should be making an announcement later today."

"Really?" Sam still showed no outward reaction.

"Yes. And we're preparing to make an arrest of a man by the name of Kevin Moore for his involvement in the murder of Henry Hayes. He goes by Kimo."

Sam's brow furrowed a bit and he nodded. "Kevin Moore? Who's he?"

Big mistake, she thought. He'd have been better off to just own it. "You ought to know. According to the records I received this morning, he signed in for your discussion group at Lincoln Hills fourteen times."

For the first time she seemed to throw him off. Her knowledge of their association clearly surprised him so Tia let it fester for a moment. He cleared his throat. "So then, you've arrested him?"

"Not yet. But only because he's in the hospital with a concussion and compound fracture of his femur. He's not going anywhere. But we had a talk. Turns out he and Henry had quite a racket going, extorting men for money."

"How so?" Sam had regrouped quickly and Tia was impressed at how well he was holding up.

"Henry would have sex with men. Carefully selected men who had a lot to lose. Men like Robert Gosforth. Then he would threaten to go public, accuse them of having sex with a minor. His last take from Gosforth was for a thousand dollars."

"Gosforth?" Sam nodded and Tia saw no signs of anxiety. Then again, the guy had hidden from Sudanese death squads. His voice was calm. "That's a name from the staff list."

"It is."

"And is *he* under arrest?"

"No." Tia shook her head. "I don't think he had anything to do with Henry's murder."

"So then, what *do* you think?"

"I think Gosforth was bait."

"Bait?" Sam did his best to look confused.

"When I first spoke to Mr. Gosforth, he told me Reverend Mills invited him to the retreat. I just assumed he was talking about your father." Tia paused and saw that Sam realized another piece of the puzzle was slipping into place. She leaned in closer. "But it was you. You invited him."

When Sam only sat wordlessly she pushed a little harder. "I take it Kimo had let you know about Gosforth. That he and Henry had a live one. That they were working a schoolteacher. Turned out to be a churchgoing man. That's when you decided to visit Gosforth's church. Get with him one-on-one and invite him down to the retreat. Then you could get Kimo to bring Henry to the woods."

"I'm sorry, I'm just not following you, Tia."

She ignored his denial and continued, "After his release from Lincoln Hills, you and Kimo stayed in close contact, right?"

Sam stared back; once again Tia was impressed by his ability to remain calm. His voice was deliberate and clear.

"Sounds like you've come to the conclusion Henry Hayes was some sort of predator, exploiting the frailties of others."

"He sure was. He was a real son of a bitch. And if this was the Sudan or maybe even Afghanistan he'd be taken out, no questions asked. But this isn't North Africa. This isn't a war-torn country in the Middle East. It's Wisconsin."

Sam stared back and sat quietly. He mulled over his thoughts and Tia wondered what he might say next. When he spoke it became obvious to Tia he knew she was closing in.

"Everyone, Tia, and I mean *everyone* is fine with the conclusion that Henry Hayes killed himself. The medical examiner, the mayor, the media . . . even members of your own department." A desperation came over him. "I don't make any excuses for the likes of Robert Gosforth, but what is your obsession with this case?"

"What about the likes of Ezekiel Mills? Do you make excuses for them?"

Sam finally reacted. "I'm not entirely sure what you are implying but I think—"

"How long had Henry been blackmailing your father? It must have started before Henry went to Lincoln Hills, right? How much has your father given him over the years?"

"I think it would be best if you—"

Tia had Sam in a corner and she thought he might be ready to walk out. She kept at him. "Did you encourage Kimo to get close to Henry? To be his friend? His protector? Was that your doing, Sam?"

Tia could see Sam begin to scramble, trying to throw off her rhythm. "Why would you think that Henry could extort my father?"

There it was. Sam's lifeline. His certainty that Tia didn't know about his father's history. She took no pleasure from what she was about to say.

"I know Detective Coleman from Chippewa Falls reached out to you. Let you know we were sniffing around about the report involving your father."

She waited, but when Sam sat silent, Tia went on. "You tipped off the media. Did your best to shut us down. But, we found him anyway, Sam."

"Found who?" She could see in his eyes, he already knew.

"Owen Vickers."

Sam's voice grew thick. "Owen Vickers is a liar. And if he said anything to you, I'll have his last dime."

A new side of the man was coming out. An ugly side. Tia knew she could exploit it. "Is that what you've told yourself all these years, Sam? Vickers made it all up?"

"Nothing was ever proven," Sam said. "No charges were ever filed."

"Then along comes Henry Hayes and it starts all over again. But Henry wasn't some innocent fourteen-year-old boy, was he? Henry wasn't going to be silenced. Henry was nobody's victim."

The color drained from Sam's face.

"Your father was being extorted by Henry Hayes—until Henry was sent off to Lincoln Hills. But that would have been just a short reprieve, wouldn't it? You knew he'd be back."

"I've heard enough," Sam said, standing from his chair.

Tia pulled a sheet of paper from the manila envelope and slid it across the desk for Sam to see. "We knew the shotgun recovered from the scene was the weapon used to kill Henry, but we also knew Henry couldn't have used it to kill himself."

"And what makes you think that?" Just as Tia had hoped, Sam couldn't just walk out. He needed to hear more.

"Math," Tia said with a shrug. "Two plus two kind of stuff."

"I don't follow you."

"The gun was too long for Henry to turn it on himself." Tia let her words take hold then went on. "It was his gun and he brought it to the woods. But he didn't shoot himself with it."

"Then who did?"

Tia remembered the moment she told Carla Hayes her son was dead. She recounted Owen Vickers's gut-wrenching disclosure of the darkest time of his life. She thought of Robert Gosforth and the personal anguish he would face with his family. It had been an emotional case and now, it was over. She felt no sense of victory.

"We lifted DNA from the shotgun. I had the lab compare it to DNA I collected from a juice can your father drank from when he visited Chief Sawyer."

"What are you saying?" Sam picked up the one-page report, prepared to fight back against information he knew was flawed. "You found my father's DNA on the shotgun?"

"No," Tia said. She let Sam keep reading. "You know we didn't. But, we did learn something very important."

Sam read, until he let the report drop slowly to his side.

"The test proves a familial match," Tia said. "The DNA on the weapon doesn't come from your father, but from a very close blood relative."

Silence. "It's your DNA, isn't it, Sam?"

"Henry was going to ruin him." Tia wouldn't have recognized Sam's voice if she hadn't seen him speak the words. "He was never going to stop. He would have destroyed everything."

Tia knew those words amounted to a confession. Sam knew it, too, but Tia still wasn't satisfied. "All of this, Sam? Kill a seventeen-year-old boy? Just to protect your father?"

"I wasn't protecting my father. It isn't about him."

Tia said, genuinely confused. "Then who? Who were you protecting?"

"Don't you see? This isn't about my father. It's about Darby. It's about her family. Her neighbors. Who will look out for them, Tia? You?"

"This is about your work?" Tia shook her head.

"Is that so terrible?" It was the first time his voice cracked. "That I recognize the greater good here? That I understand what's really at stake?"

Tia waited, hoping he'd dig himself in just a little deeper. "All of this, Tia, all of what we're trying to accomplish, none of that is possible if my father's work is destroyed. Can't you understand that? I can control him, Tia. I won't let him hurt anyone."

"That's not a choice you get to make, Sam."

He looked toward the door. A minute went by before he spoke. "So, am I still free to leave, Tia?"

"Actually, you are," she said. "Or we can go upstairs, I'll Mirandize you. And I can record your confession for the murder of Henry Hayes."

"And if I choose not to?"

"We'll maintain surveillance of you while we finalize the DNA results. Interview Kevin Moore, probably your father too. Seize more phone records. When we're ready, we'll arrest you in a public place. It will cause quite a stir and in the end the results will be the same."

"Can I suggest a third alternative?" Sam almost smiled. "A compromise of sorts?"

"What's that, Sam?"

"Let's take a drive. After that, I'll tell you what you want to hear."

FORTY-SEVEN

Tia sat on the couch with Connor, listening to Ben deftly handle every question the media lobbed his way. The announcement of the arrest of Sam Mills for the murder of Henry Hayes reignited the story that had simmered all week. Behind Ben stood Dr. Kowalski and Mayor Andreasen. Both of them had already bitten off huge pieces of humble pie and it was obvious to anyone watching that this was Chief of Police Ben Sawyer's press conference.

Earlier in the evening, Tia had invited Livy over for dinner; she was pleasantly surprised when Livy asked to bring Rich Puller along. The four of them had enjoyed burgers and brats off the grill, and Rich and Conner seemed to really hit it off. Tia was glad to hear that Livy was back on full duty and Kowalski had apparently spent much of the day in a private meeting with the chief county medical examiner.

Before they left, Rich pulled her aside. "The Chief said I'm back on Patrol starting Monday and that as far as he's concerned, my training is complete. I want you know how great it was to work with you, Tia. You're a hell of a cop." She didn't doubt he had a long career in front of him, hopefully with Newberg PD.

The press conference was winding down when Tia heard a knock at the door. She figured Rich or Livy had forgotten something so she was a bit taken aback when she saw who was standing on her porch.

"Travis? What are you doing here, man? Don't you have a flight in the morning?"

"I just wanted to stop by," he said. "Congratulate you and all. Amazing work, Tia."

They were talking through the screen door with a june bug buzzing between them, banging on the mesh. Tia stepped outside and they stood together on the porch. The summer evening was warm and fireflies blinked on and off in the surrounding field.

"I'm glad you came by," she said. "Such a crazy day, we didn't get much of a chance to talk."

"How did Mills hold up during booking?"

"Pretty well, actually. I agreed to let him go back to the church for one last time. He wanted to swing by the construction project he's been working on."

"Damn," Travis said. "That's a bit unusual, isn't it?"

"What? Like you're still my sergeant?"

"True. I guess you got me there."

"But don't worry, I took Rich with me," Tia said. "And I had a two officer marked unit follow us, plus I gave Milwaukee PD a heads-up. You good with all that, Sarge?"

Travis rolled his eyes and shook his head. "Well done."

"I know it seems strange," Tia said. "But I just knew he wouldn't try anything. I guess I kind of trust him, you know? And besides, he kept talking. Got some really good statements. Said Henry had been extorting his father for over a year; close to ten grand. It was never going to stop. Once we got back to the station his lawyer showed up, so that ended all communication. But based on the noncustodial interrogation, and now that we're moving forward on the evidence, we'll have a solid case."

"Sorry I wasn't more help," Travis said. "I feel . . . I don't know. Like I let you down. Like I'm running out on you."

She smiled at him. "Well, you are running out on me, but you've never let me down, Travis. Not ever."

"I hope you know, I had to do this. For my family, even for myself. The only real regret I have is I won't be working with you."

"You're going to do great. I'm happy for you."

"Well, like I said, I just wanted to stop by before I left. Molly isn't flying out for another week."

"I'll stop in and see her before then," Tia promised. He headed down the steps. "Travis?"

When he turned back to her, she saw a glimmer of the boyish face she'd known most of her life.

"Stay safe out there. And you know, you can always come back, right? I did it. You can, too. Don't forget that, okay?"

"I won't, Tia."

She closed the space between them and hugged him tight. "I mean it. Promise me."

"I won't forget, Tia. I promise."

EPILOGUE

Ten Weeks Later

Tia pulled another bushel of corn from the back of the pickup and carried it to the sales stand. These were their last thirty ears and it wasn't even 10:00 A.M. There was just no way to keep up with demand. Connor tended to the rest of the stock, which included tomatoes, bush beans, squash, and a half-dozen other vegetables.

The 53206 Farmers Market was in its third weekend of full operations and continuing to gain steam. Alex Sawyer had set up a bistro on the first floor of the building, serving free-trade coffee and pastries made on site. She'd hired a dozen women from the neighborhood to staff the store seven days a week. Some of the same men who had worked on the construction project were now manufacturing coffee tables and cutting boards shaped like the state of Wisconsin. Sales were good. A family-planning clinic and day care center had opened, and plans were under way to bring in teachers to offer preparatory classes on job interviews. The 53206 Transformation Project was but a fraction of the original vision, but it was up and running.

"I've got a couple of fresh oranges in my backpack. Think we could work a trade?"

Tia stopped arranging the corn and looked up to see a familiar face. She came around the fruit stand and hugged his neck.

"I heard you were in town. How are you, TJ?"

"I'm good. Missed you at graduation, you little shit."

"I'm sorry, man. I really wanted to make it but I couldn't get away. It looked like we were headed for trial but Sam ended up taking a plea."

"I heard. Forty to life, huh?"

"Yep. He'll do a minimum of eighty-five percent," Tia said. "And we never even had to pick a jury."

She and Travis had stayed in touch while he'd been away, keeping each other up to date. He'd filled her in on his progress through the academy; she'd briefed him on the legal proceedings in the case of the *State of Wisconsin* v. *Sam Mills.*

"What about that other guy?" Travis asked. "The kid from Lincoln Hills?"

"Kimo also took a plea. He'll do nearly as much time as Sam," Tia said. "Saved himself a few years by becoming a cooperating co-conspirator. Sam's phone records were a gold mine, too. Showed dozens of calls between him and Kimo in the weeks before Henry was killed."

"Who called nine-one-one that night?"

Tia smiled. "That was Kimo. Can you believe the dumb ass went and got all sentimental? Couldn't leave his boy there in the woods. Made the call, then hightailed it out. 'Course, he didn't realize Youngblood had to get his clothes back on."

"How is Jimmy?" Travis asked.

"Got his job back." Tia shrugged. "Ben was pissed. Police unions, ya know? Our own worst enemy sometimes. But Rich Puller is working out great. Doing some good police work. Him and Livy are still going hot and heavy."

"Hey there, Hollywood." Connor came over to shake hands with Travis.

"Hey, Connor," Travis said. "You're looking good. Damn man, you got a better tan than most people in San Diego."

Connor smiled at Tia. "Outdoor living will do that. I'm a full-time farmer now."

"So I've heard." Travis asked, "You miss working at the Pig?"

"Nah," Connor said, looking around at the crowd. "This is working out great. I've got almost fifty vendors coming in every weekend. Selling like crazy."

Tia beamed. "The whole 53206 Farmers Market thing was Connor's idea. He's gotten some great press about bringing fresh produce to the inner city."

"That's awesome, Connor," Travis said.

"People have to eat." Tia loved hearing the pride in Connor's voice.

"It's kind of weird to think of it this way," Tia said, "but you can thank Sam Mills for all this."

"How's that?" Travis asked.

"All those victims coming forward meant the end of the Church of the Rock. Sam had his lawyer work it out so that the Church of the Rock assets would be dissolved. Most of the money went to a victims' fund, but he took a slice and formed a nonprofit. The 53206 Transformation Project. The board of directors is made up of folks from right here in the neighborhood."

"Where is Ezekiel now?" Travis asked.

"Out on bail, on an ankle monitor, doing everything he can to put off going to trial as long as possible. Eventually he's going to have to answer up, though, and last I heard, there were over a dozen victims going back twenty years. Most of them pretty damn credible. When they get done stacking the charges, he'll be looking at more time than his son."

"Sam Mills went from social activist to murderer," Travis said, looking around, "and back to social activist. You have to wonder how something like this comes together."

Tia surveyed the hundreds of people around them. Most were from the neighborhood, but some had driven in from the suburbs, and the diversity of the crowd was impressive. She thought back to her first visit with Sam Mills. She was saddened by the waste of his promise, but she still felt that same sense of hope in the air.

"Mysteriously, TJ," she said. "Very mysteriously."